My Canadian Exile

a novel

by

Edward Charles Bagley

First Ted's Pad Edition, May 2016

www.tedspad.com

ISBN 978-0-692-74483-3

1. Thriller
2. Immigration Issues
3. Canadian Noir
—Fiction

To Mum and Dad. Of course.

Table of Contents

I. Mashup

Chapter 1 – The Checkstop

THE HEADLIGHTS LIT UP the white lines as they flew under the truck. We were on the highway, ripping north up I-25 about ten miles over the speed limit, and making pretty good time. The darkness and the warmth of the heater and the lights of the dashboard and the long day we'd just had started to work on me all together, and my eyelids started to fall, just like they had on the plane that morning. I was already in a deep dark slumber when some internal gyroscope told me the truck had slowed and was changing direction.

"What's up," I asked, all groggy and thick. A river of drool had already started out of the corner of my mouth and I wiped it away quick with the back of my hand.

"Check-stop," James Quintana said, looking straight ahead.

"Drunk drivers?" I asked, not understanding.

"Border Patrol," he said. "Looking for illegals and drugs and what-not. They're always doing that around Cruces."

"We're in a State car," I said, still not fully awake, thinking we were okay, forgetting how we had gotten there.

"This is my truck," James said, reminding me.

I struggled up into my seat now, and saw the line of cars in front of us inching forward guided by orange emergency cones toward a high metal canopy, white and green Border Patrol pickup trucks and vans up at the front of the line parked on either side of the thing. There were a score or more paramilitary agents in green uniforms walking the line of cars, each one wearing jackboots and a sidearm, every other one it seemed with a drug sniffing dog on a lead.

"What're they doing here?" I wondered out loud. "We're miles from Mexico."

"There always stopping you on this road. It's a permanent check-point—a real pain in the ass."

"They can't just *stop* you," I said, getting rather shirty and feeling a tad indignant. I'd never run into one of these animals, you see. My work was all in the northern part of the state, hundreds of miles from the border—it was Judge Smith based out of Cruces that made us have the trial away down here.

"Preaching to the choir, brother." He shook his head slowly. "Ever since Nine-Eleven Homeland Security has more money than they know what to do with. Border Patrol's the biggest law enforcement agency in the country, now. There's tons of these check points anytime you get within a hundred miles of the border. It's the same up north. You start to get close to Canada you run into them all the time, too—I got pulled over when I was up there back in July."

"You got to be kidding me."

"Hell, no. A hundred miles from any border is a Constitution-*free* zone my friend. I heard the CBP even walk busses and trains and stuff when they pass close to the border, waking you up and asking where you're from and where you're going and all. I can't believe more people aren't seriously pissed off about it. You know, I had this girlfriend, a real firecracker. She was riding a train in upstate New York one time and had a light shined in her face by one of these guys on the Amtrak. She told him to go fu—"

Suddenly, up at the front of the line, one of the sausage necked Border Patrol thugs spotted us, and took a step closer. He waved over a colleague, and that agent looked as us too; then they both signaled to us to

4

pull out of line and over to a siding marked "secondary inspection area" situated next to a small white clapboard building.

"Goddamit, how long is this going to take?"

James grimaced, as if he knew I wouldn't like the answer.

It wasn't the Border Patrol I was worried about, mind you. That seemed a prosaic concern just then. I'd been living so comfortably in the U.S. for so long, you see, that the notion I'd ever come a cropper with the immigration folks was fantastic. Hell, on occasion I actually had to remind myself I was still Canadian.

No, it wasn't my papers I was worried about—they were all in order: my green card locked up tight in a safe-deposit box, my current and valid passport sitting comfortably next to it. It was money. Money and a woman.

Of course a woman.

Well, she wasn't a woman, *exactly*…

Chapter 2 – Stuck in Cruces

I'M AN ATTORNEY. I should probably mention that first. Not a real lawyer—I'm a lawyer for the State, which means that although I'm a licensed attorney, a bona fide counselor at law, a member of both the State and federal bars and commissioned by the Attorney General, what I do isn't really the practice of law. There's law in it. Mostly, though, it's poorly paid bureaucratic paper-pushing enlivened with the somewhat more rewarding exercise of counting off the days until retirement. On the day of this particular night, though, instead of inhabiting my pathetic cubicle, I, along with about a dozen other Special Assistant Attorneys General had been off on what the plaintiff's lawyers like to call a "detour and frolic"—a field trip to the federal courthouse down in Las Cruces, New Mexico, where our most excellent Magistrate Judge Veronica Smith had taken evidence on what is referred to in the recent vernacular of the newspapers and editorial columns as the Copper Pit Rule, more correctly referred to as New Mexico's Copper Mine Groundwater Regulation, and in the deliberately obtuse code-talk fancy language of lawyers as Administrative Code Section 20.6.7. But whatever you want to call it, Pit Rule, statute, or political football, as a practical matter it's the law that allows the mining industry to get out from under any number of pesky regulations and pollute the groundwater of the state without liability all the livelong day.

6

We were the lawyers for the Environment Department. And Yes, we were actually *defending* the rule.

Funny thing for the Environment Department to be defending, you say? Well, yeah—but life had changed pretty dramatically at my Agency with the new administration. Our Tea-Party Governor had some major obligations to pay off to the ranchers and oil and gas guys who had supported her run, and this was just the beginning. Indeed, almost overnight, the Environment Department had been turned on its head, and instead of protecting the environment, we had a new mission. Not unsurprisingly, the demographics of the office had changed dramatically, too. As a perfect illustration of the old saw that elections have consequences, an unwashed horde of lightweights and evangelicals swept out most of the old guard—those public servants who had committed their careers to the law and protecting the lands and waters of the state for little pay and no recognition—in record time. This was a New Order, and those few of us who survived the Blitzkrieg found ourselves going along to get along.

Am I proud of that? Are there better people than yours most very truly? Sincerely.

But in my defense, it's amazing how quickly a bureaucracy can be turned on its head. Blink and you miss it. A lot of damage can be done in almost no time at all, and suddenly those of us who need to keep our jobs become part of the problem. It's the Eichmann scenario.

Well, maybe not Eichmann, exactly, but there was definitely some moral ambiguity going on.

What does any of this have to do with my current situation? Nothing. Nothing at all. All of the preceding was window dressing. *Mis en scene*, as it were. My problem, the real problem, the issue of the day, and the reason I fetched up at this internal Border Patrol checkpoint right at the burning center of Satan's butthole was this: an ATM card was on its way to me, and I needed to be in Santa Fe early the next morning to receive it.

Simple as that. Problem was, for that I first had to get back to Santa Fe.

7

After the trial we had wound our way *en mass* out of the courthouse and around the corner in a celebratory mood, looking for a place to drink and debrief, fetching up at some storefront dive with dollar drafts and what looked to be a decent bar menu. We captured a Formica table near the faux stained glass window and settled into a retrospective of the day's events. I was essentially broke (see above), although all that was about to change—my poverty soon to be mitigated by the arrival of the aforementioned ATM card. And although the card wasn't coming in until tomorrow, and I was down to the very last of my cash-in-pocket, I parted with one of my precious crumpled up dollar bills for a Pabst Blue Ribbon anyway, and nursed the beer along as the evening progressed.

Early enough, the subject of getting back to Santa Fe came up.

"Bad news. Looks like we'll have to stay down here tonight," our Chief Counsel said, holstering his I-phone. "Plane's got some kind of electrical thing. Joe's made arrangements for us over at the Best Western round the corner."

"What about tomorrow?" Madstone asked.

"The Las Cruces office has two fleet cars available for us tomorrow. New logos, and everything. We'll just drive back to Santa Fe in the morning."

"What time tomorrow," says I, in a sweat about my Fed Ex package. I knew they delivered first thing in the morning, and I'd have to physically be there to sign for the thing. Then get to an ATM, then get the cash to the bank and into my account stat so I could wire the dough to the finance company and get the car released. Easy-peasy. It'd be tight, but if luck was with me I could get a ride out to the yard, pick up the car, and be driving again by tomorrow night.

So long as I was back in Santa Fe early tomorrow morning to receive the Fed Ex package, that is.

"Should get back to Santa Fe after lunch," the Chief Counsel said, as if time meant nothing in the world to him, which I suppose it didn't.

"*Shit!*" I said, a little more forcefully than I should have.

Everyone suddenly looked at me, so I shrugged and lamely tried to dial it back a bit: "Yeah. I've got a thing in the morning."

8

The Chief Counsel nodded with something like sympathy. "Well..." he trailed off helpfully.

It was a brilliant observation, but of course it totally begged the question of how *was* I going to get back by tomorrow morning. Before I could contemplate the question further, someone hailed me from across the room.

"You can ride with me," James Quintana, our resident horsey-guy and sometimes hydrologist shouted.

He was at the far end of the next table in cowboy boots, a neat flannel shirt and a bollo-tie with two of the other expert witnesses who'd testified for our side, three empty pint beer glasses in front of him already. "Your beer," said the waitress to him at that exact moment, setting down a fourth. He thanked her for it, then suddenly belched loudly. It was a long, robust belch—deep, soggy and entirely unselfconscious.

My first reaction was thanks-but-no-thanks, but as I weighed the other options, I concluded there were none. Reluctantly I waved thanks at him. "Sounds good," I shouted back. At least he'd get me back to Santa Fe tonight, I thought, and as the barmaid passed our table, parted with another precious dollar for a second pint of Pabst. I rationalized that I'd probably need it if I was getting into a car with James Quintana. But if all went well I'd be rolling in the chips tomorrow, and a dollar spent now would be of no real consequence.

Eventually, the party faded, and most everyone else had wandered off to their rooms at the Best Western, so James and I sucked back the last of our beers, and walked outside, and down the street to where his vehicle was parked. It was a pickup truck, as it turned out—big, old and blue.

"A '72 Chevy," he said, proudly.

"Nice," I said, feeling rather obliged to make some kind of admiring comment.

"Bought it up in Calgary, Alberta, of all places. I was up there for the Stampede. Back in July."

"Really?"

9

"Yup. It's on its third engine—the original was a 350. This one's a rebuilt 302, and..." For about ten minutes he gobbled on about the thing—how the last engine threw a rod, or something, and how he wanted to get a rebuilt motor anyway because the old engine burned oil like crazy, and how the blue paint was the same kind they used for the Air Canada jets, and how the wooden bed was good for transporting car engines 'cause it wouldn't crease the oil pans the way a metal truck bed would. Eventually he ran out of steam, though, and we climbed up into the cab.

And it *was* quite the relic. The dashboard was metal and the windows rolled down with a crank. The seat was the old fashioned bench seat, the kind they used to have, but have no more—it was like sitting on your living room couch, if you really want to know. He screwed the key hard into the socket on the dashboard, and the engine erupted with a roar.

He reached up and pulled down the shifter on the steering column into the "Drive" position, and we lurched forward into traffic.

"Don't worry, boss," he said. "I'll have you back in Santa Fe in no time.

Chapter 3 – Papers, Please

HE DIDN'T, OF COURSE.

Fast-forward about fifteen minutes, and about ten miles north along Interstate 25 to the Border Patrol check-stop in the middle of that dark dusty nothing north of Cruces, and to the sausage-necked Border Patrol Agent who had just directed us over to their secondary inspection area:

"Why do you suppose they're picking on us?" I wondered, out loud.

"Probably 'cause the truck's still got the Canadian plates on it," James Quintana said.

"What?"

"Yeah. Like I told you, I bought this truck in Calgary. I was up there for the Stampede, and my old beater broke down while I was up there, so I bought this one. It's still got the old plates on it."

I was afraid to ask, but I did anyway. "Why didn't you change the plates?"

"Vehicle emissions stuff," he said, as if it were obvious. "I couldn't get EPA to waive off on it 'cause it's so old. Not that it's any of the government's business anyway. I just figured I'd drive it 'till the old tags expired at least. Then I'd figure something out."

Marvelous.

I turned slowly and looked at him hard for a long time, though he didn't seem to notice. Eventually another Border Patrol Agent in a green uniform and strapped with the apparently ubiquitous sidearm came over and knocked on the driver side window. James cranked it down for him.

"You fellas are a long way from home," he said. "Where 'ya from?"

"Santa Fe," we both said, in accidental chorus.

I reckoned rightly that there was probably no town called "Santa Fe" in the Canadian province of Alberta, but he didn't look confused. He didn't look anything. "Your plates say Alberta," he said evenly.

"Yeah, Wild Rose Country!" James said with a shit-eating grin, and launched into the inevitable "Story of the Truck," making an even longer and more tedious job of it than he had just twenty minutes before to me, blabbing on about the paint and the engine and the fucking wooden bed.

"…And this is the last model year before they went to the more square-ish body you see, like with the '73's, but it was still before the gas crisis when they made this baby so the body is like quarter inch thick steel all around, and—"

"Okay, okay, okay," the Border Patrol agent said, finally waiving him off. "Are you an American citizen?" he asked.

"Not that it's any of your business, but sure," James said, handing the man his New Mexico driver's license. "Born and raised in Albuquerque."

He looked at it, then handed it back to him. "You?" he said to me.

The word hung in the air.

If I only knew then what I knew now, I would have answered differently. Unfortunately for me, I have a nasty streak of truthfulness in me that I've never been able to shake. It's my secret shame.

"Canadian," I said, handing him my New Mexico driver's license.

He looked at my license, then back at me. "You got your papers?"

He really said papers.

"You mean my visa?"

"Visa, passport. Whatever. You need to establish you are here in the country legally, sir."

"I don't carry my visa with me everywhere. It's in my safe deposit box back in Santa Fe."

"Could you step out of the vehicle, sir?"

12

It wasn't really a question.

Chapter 4 – Annie

MY LIFE IS CHAOS, in case you haven't figured it out yet.

They bundled me into the small white clapboard building, which was a pretty depressing place, truth be told, with fluorescent lights above and institutional walls painted all white, but smudged and dirty, of course. They bade me sit down in one of the cheap plastic chairs lining the wall, and Customs and Border Protection must have been having quite an evening of it because there were maybe a dozen other people waiting there too, their faces uniformly downcast and worried looking. A couple of 'em did look slightly savage, with a thuggy looking fella at one end under the window and another guy openly talking to himself, but mostly they just appeared to be garden variety nice, rather anxious looking people.

Kind of like me, I hoped.

There were still a few empty chairs, and I scouted around for a good place to light, and quickly identified a seat next to a little red-headed girl of about nine years old. She looked very small and alone, as you could imagine, and I wondered briefly what sort of rotten swine would leave a little girl like that in a roomful of adult strangers like this. Hopefully her mum and dad had only been pulled aside for some paperwork nonsense or a car search, and they'd be back directly.

"Okay if I sit here?" I asked.

14

She looked up at me all doe eyed for a moment, and then nodded. I smiled at her and sat down. She was wearing a red hoodie and had a stuffed bunny under one arm and a plastic Hello Kitty backpack on the seat next to her.

"I have a daughter about your age."

She smiled shyly.

"I'm Canadian," I said. "They pulled me in here on account of I'm Canadian."

She looked at me again. "My mom and dad are Canadian."

"Oh," I said, in an interested-sounding voice. "Well that's okay then."

I reckoned this was an opportunity to build some good karma, so I decided to keep up with the cheerful commentary to encourage the little tyke.

"They should be back here in no time," I said. "Should be the same with me. Everybody likes Canadians, you know…"

I found the talking was actually making *me* feel better, so I went on with my growing happy-ass stream-of-consciousness narrative: "They probably just want to make sure our paperwork's in order," I continued, "After all the terrorist stuff…they just want to make sure everyone's here legally, I suppose, and I reckon just about everyone in this room is in the same boat as us." I paused, and turned to give her a comforting smile.

She looked at me for a long moment. I opened my mouth to continue with my monologue, but she cut me off short.

"Do you ever think of anything you don't say?" she said.

"I uh, I uh…" I gobbled. "Sorry," I added, lamely, and sat back in the plastic chair, and tried to look out into the room.

"It's okay."

"I was just worried," I added after a brief silence.

I held on for about thirty more seconds, then found I was completely unable to shut up: "I mean, a little girl like you in a detention center like this seems like something—"

This time she sighed loudly, cutting me off again.

"Look, dumbass. My mom is in the other room. I'll be *fine*."

She said this last with real finality.

I nodded, a little shocked, and this time actually did manage to shut up.

The seconds ticked on. And then the minutes. I leaned back against the wall, and looked out into the room. For a few minutes I watched my fellow detainees, and the longer I watched, the more they started to gel into distinct individuals. Out of rank boredom, I shortly found myself mentally creating little back stories for each of 'em: the fat guy opposite me was a German tourist smuggling black market sausage; the willowy blonde of a certain age to my right was an international prostitute with an outstanding warrant from INTERPOL—a person of interest in the auto-erotic asphyxiation of a European finance minister; the teenager in a Fedora under the window was a Mexican pimp; the hillbilly looking guy with the mullet and marijuana belt buckle was on the run from a bestiality charge in Arkansas, having left a trail of confused and traumatized razorbacks across half the Mississippi delta...

The minutes ticked by. I inevitably became bored with my little game and cast about for something else to occupy me. For a while I played with a loose thread hanging from the right sleeve of my suit jacket. I vaguely wondered if James Quintana was still waiting for me, or if he'd continued on to Santa Fe. I discovered the possibility suddenly worrisome. I fretted about it rather acutely for perhaps a quarter-hour, then eventually, lacking any other diversion, considered re-initiating a dialogue with the little red-headed girl when a thick-set woman in the green Border Patrol uniform stepped over to us, and peered around the waiting area. She had the sympathetic face of a concentration camp matron.

She glanced down at the clipboard in her hand. "Mr. McKenzie? Robert McKenzie?"

"I'm here," says I, standing up. I was surprised they'd gotten to me so quick. I reckoned I couldn't have been cooling it in their charmless waiting area for more than an hour. Most of the others around the room looked like they'd been there considerably longer.

"Come with me."

16

I looked back down at the little girl with the red hair and Hello Kitty backpack. "Sorry about the chit-chat," I said to her.

She looked back at me for a bit, and then nodded.

I left her behind, kicking her little legs back and forth under the plastic chair, and followed the concentration camp matron across the room to a long counter lit cold and bright under the fluorescents. Away on the other side of the counter was the exit door and freedom beyond. My heart leapt a bit at the thought.

Chapter 5 – Interior Checkpoints

SHE USHERED ME OVER to a youngish-looking officer in rolled-up green shirt sleeves. Except for the gold badge, the embroidered CBP logo above one shoulder and the words "Border Patrol" over the other he appeared entirely civilian-like, and actually had the air of a slightly beaten-up white collar professional about him, although I suppose he was much the same sort of quasi-law enforcement agent as anyone else working at that check-point—I already had a sense that these Border Patrol types were sort of inter-changeable. He must have had his para-military jacket and unnecessarily large side arm stowed somewhere out of sight away at the back. He was organized, though, I'll say that for him, with a thin folder and a couple of papers set in a neat pile in front of him. In one hand he was holding a document that looked to be a computer printout, which he was examining intently as I stood patient and contrite before the counter.

"Mr. McKenzie," he said, more to himself then to me, and continued to look at the thing. There was a long pause. "Okay," he said, putting it aside. "No visa, right?"

"No, I have a visa,…" I started.

He was shaking his head. "No, I *know*. I know you *have* a visa. We ran your license and a Robert James McKenzie with your birthday comes up with a valid A-series green card. You came to the States in 1964, your permanent resident status hasn't changed since then, though it does

18

appear you came in and got a new card in, what…" he glanced over at the paper again, "in 1979 it says here, thirty years ago. At the INS office in Chicago—back when we *were* the INS," he added. He set down the paper, and looked at me directly. "So, Mr. McKenzie, based on everything we have in our records, it appears you are perfectly legal—that is, your *status* in this country is perfectly legal," he added, quickly correcting himself.

"That's a relief," I said.

"—*Except*," he added abruptly, "that you aren't carrying your green card."

"Right. About that…"

"You know you have to have your visa with you at all times, don't you, Mr. McKenzie?"

"I *do* have it—it's at home."

"It has to be on your person, Mr. McKenzie. At all times. Not at home. Not at your office. Not in a safe deposit box."

"Thing is I really don't want to lose it, so I keep it in my—"

"Mr. McKenzie, the rule is—the *law* is—you have to have your visa on you at all times. Always carry it with you on your person. *Always*."

I dropped back ten and punted. "I'm sorry," I said sincerely, sensing that accommodation made the best sense with this guy, since despite his strident tone he seemed like he might actually be an alright sort. I've actually got a pretty good instinct for that sort of thing. Comes with the practice of law, I suppose. "I guess I didn't know that." I added soberly. And to my relief he seemed to stand down a bit.

There was a commotion on the other side of the room.

"*GOT A COUPLA' TONKS HERE!*" a burly Border Patrol type shouted, entering through the glass doors. He was marching in two young gentlemen of what appeared to be east Indian descent.

My desk agent winced a bit at the word, although I couldn't make out if he was offended or just irritated his colleague had let the mask slip a bit. He glanced over at the newcomers as they were being seated in the waiting area I had just vacated, and sighed, took a moment, then looked down at my stats again. "Look, we're packed tonight. You don't seem to be a serious villain, and I don't want to say that this is okay, not carrying your visa. But let's just call this one a mulligan."

"Really?"

"Yeah, you can go," he said, handing me back my driver's license. "You're free to leave."

"Thanks," says I.

"The exit's just there, Mr. McKenzie." He waved me vaguely toward it with one blind hand. He was already looking back down at another set of papers, preparing for an interview with the next detainee, I suppose.

I hesitated for a second, but before I fully turned away from him, I had to ask:

"Hey, can you tell me something?"

He looked back up at me from his documents.

"How about that little girl?"

He had a blank look on his face. "What little girl?"

"The little girl just over there," I said, gesturing back at the waiting area. "The kid with the red hair, nine or ten? Stuffed bunny? 'Hello Kitty' backpack?"

"Oh, yeah, yeah," he said, his face brightening a little with recognition. "Of the tinted persuasion. Sure, I know who you mean. What about her?"

"Well, she's all alone over there. Do you know what's going on with her parents? With her?"

"Oh, that kid? No—not to worry. She looked like a Mexican at first, but it turns out she's a regular American, alright. I processed them—her and her mom. They were standing here at this same desk about six hours ago. The two of them are on holiday. They said, anyway. Must have got a little off track and came through here tonight. Mom's leaving for El Paso right now."

"El Paso?"

"As we speak. Detention Center in El Paso. She's an undocumented Canadian national, so we'll house her in El Paso until we can get a removal order."

20

"Wait, what?" I was confused and appalled in equal measure.

"Yeah—kid's an American, mom's undocumented."

"So the mom's a prisoner?"

"No," he said, a touch irritably. "She's not a prisoner. Immigration offenses are civil, not criminal. People are held only to affect a removal."

"But you said they're taking her to El Paso?"

"Yeah. To the Transitional Center there. She's illegal, so they'll keep her until the removal hearing. Yeah, the mom's got real problems," he said, shaking his head.

"What about the girl?"

He thought for a minute, then shrugged. "Dunno. The kid's an American, so it's not my department. She won't get deported, that's for sure. A local case worker'll probably come in for her tonight, and take her away—State foster care, I suppose. We see a lot of that, by the way. Illegal parent, American kid. Happens all the time, actually. Really splits up families. It's never pretty," he added brightly

"What about the father?"

His eyes narrowed. "Are you a relation?" he asked, in a voice that had become dangerously flat.

Startled, I took a step back. "No. I just saw her over there," I said with a shrug, affecting a disinterested tone. "Just wondering."

He seemed mollified, and his eyes returned to normal. "Yeah, it's rough," he said, evidently having decided I wasn't a threat, and returning to his papers. "The exit's just there, Mr. McKenzie."

What about the father?

"Mr. McKenzie—*the door*," the Border Patrol Agent said to me again rather pointedly, realizing I was still hanging around. Apparently they were insisting I release myself back into the wild. At this point I didn't need to be asked twice, and in an instant I was outside.

I put that last bit of weirdness out of my mind—maybe he was right to get touchy about unauthorized questions about the kid's father; what was it my business anyway?—and tried to orient myself, but a Border Patrol van was blocking my way. I began to step around the awkwardly

21

parked thing, and with more than a little relief saw James Quintana's big blue Chevy pickup truck parked just beyond, still in the secondary inspection area.

"Thank god," says I, aloud, and began walking toward it.

Before I could make it two steps, though, I came smack into two giant Border Patrol Agents escorting a prisoner. And that other Border Patrol Agent, the one back inside the white clapboard building, he can go on all day about how immigration violations aren't criminal, that their detentions are merely civil in nature, but I've been a lawyer for a long time and they don't haul you off in chains for a civil matter.

"Why do we gotta' bring her around front?" one of her guards complained.

"You know why," the other said all irritable.

"'Cause the holding cells are full and the parking area around back is full, too," the first one said in rote fashion suggesting both these idiots had just received the same lecture.

"That's right. We gotta' move more of these guys out to El Paso or shut down the checkpoint," he said, shaking his head.

Well, that'd be a shame, thinks I, and then got a look at their detainee. She was pretty as hell, a tiny beauty between two hulking guards, which would have caught my eye in any event, but it was her red-hair that knocked me back. Having seen the little girl, it was clear right away that this person being taken to the van was her mother; her red hair was just the same color as her daughter's, and I'll say it again, the woman was a knockout, with freckles all over her young face and a cute upturned nose; I already knew the memory of it'd be sticking in my head for a while. It's that way with a beautiful woman sometimes. She was maybe early thirties, if that, and would have been striking in any setting, despite the fact that her jaw was slack and her mouth was hanging open just a little bit, and her eyes were cast down, as you'd expect to see with someone in chains.

She had her manacled hands folded up under some kind of scarf or something in such a way it was obvious she was trying to hide the chains.

22

And that would have been it. It would have ended there, I suppose.
I could have turned and walked the other way, or stepped well around her
jack-booted custodians and escaped into the parking lot. I could have
never looked back, and that would have been the end of it. But at that
exact moment, before I could make good my escape, I stole another
glance.

And this time, it wasn't her hair or her freckles that caught my attention. It wasn't her expression, either. It was her eye. Her right eye. The
eye itself.

It was black.

Now I boxed a little in college. I was never very good, and I mostly
got my ass kicked. But what I learned from that painful experience was,
one, I should never, ever box. And two—only a human fist can paint a
lurid sunset like that.

The red haired woman in chains sensed my looking at her, and in
that very instant she suddenly looked up at me herself, and met my gaze.
Her velvet eyes locked hard with mine, and butterflies instantly filled my
stomach. I was immobilized. She glanced down very deliberately, and
my eyes followed her lead: from underneath her scarf, or whatever it
was, she dropped something.

"Monsieur, these are not mine," she said in a husky French accent.
"*Please*, get them to my daughter."

Two rainbow colored mittens lay on the pavement.

"What the f—" one of her handlers began, noticing.

"*Please!*" she repeated to me over her shoulder as they hustled her
up into the van. "She's just in there—"

The look on her face knocked the stomach right out from under me.
I was frozen on the spot. Here was a mother being physically separated
from her child, reaching out to her little girl one last time through the
hands of a stranger.

"Watch your head," one of her green jacketed handlers said.

The first guard hesitated, glanced down at the mittens, then glanced
at me, shrugged, and followed the two of them inside the van. I could

23

just see her over his massive shoulder, but she never looked back, and in an instant she was gone, up the step and into the darkness.

I hesitated for a moment, then I reached down and scooped up the mittens.

My jaw was still hanging open just a little as the van started up its engine, and drove away.

II. Detainer

Chapter 6 – James Foolishly Lends Me His Truck

I'VE NEVER HAD MUCH of a social conscience, that is to say, I've never worked with the handicapped or felt a compelling need to be a foster parent, and even my statutorily required pro bono work has tended to be along the lines of sitting on the board of some artsy-fartsy "non-profit" and donating a lunch or two a month to wanna-be socialites and like-minded blue hairs to advise 'em about forms of property ownership and the perils of deferred compensation. Not that I don't care about the disadvantaged among us—I really do, in a general, sort of John Donne-ish no-man-is-an-island kind of way—but at the end of the day, my charitable works have consisted almost entirely of applauding the efforts of others. I assume someone is out there doing those things. In any event, best to leave the good works to the professionals, I say, but despite all that, I've got to tell you, the plight of that illegal Canadian woman and her little American girl really got under my skin.

Why had she trusted the mittens to *me*? Why hadn't she passed 'em off to an agent, instead? Why did she wait until they were actually loading her into the van to hand 'em off to somebody?

In the end I reckoned that after all it was probably nothing more than just happenstance; she had looked up and I was there. Just by accident. I was the anonymous guy in her line of sight. And at that exact moment the horror of being torn away in chains, of leaving her little red headed daughter in the hands of malevolent strangers, came pouring from her out at *me*. It was profound, yes, but in the end nothing more than a pure and simple a cosmic coincidence. I just happened to be the guy standing there.

But I'd be lying if I didn't say it sure felt like something more.

I stood there then, on that empty blacktop apron looking stupidly at those tiny woolen mittens in my hand for about a minute. Finally, the sound of a horn honking woke me from my reverie—James Quintana was getting impatient. I looked at him up there in the cab of the truck, then down at the rainbow colored mittens, then back at the door to the white clapboard building I had just left. James had been patient as hell waiting for me and all, I rationalized, plus the Border Patrol had all but kicked me out of there just moments ago; going back inside to deliver the mittens might cause them to revisit their earlier decision to call my immigration infraction a "mulligan." I felt like a bit of a rat, but decided that here and now at least, discretion was indeed the better part of valor. I shoved the gloves into my coat pocket and headed over to the truck.

We got back to Santa Fe really, really late, of course, maybe 2:00 a.m., maybe later, I don't even know. James dropped me off in the middle of my empty, conspicuously car-free gravel driveway, and thanked me again for my company.

"Dude, do you have car issues?" he suddenly asked through the open driver's side window before turning the truck around.

I don't know if it was the exhaustion, the late hour, or just the fact that James Quintana was such an up-front straight ahead guy himself, but before I could really think about it I went against type, and blurted out the truth: "Car got towed Friday," I admitted with a sheepish shrug. "Got a few payments behind."

He nodded sympathetically.

"But I'm getting it back tomorrow. I bring the note up to date and I'm golden. Then I'll go across town to pick the thing up. That's why I had to get back tonight. To get my car. Well, actually so I could be here in the morning to receive this ATM card. You know, so I could get money out of the bank so I could get my payments current so I could get the car back…"

I took a deep breath, realizing I was well past the point of "Too Much Information." The little red headed kid suddenly came to mind again.

Do you think of anything you don't say...

James paused for second. "How are you going to get across town?"

"Take a cab, I guess. I think there's a bus out that way, too."

"Take the truck," he said, already climbing out of the thing.

"What?"

"Here," he said, handing me the keys. "I have a used Mustang at home. It's a '66, kind of beat up. But it runs. Ragtop, too. I slap the wheels back on her, and she'll be okay."

"But how will you get home now?" I was so stunned I truly had no idea how to react. It was too much, I knew that. On the other hand, having a motor vehicle tomorrow would make my life so much easier.

"I only live a half mile up the river," he said, already walking away. "Up on Don Diego. I'll hike it. It's no big deal. Just fill her up with gas when you're done and we'll call it evens."

"Dude! No! I can't...I mean—I don't know what to say."

He was already at the end of the gravel drive, half in darkness, but he turned to me and smiled. He rounded the corner of my house then, out of sight, leaving his grin hanging in the air like a Cheshire Cat.

I was flabbergasted. And part of me knew it really was too much. But the deal was done, and I waved him "goodbye" even though he was already gone, and stepped through the door and into my house.

And I have to say, it was a welcome relief to be back in the safety of my old home-sweet-home. It really did seem a jolly little cottage after my brief detention. All the lights were still on from when I'd left in the morning, and the whole presented as a very homey, very occupied sort of place: books scattered on the couch, magazines and papers on the coffee table, my daughter's drawings and craft projects set about on various kitchen surfaces, cards and pictures posted on the fridge. Indeed, it truly *was* a happy little home, even if it was quite a bit more than I could afford at this exact financially strained point in my life.

Okay, I thought to myself—it's Tuesday morning already, even if it is still dark out. I have about five or six hours before the Fed Ex man begins making his rounds. I set the alarm for seven, kicked off my shoes, shrugged out of my jacket, and laid down on the bed otherwise fully dressed. I pulled the comforter over me, and was asleep in an instant.

As it turned out, the next five or six hours were every bit as wearying as the previous twelve had been. I dreamt vividly of being chased by giant concentration camp matrons up and down nightmare government hallways, and back through darkly shadowed film noir waiting rooms, desperately searching all the while for vaguely remembered identity papers that I hoped existed somewhere in space and time, but somehow knew were forever beyond my reach. It was an exhausting Kafka-esque dream circus of bare lightbulbs and dirty walls, with the only thing missing being a soundtrack of sinister off key organ music. The whole fetched up ultimately at a the end of a narrowing hall at a tall white door with the word "THE KID'S FATHER" on it. The thing loomed high above me, and started to open silently, and I was frozen on the spot with a scream stuck gasping in my throat, so it was with some relief that I finally awoke, tired and unsatisfied, to the beeping of my electric alarm clock.

I sat immediately upright, and shook off my grim night-sweats. It was time to get organ-a-zized. Today was ATM day.

Chapter 7 – London Calling

THE WHOLE ATM CARD thing was a one-off, of course: a magical resolution to my insolvency by way of the loss of a family member. In short, my Uncle had died the year before and had left me a legacy. He was a great bear of a man, much loved and much lamented, but I'd be a liar if I said I wasn't desperate for the dough. It had taken twelve months, but the Friday before the trial, the Friday just passed, probate in Ontario had finally been concluded, and they transferred the funds into my London savings account. I was saved! Unfortunately, my relief was quickly tempered by frustration when I realized I still had no ready access to the money. It was in my bank account, yes, but with the teller window being two thousand miles away on the other side of an international border. Writing a check wasn't an option 'cause it was a savings account, and short of driving a very, very long way, I had been at a bit of a loss as to how I'd get a hold of it.

After a brief period of hand wringing, though, I finally clicked: there was a thing in our modern world called a wire transfer. Duh! The instant electronic cure to my chronic insolvency.

And despite the fact that I ultimately didn't get the wire transfer I'd hoped for, I eventually scored the next best thing, though only after the worst kind of heartbreakingly obnoxious phone call you can only have with a bank—make that a Canadian bank, because on the afternoon of

31

the Friday before the trial I picked up the phone and dialed London, Ontario.

"My name is Chandra, what can I do for you today, Mr. McKenzie?" the faceless gatekeeper said after we had exchanged introductions.

"Hello, Chandra. I'd like to wire some money from my account in Canada down to my bank here in the United States."

"Okay, Mr. McKenzie," he said, in a positive sort of way, lifting my heart for a split second. "First I'll need to…" He paused dangerously. "Oooh—wait." He paused again. "Please excuse me for just a moment, Mr. Mckenzie."

My heart dropped back down again. And that's the hell of it, really, they give you that false hope. But to be truthful, the worldly part of me was fully expecting them to shut me down anyway, so anything short of that was good. It had seemed just a little too easy. And the truth will set you free, as they say.

Chandra vanished from the call for a bit, and I was put on hold to listen to some crappy sort of music that did not come across the phone lines nearly as clearly as Chandra's voice had. God knows what they were listening to up there north of the border, but judging by the snippet they were feeding me here, I sure wouldn't want a steady diet of it. Fortunately, I didn't have to listen for too long, and he came back on the line.

"Mr. McKenzie, you have to come in to the branch office, sir," he said. "We can't wire your money to the U.S. unless you come in to the branch."

Good. It was inevitable that I was going to get screwed, and now at least I knew how they were going to do it. Still, I bristled at the stupidity and unfairness of it.

"You are in London, Ontario," I said through clenched teeth, keeping my voice under control.

"I know, sir. I'm sorry Mr. McKenzie. Can you come in to the branch?"

"I'm in Santa Fe, New Mexico."

"I'm sorry, Mr. McKenzie."

"It's like two thousand miles! Look, why can't you just wire me the money without me having to come up there? You must know it would be terribly inconvenient for me to have to do that."

"I'm afraid you have to come into the branch."

"Why? Explain to me why."

"I've told you why, sir. We can't wire money from your account here in Canada to your bank account in the U.S. unless you come in to the branch office."

"Your branch office is literally on the other side of the continent!"

"Yes, I'm terribly sorry Mr. McKenzie. You have to come in to the branch."

Sensing I was losing badly, I shifted gears and adopted a more rea-sonable tone: "Look, you're not questioning that it's me on the line, are you? There's no question I have money in the account. If you like, I can mail you a letter over my signature requesting that you wire me the mon-ey in writing. How about that? Can you wire me the money if I ask you to do it in writing?"

"No, we can't do that Mr. McKenzie."

"*Aaarrgh!*" I said in my head.

Why?" I said aloud.

"We can't wire you the money unless you come in to the branch."

"That's not a reason, that's just arbitrary

"It's not arbitrary. We can't do that."

"Do you know the definition of arbitrary?"

"Yes."

"Let me talk to a supervisor," I said.

"I'm sorry, I'm not going to do that."

I was taken aback. In America they give you the supervisor without question. It's your unquestioned, inalienable right to talk to a supervisor. In America.

"Let me talk to your supervisor," I repeated.

"My supervisor will give you the same answer. I'm sorry."

And the hell of it was, he actually did sound sorry. Worse yet, he was not the least bit snotty or petty about it. And even though he sounded like he was starting to get into a bit of a sweat over this increasingly ugly little interview, he was nevertheless relentlessly polite—genuinely, sincerely, nicely polite. It was infuriating.

I ranged about for the next logical thing. What do you do when you don't get satisfaction, and they won't give you their supervisor? In my pathetic heart of hearts I was already writing off the Canadian account; I was never going to see a dime of it. And all I really wanted now was not the money, it was somebody's supervisor, somebody just a notch further up on the food chain to get on the phone and tell me no. Then the universe would be back in balance. Then I could give this project up as a bad job, and like any other good American I could admit I was screwed, and this weird, horrible exchange could end.

I was at the end of my rope, and both of us knew it. All I could do was reach for some thread or fig leaf to clothe my humiliation.

"What's your name again," I asked, trying to sound as if I had a pencil in my hand.

"My name is Chandra, I'm in the London office and my badge number is L 08127. Is there anything else I can do for you, Mr. McKenzie."

"No."

"Thank you for your call, Mr. McKenzie."

There was a silence on the other end of the line while he politely waited for me to actually end the phone call.

"Go to hell," I said, evenly.

There wasn't even a sigh on the other end of the phone line. He was decent and proper right up until the very end.

And then there was nothing left but a goddam Canadian dial tone.

I sat there staring into space for a full minute. It was quite jarring, I have to tell you, to come up against an unbending rule follower like that. An American would at least have given a nod to the fact that this was all bullshit. But not Chandra from London, Ontario. Young Chandra had a rule book, and by god he was going to follow those rules no matter how silly they might seem. To the letter and unapologetically. And frustrating as it was, I supposed there was a certain honor in that.

I was still swearing at the air when the phone rang.

34

It was Chandra.

"Mr. McKenzie?" Chandra said. "Is this Mr. McKenzie?"

"Chandra?" I said. It couldn't have been five minutes since I'd told the young Canadian at the branch office to go to hell, and I realized I was feeling rather badly about that. He was just some poor mother's son trying to make a living at a shitty phone bank job. I can be a real asshole, sometimes. I really can.

"Yes, Mr. McKenzie. I'm sorry to bother you, but I did speak to my supervisor, and she instructed me to tell you that while we cannot wire you your money down there to the United States, we can send you a bank access card and a password that will work on most ATM machines down there."

"You can?"

"Yes."

"And I can get my money out that way?"

"Yes."

"Well, I'm speechless, Chandra," I said.

"Shall we do that then, sir?"

"That would work just fine."

"If you give us the address where you'd like it sent, Mr. McKenzie, we can courier it down and you could have it by…it would be an international delivery…so, say, Tuesday morning?"

Halleluiah!

I promptly gave him my home address, and he provided me with certain vital information on the use of the card, and then we reviewed the main points: item one, Fed Ex; item two, Tuesday morning delivery; item three, activate the card at any nearby automatic teller machine; item four, the money's mine.

And that was that.

After we hung up, all I could do was rest back in my chair and buzz. I was soon to be solvent!

But a certain puzzled irritation remained—why had he put me through all that? Was he just messing with me? It made no sense. Perhaps that's just how they all were up there in the Great White North—rules were rules, but *Jesus Christ*...

Then I relaxed.

Hell, I said to myself. They can't all be like that.

And now that it was Tuesday morning I spared a thought for Chandra and wished him well.

That done, I put on the kettle for tea—no coffee in the house, on account of my soon to be alleviated poverty—and while I waited for it to boil checked my e-mail. Sure enough, there it was: my brand new password for my brand new ATM card. Now it was just a matter of waiting for the delivery guy.

Chapter 8 – Secure Communities

AND AS IT TURNED OUT, there was nothing much to it. The Fed Ex guy arrived at the house at eight-fifteen and I ripped open the envelope and had my new Bank Access card in my hands by eight-sixteen; I was downtown at my bank half an hour later. Suddenly, I was cash rich.

I drove James Quintana's big blue Canadian truck across town to the wrecking yard identified by the tow-truck driver's grease stained business card, and redeemed my vehicle. It was actually as easy as that. One, two, three. I had my car back before lunch.

It was a good news day.

There was the issue of James' truck, however. Like an idiot I hadn't properly thought through the logistics of the thing, and now found myself with two vehicles on the far side of town. I sought and obtained permission to leave the truck parked for the afternoon out front of the wrecking yard, and figured I'd have to return in a couple of hours with someone, or alternatively take a cab back here to retrieve the thing.

Nothing's ever easy, by the way, there's always one more step.

That little wrinkle aside, though, I was smiling as I piloted my little green box-car back up Cerillos Road, and reckoned this minor success at least was cause for some kind of celebration. Austerity had been the rule for too long now. I contemplated dropping in over at the Bull Ring and parting with twenty or so of my new found dollars for a lunchtime cheeseburger, some green chili stew and a Martini.

37

That was when I saw the cherries in my rear-view mirror.

What now?

I pulled over in front of a Denny's restaurant to let him pass, to head off after what I hoped were the real bad guys. Maybe it wasn't for me, I thought to myself, hopefully. But of course he pulled up high and tight behind me with his emergency lights still raging and the headlights blinking back and forth and with sinking heart I knew I was his target.

He sat in his black squad car for an overly long time, the way they always do, and I waited. In the interim I mentally ticked down the checklist of reasons why people get pulled over: expired tags, cracked windshield, hot looking female driver, failure to signal, weaving in and out of traffic, teenage driver, speeding, headlights not on, dark skinned driver....Not one of 'em seemed to fit. Finally, I saw him get out and start walking up the sidewalk to my passenger's-side window.

"Afternoon, sir."

"Afternoon, officer."

"Could I see you license, registration and proof of insurance, please."

I spent a few seconds rustling around in my hopelessly messy glovebox looking for 'em, realizing, of course, that this is what I should have been doing before instead of daydreaming. Now that I thought of it, that was probably the reason they generally took so long to come up to the car, to give you time for that. Good to know, I thought to myself, and filed the realization away for future reference while I kept searching. I eventually found the relevant documents (I knew they had to be in there), and handed them over to him through the window.

He took them in his hand, spent a few seconds flipping through the little cards, and then nodded.

"Okay. Mr. McKenzie, the reason I pulled you over is there is no license plate displayed on your vehicle."

"You're kidding me!" I exclaimed.

"No, sir."

"Are you telling me they aren't there?"

"Yes, sir. There are no plates displayed on your vehicle."

With his permission, I climbed out and had a look for myself. Just as he said, there was nothing there.

"Look, I just got it back from the wrecking yard—"

He was nodding before I even finished. "People swipe plates from the yards. Happens all the time." He took several seconds to double-check my registration, then looked back up at me, flicking the registration contemplatively with his thumbnail. "Well, that's just some bad luck," he finally said, deciding not to write me up. "I'll give you a warning now, but get over to MVD, okay. Do it today. Get new plates ordered and the temporary notice up on your back window, or you run the risk of getting pulled over again."

"Will do," I agreed, earnestly.

"Okay," he said, and handed me back my documents. "One last thing, Mr. McKenzie. Governor's got this new Executive Order…" He made a "this-is-stupid" face as he said it, like he didn't think too much of whatever this next thing was about, and at the same time pulled a crisp three-by-five card from his breast pocket. "She's making law enforcement ask everybody about their citizenship status when we pull 'em over now." He held the three-by-five card up to his face. "So," he began, commencing to read: "Mr. McKenzie, are you an American citizen?"

He read the question in an uninterested, perfunctory sort of way— purely pro forma. I noticed he wasn't even looking at me anymore; in his mind our interview was already done, and his hand was already poised with a pen over the same box he always checked off when the driver was white and well groomed and spoke American English with a Midwestern accent. And I've got to be honest with you, at that exact moment I mentally flirted with the notion of just telling a lie. After my recent experience with the Border Patrol, it was the only thing that made sense. A one word lie: "Yes." That's all it would have taken. After the horror-show of the night before it would have been so easy, but frankly I just didn't want to do it—the notion of lying about who I was really stuck in my throat.

"No," I admitted flatly. "I am not."

"Okay, Mr. McKenzie. You're free to…Wait—what?"

"I am not an American citizen."

With the benefit of hindsight, my response might seem a bit foolhardy, but I reckoned though the Border Patrol was one thing, the local cops weren't going to actually ask me for my papers. I'd certainly never heard of such a thing. Plus, I have to tell you, I was feeling a little ballsy, what with getting my car back and my bank account restored to solvency and all. It's funny how a little good luck will grow your *cajones*.

"Oh," he said, somewhat uncertainly. "Shit. Okay..."

He was rebooting. I had caught him by surprise, obviously. The Governor's question was for poor folks in crappy cars with weird accents and foreign tattoos. But he had to follow the script they'd given him, and so he resorted to the card again.

"Okay," he said, commencing once more to read from the thing. "Where are you from?"

"Santa Fe."

"No, no, no—what country are you from?"

"Oh, sorry. Canada. I'm Canadian."

The Mapleleaf, Forever! I *was* Canadian, goddamit; I was proud of it, and I was here legally. I *did* have a visa; I was a tax paying, law abiding, moderately sexy member of United States' society, so why shouldn't I be honest. Would any of the hundreds of thousands of Americans working in Ottawa or Toronto or Vancouver have to lie and say *they* were Canadian to get out of a traffic stop? Hell no!

"Right," he said, writing it down very deliberately in his little metal notebook. "And are you in Santa Fe on business, or pleasure?"

Part of me couldn't believe I was being asked this. It was just like I was at the border going through customs, only I was four hundred miles from the nearest port of entry. "No," I answered. "I'm here in the States as a permanent resident. I'm a lawyer in town here. I actually live just up the street on Alameda...well, you saw my license."

"Right." He nodded gratefully, and wrote something else into his little book. It was pretty obvious he wasn't trained for this, and I actually was starting to feel kind of badly for him. The Governor and her Tea

Bagger crowd had corralled this guy into being a customs agent, and that clearly was not what he had signed up for when he joined the force.

He referred to his note card one last time: "Do you have your pass-port-slash-visa."

Gulp.

I suddenly felt a bit queasy. It was clear he wasn't asking me if I legally possessed one; like the Border Patrol last night, he wanted to know if I physically had the thing on me. "No," I admitted, realizing I hadn't properly thought this through.

"In your glove compartment?" he suggested, reasonably.

"No, I'm afraid I don't have it with me," I said. I knew now I had badly miscalculated, but what were the State Police doing asking about my visa? Hell, I thought to myself bitterly, I should have retrieved my Green Card first thing—before getting the car back, even. And I'd just been at my bank. *I'd been there!* Five minutes and I could have visited my safe deposit box and gotten the thing out and I'd have had it on me now.

"You must have a visa," he said, obviously trying to find a way out of the situation. "You said you were a lawyer. You can't be a lawyer in New Mexico without—"

"I *have* a visa," I said, suddenly desperate and scrambling, my earlier bravado long gone. "A passport, too. They're in my safe deposit box. We can go over to my bank right now and—"

"*Sonovabitch!*" he blurted, and turned on me. "Are you fucking kidding me. That's no good. What kind of lawyer are you?"

"They're important identity papers," I said, rather defensively. "I don't want to lose them."

"*You have to have them with you.* Do you know how much paperwork this is going to take me. I'm a cop, not a border inspector—"

He pinched the bridge of his nose between his thumb and forefinger like he had a bad headache and clamped his eyes shut for a second or two. When he reopened them, he seemed much calmer. He started again: "Okay. Look, I'm sorry. I apologize for the bad language. I'm just a little upset at having to do this. Our genius Governor thought that

41

us joining on with the Feds, and signing up New Mexico to be involved in this "Secure Communities" program would be a good idea, but…" He looked at me for what seemed like a long while, tapping his pen on his metal notebook, obviously thinking about what to do next. He sighed deeply, and I thought I heard him curse once more under his breath, though I could tell his anger wasn't entirely directed at me.

"Okay, please turn around and put your hands on the vehicle, Mr. McKenzie."

"No, wait!" I pleaded, having a pretty good idea where this slippery slope would fetch up. "Seriously, we could run downtown right now and—"

"If you don't have your papers with you, Mr. McKenzie, you're in violation of the law and I have to take you in. Now, do you have your visa or passport with you today or don't you?"

I admitted I had not.

"Then I have no choice but to take you into custody."

In an instant I'd been frisked, trussed up in handcuffs and tossed into the back of his cruiser.

"…Coming off the street with an immigration violator," he called into his police radio. "Please alert other units…"

Chapter 9 – "ICE Has a Detainer on This Guy . . ."

I'D BEEN IN WORSE SITUATIONS, I suppose, but I couldn't think when. It was very depressing, not the least because I knew my car was almost certainly going to get towed again. I sat in the back of the cruiser, contorted to one side to accommodate the hands cuffed behind me, and I've got to tell you, it wasn't the nicest of spots, either—the upholstery was threadbare and stained, and the space between where I was and the front seat was separated by a thick wall of scratched up plexi-glass with a narrow sliding pass-through. Frankly the lack of any inside door handles in the back was troubling, too, though it shouldn't have been a surprise when you think about why they have back seats in police cars. All the drive long the radio kept scratching out noise, messages from the home office for different cops or all the cops or this particular cop, and some-times he answered those, though now he ignored me completely:

"Do you arrest many people for this?" I asked at one point.

No answer.

"Probably keeps you busy, though, having to stay on top of all these ant-immigrant directives from the Governor?"

Nothing. Our relationship had changed, you see. I had become nothing much more than a package to be delivered. It really kind of shocked me, as I am by nature a pretty gregarious guy, and wasn't used to being beneath contempt. I can't say I liked it. At least the ride was short, though, but at the end of it, not surprisingly, the Santa Fe cop-shop

43

proved to be yet another depressing shit hole very much like the Border Patrol checkpoint I'd been in the night before: same institutional lighting, grimy walls, stale smell of fast food and sweat and of course plenty of law enforcement types lolling about with badges and guns prominently displayed.

And lots of waiting. Lots and lots of waiting. It was an environment that to my dismay was starting to feel all too familiar.

It was a busy place, too, and when you're being directed from spot to spot, like they do when they take you in, pretty soon you start to *feel* like a prisoner. No doubt it's specifically designed with that in mind. We hovered around the front for a good forty-five minutes while they started the process of booking me in, and then they took my fingerprints and my photograph and so on. It's a very structured process, so you know, much more than most people would care for. It manages to be both humiliating and profound at the same time: humiliating for all the obvious reasons, and profound 'cause it's like they're taking away your very identity, a chunk of your soul, and giving you a strange new one. Getting that mug shot taken, you can kind of understand how the Indians used to get jacked up at folks who took their pictures, and probably for the same reason. Maybe there's some truth to it, too, that a camera really can swallow you whole, and you're not the same person at the end of it—you definitely feel...smaller. The whole thing makes for quite a transition, in case you want to know, and maybe not so bad for someone tougher than me, but I sure didn't like it.

I was surrendering my wallet and keys and belt and shoelaces when the question finally got asked:

"What's he being charged with?"

"ICE has a detainer on him," my arresting officer said.

Detainer? What the hell was that? I knew a detainer couldn't be good. I was already in a sweat about a whole lot of other things: my visa, my job, my law license. Now I had this "detainer" thing to worry about!

"Yeah. But what're you booking him for?"

"Governor said we're supposed to bring these guys in."

44

"Sure, but he hasn't violated any New Mexico law, has he? We're just supposed to hold him. We alert immigration, they put a detainer on him and ICE comes by to pick him up. It's not a criminal thing."

Sure feels like one, I thought, but didn't say it out loud.

"Well somebody could've told me that."

"Forget about it. Look, cells are full anyway."

"Cells are full?" my cop repeated, sounding a little aghast.

"Toilette's broken in one, and yes, the others are full. We were sued for overcrowding last year, so we can thank the ACLU. So if he isn't criminally charged with anything, or technically even under arrest, for now just put him in the Bullpen. There's five or six of them in there already."

"Up," he says. He said it without looking at me.

Up?

"Cells are full, so we're putting you in the bullpen," he said, like I hadn't heard the other guy. "Let's go."

I made to follow him, and he walked me down the hall, me awkwardly holding up my sagging beltless pants up with one hand, shoes flapping lacelessly on my feet below.

"Can I ask you what I'm being held for?" I ventured.

Surprisingly, this time he answered me. "Hell, I don't know, guy. 'Cause ICE has a detainer out on you. We told Immigration and Customs Enforcement we had you in custody 'cause you didn't have your papers, and they immediately put a detainer on you. That's how it works with them. We tell them we found someone who might be illegal, they immediately put a detainer on you. Then we hold you until they come pick you up."

"How long does that take?"

"Days sometimes. But I know they're already coming up for someone else, so you're not gonna' be waiting long."

"When do I get arraigned?" I asked, still woefully naïve about the world of immigration law.

The cop just laughed.

45

"My bond hearing, then?" I said, straightening a little as we walked. I was an attorney after all. I've never done any criminal work, mind you, but I knew from law school the amount of due process I was entitled to. They had to take my plea and set my bond. It was in the Constitution! These were things I had a fundamental right to demand. Then I remembered what the CBP guy had said the night before at the permanent checkstop:

She's not a prisoner—Immigration offenses are civil, not criminal…

The intake officer at the front just before had echoed the same: *It's not a criminal thing*, he had said.

This whole process was starting to sound like bullshit. And the grim understanding that I had possibly found myself in some dark loop-hole to the Bill of Rights began to grow in me. With a sinking heart I realized I was a lawyer who was going to need a lawyer. Worse, I was probably going to have to write some rather large checks to pay for that lawyer. And while thanks to the recent legacy from my Uncle, and my recently arrived ATM card (which I had just surrendered to the cops), I could probably do that now, parting right away with that cash to get back to even was not what I'd had in mind. This couldn't be happening.

Without further comment the cop ushered me into some kind of storage room with empty shelves lining one wall, and a big metal door at the back where under normal circumstances they probably got deliveries of whatever it is cops get deliveries of (bullets and body armor and such like, I supposed). It had been hastily converted into a waiting area, and there were maybe a dozen mismatched chairs that looked like they had just been brought in, lined up in disorderly rows, about half of 'em occupied.

"Wait here," the cop ordered, and disappeared.

"*Dammit!*" I whispered, half to myself, shaking my head.

I sat down without looking around any further. I could sense the other malefactors in the room seated around me, but didn't much care to become acquainted. Neither did they, apparently, and I didn't bother to survey 'em about it, neither.

This was a hell of a thing, I thought to myself indignantly, the way they treated a body just for being in the wrong category. It should take more than that to lose your liberty, for as anyone who's been locked up will tell you, being incarcerated is a BIG deal. Even a short captivity will remind you pretty quick of what's important in this short life. And with no arraignment, and no bond hearing, I was beginning to understand just how desperate a situation I was in. It suddenly occurred to me they hadn't even offered me a phone call—

Mid-thought something caught my attention.

Just out of the corner of my eye, just within my peripheral field of vision, something hooked me. Something small, something color-ful....Something very familiar. I turned my head slowly to look.

Red hair, stuffed bunny. Hello kitty backpack...

The little nine year old girl from the night before was looking up at me with disbelief. For a second we both sat there speechless. Then the penny dropped.

"*You!*" we cried in unison.

Chapter 10 – CBP Translators

I'VE GOT TO SAY, after the shock of it wore off, I was glad to see at least the kid's condition was still okay, if not exactly improved. I couldn't for the life of me come up with a linear explanation for why she should be in Santa Fe, though, and reckoned, rightly, that there was a story there. Before I had a chance to ask her about it, though, a burly woman police officer stepped into the room. Immediately behind her walked in a great big bear of a fellow wearing the now familiar green uniform of the Border Patrol.

My heart sank. The broad shouldered prick was probably there for me on account of my "detainer." My brain sensibly noted that he was Border Patrol, however—my own arresting officer had just said it was the ICE that was coming to get me. Both entities were part of Homeland Security, of course, but the distinction between ICE and CBP seemed somehow significant in the strange new world I'd found myself in. Nonetheless, I found myself experiencing a Pavlovian reaction to the green Customs and Border Protection uniform, and in spite of my rational conclusion he probably wasn't there on my account, my mind went back again on a jag through what exactly this sinister *detainer* might imply—probably immediate escort to a "transitional facility" for a lengthy detention prior to my removal from the country, or some such other personally apocalyptic thing.

48

The two of 'em stood at the front of the room for what seemed like an eternity, looking around at all us pathetic chickens, and conversing between 'em in whispers. You really got the sense they were debating which of us to eat first, until I realized their eyes hadn't moved from the seat next to me—the one where the little red-headed girl was sitting.

The CBP agent said something to the woman cop I couldn't quite make out, both of 'em still looking directly at the red-headed nine-year old. The woman cop nodded quickly, setting aside what looked like it could have been unease, then shifted her vision, looking around at the the room as a whole:

"Okay, translator's here," she announced.

I noted that the title "translator" also seemed at odds with any mission related to gathering me up. I shook my head to clear it, and decided to hold my water and wait and see what developed.

Border Patrol immediately stepped out in front with an air of authority and a gigantic smile that his eyes didn't share. He boasted the familiar sidearm and jackboots, and a gold badge on his broad chest that read "Honor First."

"Who here speaks Spanish?" the giant says to everybody with fake bonhomie in a bluff voice as deep as gravel. Then he repeated something like it in *Espanole*, with "*akis*" and "*por favors*" peppered about.

I looked around at the others in the room, and saw hands instantly fly up into the air. They were the ones this Border Patrol "translator" was speaking to, of course, and I suddenly clicked. His audience was everybody in the room *but* me. But me, and probably the little red-headed girl.

No, his audience was the darker, Mexican looking folks, about half-a-dozen in number, every one of 'em the sort you see down at the corner of Guadalupe and Agua Fria early in the mornings, day workers hanging about in canvas jackets and work boots waiting for pick-up trucks to take 'em to off-the-books jobs at construction sites and ranches. For all I knew, Guadalupe and Agua Fria was where the cops had actually gathered these guys up. They all looked pretty harmless to me, and I suspected they had been pinched by the local PD for a variety of non-existent misdemeanors—loitering while brown, doing fifty-five in a fif-

49

ty-four, that sort of thing—a regular quota-filling exercise, a bleak bi-weekly dragnet of the vulnerable, foreign looking folks on the edges of Santa Fe society that was designed to bolster the department's monthly numbers.

And since these guys by and large couldn't communicate directly with the local cops because of language barriers, and were probably at their most vulnerable right now, it was simply a matter of putting two and two together to conclude that the CBP Agent was there playing a double game. It's an attorney's job to be suspicious, of course, and the idea that Border Patrol Agents were kindly offering to come all the way up here from their home base five hours away down in Las Cruces solely to interpret for any tired poor huddled masses that needed their services didn't ring true. They'd translate, no doubt about that—ostensibly to help these poor prisoners present their side of things to the authorities—but in the meantime, they'd screen 'em for possible immigration violations, too. What a dirty trick.

Papers Please!

Seeing the many hands raised, the Border Patrol agent launched right away into an Hispanic soliloquy that went on for quite a bit. God knows what he was telling 'em. The whole thing really didn't sit well with me at all, but the audience of bland faces nevertheless woke up as he spoke, and looked suddenly plugged in. It was hearing the Spanish that did it, I'm sure, and after what was probably hours of people talking overly loud to 'em in words they didn't understand it must have been quite a relief to hear their own language.

When he'd finished, several of the prisoners started up, chattering over each other in Spanish themselves, with statements or questions, and it became apparent they were anxious, even eager to engage with some-one—anyone—who could understand 'em. I didn't get a word of it, of course, but it was still kind of pathetic, 'cause by their tone you could sense the desperate nature of their entreaties.

Watch out! I wanted to scream at 'em. *How can you be falling for this!*

50

The CBP Agent received a question from a likely looking fellow in red Chucks, held up his hand for the gentleman to wait, then whispered the English version of the man's question into the stout woman police officer's ear.

She seemed visibly offended.

"*No*, you can tell him he's definitely *not* entitled to have a lawyer appointed for him!" She said the words loudly, in the final and non-appealable cinderblock tone used by civil servants the world over, even though there was no way red Chucks could possible understand her. "He can pay for one himself," she explained, her tone becoming more controlled, "but he's not criminally charged with anything, so there's nothing here that would allow him free counsel."

The Border Patrol Agent repeated her answer to the room in Spanish, and the room buzzed again with subsidiary questions. However, the Border Patrol Agent held up a hand to try to settle 'em down. The cop stepped up then with an air of finality, and cut 'em off neat as you please:

"OKAY, UP-UP-UP!" she said to the group, staccato voiced and a tad impatient. "That's enough. Let's go! You'll each get your own individual interview with the translator."

The "translator" repeated it in Spanish, and the six or so Mexican men in the room got up and followed him and the police officer out the door. As the one in the red chucks—the one who'd asked the question about the attorney—passed my chair, he paused and turned to me.

"Welcome to my world," he said in perfect midwestern English, his eyebrows raised and his brown eyes locking briefly with mine. And before I even had a chance to process this cognitive dissonance, he was gone with the others.

Off to their individual self-incriminating interviews, I expected. And from there, in chains to a distant detention center—probably without any kind of notice to loved ones, either. While it was a sight to make any immigrant-hating right-wing conservative stand up and cheer, to me it seemed really low, a cruel trick, and a dishonest one, too. An image of their fatherless children and soon to be destitute families flashed in front of my eyes.

51

Before I had time to properly think on it any more, though, the lady police officer popped her head around the corner into the room to look at me, and then at the kid.

"Young lady, Annie," she said, "you stay here, okay?"

The little red-head—Annie by name, apparently—nodded sweetly.

"We'll be right back for you, sweetheart, okay?"

And with that, the cop's head disappeared back 'round the corner, and she followed the receding parade down the hall.

From a little ways off, over the diminishing tromp of boots on linoleum, I heard the deep, gravelly voice of the gigantic Border Patrol Agent remark to the police office: "*You know, ICE has a detainer on that guy...*"

It was a sock in the gut, a reminder that smelled of Gestapo basements and endless institutional hallways, but in truth, I decided I really didn't much want to find out what it meant. By hook or by crook, I had to get out of there. I was an attorney, a functionary of the State of New Mexico—surely my status in the community, such as it was, could protect me. How to bring those assets to bear? I needed to square some legal representation, and double-quick, too. Judging by the lady cop's recently translated comments, and as I had actually already surmised, they weren't going to pay for my attorney. But presumably I was still entitled to call one before they shipped me off. Like I said before, I did have the dough for representation now, and I knew a lot of lawyers, of course, but no one schooled in immigration law, except maybe Madstone. Madstone'd help me out. He *had* to help me out! In fact, I'd been weighing my options since they'd tossed me in the back of that police car, and had already come to the conclusion that Madstone was my only hope. He might represent me himself, or if for some reason he couldn't, he'd put me on track to find someone schooled in immigration law who could.

Good news. But frankly, it pissed me off to think of my Uncle's legacy circling the drain for such a thing. I'd been lifted out of destitution for about a nanosecond, and now I was looking right back in to the abyss. I never even had a chance to get that Martini and hamburger!

52

Sonovabitch, I thought bitterly. The day had begun with me newly solvent, back in the driver's seat of my freshly redeemed car, looking forward to being a daddy once again and picking up my daughter in a few days after a having missed just one weekend of visitation. I'd thought I'd been climbing out of the hole—now it would appear my situation was worse than ever.

Before I could think on it further, though, next to me, I heard a snuffle, and turned to see the poor little kid next to me was crying.

"Oh...hey...don't cry," I said reflexively.

"They took my mom away."

"What? Oh. Hey, well, but..." I stumbled awkwardly.

"My mom's going away, and they're sending her to Canada," she snuffled.

Well, there was no response to that. The hell of it was, Annie, as the cop had called her, was probably right, and frankly I'd have been crying, too. I cast about for something I could say.

"They'll get you back to her," I lied. "You don't think they actually want to split up families, do you?" I looked into her little face as earnestly as I could, but even then I sensed she was too smart for me.

"That's not true," she said to me tearfully, in a voice almost too quiet to hear.

The kid's waterworks continued, and I struggled with how to deal with it. My own daughter I would have hugged and comforted, but fortunately her tears were spent on things like lost toys in the back seat of the car or the unfairness of a perceived rebuke. Weeping over the loss of a parent was far more profound thing, and possessed of a certain existential dignity. Perhaps it would be better if I just stood aside and respected the tears?

My uncertainty was quickly rendered moot, though, because she suddenly went silent.

I realized Annie was staring at something and I followed her gaze. She was looking across the room at the big delivery door, and it was pretty forbidding, too, if you really want to know. As doors go, it was oversized and armor plated, with that vertical metal lip over the door jamb to keep anyone from trying to jimmy the latch, and it looked like people had tried pretty hard, too, over the years, to jimmy that latch. There were deep scratches in the metal, and chunks and dents, and places where rivets had been replaced. All in all, it was a junkyard dog of a door that looked like it had been tested pretty thoroughly, and come through not wanting much, either.

"They never said not to go out the door," she said, tentatively, as if she had found a loophole.

"I don't think they're too worried."

That made her suddenly very excited. "So you didn't hear 'em say anything about the door, either?"

"It'll be fine. Just sit tight."

"*They're—sending—my—mom—to—Canada,*" she said, enunciating each word like I was some kind of idiot, and hadn't remembered.

She got up, and walked over to the door and stood before it with her 'Hello Kitty' pack strapped on her back, and her stuffed bunny under her arm. She stood there for several seconds, contemplating the thing, then lifted one hand, and extended it toward the door with the forefinger out. She didn't actually touch the door, mind you, but just held her finger suspended, hesitating, the tip of it maybe an inch away from the cold metal.

"C'mon, kid," I said. "Sit down, why doncha'..."

She turned and looked at me, then turned back to the door, and gave it the slightest push with the tip of her finger. To my amazement, and without any more than that, the massive thing swung open. It swung heavy, slow and silent, all the way open, nice and easy and without a sound.

What the hell, I thought—an open back door? What kind of police were these?

She turned to me with such a face—her mouth wide with surprise, her eyes lit with triumph!

"Don't go out the door, kid," I said, wearily. "They said they'd be back in a minute. C'mon, you're gonna' get us into trouble..."

She shrugged, and took a peek around to look outside.

54

"C'mon kid—quit messing around. Close the door."

"Make me," she said.

"Seriously?" I said, getting up. "Make me? Really?" I was getting a little hot—I mean, after all, who needs this. It's not that I wasn't sympathetic, but I had troubles of my own, and the last thing I needed was some kind of accidental abetting escape charge to deal with now. I didn't even want to think what the cost of defending a charge for something like that would be. "You're *going* to get us into trouble," I added, realizing immediately that the words sounded quite whiney even to me—it made me feel like a bit of a nine year old myself.

Her eyes narrowed and her jaw set. "I'm *going* to find my mom," she said. Then lickety-split, just like that, she was round the door, and out. It's amazing how quick kids can move when they want to.

The door hung open behind her. I shook my head. I weighted my options, but there was nothing for it. I was the adult here, so I reckoned I'd have to grab her and bring her back before the cops returned to the room—it was for her own good, after all, and mine as well.

"Shit," I muttered, and stepped out after her.

I found myself in what was your basic garden variety back alley, with a tall cinderblock wall topped with razor wire along its length, and some soggy boxes scattered in a pile, and at the end of it, about ten yards away, a heavy-duty chain link gate that blocked the exit. The little girl at that exact moment was standing in front of that gate, eyeing it up very deliberately. I took a quick look behind me, and saw the heavy metal door was slowly closing. I thought briefly about propping it open, but time was of the essence, plus at the rate it was moving I reckoned I'd have a good several seconds before it shut, so I gauged the distance, and took a couple of tentative steps away from the door and toward the little girl, the better to persuade her.

"C'mon, kid. It's a *police station*. The gate's locked. Let's get back in before you get us both into more trouble."

"No."

"We'll get stuck out here if you don't."

She ignored me, and gave the chain link gate a push, and sure enough, that goddam thing swung wide, too.

"*Jesus Christ,*" I hissed.

What kind of cops were these?

Before I could say another word—or move another step, for that matter—she was through the gate and out.

What the hell! I stood there, and wrestled for a moment with the notion of just letting her go, but she was so tiny. I mean, she was just a little kid, a defenseless little nine year old running out of some back alley into the New Mexico desert at night. Man or girl, it doesn't take much imagination to conjure up the bad things that can happen to you in New Mexico after dark. And it is a pretty scary place, too—just for a kick-off, there were hoboes, rapists, gang bangers, child molesters, feral dogs, hoodie wearing teenagers...

I imagined my own little girl, and knew what I had to do.

As it turned out, my time was up anyway. Behind me, the heavy metal door clanked shut with a terribly finality. Instantly, an alarm ripped open the night air.

"*Jesus Christ!*" I said aloud, though over the claxon you couldn't possibly hear me. I weighed my options once more, and in a split second I called it.

I launched past the chain link gate, and after the girl.

III. Run!

Chapter 11 – Escape!

THE ALARM FILLED the dark night air, rising and falling.

"Hey!" I shouted after her, "HEY!" but you couldn't hear a thing on account of that terrible noise.

I ran hard, following her out into the back parking lot, but not closing any distance. That little kid was fast as hell, I gotta' tell you. She disappeared amongst the police cars, but there was only so far she could go—I hoped.

Twenty feet behind me a couple of cops had already emerged from behind the chain-link gate we had just exited, with the bear-like Border Patrol Agent standing head an shoulders taller in the middle of 'em. The lot were peering out into the night, obviously not having clicked to who exactly had gotten out or where we had gone. I weighed my options, and the only reasonable one was to call 'em over and explain things. This was just a misunderstanding, after all—they'd mostly be interested in the welfare of the little girl. Maybe my assistance would earn me their indulgence on the detainer thing.

"WAIT—OVER HERE!" I shouted at 'em, trying in vain to sound earnest and unthreatening above the wailing alarm. "I'M OVER HERE!"

I had my hands up, and contemplated dropping to my knees, like I'd seen 'em do in some movies, 'cause I knew the main thing was not to appear threatening. I realized I didn't actually know the right thing for sure, though, and decided instead to start walking slowly toward them, thinking it'd at least be easier to communicate with them that way.

"SHE'S JUST OVER THERE," I shouted, "AND—"

To my surprise, two more green Border Patrol uniforms appeared outside, joining the growing law enforcement milieu, and immediately shoved their way to the front. How many of these CBP guys were hanging out here in Santa Fe? If I hadn't know better, I might have thought they were running the show.

One of 'em heard my shouting, and pointed at me.

Here we go, thinks I. Maybe now they'll turn off the alarm. Then I saw him pull out his sidearm.

Pop! Pop!

I looked down. The dust had kicked up two little clouds right in front of my shoes, and spattered my pants with sand. I looked back up. Another one of the Border Patrol Agents had his firearm out, and was aiming at me, too.

"*Christ!*" I blurted. "DON'T SHOOT!" I threw my hands even further in the air. "DON'T SHOOT!"

"Get him!" I heard the deep, gravelly voice of the bearlike CBP interpreter cry out over the surging alarm, and suddenly there was that popping sound again.

Pop! Pop! Pop-Pop!

"*Jesus Christ!*" I cried out, again.

Instinctively, I ducked and ran.

Looking for any kind of shelter, I scrambled over to where the police vehicles were parked a few yards away. I made for 'em in a sort of desperate, panicky, waddling half-crouch, waving my hands and arms in the air over like an Orangutan's. Around me bullets were pocking the dirt; clods and pebbles filled the air.

Why weren't the Santa Fe PD guys stopping these crazy Border Patrol bastards? *What kind of cops were these!*

I scrambled between the cars, hearing the occasional *Tink!* as a round hit the metal body of one of the vehicles, or a discrete crash as a window or mirror was shattered. I was breathing fast and shallow, and my heart was pounding like a hammer.

I whipped around behind a parked police cruiser, making sure to keep my legs and feet lined up with the tires so I didn't get shot from underneath the car. I sat tight there for a moment, trying to think. I wasn't sure, but there was a good chance I'd already pissed myself.

I suddenly realized I was still pissing.

I held my breath and peeked round the side of the vehicle. I could see the local cops were becoming very animated, and it was clear some measure of dissension existed between the different branches of law enforcement. There was shouting between 'em, and now one of the local cops was way up in the face of one of the green Border Patrol agents. There appeared to be a real confrontation brewing: boys in green versus boys in blue. I didn't have any more time to dally and watch, though, 'cause despite all that the bullets kept coming.

I pulled my head back out of sight. The alarm was still howling, and behind me I imagined 'em closing in, military style, all professional and icy. Some of those guys were probably ex-Navy Seals and such like, I thought to myself. I was a *deadman!*

"Hey," a falsetto voice cried at me from the other direction.

I looked up, and there was Annie calling to me from the window of one of the unmarked cop cars. She was waving me over in a vigorous manner, her brown freckled face all wide and excited. I didn't have to be asked twice.

I scuttled over, and scrambled up into the car through the passenger side door. To my surprise, Annie was sitting up in the driver's seat, and the vehicle itself was actually running.

"Look what you did!" I hissed. "I told you not to leave the—"

The little nine year old didn't say a word, but dropped down out of her seat onto the floor of the car with a thump, throwing both feet onto the accelerator as hard as she could. The car shot forward.

I flew back in my seat.

Looking over I saw that her little head had dropped down well below the level of the dashboard—we were driving completely blind!

The vehicle careened wide to one side, then wide to the other and then drunkenly over toward a gigantic back SUV. The thing grew large in the windshield, and I grabbed the steering wheel in terror. I pulled it hard to the right, successfully rounding us past its rear bumper.

Immediately I swung the wheel hard the other way and tried to straighten us out. Before I could, though, Annie must have jammed down hard on the accelerator again, 'cause once more I shot back in the seat, the tires squealed, and I swear to God we lifted up on one side for a split second.

We went back down with a thump, and I realized she had miraculously gotten us pointed down the fairway between orderly lines of parked police cars. We shot down the middle of the blacktop parking lot gaining speed and heading rapidly toward god knew what. To the side, I caught a blurry glimpse of one of the big kill-crazy immigration guys in his green uniform standing tall in the midst of all those dismayed cops. He spread his legs apart into a target shooting stance and lifted his pistol, and I know it's not even remotely possible, but I got the distinct impression he was somehow aiming it through the dark and dust and flying gravel and directly at my head.

Was this all over a *Detainer?*

Then suddenly the parked cars were whizzing by us almost too fast to see and I leaned over and desperately tried to steer, and Annie held down the gas, and then suddenly we were at the end of the road.

BAM!

Behind us a chain link gate flew backward spinning through the air, and we were out.

I held tightly on to the steering wheel, trying desperately to keep us going straight down whatever no-name County access road we had suddenly found ourselves on, and Annie must have been keeping her feet firm on the gas, too, 'cause we weren't slowing down at all. We were shooting forward into the darkness, without headlights and with no idea where we were headed. I knew they'd be after us in no time, too, and I stretched over to get a look in the rearview, but couldn't manage it. I didn't hear any sirens yet, for whatever that was worth.

Up ahead I spied a well lit intersection, and reckoned job one was to stop for oncoming traffic. I didn't fancy the notion of getting t-boned by some hillbilly in a pickup.

"Let's pull up at that stop sign," I said, cutting her off. I figured once we got safely through the intersection, pretty quick we'd have to find a spot to pull out and lie doggo for a bit so I could switch out with her. At least then I could get into the driver's seat, though god alone knew where we'd go from there.

"Ohhh-kay," she said, rather tentative. "How do I stop it?" She asked the question like it was the most reasonable thing in the world, which I suppose it was if you were a nine year old kid that didn't know about brakes.

There was no time to explain.

I cursed, and tried to get my leg over the hump so I could shove the brake pedal down, but it was an awkward maneuver, and before I could do it we had shot through the intersection and were on the other side of it. Behind us, the air-horn of a swerving semi-trailer truck blasted at us angrily.

I jammed my foot down on the left peddle a little too hard, 'cause the brakes immediately bit down and locked up, and we lost control.

We went into a spin, and for a moment were facing down the road backward, then frontward again, then backward, then over a curb with a horrible thump and a scraping sound. We thrashed through some scrub, then clattered down a shallow embankment, and for one terrible moment I thought we were going to roll, but we righted again, only to rumble blind down several more yards of corduroy, and *thump!* into an arroyo.

We fetched up in the loose, dry sand at an odd angle, but at least we weren't moving forward anymore, though the wheels were still spinning with a high pitched whine at about a hundred miles an hour—one of 'em entirely up in the air.

I saw that Annie was still shoving down on the gas with both feet, her arms braced hard up against the dashboard, her face locked in a horrible rictus grin. She was proving to be a pretty intense little kid, this Annie was.

"Easy, easy," I said to her. "Throttle back, kid, we're not going anywhere."

Slowly, slowly she lifted her two feet off the gas pedal, and the engine's high pitched whine eased off to a moderate hum then to a quiet idle then stopped altogether. I gently reached over and switched off the key.

After a moment she climbed back up into the driver's seat.

My heart was galloping and the pulse of it thudded in my ears. I could actually feel the zing of the adrenaline levels peak, and then start to recede. For many long seconds we just sat there next to each other, breathing heavily, and feeling the sudden quiet take hold.

As the seconds ticked by, gooseflesh raised up on my skin. I shivered hard.

With a jolt, Annie jerked herself erect and vomited on the driver's side door.

Chapter 12 – The Arroyo

WE'D NEVER BOTHERED to turn the headlights on, and it was dark as hell down in that arroyo, though high up above I could make out the brush we had just ripped through that rimmed the high banks of the dry water-course, the Chamisa and Rabbitbush and clumpgrass silhouetted nicely against the stars. Above and beyond the ghost-cloud of the Milky-Way was almost visible.

"Well, this is pretty good," Annie finally said, looking around, and nodding her head in a satisfied kind of way.

I was puzzled, because her words didn't make any sense. For a moment, I thought I'd had a stroke.

"What's good about it?" I asked stupidly, feeling numb.

"Well," she said, putting a forefinger to her lower lip, considering. "We're out of jail. That's good."

I felt the hysterical urge to laugh. This was definitely *not* good. It was the opposite of good. It was catastrophic. We were alive, yes, but the wrecked and broken laws that littered the path behind us were sufficient to get me locked up indefinitely. I ticked 'em off in my head one by one: escape, resisting arrest, theft, aggravated theft, theft of a police vehicle, endangering a minor…

There were more, of course, but there wasn't any point thinking about the rest. The prosecutor would undoubtedly list 'em for me.

Off in the distance, I heard the first police sirens start to rise.

"We've got to turn ourselves in," I said. "You know that, right?"

"*I'm* not going back there."

"We can't just break out of jail and steal a police car. We have to go back there and sort this out."

"They were shooting at us."

There was no denying the girl had a point. I thought about it for a bit, and realized that if we went back to the Santa Fe cop shop right now they probably would kill the shit out of us. Or me, at any rate.

"Okay then, we get an attorney to negotiate our surrender," I said, acknowledging the reality of our situation. "We get out of here, and get someone good. My partner Madstone did a lot of criminal—"

Already she was shaking her head. "I'm going to find my mom."

Up above, the sirens were getting closer.

Annie gathered up her backpack and stuffed bunny. "I want to get out of the car."

"Yeah—okay." I shoved open the door on my side, and climbed clumsily out of the tilty vehicle myself. With my feet sinking a bit into the flat, dry sand of the unnamed arroyo, I reached back in and lifted Annie out and onto the ground.

But now the emergency sirens weren't off in the distance anymore; they were unmistakably overhead, rising along the road up above us. They were loud as hell, and it sounded like there was about ten-thousand of 'em up there. Just as they seemed to be right on top of us, angular headlights lit up the brush along the high rim, along with bright rotating circus-wheels of red and blue and I knew then we were done for—they'd be thrashing down here in seconds, throwing spotlights on us and bringing our misguided flight to a sticky end straight away.

But almost as fast as they'd come up, the lights kind of shifted away, and the sound of the sirens started to dim. They'd passed us by, and were flying toward downtown Santa Fe at top speed. They hadn't spotted our detour and were off in the distance now, following nothing down the road.

Annie uttered an unmistakable sigh of relief.

Well, there's one lucky break at least, thinks I.

66

A thought immediately followed by how long will we have until they realize their mistake and started backtracking? I briefly wondered if they had some kind of active GPS in the stolen cop car we'd just abandoned—something that would draw a Sat-Nav target on us, and bring that mob of law enforcement types back our way. Probably not, since they wouldn't have passed us up so easy in the first place if they'd had such a thing.

Would they?

In the immediacy of the Hue and Cry, perhaps they just hadn't thought to use it...

But Sat-Nav or not, there was nothing for it but to get out of there as quickly as possible. We started walking up the soft sand away from the swamped squad car. I fully expected the sirens to return, and kept looking over my shoulder for the headlights up top to come back, but they didn't.

My eyes were getting accustomed to the dark, and I could see now there were houses all up and down the length of the arroyo. They were widely spaced, and mostly up high, screened by trees and bushes and set back some distance from the edge of the wide ravine, too, creating the perception of privacy and seclusion down where we were. It was an illusion. There was no knowing who might be out in their back yard having a drink or a barbecue, who might at any time idly drift over to the far end of their back yard and have a look down into this sandy mini-canyon at just the wrong time; look down and see us down here moving about and associate us with the police sirens.

I took a deep breath, and halted. "Okay, so what are we doing here, kid?"

"Running from the police," she answered, matter-of-factly.

The shameless truth of the statement made me want to laugh. "Look, we have to go back to the police station. We really have to turn ourselves in to somebody right now," I said. "*Before* they come and get us."

"*I'm* not going back there."

"Kid, we have to!"

67

"I'm going to find my mom," she said. She said it flatly, without emphasis, in the manner of an established fact.

I sighed heavily. We needed to clear up this horrible misunderstanding with the cops, but obviously the kid was going to be a problem. I had no plan and the situation was dire. "Shit," I said. *"Shit, fuck, goddam…"*

Next to me a heard a sharp intake of breath.

My face flushed red in the dark and I immediately felt like the one foul mouthed parent at a little girls' soccer game. "Sorry," I said. I wouldn't cuss in front of my own daughter and I decided right then and there I should extend the same courtesy to nine-year-old Annie…

Look, dumbass. My mom is in the other room. I'll be fine.

…Regardless of whatever she may have been exposed to before this.

"Look," I continued, "we gotta' figure something out. You ain't gonna find your mum down in this arroyo and I'm not going to get things straightened out with the cops from down here, either." She caught the thread, and nodded at the sense of it. She looked up at me expectantly: "Okay," I went on, "I'm just thinking out loud, trying to work my way through this thing. What can we do that'll work for both of us?…" I wasn't new to this game, by the way. Sometimes working through to a compromise is the only way forward. And the image of those crazy-in-the-head Border Patrol guys shooting at us was still fresh in my brain.

"So kid, you were right before, trying to just go back and explain things now would definitely be hazardous to our health. So the first thing that flows from that is we have to lie low. At least for now. Second is, we gotta' get some legal advice. Help, right? Legal help? And right away, so I'll try Madstone tomorrow and see what he thinks."

She was already shaking her head. "I'm going to—"

"I know, *I know*," I said, cutting her off. "You're going to find your mum. So the third thing has to be that, I guess. Not going chasing after your mum quite yet, but maybe Madstone can find something out about her while he's looking into this other stuff about settling things with the cops."

That seemed to catch her interest.

"We'll lie low and stay out of the way of the cops until we can talk to Madstone. Then see if he can arrange my surrender, number one; then find out what's going on with your mum, number two. Sound okay?"

"She's in Canada. They sent her back to Canada."

"Maybe. Yeah, maybe they already sent her to Canada. But Madstone can find out about that for sure. And if she is up there, maybe he can find out where exactly she is. I mean, it's a huge country. You can't just 'go to Canada' and find somebody. You gotta' be sensible about these things…"

Even in the dark, I could see her calculating. The silence went on for a while, but I held on. There's an old saying, never interrupt a judge when she's ruling for you. And with that, the red headed nine-year-old of the tinted persuasion that the Border Patrol desk jockey back in Cruces thought was Mexican but who turned out to be "regular American" stuck out her little hand.

"We won't go back to the police?" she said.

"I promise."

I shook her hand then, and we two just stood there. We had sort of a plan, now, and had made something of a pact. But I still had no real idea of what to do next.

"Well, we can't stay down here until tomorrow," I finally said, thinking out loud.

"Can't we go to your house?"

"It's way on the other side of town. We got no way to get there. Plus, there's a very good chance they'll eventually come looking for us at that address. It's on my ID, after all. Although this *is* New Mexico…" I looked around one more time, and then called it. "You know, I left the truck in the parking lot at the wrecking yard this afternoon."

"What truck?"

"It's a long story. My friend's truck. James Quintana's truck. He let me borrow it and I left it parked on this side of town. Not far away from here at all. I'm thinking if we follow the arroyo a half mile or so up, it'll take us to Airport Road and we can walk the rest of the way to the wrecking yard up along the blacktop."

"Won't they see us?"

"It's light industrial along in there. And it's after dark—should probably be pretty quiet. We'll just hug the shadows after we climb out of the arroyo…"

She was already walking again, so I shut up and got a move on myself. Behind us, the abandoned police car sat empty, perched at a wonky angle with one door open. I turned away and didn't bother to look back again.

It was less of a hike than I anticipated, and we couldn't have gone three-hundred yards before we came to a culvert under a road that proved to be the one we were looking for. As it turned out, there was more traffic up above than I would have liked, but we scrambled out of the arroyo to street level, and stayed well back in the shadows. We picked our way along carefully in the dark, keeping our top eye out for bad guys, and made the wrecking yard in pretty short order.

I spotted the truck straight away. The big blue machine stood alone in the parking lot. Outdoor security lights were on, though the windows of the double wide trailer that served as the wrecking yard's office were all dark, and it was plainly apparent the place was closed; the operators of the establishment had all long gone home.

I reckoned there might well be a guard on duty somewhere, maybe some dogs in the back or something, but they'd be focused on protecting the stuff in the yard. That's where the assets were—the stuff worth watching over. It'd be surprising if anyone was watching the front parking area.

"That's it," I whispered to Annie, though there was no need to be quiet really.

"It's a truck, alright," she said, nodding.

Like a magnet it drew us across the pavement. There was a vague fatalism to it, like some kind of karmic tipping point was approaching that we'd jointly have to pass over. And as we came up to the big blue machine, I hesitated once more. Did we really want to run? Wasn't this actually crazy—a very bad idea? The little voice in the back of my mind was still whispering: "you should go back and straighten things out now,

70

it's not too late; don't be a schmuck, trust the authorities, do as you're told…" It just wouldn't be silenced. And despite the bargain Annie and I had struck, I was getting a really heavy feeling about this.

Annie stood opposite me in the dark and could sense my hesitation; I could feel her staring. She knew what was going through my adult brain.

"Chicken."

"I'm not chicken, I'm—"

"You're chicken."

"It's not about being chicken; it's that—"

"Chicken." She turned her head and crossed her arms and started making "*Bwalk-Bwalk*" chicken noises at me.

"*Shhh!*—" I hissed at her. Kids can drive you nuts sometimes.

She looked around the yard, and over at the distant windows of the neighboring businesses. "Ha!" she cried, triumphantly. "There's no one to hear. Chicken. *Bwalk-Bwalk…Bwalk-Bwalk…Bwalk—*"

She actually started prodding me with her forefinger.

"Knock it off!" I said, pulling out of reach. "I'm not a chicken. Look, we don't have the key."

"How can you not have the key?"

"The police took all my stuff when they arrested me. My wallet, my keys…" My belt, I thought, yanking my pants up for about the twentieth time.

Annie reached up and grabbed the passenger side door handle. She shoved her thumb down on the over-sized button and with a loud "click" the door came unlatched. She pulled it all the way open with a loud creak.

"*Sonofabitch*," I whispered, under my breath.

"What?"

"Nothing. Look we still can't start the engine—"

"The key's right there," she said, pointing to the ignition. And fuck me if it wasn't. What the hell had I been thinking of leaving the key in there.

71

"Look, we can't take my friend's truck and go on the lam with it. People just don't do that sort of thing." This was just temporizing, and I knew it. So did she.

"We'd just be borrowing it. We'd bring it back," she said, reasonably. "And we can't just stay here. *Come on...*" she said, bouncing up and down with an urgent *tremello* flourish. "You *said* so."

She was right, of course. That was the plan, and there really was no good alternative. In any event, we couldn't very well stay out there cooling our heels in the parking lot forever. Time was not on our side. The cops would eventually find their cruiser abandoned at the bottom of the Arroyo a quarter of a mile away from where we presently stood, with our footprints giving them a clear trail up the dry sand. Waves of squad cars and SWAT teams would follow shortly afterward, along with helicopters and spotlights from above swooping down over this very neighborhood. I did want to turn myself in, but not *that* way. It made a lot of sense to flee from ground zero and buy some time so I could get things straightened out. If we "borrowed" James' truck I could call Madstone from some safe haven—somewhere outside of Santa Fe, beyond the immediate jurisdiction of the local PD—and he could get things squared away with the authorities: *Then* I could come back and turn myself in...

Time was not on our side.

"You already ran," Annie observed.

"*After you*, yeah. I ran after you. And where would we go, anyway?"

"Canada!" Annie said, grinning her big nine-year-old grin.

"We're not going to Canada!" I said, my voice inadvertently jumping an octave or so.

"My mom's in Canada."

I was done playing Hamlet.

"No! Look, we got a deal, right? I call Madstone tomorrow and find out about your mum. We don't even know for sure if she is even in Canada yet." I didn't hear any sirens, nor anything else stirring, either. The calm was close to perfect, and the Autumn air was crisp—the frost was on the pumpkin, as they used say.

72

Without another word lifted Annie up into the passenger side seat.

"*Yesss!*" she hissed, and did a little fist-pump.

"Buckle your seatbelt, kid."

She placed her Hello Kitty backpack down on the seat beside her, and her stuffed bunny rabbit next to that, and began working the lap belt across her legs. It was one of those big clunky stainless steel belt buckles that just hangs loose on the seat when you're not using it, very old school, with no shoulder belt, and no mechanism to roll it back out of the way. Early safety technology at best, and I made a mental note to drive *very* carefully.

The door creaked loudly as I slammed it shut on her, and then I walked around to the driver's side.

I climbed into the cab, and sitting down in the driver's seat I felt an unfamiliar lump in my pocket, and reached in and pulled up a pair of rainbow colored mittens. They were the very ones Annie's mum had dropped on the tarmac the night before, and I realized I hadn't thought about 'em since the event, almost twenty-four hours before. Hell, had it only been twenty-four hours? What a crowded day.

"Hey, those are mine!" Annie exclaimed, swiping 'em out of my hands.

"Oh yeah—I mean, I know. I totally forgot about those."

She gave me such a look.

"I'm sorry," I said. "Really. I'm sorry. Your mum dropped 'em last night, and wanted you to have 'em."

Her scowl waned a bit.

I looked at the things as Annie pulled 'em onto her hands. Patterns between the broad rainbow stripes resolved themselves into big rainbow numbers. They were subtly knitted into the pattern with remarkable precision.

"What's with the numbers?" I asked, pointing at 'em.

"What numbers?"

"On your gloves? Between the colors?"

"Dunno," Annie said, yawning. "They're cute. Mommy calls them her register,"

73

"Well, they sure are pretty," I said nicely, thinking what a lovely Madam DeFarge her mother must be.

Apropos of nothing, I suddenly realized I was pretty well exhausted. Hungry, too. Plus the cops had taken my belt, wallet and shoelaces—I was totally saggin' and baggin'. We were broke and on the run from the law.

God I was so screwed.

I pulled the key out of the ignition for a moment and looked at it. Even in the imperfect light of the cab of the truck I could easily see the letters "GM" stamped on the thing. It was a very old key, probably the original one that came with the truck when it was sold new back when Richard Nixon was President, and you could see the brass in places where the stainless steel had worn away.

I shoved the thing back in the ignition.

"Alrighty then."

I turned the key hard and the engine roared. Say what you will about those old V-8s, you could really feel that power under the hood.

Chapter 13 – On the Road Again

AND SUDDENLY ANNIE AND ME were on the road in a giant blue pickup truck with Canadian plates and a Jesus Fish on the back.

It was the middle of the night now, and the streets at least by the wrecking yard were completely deserted. I headed us up Airport Road past the Santa Fe Country Club, feeling like a target all around, taking great care to keep my speed right at the posted limit of thirty-five. Not too fast, not too slow. I scanned the gauges and saw the tank was full; everything else looked normal, too. That's one of the great things about those old vehicles—the dashboards only have about three items, a speedometer, an odometer and a gas gauge, so staying on top of 'em is easy.

We glided steadily along and I kept rotating my attention in thoroughly paranoid fashion from right to left, from mirrors to windows to mirrors again, looking up streets, into yards and empty lots, watching, expecting—anticipating—the inevitable Bogies. Of course, I had no idea what I'd do if I actually spotted a cop car. Or worse yet, saw its cherries come on and leap after us. It's not like we could have outrun anything in this ancient bucket of bolts, but forewarned is forearmed, I always say…

I shook my head to clear it.

Instead of worrying about that over which I had no control, I tried to focus my thoughts into a more productive line—what would we need on this trip if we actually made it out of town? What should we anticipate, so to speak, on the road? I started checking off all the boxes I could think of, and mostly, I reckoned, what we could expect was just driving. If we were going to lie low for a day or two, after all, we'd be wise to do it away out of the way—beyond the reach of the Santa Fe PD, for sure; ideally beyond the reach of Child Services, too, or any other New Mexico authorities that might be coming after Annie. So where did that lead? The Colorado border for a kickoff. I hadn't thought about the benefits of getting ourselves out-of-state until now, but if we were fleeing the jurisdiction anyway, there was no point in making a half-assed job of it. So driving and driving and more driving was our near term horoscope; we'd have to get food later, of course; and eventually gas, too. And as soon as we could I'd have to call Madsone—

Madstone!

The thought brought me up quick, 'cause it suddenly occurred to me I didn't have a cell phone. How in the world was I going to call Madstone?

I slowed to a stop for a red light. There was a trickle of traffic now that we were closing in on the main drag, drunks going home from the clubs, I supposed, single mothers getting off the late shift at Wal-Mart, and I felt marginally less obtrusive. I glanced over at Annie in the seat beside me: she was staring straight ahead, holding her stuffed bunny against her chest, quiet as a little mouse. God alone knew what was going through her head. At that exact moment in time, I was just glad she wasn't driving.

While I waited for the light to change, I tried to remember where my cell phone was. It was no longer about my person, that much was certain, but where exactly we had parted company was a bit of a mystery. The cops had taken all my belongings when they were in the process of trying to book me in—shoelaces, belt, wallet, keys; but now that I thought of it, I didn't recall handing over my cell.

The light turned green, and I pulled slowly into the intersection, and turned left.

As I headed north up Cerillos Road, courageously hightailing my way out of town, I suddenly clicked to it: I'd left it in the car! My car!

When they'd pulled me over, I must have just set the thing down on the passenger seat. I had to have done. That was my usual *modus operandi*, by the way, setting my phone down on the seat next to me when I wasn't using it. It was worth a look.

But was the *car* where I had left it?

That seemed perfectly unlikely. The cops wouldn't just leave an abandoned car there. Surely they would have towed it. Such a thing would be a hazard, a toilet for hobos, a target for vandals...

However—and I can't emphasize this enough—we *were* in New Mexico.

The cop had pulled me over on Cerillos, about a mile up from where we were at that very moment; had pulled me over right in front of the Denny's, as a matter of fact. And the Denny's, as I knew from having driven up and down this same road about a million times, would be coming into view shortly.

Up ahead the Denny's sign suddenly did pop up, looming large and yellow in the distance. Already from where we were I could see cars moving in and out of its parking lot, and as we got a little closer, I could see, still at a distance, on the street just beyond the entrance to the parking lot, my old green Scion XB right where I had left it.

Incredible.

Now the only question was whether some passer-by had seen the cell phone through the window, lying in there on the front seat; seen it, and reached in and pinched it. Hell, in all the excitement of getting arrested, there was a good chance I hadn't even locked the car door. Since I didn't have my keys anymore, that would actually be a good thing.

From a couple of hundred yards out I started to slow the truck down, and tried to do a quick mental risk assessment. Stopping and getting out of our vehicle while we were still in town was definitely *not* part of the protocol, and especially not if front of a goddam Denny's teaming with gawking insomniacs. Probably some of 'em cops, too. On the other hand, our lives would be so much easier with a cell phone. Contacting a lawyer—contacting *Madstone*—would be made more certain. And if need be, I could give my ex a call, too; undertake some damage control regarding any short term complications with my daughter's visitation that might come up. Hopefully this whole *fracas* would be resolved long before Friday. But better safe than sorry. It would be nice to have the luxury of a cell phone, and the ability to cover my parental behind on that score if and when the time came.

So that was it—I had to have my phone. For any number of reasons, I had to have my phone.

I swung our big blue behemoth over, tucked it right in behind my own green car, and threw the shifter on the steering column into park.

"Stay here, Annie," I said, and leapt out before she could comment.

The chrome-yellow light from the street lamps lit the pavement up like it was day time, and in an instant I was round the passenger side of my car, lifting the handle.

Praise Jesus, *Hallelieulia!*—it was open!

I glanced down and felt the sudden glow of triumph in my chest: my sweet, life-giving I-phone! It was sitting right there on the passenger-side seat just as I had left it, just as pretty as you please. It was like it had been resting there, waiting for me the whole time.

I shook of the sentimentality, and swiped it up in one hand. Then I checked in the glove box.

Bonus! Phone charger and checkbook. We might well need these before this was done (not the least because the checkbook was fat with two hundred dollars in new twenties I'd gotten out that morning when I'd swung by the bank).

I shoved the lot into the jacket pockets of my sport coat, shut the door, and headed back to the pick-up.

I was careful not to move too fast or too suspicious, and also not to look up to see if any of the Denny's customers were looking out the window at me. I'd learned that from *The Godfather*, by the way—that when you commit a crime in public, don't make eye contact with anyone as you walk out of the restaurant. That's how Michael Corleone did it. And even though I wasn't assassinating a dirty cop, or actually walking out of a restaurant, or committing any sort of crime by retrieving my own phone, really, I reckoned rightly the situation was still kind of like that. I was a wanted man, after all. In any event, not making eye contact was probably just good protocol. There was no downside.

Annie was looking at me wide-eyed when I got back in the truck, and I realized maybe I'd freaked her out a bit by jumping out without explanation. Was she worried maybe that I'd abandoned her? The rest of the adult world had been busily shitting on her for the last few days, so why not me, too, right?

"Had to get the phone," I said, holding it up to show her, trying to put her at ease.

She settled back down, nodded, seeming to understand. I set the thing on the seat between us, shifted the truck into drive, and pulled us back onto the road.

I made a mental note to be more sensitive in future to the fact that she really was a very small child who'd had some really bad breaks. Tough little nut though she seemed to be, right now she was relying on me—trusting me—to get us through. I hadn't thought of it in quite that way until now, but I guess I'd inadvertently taken on a fair amount of responsibility, and the weight of it suddenly struck me.

Being an adult is a hell of a thing, sometimes.

I piloted the truck on up the road, and it seemed to take forever to get out of town. Finally, twenty minutes after we had left the wrecking yard we made St. Francis, aka State Highway 84/285, aka The-Road-Out-of-Town. I pulled us up into the left hand turn lane, blinkers on, and waited for the light to change. Straight ahead I thought I could make out the dim outline of the Sangre de Cristo Mountains, backlit against a vague night sky. The stoplight changed to green, and we pulled forward, heading north on up the road—past the cemetery, past the Santa Fe Opera, over the Rio Tesuque...

And suddenly, we were out of Santa Fe.

I breathed a sigh of relief, and felt some satisfaction that we'd got this first bit of our journey down without incident. Not just without incident. With a fairly major bonus. I'd managed to recover my I-phone! I glanced over at the thing setting on the seat between me and Annie, and smiled. I reckoned I'd call Madstone at the office around ten that morn-

79

ing, after he'd warmed up to the day, and gotten his own show on the road, so to speak. But for now, all I had to do was drive. And then Annie was asleep, and the road was flowing quietly under the wheels, and I was enjoying what soon proved to be a rare moment of calm. She was snoring louder than any little girl had a right to as we passed down through the Pojoaque Valley, and crossed the Rio Grande at Espanola. It was 1:34 in the a.m, according to my phone, and I was feeling remarkably alert. We had started a new day and were driving over empty blacktop, the good people of Northern New Mexico all being safely tucked away in their beds, though in actual truth, many of those good people were undoubtedly still up carousing, with plenty of drunkenness and music and fighting and sex going on behind some of the distant windows whose lights we could occasionally see away off the sides of the road (this was rural New Mexico's "Heroin Crescent" we were driving through, after all). But at least for right now, and at least through the windshield of the truck, it seemed a clear and peaceful scene.

As Annie slept, the hours started to ease by. I reckoned maybe instead of just crossing over into Colorado, we should put a little more ground between us and them, and try for Utah, if for no other reason than I had some Mormon cousins outside Salt lake. They had a big place in a little town called Bountiful that I'd been to a few times over the years.

Yes, it made sense: Bountiful was well out of state, but it was close enough we could get back to Santa Fe in less than a day. And my cousins knew me well enough to expect something dodgy was up if I just popped in, running from an angry ex, or something in that line, but would happily take care of us anyway. Truth be told, they'd love the notion they were in on some kind of illicit caper.

We passed up the town of Chama then crossed into Colorado, where I started to feel a little better about things. I kept us moving, though, turning us onto State Road 160 and heading us west through Pagosa Springs.

Annie woke up about there, wiping her drizzly chin with her stuffed bunny, a smoggy "*where am I*" look on her face.

It was still dark and she didn't have to go to the bathroom yet, and we had almost a half a tank of gas at that point, so I reckoned we'd try to get as far as Cortez before we stopped. I'd been through Cortez a bunch of times over the years, and knew it to be a reasonably good sized place, as good as any to gas up in, anyway, and maybe buy some breakfast. I thanked my lucky stars for having remembered to grab the checkbook and my cash from out of my car. I shuddered to think where we'd be if we'd got to Cortez with no cash.

The mountains and desert of southern Colorado rolled on by, the pearly-gray light of pre-dawn starting to come on about then, and bit by bit, out enforced familiarity and severe boredom, Annie became a little chatty. Her favorite topic, it turned out, was her school back in St. Louis:

"Ms. Granados gave us an assignment—we're in groups of three. Of two or three. And we get a state. And our group has to write a report on the state. We get to go on the internet—there's five computers, so there's one for each group—and we look up about the state…"

"So you get to do a report?"

She nodded her head. "A report, yes. On a state."

"Like Missouri?"

"Missouri's a state?" she blurted. It caught me by surprise, but I guess if you're pretty young, like she was, the concept of a "state" is a purely notional one.

"Sure," says I. "Missouri's a state. And New Mexico, too. We've been through two states already today."

"We have?"

"Can you name 'em."

She hesitated a bit at that, then came out ever so tentative with "New Mexico?"

"Right."

"New Mexico is a state? Okay. And the other one is…"

"Look at the sign coming up."

She glanced out the side window at the highway sign. "And Colorado!" she answered, brightly.

"Yup. That's right. There's fifty all together."

"Fifty? Fifty states?"

"Right, that's why they call them the *United* States. They're fifty states united into one country—the United States."

"The *United* States," she said, the scales falling from her eyes. She really got it, she did. And it felt quite good to shepherd her through that little piece of knowledge.

She clammed up after that though, unsure about talking to me, I guess. Her center was somewhere else, thinking about her mum I suppose, or the third grade, or the life she'd just left behind. The life she'd had before this. I guess the corollary of the Ms. Granados story she'd just told me was that she'd been yanked away from all that, yanked away from the third grade, from her home, and now from her mother; yanked away by fate or circumstances or whatever. And I already knew she was smart enough that part of her had to know she wasn't going back anytime soon (read, probably ever)—and she was moving forward into a new life that wasn't going to be half so nice as the one she left behind.

Or she might actually be thinking along more practical lines: about how she was going to put Humpty Dumpty back together again. How she was going to save her mum and get 'em both back to Missouri. Who knows? What goes on in the mind of a kid anyway? But just thinking about her fate was another gloomy reminder of the flaming pile of shit we were both currently neck deep in.

Finally about 7:30 in the morning we found ourselves closing in on Cortez. The sun broke out over the mountain tops, instantly firing up the trembling aspens of southern Colorado in a liquid Autumn gold, and I continued driving on west in silence through that breathtaking landscape, the fresh blue sky and the mountains gorgeous around us, brilliant and peaceful, a soaring reminder of all that was grand and good in the world.

"I have to go bad," Annie said, bouncing up and down a little nervously.

"When you gotta go, you gotta go," I remarked, sagely, which is what I say to my own sweet daughter.

I swung us off onto an exit that looked like it would take us into the commercial center of town, and sure enough before long we were cruising up another street that for all intents and purposes could have had us back in Santa Fe—or Cleveland, or Oklahoma City, or Pasedena, California for that matter. Wal-Marts and Home Depots and Walgreens were mixed up with gas stations and chain restaurants, which at this point, of course, was exactly what we were looking for.

Gas up first, I reckoned (prioritizing care for our vehicle, much like the old Pioneers'd take care of their horses before they themselves ate), and pulled into a handy Chevron. Being a parent of a little girl myself, I was familiar with the bathroom protocol for an other-gendered child, and I walked Annie from the truck to the restroom, made her shout out an all clear before she went in, and stood watch over the door until she came back out.

"Did you wash your hands?" I asked.

She indicated she had, and we went together to the counter to pay cash for thirty dollars worth of gas. I did a quick mental count: the purchase left us with a hundred and seventy dollars in pocket. So far, so good.

Back out onto the tarmac, Annie got back in the truck, and I stood there and pumped the gas, and it felt good to be out of the truck, and able to stretch those muscles, I've got to say. I checked the oil, too, which was a bit low, and I made a mental note to add a quart next time we stopped. And then it was time to eat.

"What's your pleasure, young lady?" I asked, with a broad wave of my hand at the ring of adjacent fast food establishments that surrounded us.

"Wendy's!" she cried, without hesitation.

We left the truck, and clambered over a couple of concrete dividers, and crossed a parking lot to get there. We walked in through the glass door and instantly my heart froze.

Cops. There were lots and lots of cops.

Chapter 14 – Amber Alert

THEY WERE IN BOOTHS and at the tables. One was coming out of the bathroom, a pair of 'em were talking quietly over by the other door, and three of 'em were still in line getting their fast food, guns bulging prominent and unmistakable high up on their hips.

"*What is this*," I whispered, feeling my guts turn to jelly.

Annie said nothing, then glanced up at me.

"Will you get a grip," she said, with palpable disdain.

Annoyingly, she was right. I realized my jaw must have been hanging open and I guessed my eyes were big as saucers. I had no idea what the deal was, but if we were to make it through this horrible Gethsemane we'd have to try to look as normal as possible, and that didn't include me standing frozen to the spot with my mouth hanging open. I shut it with a pop, but was still shell-shocked by the situation, and my face must have shown it, too.

"Snap out of it!" Annie hissed.

"I'm fine," I hissed back, defensively.

"Look, my dad showed me all about cops," she said, taking my hand.

"What's that supposed to mean?"

"We'll do the daddy-daughter thing. It's easy, you just...oh, just follow me." She yanked me over to stand in the line with the three police officers, and I followed along robotically.

84

I was failing—this was too much. But if we didn't put a good face on things, and right now, our situation could go south real quick. I shrunk in my shoulders, and stooped a bit, struggling to become as invisible as possible.

We parked ourselves behind one oversized number in a Colorado State Police uniform—he was just enormous, of course—and I desperately tried to channel my daddy persona.

"What would you like, sweety?" I said to Annie, my voice trembling slightly.

"A hamburger and a milkshake, please Daddy," she answered, pert and pretty as you please.

It made me start to hear her sound so normal-like, and I looked down and saw a sweet, shit-eating nine-year-old smile. She was amazing, cool as a cucumber. Good thing, too, as it kind of helped bring me around. It actually turned out to be an easy switch for me, since I *was* the father of a little girl, so it didn't take much to step back into that role, particularly with so much depending on my performance.

The giant cop in front of us turned at the sound of her voice.

"Well hello, cutie," he said to her with a big smile, bending down toward her. He was so seriously massive it was like that giant from the story, leaning down out of the clouds to squint at Jack.

Annie hesitated a moment, appropriately shy. "Hi," she finally said, softly. "How are you," she added politely, extending her hand. It was the perfect touch.

The giant policeman threw back his head and laughed. It was a deep rich laugh, and he took her little hand in his, and shook it. "Well, aren't you a polite little girl," he said. "You must have a very good Daddy to teach you such excellent manners."

"He's the best," she said, beaming up at me.

My god, I thought to myself. Oscar clip.

Out loud I said, "Well, she's a pretty good little kid, herself. I wish I could take all the credit for it, but her mother does the heavy lifting."

"Well, you're for sure a whole lot better parent than the guy we're looking for," he said leaning into me, his tone suddenly changing. He glanced down at Annie to make sure her attention was elsewhere, and whispered to me, all confidential: "Sonafabitch kidnapped a little girl out of Santa Fe. We're all here scrambling on an Amber Alert. They think he's heading out of State, so we're lining up all along our side of the border in case he comes our way."

Amber Alert! And here we were in right in the middle of the net. What were the odds? Well, pretty good, frankly, since I actually *was* that guy, and the net was set specifically for me.

"God only knows what he's doing to her, sick bastard."

"I sure wouldn't want to be in his shoes," I said, quite sincerely, noting all the capable and motivated law enforcement officers around the room.

"You got that right, friend," the cop agreed, the expression on his face suddenly going very hard. "I got two kids of my own. When we get him, I'm afraid there's some stuff going to go down out of sight of our dash-cams, if you know what I mean." He patted the baton at his side.

"He's got it coming, alright," I agreed. "What kind of monster would—"

"*Next!*"

The cop stepped up, and placed his order. And just like that, he was gone, with an overflowing tray full of food and a gigantic oversized beverage. I let out a long breath. It had been easy to stay in character while I was talking to him, but now our encounter was over I realized I was visibly shaking. Part of me wanted to cry. I parted with one of our twenties for a couple of Frosties, two large fries, and two singles with cheese. Screw the breakfast meal.

"Would you like that for here or to go."

"To go," Annie and I said at the same time.

We were back in the truck, on the Highway and over the Utah border before I was breathing normally again. What the hell had just happened? How had we gotten out of there? Divine intervention was the only thing that explained it—I mean, an Amber Alert for a middle aged white man and a little red-headed girl, and we run smack into the cops charged with enforcing it *and they don't even notice us!* Not so much as a question.

Where are you from, sir? Where are you folks heading?—something like that. In the end, all I could do was chalk it up to blind stupid luck—and Annie's sterling performance, of course. It was that Shirley Temple bit that really did the trick.

"You were pretty good in there," I said.

Annie said nothing, but clutched her bunny tight to her chest and stared straight ahead through the windscreen. I waited a bit for a reply, but she stayed silent.

"Sounds like you and your dad must have had fun with that daddy-daughter skit," I persisted, somewhat awkwardly.

"My dad's scary," she said, punctuating our exchange with a full stop.

Dead air hung in the space between us. Inert and final, it nevertheless added to my questions about her father; I mean, "daddy-daughter thing"? What kind of weirdo needs a standard con in the bag to pull out whenever the cops are near?

Well, me for one, obviously, but that was beside the point.

What about the father?

The Border Patrol clerk down in Cruces had sat up straight at the question. And now I was finding out the old man liked to involve his daughter in sketchy games with the cops. Well, whatever the provenance, I had to admit the daddy-daughter thing really had worked a treat.

I made a note to be more careful next time, though, cause it was painfully obvious I would instantly fold under questioning. I looked over and saw Annie had already gobbled down her food, and I reckoned I better eat mine, too, though as I shoved the burger and fries into my mouth there was nothing pleasant about it. It was simply a refueling exercise. We drove along in silence, heading up 491 into canyon country, though unfortunately those fantastic red rock formations didn't do much to lift my spirits—I was way beyond that. Tall mesas and proto-arch formations zipped by; off in the distance I recognized Six-Shooter peak, but had no attention to spare for it; I wasn't just anxious now; I was genuinely frightened. This whole mess could end very badly. *Very* badly. Federal super-max prison badly. And up until Cortez that wretched ending had only been a distant and abstract possibility. But now, after running into those cops it suddenly seemed very real. Quite likely, in fact.

"I love my daddy," Annie suddenly said in a voice that wasn't much above a whisper.

She'd said it so quietly, I wondered if she was aware she had actually uttered the words out loud, but before I could consider it further I was distracted by a late model Buick slowly passing us on the left. On the passenger side of the vehicle, a middle aged wife sporting a beehive hairdo was squinting though her window directly at me and Annie with a level of interest that seemed inappropriate. Unable to help myself, I stared back at her, and decided her name must be Gladys. The moment lasted a lot longer than I would have liked, and then she abruptly turned her head from me and Annie to talk at her husband in the driver's seat, a man whose name undoubtedly was Abner. She was gesturing quite animatedly.

I tapped the brakes and let them slide by, desperately hoping that Gladys's unwanted attention wasn't related to the Amber Alert.

What else could it have been, though? Were people all the way over here in Utah—two states away from New Mexico—on the lookout for us now, too? I puckered more than a little at the thought we could still easily get pinched even this far afield. I couldn't do prison, I thought to myself, pathetically. Filth and violence and hopelessness. Rape and communal showers and vile food. It was so unfair. This was all just a horrible mistake, after all. The rank injustice of it made me want to cry again.

Godammit, I was only five years from retirement!

I eased off our speed even more, and allowed the Buick with Gladys and Abner in it to recede slowly away from us. They were a good half mile in front when I found I was piddling along at less than fifty miles per, but my instincts told me to hold steady and let 'em widen the gap. We were violating protocol by cruising so far below the posted speed limit, but first and foremost we had to stay clear of unwanted attention like theirs, at least until I could call Madstone. And now I was starting to think that as far as safe harbors go, my cousins in Bountiful or a hotel room in Salt Lake or anywhere else in Utah just wouldn't cut it at this

88

point. I could see now it wasn't far enough away from ground zero in Santa Fe.

Plus, and I hated to admit it, the notion of dropping in on the family in Bountiful wasn't fair to my cousins. They'd have my back, alright, they'd let us stay, and be happy as hell to see me, too, but there was no way I could let 'em do it. The downside for them was just too grim— and too entirely possible.

"Annie, check in the glovebox and see if there's any maps in there."

She opened it up and seemed to do a double take when she looked in, like there was a snake or something coiled in there, but before I could say anything her expression returned to normal. The transition was so quick I wasn't sure I'd seen it right. Just a trick of the light, I reckoned.

Sure enough, though, she said there were maps, and in an instant I was trying to pilot the vehicle while dangerously looking over at the Western United States spread out in the little girl's lap.

"There's Canada!" she said, pointing at the top of the map.

"We're not going to Canada," I said irritable, glancing back up at the road; the Buick was nothing but a distant dot on the horizon, now.

"Why not!" she said, rather petulantly.

"Because we eventually have to go back to Santa Fe and straighten this mess out."

"Are we going back right now?"

"No. We talked about this, Annie. We've gotta' wait until after I talk to Madstone."

She thought a bit about that while I examined the map. "Well, why can't we wait in Canada?" she persisted.

"'Cause it's too far, and plus that's exactly where they might expect us to go."

"Well, where do *you* think we should go, then?" she said in a challenging mister smarty-pants sort of way.

"How about Seattle," I suggested lamely, reaching over and pointing generally at the Pacific Northwest.

"That's further away than Canada!" she said in disgust, as I righted the car. We'd drifted into a work zone and I'd begun scattering orange emergency cones

"Look," I said, a little defensively, "we don't know if your mum's even in Canada yet. Right? For all we know, she could still be in El Paso. Or maybe somewhere else in the U.S. still. And if we leave the Country it'll be that much harder to get you to her."

"She's in *Canada!*" Annie insisted, with the absolute certainty of a nine year old. And the thing was, she might have been right. I didn't really know, and had to allow the possibility of it, at least. She could have been up there.

"Look," she added, "we're already on the road that goes up to Canada. See—" She traced her little finger along the map up Interstate Highway 15 from the point where we were now, just north of Moab, Utah, up through Idaho to Great Falls, Montana, and from there a short bit further to a border crossing at the bottom of the Canadian Province of Alberta. It was as close to a straight line as you'd ever find on a map.

"Okay," I said in frustration. "We'll keep going up 15—*Not* to Canada, though!" I added pointedly, seeing the look on her face. "We'll go as far as Great Falls, okay. That looks to be about a six or eight hour drive, and it gets us far away from here."

I knew we had to get moving, you see, whichever way we went, and Montana seemed like some sort of compromise at least. Annie seemed grudgingly satisfied, and with that we had a destination.

The Buick was gone from my field of vision now, off to wherever it was Gladys and Abner were going, so I shoved down on the accelerator, and we surged forward.

Annie put her hands in the air.

"Geronimo!" she cried.

Chapter 15 – Great Falls

A SIGN FOR Arches National Park zipped past us on the right, indicating an exit. I could see the road to the Interpretive Center switchbacking away high off up over the hills. Above, the sun was rising to its Autumn meridian and all around us the shadows were shrinking to nothing, the red rock mesas slowly shifting their shapes under the desert sun.

Annie had already become chatty again, getting a little kooky, and soon launched us into a game she called "Yellow Car." Its rules were simple: you sang out whenever you saw a yellow car.

"Yellow car!" Annie said, as a yellow Subaru passed us by in the other direction.

There was a brief pause. "Yellow car!" she yelled again; this time she bagged a yellow Toyota FJ. She was quite good at spotting 'em, I've got to say.

I was behind in the count. I scanned the road up ahead. Above I noticed a billboard coming at us. A brand new yellow Mustang was on offer at some nearby Casino. "Yellow car!" I shouted, pointing at the thing.

"Where?" she instantly demanded, then seeing where I was pointing, sighed in disgust. "That doesn't count."

"It's a yellow car, ain't it," I said.

"It's a *picture*. Pictures don't count. It's got to be a real car."

"Is that *really* the way you play it?"

"Yes. It's got to be a real car."

"*Dammit*," I whispered under my breath so she couldn't hear.

As the game progressed we had to go through a few other clarifications, usually with regard to marginal "yellow car" claims of my own—mustard colored cars, for example, didn't count at all; school buses counted as only one point, but Penske trucks counted as two. The sport of it was surprisingly diverting, and really chewed up the miles. I'd gotten us back up to the speed limit now, not wanting to get pulled over, but not wanting to go so slow that we'd draw attention, either. It's not that easy, by the way, staying exactly a mile or two over or under the speed limit. Just try it some time.

"Say, kid, you never did tell me how you wound up in that police station," I said, shortly after she bagged three yellow school busses traveling together in some sort of high school sporting event convoy.

Annie actually snorted at that. "Those ladies back in New Mexico wanted to take me away from my mom so I ditched 'em." She hesitated a moment, and looked at me, considering whether she should share her secret. I guess I must have passed her test, 'cause she went on: "They drove me to all the way to Santa Fe, and they said I was going to stay at a *facility*. And I didn't want to stay at any 'Facility.' I told 'em I wanted my mom back. And they said no. So when we got to Santa Fe I said I had to go to the bathroom and we went into a McDonald's and I pretended to go into the bathroom, but they weren't watching, so then I just went out the front door."

She sounded quite proud of it, and I can't say I blamed her.

"What'd you do then?"

She shrugged her little shoulders. "I just walked all night. It was night time and I tried to walk north, which is where Canada is, but I wasn't really sure. If I was going north. And I walked for a long time. But then a policeman saw me. I went behind a trash barrel and tried to hide like I'd been doing, but he saw me. He was really nice, though, and I made up a name to tell him. But they figured out I was Annie Chretien anyway. I'm not sure how. And they took me to the police station where you were. They took me there so those ladies could pick me up again."

"Wow. You're pretty brave," I said, resolving to keep a much closer eye on this slippery little fish. The notion of a tiny kid like Annie taking off on her own hook and putting herself at the mercy of the world was…unsettling.

"It was scary," she allowed matter-of-factly. "Them taking my mom was scarier, though." She paused again, then shouted: "Yellow truck!"

It was a goddam Penske van. Two points.

I kept a weather eye on things, and piloted us up through the remainder of Utah, toward the Idaho border. We crossed uneventfully into the Potato State, thankful we'd encountered no more "Abners" or "Gladyses," and Annie was asleep again, slumped down into the seat next to me, chin tucked in to her chest, stuffed bunny clutched close. I was growing more and more road-weary myself as time marched heavily onward, and as the shadows gradually lengthened I had to force myself to stay alert, pushing us on through the day further and further north as the little red-head snoozed away beside me.

Over the next few hours the eroded sandstone monuments of Utah gave way to the gently rolling hills of Idaho, and we passed on up through that great ocean of grassy nothing, eventually past Pocatello, where hours later the landscape started to change again.

Mountains grew up around us, and some hours later we passed up signs for Yellowstone National Park, finally crossing over the Montana state line. Annie was awake again, and we knew we were getting close, now. By the time we stopped in Helena for gas an hour later, the sky had been full on dark for a while. We got out and stretched our legs there for a bit. The Montana air was noticeably cooler than it had been nine hundred miles south in Cortez, and I reckoned we'd be wanting jackets if the temperature dropped any more—the sunny, relatively warm southwest was well behind us now.

Not surprisingly I was thoroughly wiped at this point. As it turned out, it had been damn near close to twelve hours driving from Moab, when we'd decided to come north, to where we were now in Helena, and my ass hurt, and I was borderline numb, sluggish and completely exhausted.

Once our break was done it was only through pure force of will I was able to switch the truck engine back on again; I knew full well the last bit of this drive was going to be unambiguously the most brutal. Frankly, a bed would have been nicer. *Oh my god, a bed would have been absolute heaven*—but it was not to be. At least for a little while longer.

I kept the thought alive in my head, though: a bed at the Holiday Inn in Great Falls. Beds, a swimming pool, a hot tub, a television. A drink. The works.

And just under a hundred miles to go.

I was moving in slow motion by now, my reaction time thoroughly dulled by lack of sleep. My judgment was undoubtedly suffering, too, and I had the sense I was only a step or two away from actually hallucinating. In retrospect, and to be honest, at this point I probably shouldn't have been behind the wheel of a vehicle at all. I drove on, though, amazingly without incident, and we finally made Great Falls.

It was about nine o'clock at night, and I had nothing left. It had been fifteen hours since we'd left Cortez, and probably about twenty since we'd left Santa Fe, and to tell you the truth, if you'd asked me before, I would never have guessed I had the capacity for such an epic drive in me.

Annie and me saw the Holiday Inn from the highway at the same time. It was half a mile before the turn off, but I set the blinker going anyway. I gave her a nudge, and she smiled at me as we listened to its old fashion *chink-a-chink,chink-a-chink,chink-a-chink...*

We got to the turn off quick enough, and glided up to the top of the highway exit ramp, waited at the stop light there, then turned and cruised toward the big green and yellow Holiday Inn sign. The gigantic box shaped hotel behind the deliberately obtrusive sign was a square-ish cinderblock insult to whatever local architectural style might exist in Great Falls, but I didn't care. There were beds and a pool and probably a bar, and best of all we'd be able to get out of the truck for a while.

Yet again I marveled at how much my ass hurt.

These next were not moments I ever want to live through again.

We were still about fifty yards out, but just before I clicked the blinkers on, I caught myself. I could see there were flashing lights swirling around the place, lighting up the pavement and washing blue and red up against the hotel walls. It didn't take much analysis to recognize them as coming from emergency vehicles. Despite my fatigue I was on my guard immediately.

We drove past apron of concrete that marked the entryway as unobtrusively as possible. Front and center there were three blue and white ICE vehicles parked there with their lights a-flashing. Immigration and Customs Enforcement. Before them, lined up against the high brick hotel wall, were about ten dark skinned men, dejected looking and handcuffed. They crouched on the pavement in front of the hotel, and were pretty obviously under arrest.

The Bulls were walking amongst them, wearing blue windbreakers. On the backs of the windbreakers, even at that distance I could see printed POLICE above, and ICE below in big white letters.

Who knew what the deal was. Maybe Gladys and Abner had gotten here just ahead of us, and called the cops when they noticed a bunch of immigrants were staying at the hotel? Or perhaps these guys were owed money for some post-season job up here and a cheap and vengeful employer had turned 'em in? Or maybe they were just some innocent farm workers with time to kill after the end of the long season, looking to connect with family in Great Falls only to find themselves caught up in a routine sweep? Or maybe it was something else entirely? But one thing I did know, now that I thought of it: we were closing in on the Canadian border. It was totally to be expected that we'd see Border Patrol and Immigration and Customs Enforcement activity: vans and roundups and checkstops and so on. It was what they did, after all—just like down in bloody Las Cruces. We were once again within a hundred goddam miles of a goddam international border, and incredibly, for the second time in less than a week, I'd put myself in the bloody red zone of immigration enforcement. We'd fumbled our way into another *Constitution Free Zone!*

Idiot that I am, I'd brought us across half a continent just to put in the very same danger from the immigration authorities that we'd been in just two days before on literally the other side of the country.

"We can't stay here, Annie," I said.

We had no choice, and she saw the sense in it. The fear of these immigration guys was already ingrained in her, too. I didn't say a word, and we drove on in silence, leaving the hotel behind, not going anywhere in particular, just away from those blue and white vans.

I was as depressed. As depressed as I'd been since our adventures had begun two days before, and with nothing at all in mind at all I pulled the truck back on to highway 15, heading south, leaving behind Great Falls and the Holiday Inn; leaving behind the pool and the prospect of our free breakfast. For about five minutes we were just about to live like human beings again, and then, suddenly, not.

I looked over at Annie; she was crying.

Chapter 16 – Canada

THE LITTLE GIRL was silently sobbing, looking out the passenger side window, and I guess I felt about as blue and lonesome at that exact moment as I ever have before in my life. This whole trip had been a nightmare, and our future looked bleaker still. Worse, I knew from past experience that whichever way we went, being in a Constitution Free Zone, around the next corner or past the next mile marker there *would* be a checkstop. To a certainty. And there was no question but that they'd pull us right away out of whatever line we were in. We had no IDs, no luggage, there were arrest warrants out for us in New Mexico and probably in Colorado and Utah, and maybe Idaho and Montana as well; hell, who was I kidding: the warrants were superfluous—*Homeland Security already had our stats!* It was DHS that had a Detainer out on me. They knew what we looked like and who we were.

The only thing they didn't know is what kind of car we were driving.

But there was no question if the immigration authorities stopped us for whatever reason, we were done for. This time, though, it was really too much to hope that we'd squeak by like we did at the Wendy's in Durango. How many times can you count on blind stupid luck or the authorities just dropping the ball?

But then something occurred to me. The CBP checkstops were just set up to look for cars coming *into* the United States. They wouldn't look twice at one that was on its way out. *And, once again, they had no idea what kind of vehicle we were driving!*

"Annie," I began, unable to believe the words that were coming out on my mouth, "what would you say to us going to Canada?"

She looked at me for a moment, making sure she'd heard right.

"Yes!" she yelped, eyes suddenly coming alive. She wiped her forearm across her snotty face, swiping away her tears, and grasped her stuffed bunny close to her chest. I pressed down hard on the accelerator, swerved across two empty lanes and onto a handy off-ramp, getting us neatly turned around and headed north in only so long as it took us to drive over the highway.

Annie sat up tall in her seat, looking through the wide windshield into the darkness ahead.

I added it all up. Crossing into the Great White North kept coming up cherries. We were driving a Canadian truck; it had Canadian plates. We were both Canadian (Annie as a matter of law claiming citizenship through her parents)! They'd have to let us in!

It was a safe haven, too: a Canadian world; a world with no Border Patrol, no ICE, no Department of Homeland Security—no checkstops, no roundups, no "papers please" every time you got pulled over for a busted tail light or expired tags. We could much more easily cool it up there hassle-free for a few days until Madstone told us to come back. My brain was working slowly through very thick cobwebs, I must admit (I was frankly having trouble just focusing on the road), but the more I thought of it, the more sense it made. Of course, there was the pesky issue of getting back into the States after Madstone got things squared away for us back in Santa Fe, but we could figure that one out later. The challenge for the moment was not getting pinched by the American authorities, *and we could not allow ourselves to get pinched!*

Canada it was!

We drove up into the northern Montana night, and I swear to god I felt it getting seriously colder. Whatever happened, somehow I knew Annie and me would be getting warmer clothes before we were done.

There's not much to see between Great Falls and the border crossing at Sweet Grass, by the way, particularly at night; nothing but speed limit signs and mile markers break the journey. We passed up a couple of towns, and the drive took us another hour or so, but after the continental scope of what had come before (not to mention the terror and nail-biting uncertainty that had dogged us every step of the way), this last little bit was nothing, and we arrived at the border crossing with Annie still sitting high up in her seat all attentive, eyes shining, stuffed bunny clutched close.

"Remember, we're both Canadians," I said to her as we approached the booth where the Canadian border folks question you.

"But I'm an American," she said, perfectly reasonably.

"Yes, that's correct. But as a matter of law, you're also Canadian."

"I'm also Cana—"

"That's right," I said, cutting her off, needing to make sure we got our stories straight before they quizzed us. "According to Canadian citizenship law, your mother's Canadian so that makes you Canadian, too, see?" This was actually true, by the way, but I could see by her vacant expression she wasn't getting it. "Okay, see first generation children born abroad with one Canadian parent, which you are, have a right to…And your dad's Canadian too, right, so that makes you…oh, never mind. Look, just say what I say."

My throat got tight as we pulled under the high metal awning, and up next to the little kiosk the immigration officer interviews you from. She gave us a sharp look up and down, and then asked: "Destination?"

"Calgary," I said, having thought out that one, at least.

"Purpose of the trip?"

"Just going home."

She took a quick step outside to look at our license plates, and seemed satisfied. We continued on through the usual why were we abroad, nationalities of the parties stuff, and then came the big one:

"Identification, please."

I had nothing, of course. Scrambling, I said, "Her mother has it."

The Canadian customs officials looked at me with a gimlet eye, and it was clear she smelled something off. "So where's her mother, then?" she asked, all flat and neutral.

There was a protracted silence after that, as she looked at me hard and steady, without so much as a single blink. I was feeling the heat of it, too, and I'm ashamed to say for about a nanosecond I flirted with the notion of telling her the truth. Fortunately the experience of the last couple of days had cured me of that.

"We're getting divorced," I blurted suddenly, out of the blue. "My daughter and I are moving back to Calgary, and she's staying in Great Falls. Her mum, that is. With her boyfriend," I added.

Believe it or not, the words had come unbidden to my mouth—I hadn't thought about it at all, and just said it. But it was clearly the right thing to say, for her face fell, and her attitude changed on a dime.

"Oh, I'm so sorry, Mr. McKenzie. Please, pull your truck over here and we'll get you squared away."

It's lovely to see the humanity in people, it really is. Even if what I had said to her was a complete lie—and of course, it was—it took nothing away from the thing, 'cause her reaction was sincere. She bade us get out of the truck, and led us over to the main building, where they entertained Annie with crayons and books they'd obviously stowed for the little kidiwinks who came through their office, and worked me through a few pro-forma questions that were clearly designed to lead me into the country.

It couldn't have been much more than ten or fifteen minutes before we were back up in the truck waving a pleasant goodbye to the customs lady.

"Welcome to Canada," she said with a broad smile, and we drove under the Maple Leaf flag and up into the great western province of Alberta.

IV. Canada

Chapter 17 – Annie's Got a Gun

IT MAY SEEM ODD that Canadian customs would let us in so easy, but they were welcoming us home, you see.

It was the license plates first and foremost, of course. And our faces too, I suppose: Annie's red hair, my white middle aged lawyer's paunch—they were about as old school Canadian as you can get. Plus, we were going in the right direction through a remote and otherwise deserted border crossing at night and had the great good luck to get a customs official who actually seemed to have a human soul.

A first time for everything, I thought, remembering the casually heartless bureaucrats at the Las Cruces checkstop that had stripped Annie from her mother.

The thing that puzzled me most in retrospect, though, was what had happened to Homeland Security. Where was DHS on this? Or any of the other branches of law enforcement we'd crossed in the last forty-eight hours. Surely any of them could've queered the deal—a call to Canadian customs and we'd have been done for. Annie and me were malefactors enough for the Border Patrol to use deadly force to try prevent our escape from the Santa Fe lockup, and for New Mexico to throw up a multi-state Amber Alert to thwart our getaway. Despite our recent success crossing the border I had no illusions whatsoever that we'd fallen off anybody's radar.

But whatever the reason, we were past the hump.

And with that, we were in Canada. My home, my Country, the place of my birth. The land of my father!

On the ground, the Montana town of Sweet Grass morphed into the Alberta town of Coutts, which at first glance appeared to be a desperate nowhereville of Quonset huts and chain link fences dropped at random onto the dark western prairie. I piloted the truck slowly up the street past the closed Duty Free Shop and the silent currency exchange, and right away we came upon a one-story motor inn called the Doubletree. I pulled into the parking lot under its big yellow sign, and up into a space in front of the door to the reception desk. It was eleven-thirty.

"Well," I said to Annie. "Whaddaya think?"

She put out her lower lip, and nodded her head thoughtfully. "We're in Canada."

"We are in Canada," I agreed.

Our financial situation had been seriously bruised from our travels, but the notion of sleeping in the truck was just too much. "Shall we see if there's a room?" I said.

Annie nodded her head again, and yawned.

Twenty minutes later we were set up in a small room with two beds, frankly not even half as nice as a Holiday Inn in Great Falls probably would have been, but a whole lot safer. There was no hassle with the desk clerk about checking in with cash, either, but now money was definitely an issue.

Like Scarlet O'Hara, I'd think about that tomorrow.

Neither one of us bothered getting undressed, and we were both asleep in minutes.

* * *

I didn't wake up until nine forty-nine the next morning, at least according to the red numbers on the plastic clock next to me on the night table. Annie was still fast asleep, snoring lightly, so I climbed out of my own bed as quietly as I could and padded over to the window, and pushed aside the curtains to have a look at the new day. Surprise, surprise! There was an inch of snow on the ground that hadn't been there when we checked in. The sky was gray, too. I felt the glass, and shivered.

We were definitely going to need jackets.

I went to make the coffee and it bubbled out its two motel-room cups in short order, and I sat in the dim light sipping the raw black brew while I considered our circumstances. It's always best to make a list, I thought to myself. On the minus side, we had no ID and no credit cards; for the third day in a row I still had no belt or shoelaces, and we were low on gas. At most we had maybe fifty dollars in American bills left from the wad I'd had in my checkbook when we left Santa Fe.

I glanced over at Annie.

And we're missing a mother for the little red-headed girl, I thought to myself, adding to our grim list of deficiencies. Other than that, though, we were great.

But the coffee's not bad, I reflected, leaning back in my chair and taking another sip. I love the smell of coffee as much as I do the taste, and I lifted the warm cup in my hands up to my face to savor the aroma. Continuing my mental inventory, I had to say on the plus side we did at least have the truck. I struggled to think of anything else we had on the plus side, and was having a pretty hard time of it, too, until suddenly I remembered my famous Canadian bank account.

Holy Crap!—my Canadian bank account! In all the confusion of the last forty-eight hours, I had completely forgotten about it.

It was only five days before that I'd had my landmark conversation with good old Chandra of the London, Ontario branch, and made arrangements to get access to it. And after all we'd gone through I'd immediately lost the Access Card they'd sent me, seized by the Santa Fe PD along with my belt, ID, shoelaces, etc. when they booked me in, but maybe there was some other way to get at the funds—I *was* physically in Canada after all.

Mr. McKenzie, you have to come in to the branch office.

I assumed the "branch office" Chandra had been referring to was the one where he worked, two thousand miles to the east in London, Ontario.

But maybe just being in Canada was enough. Maybe I could get my money out at a branch in Calgary, for example. My recollection of Canadian Banks was there were only about eight or ten, all told—Toronto Dominion, Scotia Bank, Banque du Montreal, and so on—but that they each had offices everywhere all over the country. With that in mind, I knew there had to be one of my particular brand somewhere in Calgary. It was worth a shot, at least. Hell, if I could tap that thirty-thousand, Annie and me could stay up here in relative comfort for six months at least. Not that we'd need to; I was all but certain Madstone would have us back in the Land of Enchantment within a couple of days.

Calling Madstone. That was next. But how to do that? I'd already tried my I-phone, and north of the border it didn't work quite right. I'd been down this road before over the years, and knew that crossing a line on a map can play hell with your coverage, but just for giggles I tried Madstone's desk number back at the Agency—punching in one and the area code and everything—and all I got for my troubles was some kind of busy signal I'd never heard before in my life. So for an international call it appeared I was going to need a landline, and the only one going was the old school rotary motel phone sitting on the nightstand. But with no credit card to charge an offshore call to it was as useless as the kitsch Indian prints they had hanging on the motel room walls. But maybe I could slip the Innkeeper some cash to let me slide and use the phone in the room. It was worth looking into.

I got up to refill my coffee, and heard Annie stir.

"Wake up, sleepyhead," I said reflexively (it was the standard morning greeting at my house).

Annie smiled sleepily, and said something muffled. Then, still half asleep, she climbed out of bed and made her way to the bathroom.

It was ten-fifteen. Checkout time was noon according to the sign posted on the inside of the room's door, but we'd want to be on the road well before then. I did some mental calculations, and reckoned if we took an hour for showers and getting ready and such, we could be out the door and on the way to Calgary a little after eleven. Surely that would get us there before three -- enough time to take care of business before the banks closed.

"Alright, Annie," I said, as she came out of the bathroom. "We need to get ready and get on the road in an hour. Shower?"

She nodded.

"Okay, then. Why don't you hop on in. Do you want me to turn it on for you? No? Okay. I have to go talk to the front desk for a bit. Will you be okay if I run down there for five minutes?"

* * *

I stepped outside and shut the door behind me, being very careful to lock it. My breath made little puffs of white in the cold air as I stepped lively up the pavement, keeping the door to our room firmly in my line of sight, despite having locked it. By nature I am a paranoid parent, though if ever there was a nine year old that could take care of herself, it was Annie.

I had a short talk with the desk clerk, and after a little pro-forma grumbling he accepted an American twenty for a thumbs up on a long distance call to the States from the phone in our room. I got the sense that he wasn't entirely unhappy to get the cash, as he probably reckoned rightly he was making a smart profit on the deal. As an afterthought I asked him if they had any disposable razors and toiletries available for the guests, and he produced a little plastic bag with mini-toothpastes and such in it.

"Dial nine for an outside line," he said.

When I got back to the room the shower was still running, and steam was accumulating lavishly around the ceiling outside the bathroom. The door was slightly ajar.

"I'm back!" I shouted.

"Thanks for the information!" she shouted back.

A few minutes later she came out of the bathroom wrapped in towels and walked over to her bed to retrieve her Hello Kitty backpack, and opened the thing and commenced rooting around inside it. She's proba-

107

bly got a change of clothes in there, I thought jealously. Even some fresh underwear and socks would be nice. My own were definitely getting a bit ripe.

"Get dressed, Annie, and I'll go in and get my shower out of the way," I said to her, standing up. "I should probably see what we have left of our funds, first," I added, hoping we had at least the fifty I thought we still had, but starting to worry about whether my count was off. I was becoming concerned about what we'd need even to get to Calgary. "Best to be sure of what we have before we go to spending any more," I said, sounding like my mother.

"I've got something I should probably tell you," she said.

"It's always less than you think," I added, pulling the noticeably de-pleted bank roll out of my pocket.

"Actually, it's more something I should probably *show* you," she said reluctantly, continuing to dig into her backpack.

"What's that," I asked, still not really paying attention, carefully counting the money.

"Don't get mad," she said, hefting something big and black out of the little backpack and up into view.

I looked over. It was a gun.

"What the—" I gobbled. *"What the F*—What is that!" I couldn't have been more stunned if she'd pulled out the Pope's hat.

She looked at me rather sheepish. "I'm really sorry. I put it back in my backpack last night, when we got out of the car. Here at the motel. Yesterday. It was in the glove compartment. I saw it in there before, back when you had me get the map out, and…"

So the thing had been in the glove-box. I didn't have to range about too far to put the pieces together for that. James was a gun nut, alright. A right-wing Evangelical talk radio dyed in the wool gun nut. That he kept a revolver in his glove box certainly was consistent with that. And the little red headed swine I was traveling with had grabbed it from out of there while I wasn't looking.

"Remind me not to take my eyes off you again," I said to her, a little chagrinned. Then the other shoe dropped. "Jesus, we crossed the border

108

with a firearm!" The thought flashed through my brain and made me feel a bit sick. I sat down on the bed. "Is that thing loaded?" I wondered, weakly.

"We made it across okay," she offered, trying to look all winsome and sorry.

"Yeah, talk about blind stupid luck," I said, not buying it. Not that it was her fault, mind you, but she was a happy little messenger, nonetheless. I gently took the gun away from her, making sure the safety was on. "Goddamit, it *is* loaded. What are we going to do with this thing?" I said.

Annie shrugged. "You never know when you're going to need a gun."

"There's a comforting thought," says I. "Let's just hope we *won't* need one."

I sighed. The big problem was, there was no easy way to dispose of the thing now. We couldn't very well throw it away. We certainly couldn't leave it there in the room. "What are we going to do with this," I said once more.

"We should just keep it," Annie said. "Just in case."

"Yeah, keep it," I repeated sarcastically. "That's just what we need to do. Look, I'm going to call Madstone, and find out about your mum. Meantime, you go get ready, okay. And leave the gun alone. We'll decide what to do with it before we leave. Just—here, just take your stuff into the bathroom and I'll call Madstone now. I'll take my shower after."

She bounced off to the bathroom to do her hair, and I looked over at the motel phone on the nightstand. I was nervous to do it, if I'm honest, to make the call to Madstone. No situation is so bad it can't get worse, that's my motto. But being a lawyer, I am well familiar with the grim truth that knowledge is always your friend. It's better to know than not to know. And if I didn't talk to Madstone now, I wouldn't have an opportunity to call him for another four or five hours, if then.

Time was a factor. I seized up the receiver and dialed nine for an outside line.

109

Chapter 18 – Madstone

I HELD THE PHONE to my ear with one hand. It rang twice, and then he picked up:

"Madstone," he said.

"Hey Madstone, it's me," I said. "Bob McKenzie."

"McKenzie!—where the hell are you? Did you hear about Quintana?"

This couldn't be good. I didn't know what was coming next, but my guts were already turning south. "What?" I finally said.

"He's dead, McKenzie."

"Dead?"

"Yeah. They been looking for you here all morning. I'm sorry to be the one to tell you. They found him in his bathtub."

"Bathtub?"

"His prayer group found him. Prayer group—can you believe it. He lived alone, so otherwise it might have been weeks before they found the body. Not that we'd have noticed here at work." He paused. "I mean,...well, you know. James was never really big on actually spending time at his desk. Pretty horrible."

"It was an accident?" I said, my mind racing.

"Drowned. Apparently it wasn't too pretty. They say he slipped and knocked his head."

"In the *bathtub*?" I said again, hardly believing it. Falling in the bathtub was for old people. The infirm and the clumsy. Quintana had been neither.

"Ninety percent of accidents happen in the home, McKenzie. Actually, that could be total bullshit. But Quintana did live alone. Apparently he cracked his head like an egg on the side of the tub and never woke up. Slid right under the water. Lots of bubbles, then nothing. For what it's worth, they say the poor bastard probably never knew what hit him."

I mumbled something commiseratory, then Madstone ran on about funeral arrangements and taking up collections and such things, but I could hardly hear him. Poor James. He was one of the good guys. An Evangelical right wing gun nut, but thoroughly decent for all of that.

"So, McKenzie, are you able to go to the Rosary?"

I felt my face flush red. I had to force myself to remember that Madstone had no idea we'd swiped James Quintana's truck. Not that it had anything to do with him falling in the bathtub, of course, but just the same, I felt guilty as hell. I had to remind myself that to Madstone, this was the death of a mutual acquaintance, and bad as that was, nothing more.

"I can't, Madstone."

"You can't go?"

"Well, no. I can't really go to the Rosary tonight. I would, but here's the thing—I was arrested yesterday..." I hesitated, hoping for some feedback to what seemed to me a pretty shocking statement, but there was a long pause on the other end. Was Madstone appalled? Disgusted? Surprised? Or was he simply annoyed at being bothered with something that clearly came under the heading of "not my problem"—a "not my problem" that paled significantly against the death of a close friend.

I took a breath and carried on. "It was an immigration issue. You know I'm Canadian, right. And the governor's got this new Executive Order where the Police have to ask about your status whenever they pull you over for a stop—"

"Sure, that new 'Papers Please' law," he said, finally talking again. I was relieved he was back with me, alright, and could tell from his tone he'd not gone silent out of disgust, he'd simply gone into lawyer-listening mode. "She's another Tea-Party governor who hates immigrants," he added. "Just like Arizona. I'm with you so far."

"Okay, so they booked me 'cause I didn't have my visa, and put me in some kind of makeshift holding tank. And there was this little girl in there, too, and when she..." I tried to think of a diplomatic word to use, but there was only one: "escaped, I tried to get her to come back, but the cops started shooting, and—"

"*That was you!*" Madstone blurted.

"I'm afraid it was."

"Holy shit, McKenzie, that's all over the news—*what were you thinking!*"

"It's not what it looks like. Seriously. It's really not."

"They said you had a gun."

"Madstone, I swear that's not true! I didn't have any gun."

At least, not then I didn't, I thought without saying it.

"Okay."

"Look, how could I have had a gun when we left out of there – they'd already booked me in. They took all my stuff. Wallet, belt, credit cards...Hell, what am I talking about—*I never even had a gun in the first place!*"

"Okay, okay. I'm just telling you what's in the papers," he said, matter-of-factly. "I don't doubt the cops are full of shit. Or maybe the papers got it wrong, who knows. But, look, first things first. Why don't you tell me exactly what happened. Start at the beginning, and just take your time."

And so I did. I spun my tale of woe, starting from the Las Cruces trial, and the episode at the check-stop, to my arrest in Santa Fe, and running into Annie again, and escaping police custody in a hail of bullets. Of course, I didn't mention anything about borrowing James Quintana's truck, or where Annie and I were now. But I didn't stint on any of the rest, and frankly, I wasn't too bad at telling the story.

112

Good practice for my sentencing hearing, I thought, darkly.

"Okay. So I assume you still have the kid with you."

"Yes." Off in the bathroom I could hear the water running. I suspected a mess was being made.

"And you want me to arrange for your surrender to the authorities."

"Correct. That's exactly right."

There was a long pause. Then Madstone said, "I'd be willing to do that for you. If you want."

"I'd be thankful forever, Madstone. And I'm good for it, too—hell, I'll pay you double for chrissake!"

Madstone actually laughed out loud at that. "That's a good one," he said, still laughing. It actually took him a good thirty seconds or so to fully compose himself. It's a hell of a thing, by the way, when your promise to pay don't even meet the straight face test. "Look, don't worry about it," he finally continued. "This one's on me. Frankly, I'm happy to do it. Ever since our Fascist handlers took over the Environment Department our phony-baloney jobs are only good for about twenty hours of actual litigation work a week. And only about ten hours of actual mental effort. We've become the lap dogs of industry, and since we can't go after the environmental bad guys any more it's boring as shit here. And as for myself, I've got to do something to keep myself fresh or I'd go nuts."

"I really appreciate it," I said, and meant it.

"You're the one doing me a favor."

"Madstone. One other thing," I said, remembering my promise to Annie, "the girl...right. That girl. Annie. Immigration pinched her mum at the Customs and Border Protection checkstop outside Cruces Monday night, too. Same time I was there. Took her into custody. Is there any way you can find out what her situation is? Her kid's really worried."

"What's her name? The *mother's* name?"

That caught me up a bit, 'cause even though her presence had been shadowing us for the last couple of days, and in a way the whole journey had been about Annie's unrelenting focus on her, I realized I didn't know what her name was. I clamped the receiver to my ear, picked up the phone and crossed the room.

"WHAT'S YOUR MUM'S NAME, ANNIE?" I shouted at the bathroom door

"Michelle Chretien," Annie shouted back over the running water.

I repeated the name to Madstone. "For what it's worth, the Border Patrol guy outside Cruces told me they were sending her off to a transition center in El Paso. I saw 'em put her on the bus that very night. Monday night."

There was a short silence on the other end of the phone while I imagined Madstone writing all this down with his wrecked hands, then he returned to the line and said: "Okay. Let me look into this a bit. For right now, I'm not going to ask where you are, and frankly I don't want to know. Anything we talk about is protected by attorney-client privilege, anyway—hell, you're a lawyer, you know that—but let's be as discrete as we can; let's play this real safe."

He thought for another couple of seconds, and then added practically, "What are you telling them at work?"

"Jesus, I hadn't even thought about that—"

Madstone waived me off. "Leave it to me; I know exactly what to tell them. Don't you contact work at all. And in the meantime, stay safe. Don't do anything stupid. What's your phone number?"

"How 'bout I call you later. That'd be better."

"Perfect. Okay. Chin up, McKenzie. Let me look into this, and I'll try to call you back later today. Sorry. Strike that—you call me when you can. Let's connect before COB, though."

"Thanks, Madstone." I said.

"Okay. Oh, one more thing. And this one's pretty important."

"What's that?"

"Whatever you do, don't leave the country."

"Don't leave the..." I started to repeat.

"Right. That's stupid, I know. I mean, I don't expect that you would even be thinking about such a thing. But under no circumstances leave the borders of the United States. Based on what you've told me, my guess is ICE thinks you're headed to Canada, and if you *do* get across, you'll never get back. Not without getting locked up at the border on you return trip."

"Of course," says I, thinking it best to keep the fact we'd already violated his instructions to myself for the time being.

As I hung up the phone, I spied the big black pistol sitting next to it on the nightstand.

"*Shit*," I muttered.

Chapter 19 – Calgary

HAVING TEMPORARY ACCESS to a phone, I gave some thought to trying to call my own little girl back in Albuquerque, but reckoned it wasn't the time, it being only Wednesday, and all, and there still being the barest possibility that we'd be back home and dry, or at least on our way there, when time came for this weekend's visitation. Best to play things as normal as possible, thinks I. Play things normal, and hope my name and face weren't plastered all over the news back home. Madstone had been surprised to learn it was me that was involved in the jail break, so maybe we could get this business straightened out before family and friends found out I was public enemy number one. In any event, I already had enough spinning plates in the air for one day without piling on anything additional, so I put a little red pin in the notion of calling my daughter until after we'd talked to Madstone later. At least then I might have some idea of when I could return home. Hopefully.

Whatever I did, though, the one thing I had to avoid come this Friday afternoon was having my ex and my daughter standing together in the doorway going "where's daddy?"

I took my shower, and shaved, washed and brushed up, and Annie and me headed out the door. And how'd I get the gun out to the truck, you ask? Shoved it in my waistband, like any proper criminal. I untucked my shirt, shoved it under my waistband, and Annie and me walked through the slush and snow out to the truck. The pistol hung heavy at the top of my loose pants, me still having no belt and all, and I could feel the cold steel of it against my belly, and I was a little nervous about shooting my parts off, but in the event there proved to be no problem.

The experience made me feel a little cocky, though, as carrying around a gun will tend to do, and once in the truck, I shoved the damn thing back in the glove box with some relief. We buckled up, I started the engine, and off we went, heavily armed into a brand new Canadian day.

It was a bloody cold day, too, or felt it at least. I shoved on the heater, and as we drove out of Coutts we passed up a time and temperature sign that read one. Just the number "1." It baffled me at first, 'cause it seemed cold alright, but nowhere near one bloody degree cold, and I struggled to think through just what it meant. And then I remembered Canada was on the metric system. "1" was simply one degree centigrade, which is about thirty-four degrees Fahrenheit to you and me.

Cold enough, as far as I was concerned, but at least not fucking *one*.

We hadn't had anything to eat of course, but agreed that getting some road behind us was our first priority. The time and temperature sign had additionally reported that it was exactly 11:01 in the a.m., so we were more or less ahead of schedule, and helpful signage put us on to Route 4 as the way to Calgary.

Annie wanted to do the yellow car game again, and we played that for awhile, and when that wore smooth we switched over to cow jokes for a bit. It turns out she had quite an arsenal of 'em, too.

"What goes 'ooo'?"

I thought about it. "I don't know, what goes 'ooo'?"

"A cow with no lips."

It was funny and disturbing all at the same time, but Annie thought it was the height of hilarity, which it kind of was.

"What do you call a cow that wakes you up in the morning?"

I didn't know.

"A cock-a-doodle-*Moo!*" It continued in the vein for a while, and then their quality started to deteriorate, whereupon Annie made the switch to ghost jokes: "What do ghosts like for dinner," she asked."

I was flummoxed.

"I—*scream!*"

We both ran out of material shortly after that, and tried to start up our yellow car game again, but there being not much traffic, the pickins' were slim and it was a desultory affair at best.

Alberta is huge, by the way, almost as tall as the continental United States, north to south, and the drive to Calgary, which is only about a quarter of the way up the Province, proved to be correspondingly epic— well, four hours, or thereabouts, anyway. And expensive, too. We filled up at some town called Lethbridge, and I don't know for sure what a liter is, exactly, but I can tell you it cost almost double to fill up the tank. I looked at the pathetic handful of ones and fives I had left, and sighed. We were really and truly up against it, now. If my bank plan didn't come through, we'd probably have to throw ourselves on the mercy of the court—or the Mounties, or whatsoever the appropriate authorities were for turning oneself in when there were international warrants out in your name and you were completely destitute. It's no good to be out of money, I can tell you that from bitter experience! The alternatives to having dough are very poor.

So naturally we stopped an hour later to spend what meager fortune was left us for some breakfast in Fort McLeod at a donut place just off the highway called Tim Horton's. Might as well have a little nosh to cheer us up, I reckoned. It was a jolly little feast, made all the more cosy by the snow and ice just beyond the donut shop's window.

After we finished up, and threw our cups and napkins away, we returned to the counter and spent the very last of what we had on road-sodies: a second cup of coffee for me and an orange juice for Annie.

We pulled onto Route 2, then, and right away we passed up a sign telling us that it was still another 165 kilometers to Calgary—one-hundred and sixty-five klicks straight north. I braced myself for what I hoped would be our last significant chunk of time in the car—last signif-

118

icant chunk until Madstone gave us the Olly-Olly-Oxen-Free to come back to Santa Fe, at least (which was something I didn't want to think about too much right then, as the notion of having to do this bloody drive again so soon made me a little nauseous).   Annie and I sat in silence and sipped our beverages and enjoyed the views. They weren't much, by the way, the views, it being overcast and all, and because we were driving up the middle of a sort of brown featureless rolling prairie—wide empty grasslands and low rolling hills and such. Far off to the west, just under the clouds, the Canadian Rockies peaked over the horizon, already snow-capped in mid-October. Frankly, except for the snow, Alberta was much like Idaho or Montana to drive through, though I noticed the Canadians did seem to keep their headlights on during the day.

So as not to stand out, I figured I'd better switch ours on, too. Who knew what the law was, or whether they'd pull you over for *not* doing it. Best to be careful, especially as I didn't presently have a driver's license, and it didn't cost us nothing to do it, anyway—although I have to admit I felt a bit paranoid about it just the same. Headlights on during the day just felt odd.

The ghost of James Quintana preyed on my conscience a good part of the time we were chewing up the Canadian miles—kilometers, I mean. He'd been a good friend, despite being a little righty-wing-nutty, and I realized I missed him. It was a hell of a thing. Good old James, I thought sadly. Madstone's news had been truly shocking, and this was the first real chance I'd had to think of it. It was taking a while to fully sink in. Hell, we'd just been together at the Las Cruces checkstop two nights before.

Suddenly the notion that James' death and my current adventure were somehow connected flashed through my head like summer lighten-ing. Was there some kind of nexus? James was dead and we were on the run. It was a hell of a coincidence. Was it possible that by taking his truck I had brought some seriously dark Ju-Ju down on his house? Was James' fate somehow tied up with our own? Had some sort of bloody scene then gone down inside that double-wide trailer? Had certain yet to be identified bad guys forced James Quintana to his naked knees at gunpoint in the bathtub and smashed his skull in with a ball bat to simulate the injuries of a fall? But why?—and what could something like that possibly have to do with Annie and me?

At this point I had what the professionals call a moment of lucidity, and realized all this speculating was pure fantasy. But then I remembered the shootout back at the police station, which by any measure was a pretty fantastic event. I'd never have thought something like that could happen, either.

Could all these things plausibly go down in the same twenty-four hours and not be related; could the world possibly be that absurd?

By now, as you can no doubt tell, my brain was becoming my own worst enemy. I looked out the window and tried to think about vanilla.

As the day wore on my desperation found a new focus, and I began to get into a bit of a sweat about whether we'd make Calgary in time to get to my bank (and the very real possibility we'd find no joy at the bank anyway, and wind up ultimately stranded and penniless in an unfamiliar city), but pretty soon we came upon a town called High River and then another one called Okotoks, and finally the outlying edges of the City of Calgary itself.

And at that exact moment the afternoon sun broke through from under the clouds, and lit up the prairie a fiery bright golden all around us. It was breathtaking. The purple clouds were still overhead like a broad low ceiling, but the sun was peeking out from underneath 'em, like it was looking under a blanket. It was spectacular. It lit up the sweeping stubbily wheat fields something fierce, all fresh and clean—golden—and was a sight that frankly lifted my heart.

Buildings started to grow up around us, and signs started appearing about then for the City Centre (Canadian spelling had fully kicked in, of course, with its switched up r's and e's, and gratuitous u's in words like "colour") and I followed their directions, reckoning rightly that you can always find a bank downtown. We quickly found ourselves in heavy urban traffic, and after passing through the usual light industrial zones, and outlying suburbs, ran along the bluffs over a fast muscular river (the Bow, as it turned out) and followed our way around it until we were pointed toward the skyscrapers. I made generally for a huge tower that stood in their midst that appeared to be the Calgary version of the Seattle Space Needle, though orders of magnitude less elegant—more in the nature of a giant cinderblock Olympic torch, I thought briefly. But whatever it was, it was the tallest thing going, and seemed a good landmark to head for. We drove toward it for a few minutes longer, as the stoplights and cars and so on thickened up around us, and traffic quickly slowed toward gridlock. Welcome to downtown anywhere, I thought.

But as luck would have it, bank offices of various stripes were popping up now and then every couple of blocks, so I reckoned we might as well park, and continue on foot. We were coming up on the Calgary Public Library, and I swung into an empty spot in front.

Yet again, it felt great to climb out of the vehicle. Free at last, free at last, oh Lordy—

"You can't park there."

I looked over and a middle aged man and his lady wife were eyeing us sternly. Simultaneously, the sun ducked back in, and a monochromatic gray overcast immediately re-colored the City a grim cement.

"No parking," he said, pointing at the sign over my head.

What was this, thinks I? It's none of his damned business anyway. For a brief moment a violent urge to strike the man down rose in my breast—I'd never been confronted in such an insolent fashion back in the good old U.S. of A.—but I overcame it. Instead I nodded to the two coldly. I glanced up the street and saw a branch of my bank about half a block up.

I looked back at Annie. "Take our chances with the parking?" I suggested.

"Sure," she shrugged, and we started briskly up the street, breezing by the officious couple without further comment. I reflected that the worst that could happen was the truck'd get towed and we'd find ourselves in the heart of a strange city with no money, no vehicle and no place to call home, but what were the chances? Actually, reasonably good, since the evidence was mounting that this was a country where the rules were scrupulously followed, and inappropriately parked cars prob-

121

ably got immediately towed. I decided I didn't want to think about it, and we strolled westward, on up toward my bank.

One problem at a time, thinks I.

Walking up the cold pavement, I noted the weather remained just as frosty in Calgary as it had been in Coutts, though there was no snow on the ground up here. In any event, it was definitely more winter than fall now that we were in Alberta, and Annie was shivering. She drew her arms close in around her little chest as we hustled up the street.

Chapter 20 – The Bank

AS FOR MYSELF, the continued irritation from our encounter with the two self-appointed parking scolds was sufficient to keep me warm. But it was still a relief to step inside a warm bank. The glass door slid silently closed behind us, and I surveyed the place. It looked to be about the same as any branch bank in north America, with the seasonal touch of Halloween silhouettes of witches and pumpkins and such like pasted up on the walls. It was comforting to know Canada celebrated Halloween, too.

I smoothed my hair, pulled up my loose pants and patted down my wrinkled clothes, and stepped up to their sort of concierge-cum-receptionist to present our problem. He seemed not to notice our disheveled coatless state, and bade us have a seat, stating a personal banker would be with us in a moment.

"When we go in there, don't say anything," I whispered to Annie.

"Okay," she whispered back.

"We'd probably best pretend I'm your dad, again, too," I added.

"I figured."

We sat in the comfy chairs, enjoying the lobby for a few more minutes, when a likely looking young chap in a crisp suit and tie stepped up to where we were sitting. "Hello, there. Mr. McKenzie?"

I stood up, and allowed I was, and introduced my "daughter" Annie.

"Well, that's just great," he says, making a big production of shaking her hand. "Follow me and we'll get you squared away." We wound our way down a hall and round a corner to where he had an office, and we sat down opposite him, in front of his desk.

"What can we do for you today, Mr. McKenzie?"

"Well, my daughter and I have a bit of a problem," I began. "I'm a bank customer, and we're from the States, and we're on a family trip, and I'm afraid while we were traveling up here I lost my wallet. I don't know if we were robbed, or I just misplaced it, or—"

"You left it when we went down to the pool daddy," Annie piped up.

It was the perfect touch. The banker smiled.

"Yes, that's probably it," I agreed sheepishly. "We were staying at the Holiday Inn in Great Falls on the way up here, and went down to the pool after dinner, and…Well, anyway, we found ourselves without identification or credit cards, and I'd like to get set up again with my accounts. I was hoping to get an Access Card and some checks, at least. Is that something we can do here?"

The banker had been nodding throughout, taking it all in.

"You'd just sent me a new Access card, by the way," I added, shaking my head in self-deprecating dismay. "Just this week. I was quite grateful because we needed it for the trip. I can't believe I lost it so quickly."

He looked over at his computer screen. "Indeed," he agreed. "Says here you did that through our London, Ontario branch." He looked up and down the screen for what seemed a very long minute, and then returned his attention to us. "Well, Mr. McKenzie, that's really a shame. That happened to my cousin once on her way to South Carolina a couple of years ago. It was a real mess for her, as I recall." He returned his focus to the computer screen, and banged something clickity-clack into the keyboard. "Let's see if we can make things go a little more smoothly for you. No identification?"

"That's right. Just a little cash left," I lied. "All in American dollars."

124

"Hmmm. Is there any way you could you tell me what the last transaction was with your checking account?"

Eureka! Thinks I. "Yes. I withdrew seven hundred dollars from an ATM in Santa Fe, New Mexico. Just this last Tuesday."

"And a security question," he said. "Mother's maiden name?"

"Pastmaster."

"Pastmaster," he repeated. He looked at his computer screen for a moment, smiled sincerely and seemed entirely satisfied. "Very good, Mr. McKenzie," he said. "So, what can I do for you? An Access Card and some checks, you said?"

"That would be great. Can I get an account balance, too?"

"Of course. At present you have $32,140.28 Canadian in your account."

"While we're at it, I'd like to get a little cash out, too. In Canadian bills." I looked over at Annie. "It's my daughter's birthday, you see."

Annie looked back at me and smiled.

Back out on the street I could feel the replenished wad of cash inside my pocket, now wrapped around a brand new ATM card, and twelve temporary checks.

"You did great in there," I said to Annie really meaning it.

I was coming to realize she had the natural timing of a real con artist, and I wondered if that came from her villain of a father or it was something all kids necessarily have. I'd never observed it my own flesh and blood, mind you, but my daughter and I had never tried to deceive Child Services or a police officer or customs officials, or a bank manager, neither. Perhaps I was doing my own little girl a disservice, and she was equally capable of putting one over. But either way, right now and right here during our very sudden and very weird two day Odyssey, Annie was proving to be a real asset. "What do you say to a little 'birthday' celebration?"

"Yes!" she said enthusiastically.

We fairly skipped back to the truck, which proved to still be there, and ticket free, too, notwithstanding the unsolicited caution we'd earlier received. And all things settled financially, we set off to buy ourselves some "birthday presents."

Two hours later it was already full on dark, and we emerged into the cold night air clad in new winter jackets over brand new clothes. I'd even splurged on a fairly nice middle-sized suitcase to carry our old soiled stuff in, plus fresh packets of underwear and socks all around, and a spare shirt and blouse each. Best of all, I could feel the presence of my new belt and the laces on my shoes with some satisfaction, as well as the new wallet in my pocket, too. Don't let anyone tell you can't actually feel those things. Or that you don't notice when you *don't* got 'em. I can tell you, I'd been pretty self conscious about it ever since the Santa Fe PD had confiscated those things from me, loose lace-less shoes and belt-less saggy pants and all.

By this time, our shopping spree had us parked near the bottom of downtown, by the Bow River opposite a park called Prince's Island. We were looking for a place to eat, specifically for some apparently well known spot called the River Cafe that one of the store clerks told us had great seafood. Annie said she loved salmon, and it all sounded good to me, so we commenced wandering around looking for it.

The restaurant proved to be a short walk from the bridge over to the island, and was surrounded by a patio full of large white umbrellas that the changing season hadn't caught up with, yet. It looked nice enough, but the whole damn thing was suspiciously dark.

"It's supposed to be open 'till eleven on week days," I said, reading the sign.

"What time is it," Annie asked.

"No idea. Can't be much after five, though."

We turned back to the car, mildly disappointed. Still, there was nothing to complain about. We had money, clothes, and the wherewithal to check into a decent hotel for the night. We'd get dinner squared away, too. But somehow I wasn't feeling it; I should have been realizing some satisfaction from the day's accomplishments—notwithstanding the fact that that we were still deep in the shit, stranded on foreign soil. Things could have been a lot worse.

126

But something was still nagging at me. Something I'd forgotten. Something important.

Dammit!—I suddenly remembered.

The gun.

Chapter 21 – Dennis the Killer Pimp

THE GUN. Thank god I'd remembered. It was still sitting there loaded and with the safety on back in the glove box. It would have been a disaster to find ourselves holding onto that thing if we got pulled over up here in Canada, or worse yet: if they found it when it came time to cross the border again. Getting away with inadvertent gun running once had been lucky. Twice would be ridiculous. We had to ditch it.

The question was, how. As a practical matter, like I'd concluded back in Coutts, I couldn't very well toss it out a window, or just leave it in a garbage can. It would likely be found, and someone could wind up hurt.

Suddenly the lightbulb went on! The River would do. We were in Calgary's downtown river park. This was good. The Bow was fast enough and deep enough, a broad shouldered glacial torrent. We could drop the bullets in, and then the unloaded gun after 'em. Maybe some fishies'd get hurt, but the thing'd be out of our hair. We could do it right now—get the gun, stroll over to the bridge, drop the weapon in the fast fresh waters of the river Bow, then drive off to check into a hotel and get something to eat. Perfect.

That was when Annie noticed a shadow recede into the dark.

"What was that?" she whispered, breathlessly.

Before I could answer, I saw one myself, then two more.

I was briefly alarmed, being loaded down with a new wad of cash, but then I clicked. Women of the night, they were, and for the first time I noticed the active line of cars along the frontage road on the other side of the river. There was a brisk trade taking place all around us.

"Who are those ladies?" Annie asked.

I didn't say anything, but the answer was obvious. Calgary was first and foremost an oil and gas town, and a cow-town, too, with large numbers of itinerate workers and a robust cash economy. Lots of horny young men added to a virile working culture and the libertarian politics of the wild west. Call it what you want: Economics 101, the Invisible Hand. Capitalism at work, maybe. But whatever the economic underpinnings, right now there was no denying there were lots of people exchanging sex for money down by where we were in the river park at that exact moment in time.

Focus.

We jetted back to where we'd parked the truck, I shoved the pistol under my belt, and Annie and me headed back into the park to look for a handy and isolated bridge. We passed up clumps of people who were still about, it being only five-thirty, and wandered between the bare trees, up paths lit with discrete pools of light from wrought iron street lamps. The women of the night were definitely out in force, but despite the fact I could sense 'em around us, this time I didn't actually see any.

They might be our biggest problem, thinks I, used to watching from the shadows as they were, and slipping out of sight when they didn't want to be seen. Obviously we'd need to find a moment where there was no one around to do the dirty deed, as it wouldn't do to have anyone secretly witness us tossing a weapon into the river, but how could we ever be certain none of them were looking on?

Between the naked trees I spied reflected light on flowing black water, and in the same vicinity the shadowy outline of what looked to be a suspension bridge.

"There," says I, pointing it out to Annie.

We followed the path in that direction, taking it slow, and scouting out ahead of us for people in the area. The bridge and its environs looked pretty dark and lonesome to me, so we hustled forward. The quicker we were done with this, thinks I, the happier I'll be.

As we closed in on the water, I reached under my coat and seized the revolver by the butt, getting ready to whip it out, flip open the chamber and empty the shells into my hand. I reckoned when we got to the middle of the bridge I'd kind of lean in to one of the suspension struts, keeping everything out of sight, and then release the handful of loose shells down into the dark roiling waters of the Bow. Then I'd plop the gun in. All in all, it shouldn't take much above seven seconds, and then we'd be done, and we could walk casually back to the truck.

We were close enough now I could see there was no one on the bridge; Annie and me had reached the threshold of the thing, and stepped forward to cross onto it. But before we could, though, there was a loud crash, and a woman came tumbling out of the brush.

She slammed into me full tilt, windmilling, trying to keep her balance, and the force of it shoved me back a bit. Annie jumped back like she'd been stung.

For a split second the woman's face was inches away from my own, and I could see even in that dim light she was pretty young, like a teenager, maybe. "Get away!" she spat, and recoiled awkwardly back, visibly offended. She planted her feet, and looked me up and down disgustedly—like *I'd* run into *her*!

I didn't have time to react myself, or look at Annie or comment in any way, because right on top of her followed a man. He wasn't a tall man, but he had broad shoulders and red eyes that even in the dappled dark looked sleepy. He stepped slowly out of the brush very deliberate and controlled, and says all entreatingly in a heavy eastern European accent, "Come on back, Britt."

It was a bored voice, tired and laconic, and one you wouldn't expect to associate with such a powerful entrance.

"Go away, Dennis," she says to him evenly, wiping a trickle of blood from the corner her mouth. "You're a *jack*-ass." She didn't sound scared at all, but put me between herself and her gentleman friend just the same.

"C'mon, baby. Why do you make me do you like that?"

130

"Yessss," she says, very dry, "Why *do* I do that?"

"You know I love you."

The girl laughed out loud.

"Who takes care of you, Britt?" he said, sounding very hurt.

"Who takes care of my money, do you mean?"

Everyone was standing their ground, now, and I looked down at Annie expecting to see wide eyes and panic on her face. Instead I saw she was actually staring in a funny sort of way at the face of the man who'd just come out of the brush. For the umpteenth time since we'd met, I realized I had no idea what was going in her little head, but the protective daddy in me kind of took over at this point, and I said to the two interlopers (I thought entirely reasonably) "Will you two please leave my daughter and me alone."

The words came out sounding kind of weenie, though, and it made me feel a bit flaccid, if you really want to know. But under my coat I gave the handle on the pistol a little squeeze, and do you know what, I actually felt stronger for it!

For the first time, the man deigned to notice me. "Shut up, you stupid," he says, sounding mildly annoyed.

I've never performed very well in the face out outright rudeness, and it took a few seconds to formulate a response.

"You—*you* shut up!" I finally said.

A wrinkle of mild irritation passed across his face at that, and he lifted his hand. In it a flat knife glinted. He held it there easily, balancing it in his hand for me to see, exhibiting the blade like a man who knew how to use a knife, but wasn't particularly concerned about whether or not he'd actually have to.

And can you believe it, without thinking at all, I just pulled out the gun. It was the most natural thing in the world, and it just sort of happened. And even though it was entirely reflexive, in that instant I suddenly felt like a different person. It gave me a bit of a semi, if I'm honest.

I could definitely see why people are into these things, I thought to myself.

131

The man stiffened. He wasn't fearful by any means, that much I could see, but he very sensibly froze with the safe and savage instincts of a pimp.

I ranged about for an appropriate statement. "Hold it," says I, finally.

He looked frankly offended, as if I'd committed a grave faux pas. "Who do you think you are," he says in his Eastern European accent, shaking his head more in sorrow than in anger. "This is not your business. *This is not your business!*"

"Not my business!" I sputtered, becoming quite indignant. "You came crashing into *us*."

"Get out of here. Go away," he said, dismissively waiving the knife at me. "Silly tourist."

"I will *not*! You go away."

Now, I'll be the first to admit that I was getting quite shirty at that exact moment, though if I'd had more time to think about it I would have stepped back with Annie as fast as I could, and scampered quickly away from that ridiculous scene. As a practical matter, if we'd gotten pinched by a Calgary cop right then, which was a distinct likelihood under the circumstances, all would have been lost in an instant. I didn't think of it, though, and it didn't even cross my mind until later. I reckon it must have been the immediacy of the situation plus the aphrodisiac of holding a firearm that seemed to have me in something other than my right mind.

Dennis the pimp rolled his eyes in exasperation at that, and gestured with his knife at the girl standing behind me. "*Fine!* Britt, leave them alone."

"I'm not coming with you," Britt says from behind me, quite matter-of-fact. I could tell from the way she said it she wasn't going anywhere with the guy. At least not then.

What with me holding the gun and all, it seemed like I should take some initiative here. "Look, can't you two just go off and settle things somewhere else, and leave decent people…" I started, then trailed off, realizing that Dennis was no longer listening to me. "Goddamit!" I said, waiving the gun, "Can't you even—"

And at that, I realized he was staring at Annie.

132

But it wasn't just him staring, 'cause when I glanced over at her, I realized she still had her eyes locked on his face, too. And worse, an unmistakable look of recognition was passing between 'em.

"Anna?" the thuggy little bastard suddenly said, sort of tentative-like. "Is that you?"

"What?" I said, stupidly.

"Anna? Could that be you?"

"Shut up," I barked at him, realizing this was not a good situation, and now wanting quite urgently to end the exchange as expeditiously as possible.

"Anna Chretien," he says with a huge smile, puffing out his abnormally broad chest and pointing at himself, and ignoring me completely. "*C'est moi!* It's me, Dennis. From back in Montreal! I gave you that stuffed unicorn last Christmas. Your dad and me—"

Annie didn't smile, but she kind of nodded at that. "I really liked that unicorn," she said.

"So are you okay?" he said, suddenly suspicious, now. "Why are you with this guy?" he glanced at me with obvious contempt. "What's going on, Anna? Where's your papa? Where's your mother?…"

This was a disaster. I didn't know what was going on here, but it wasn't good, and was looking frankly worse with every passing second.

"I told you to go away," I said to him, trying to take back control of the situation, desperation and expediency firming up my voice.

He turned his attention to me at that, and looked not the least bit alarmed. "This is not the first time I've had a gun pointed at me, *Monsieur*," he said, quite calmly. "So why don't you tell me what you are doing with my friend's daughter?" He started toward me, knife in his hand.

"I'll count to three…" I said, and reached down with my free hand, and clicked the safety off. The warning strip of day-glow orange instantly appeared.

"One…" says I, my hand suddenly trembling.

He took another step toward me.

"Two—"

There was a loud report. I felt the gun kick in my hand.

"Oh shit!" I exclaimed, and looked down. The muzzle was smoking.

"*You shot me!*" the pimp hissed, looking down at his foot.

I looked down, too. There was blood, alright.

"Holy shit," I kind of whispered. "*Holy shit!*—I'm sorry, I just wanted you to—"

"*You shot me!*" he says again, though this time quite savagely. He tried to move forward, but winced in pain, and sat down hard against the side of a bench. He kept glancing back and forth between the gun and my face like a serpent, gauging whether to strike and I knew he would have, too, if his foot hadn't just been shattered. He supported the wounded leg with both hands, the heel gingerly touching the ground, and it was obviously painful. Even in the dark, it looked to me like the thing was bleeding rather profusely.

He looked up at me now with a different eye—still not fearful at all, but wary and pissed. Definitely pissed. With a shudder, I realized he was staring directly at my face like he really, really wanted to remember it.

It was time to go.

"C'mon Annie," I said firmly, still holding the gun steady on the guy. I grabbed her arm. The sound of the gunshot was still echoing in my ear, and I reckoned someone must have heard the noise—time was not on our side.

"My *foot?*" he said, gesturing pointedly like he expected me to do something about it.

"Put some ice on it," I said over my shoulder.

"I'll be seeing you, *Monsieur*!" he said after me as we stepped quickly—but not too quickly—up the path. "*I'll be seeing you!*"

As we ran-walked away, I slipped the safety back on, shoved the gun into my coat pocket, and yanked Annie forward along the path.

"You said you were going to count to three," Annie said.

"I know."

"But you only gave him until two."

"I know that—c'mon, will you!"

134

"And you shot him before you got to three."

"I know, I know. It was a mistake. The gun just went off."

"But you didn't give him 'till three. It's not fair."

"I *know!* It was an *accident!*"

"Will he be okay?"

Managing a kid is exhausting, take it from me.

"Sure he will," I said. "He's got his lady friend there to help him. They'll just put pressure on it and stop the bleeding. He'll be fine." I realized now Annie had been twisting her head, looking back over her shoulder the whole time we had been run-walking along, and it made me look, too.

Britt the prostitute was skimming along right behind us.

"*Goddamit!*" I wheezed at her—I was getting quite breathless by now, between all the running and the talking. "Where do you think you're going?"

"I am coming with you."

"What!"

"You made a real mess for me back there."

"But your friend?…(*wheeze!*)…Who is…(*wheeze!*) Is Dennis going to be okay?"

"I'm not staying with him *now*."

By this time we were back at the truck, and there was no time to argue. Plus, I didn't have the wind for it. I just wanted to get out of there as quickly as possible. In a trice the three of us were sitting up on the broad bench seat of the big blue vehicle, and it was actually quite comfortable, believe it or not—roomy even with three of us in there. There really is an awful lot of room in those old pickups.

I ground the key hard into the ignition, the engine roared, and I pulled on to the mean streets of Calgary.

"Is this your bunny?" Britt asked Annie.

"Yes," Annie nodded with a shy smile.

I headed us away from the park as fast as I could, driving uphill into downtown, stopping at stoplights, observing every traffic regulation, my heart beating like a hammer. Pretty soon, though, we were on the other

135

side of downtown, driving past the Calgary Tower, and heading up Centre Street. Before I knew it, we passed up seventeenth and were into the south part of the City and far enough away I could breathe easy—or easier, anyway—and start to think about what to do next.

Next to me I heard a distinct giggle. I looked over at Annie, who was grinning the biggest little grin you ever saw.

I waited for it.

"I told you a gun would come in handy," she said.

Chapter 22 – The Britt Situation

MIND YOU, it *was* kind of funny, but I was a bit troubled that Annie could be having a laugh about the gun. It seemed like she should have been totally freaked out by the whole episode in the park—what with all the blood and pimps and knives and whatnot. But then, if the last few days had shown anything, it was that this was one little nine-year old who had the instincts of a Cook County con-man and the guts of a Navy Seal. I found I had to remind myself she was also the little girl who had broken down in tears at the sight of the Border Patrol at our hotel in Great Falls and had crossed the better part of a continent in search of her mother.

We drove around the south end of the City for a bit, decompressing as it were. Eventually we fumbled our way onto some major artery called the Macleod Trail, and it seemed to take us in the direction we wanted to go, which was basically anywhere so long as it was away from where we had been. We drove along in silence, past residential areas and well lit industrial parks, eventually passing into a broad commercial zone of box stores and clusters of restaurants and strip malls, and I realized driving around with a Calgary prostitute and a gun wasn't maybe the wisest move at this exact moment. We'd have to wait until later to do something about the gun, of course, but I figured it would be best at least now to get the Britt situation taken care of as quickly as possible.

"So, where should we drop you off," I says to her kind of tentative, feeling very badly about the whole thing. She was in an obviously shitty situation, too, just being a hooker, and all, her status no doubt made immeasurable worse by the fact that I'd just shot her pimp, and I didn't want to inconvenience the poor woman any more than we already had. The least we could do was take her to a friend's house or something.

Britt whipped around in her seat to face me, making me jump.

"Drop me off!" she cried with startling ferocity. "Are you *kidding!* You just destroyed my life."

"What are you talking about?"

"Thanks to you I can't show my face in Calgary. Not anytime soon, anyway."

"What do you mean," says I, not liking this at all.

"'Drop me off'—that'd be real convenient for you, I guess. Where the hell are you going to drop me off where he's not going to catch up to me now? You got an answer to that one?"

"Well, I'm sorry, but I don't see how that's—"

"It's *all* 'cause of you!" she shouted at me before I could even finish the question. "*You* shot Dennis. No one asked you to do that. Not *me*, right? You pulled out a gun and you shot him. Who even does that?" she added, shaking her head.

"Oh really!" says I, all defensive now. "How 'bout he pulled a knife on *me*? Did you conveniently forget about that? My daughter and I were having a nice little stroll in the park before dinner, and suddenly you and Dennis the killer pimp got us surrounded. What was I *supposed* to do?"

"Not start shooting people!"

"I'm not his daughter," Annie said in a tone that made it clear she was just correcting the record.

Britt looked at her for a minute, then back at me. "What's going on with you two, anyway? Dennis *thought* there was something weird—"

"Look," I said, cutting her off, growing very alarmed. "I'm going to pull over, and you're going to have to get out of the truck, okay. So please just tell me where a good place would be for that."

138

"Okay. How about the next police station – since you're carrying a gun and you just shot a guy. Will that work for you? Or the RCMP office downtown. Maybe that would be better. The RCMP deals with kidnappers. And I can tell you where that's at, by the way. It's right by the—"

"Okay, okay," I said, cutting her off with a sort of hysterical laugh. "Maybe we should just calm down a bit."

Silence.

"Why don't I—I'll just pull the truck over, and we can talk. Then we can figure out what to do. Is that okay?" I was speaking in soft, low tones, now, desperate not to ignite another horrible incident like the one we'd just had down at Princes Island, one that could potentially draw attention to us. "Does that work for everybody?"

"Sure," Annie shrugged.

Britt didn't say a word. I took her silence as assent, though, and yanked the truck off the road, and into a parking space in front of some storefront restaurant called the Sushi Ichiban. I switched off the truck, and we sat there, we three, on the high bench seat of the silent truck saying nothing.

"Anyone want to eat," I finally broke in kind of lamely.

"I *luuvvv* sushi," Annie said, with childish gusto.

Britt started shaking her head. "I'm not getting out of this truck," she said.

"Okay," says I, resigned to it. "Let's sort things out here, first."

"But I'm hungry," Annie says.

"We'll eat," I promised her reassuringly. "We'll eat. Let's just talk to Britt a little first. Figure some things out." I turned to Britt: "So, what do you want?"

I prepared myself for the worst—extortion, money demands, hysterics. And I don't know why this next caught me by surprise, because I'd already been flummoxed by Annie's young tears a couple of times in the last forty-eight hours, but it did. Britt was crying. Silently weeping would be a better way to describe it. Annie saw it, too, and in a touching little gesture, put her finger under Britt's chin and lifted up her face close to hers so she could look in her eyes. "It's okay," she said. "I lost my mom."

"You lost your mom?" she said, alarmed, obviously thinking that by "lost" Annie had meant dead.

"It's okay. He's a lawyer—he's going to help me get her back."

Britt turned her head at this, and her tear streaked face came in to the direct light of the parking lot street lamps. For the first time since she'd come tumbling into me out of the darkness I got a good look at her, and she was young. Real young. With a chubby face framed by a parted curtain of black hair, a tattoo on her neck and a hint of desperation behind her wet swollen eyes.

"How old are you?" Annie asked.

"Eighteen," Britt answered mechanically.

"I'm nine," Annie offered, sounding very proud of that fact.

Britt hesitated again. "I'm actually fourteen," she said to Annie. "But my birthday's in two weeks, so I'm almost fifteen."

It took several seconds for the import of *that* to sink in.

I sputtered like a motor boat as soon as it clicked. "What—who?...how did?..." I tapered off at that point, 'cause I realized I was actually speechless.

"Yeah, fourteen," she admitted, in sort of a flat, resigned way.

"But how did—you're awfully young," I said, horrified. "What about your mum and dad?"

"I didn't run away, if that's what you think," she said, kind of indignant and bucked up a little bit, sitting taller in the seat, wiping away the residual moisture from her eyes.

"Did they kick you out or something?"

She laughed bitterly. "Yeah, that was it." She paused with a certain finality at that, and gazed for a long time through the windshield at the decent folks inside the Sushi Ichiban having dinner. The silence in the cab of the big blue truck drew out.

"Do you have anywhere to go," I asked.

"It doesn't matter," she said, her expression already hardening back up.

140

"Well, I'm just asking, after all."

Flinty silence.

"Really?" I said, feeling a bit exasperated with her. She was the one who didn't want to get out of the truck, after all. Of course, having found out she was a fourteen year old with nowhere to go made me feel a little ambivalent about just putting her onto the street at this point. I mean, I didn't really have any sense of what my role was here, but my gut told me giving her the heave-ho, even if I could, would be somehow inappropriate. Dishonorable, in fact. On the other hand, what could I do? Annie and me would be high-tailing it back south any day now. Madstone was setting things up for us back in Santa Fe. And surely they had shelters and such things for people like Britt? It was Canada, after all. The very flag was a good socialist red.

"Alright," says I, changing tack a bit, "What about Dennis, then."

"What do you mean?"

"Well, I did shoot him, after all. Are the cops gonna' come after us, or?..."

"Oh. Well, maybe somebody did hear your gun go off," Britt admitted, "but I'm pretty sure we got out of there clean. It was just a loud noise in the park at night, right. Nobody's calling out the Mounties or anything."

"Well, yeah, but Dennis's got a bullet hole in his foot. There'll be blood all over down there."

"Sure," Britt agreed. "Someone will notice the blood. Maybe. But don't worry, Dennis won't go to the hospital or anything. Some of the girls'll get him out of there. They'll get him patched up. Nobody wants the cops involved in this, especially not Dennis. It'll just be a big mystery—nothing but a puddle of blood in the dark." She paused and thought for a bit. "Dennis is pretty pissed off at you, though."

"Yeah," I could see that.

"Dennis has got a lot of friends," she added, partly to herself.

"So, can we go eat *now*?" Annie asked.

There was another long pause, and I looked over at Britt. It was her show, at this point—for the moment she definitely had all the power in

141

this relationship. She had gone silent again, though, but this time it was more a reflective silence, not the gratuitous hard edged adolescent street-tough silence from before. Now she was thinking—weighing the realities of our situation (and monetizing the level of my guilt, no doubt). I wondered again about her mum and dad. How does a fourteen year old find herself fighting her way alone in the world like this? Was she an orphan? Abandoned? Despite what she'd said before, runaway came to mind, again…

"I need my stuff," she finally said. "You'll drive me over to the flat, and help me get my stuff, then we'll call it evens."

"What about Dennis?"

She laughed. "Are you scared?" She glanced at my face, and saw I clearly was scared, then gave a concerned look back over at Annie, and her mocking tone quickly changed: "Well, don't be. He's not going to be there, obviously. And all the girls are working; probably they'll be busy binding up Denis' foot right about now. And our place is just round the corner. Thirty-Seventh Street, south-west."

"So, what are we talking about?" I said, wanting to be clear about exactly what we were getting into, "we just drive you over there? To your flat? You can get in and get out? No Dennis, no one else?"

"No muss, no fuss."

I glanced at Annie. I really didn't want to put her in another situation so desperate we'd be glad we had a gun again. Britt dangled a house key in the artificial light, and it twisted and twinkled. "We'll be in and out and you guys can go on your way. And no hard feelings."

Annie and I looked at each other for a long time.

"*Let's help her*," Annie finally blurted, obviously a little disgusted with me—like helping Britt was the only decent thing to do and I should already have come out and said it.

"Okay," says I, and screwed the ignition key into the dashboard once again, and roared the mighty engine to life. Maybe this wasn't so bad after all. If we took care of this little errand we could be done with Britt. And hell, I thought, if all goes well, in three or four days time none of

142

this will matter anyway—it will all be ancient history because Madstone was on the job back in Santa Fe.

Britt directed us over the road and straight to Thirty-Seventh Street, and just like she'd said, we were there in minutes. And the neighborhood didn't look near as seedy as I'd imagined it would be. It was a street populated for the most part by old, leany, slightly dilapidated two story frame houses, the kind you can rent out for not too much to bunches of college students and such like, alternated periodically with cheap two and four-flat apartment buildings. Not high end, but definitely not too low end, either. Indeed, maybe this *was* low end for Canada, this weird northern parallel universe—in fact, it was starting to look like Calgary didn't have anything like a real ghetto; no slums *a la* Chicago's west side or the worst parts of Shanghai or Mexico City or Rio, places where the darker of the service industries usually prospered. It was oddly comforting to know that even pimps and hookers lived somewhat decent here.

Maybe that's the true mark of a civilized society, I thought to myself—that everybody lives at least sort of well.

Chapter 23 – Death and Mothballs

"PARK OUT FRONT HERE," Britt said, indicating one of the four flat buildings.

It was stucco, two stories, with twin balconies that ran one above the other the length of the front of the building.

"C'mon, c'mon, let's go," Britt said impatiently, already on the frozen sidewalk, waving us out of the truck.

"What?"

"C'mon."

"Wait," I said, suddenly alarmed, "that's not the deal. We're not going in—"

"*Hello!*" Britt said. "I've got a back thing and I'm not supposed to lift stuff. You said you'd help me."

Not supposed to lift stuff? "Christ on a pony,..." I muttered. This wasn't the deal. "Alright. Look, I didn't actually say that we'd help move your stuff, but..." Both the girls gave me such look at my hedging that my face flushed red. "Okay, then....But it'll be safe, right? You said there'd be nobody here, right?..."

"Yes, there's nobody here. You'll be totally safe, yes. I promise."

"You can use the gun again if you have to," Annie suggested, all sober-like. "It's still in your pocket."

I ignored her and climbed out of the truck into the cold dark night. Annie hesitated in her seat, not out of fear, but rather uncertainty as to what her role was. I indicated for her to come along; better with us than alone in the car, I reckoned. I didn't know for sure what we were going to run into in there, or whether we were truly as safe as Britt claimed, but so far everything she said looked like it was kind of meeting the straight face test: the place *did* look dark; hookers *probably* would be out at night earning a living; Dennis *probably* was still downtown bleeding heavily—and anyway, we had flashed out of the park so quick it was hard to see any way he could have beaten us back up here. For once, time did seem to be on our side.

Nevertheless, I patted the gun, just to be safe. I wasn't planning on using it, but Annie had been right about it having come in handy before.

We followed Britt forward toward the apartment building entrance, and on closer inspection it didn't appear quite so nice as it had from the street. Not awful, mind you, but kind of like it had been knocked around a bit, with loose shingles and some discrete graffiti and broken wall sconces—that sort of thing.

Britt stepped up to the front door, turned the key in the lock, and disappeared inside. I held Annie back for a second or two, then the lights came on.

"*Well*...Are you *coming*?..." Britt called from inside, all irritated.

It *seemed* legit, so I took Annie's hand in mine and we crossed the threshold. Immediately the sour smell of communal living assaulted my nose. I shut the door behind us, not wanting to advertise our presence to the neighbors any more than we already had, and suddenly it was like we were in an I-Spy book: there was just too much to look at. The bare light bulbs above lit up a living area that presented like a coarse dorm room, with a hodgepodge of thrift shop furnishings, and stained and mismatched sheets over the windows; there were unidentifiable marks on the carpet, and closer inspections revealed cigarette burns just about everywhere. Peppered about it all was the detritus of feminine occupation: loose hair-ties, brushes, empty makeup containers and nail polish bottles; there were discarded items of clothing that at first glance appeared specifically designed to enhance secondary sexual characteristics, as well as much indicia of casual drug use—a bong here, an overflowing ashtray with stubbed out roaches in it over there.

I could see into the kitchen too, off to one side, which was no better, with a sink full of dishes and empty beer bottles and miscellaneous crap obscuring every surface. I could detect a whiff of rancid garbage from where I was standing, and frankly didn't want to move too far in any direction for fear of slipping on a used condom or stepping on a needle. I held onto Annie's little hand like a vise, keeping her right up next to me.

"What is this place…," I started to say to Britt, 'cause it sure looked a lot like what I would imagine a crack house to be, but she had already scurried off down the hall, leaving Annie and me alone in the front room. There appeared to be two or three bedrooms down the back of the place, guessing by the number of doors I could see down the darkened hall, and I wondered if Britt expected us to follow her. Before I could think on it much more, though, she emerged from one of them with an oversized suitcase, a frying pan and a purse that she wore awkwardly around her neck like a harness.

"A little help here!"

I let go of Annie's hand, and rushed forward. "Don't touch *anything*!" I shouted urgently back at the little girl over my shoulder, and took the huge suitcase from Britt's hand.

Turning around I nicked the edge of a coffee table, triggering a brief avalanche of empty food containers onto the floor. Filthy cups and Styrofoam boxes, stained plastic utensils and chunks of spoiled food. The slide continued for several seconds, and finally stabilized in a loose, random pile on the floor.

There was a brief pause, and then a charred, bent spoon and a white pack of matches slowly slid off the remaining junk on the table and onto the pile with a hollow *Plunk!* It was the veritable cherry on top.

Great, thinks I. Heroin.

Britt took no notice. "Here, take the rest of this stuff."

"Oh, *c'mon*…," I whined, slinging the purse around my own neck and grabbing the frying pan with my free hand.

"I gotta get one more thing."

146

"Annie, don't…look just…just hold on to my sleeve."

Annie and I stood in the center of the room, loaded down with Britt's baggage and shrinking away from every surface except the carpet. I prayed the soles of our shoes would keep us safe from whatever was incubating amongst the matted fibers of that sweaty pile. I briefly wondered what inspection with a black light might reveal, but had no time to think anymore about it 'cause Britt was back in seconds.

This time she had a lockbox under her arm.

"Okay, let's go."

We hustled out of there double quick, then—me shoving Annie forward first, wanting to get her out of that greasy Hep-C hell-hole as quickly as possible. In an instant we were back on the pavement, loading Britt's belongings into the back of the truck. All except the lockbox; that Britt held tight in her lap. Minutes later we were back on MacLeod Trail heading south.

I had no idea where we were going. We rode along in silence for awhile, driving and listening to the truck heater blow warm air into the cab. And it was oddly relaxing, too, if you can believe it. Even after the insanity we had just been through, and even with all that we had yet in front of us, for a bit I was able to just let my mind go blank. It's like that sometimes; those eye of the hurricane moments when you just have to go with the flow and enjoy the peace and quiet, even if just for a few minutes.

Your red hair's really pretty by the way," Britt said to Annie.

Britt and Annie. The parallels between the two were impossible to ignore. I glanced over at the 'em. What was the difference between the two really but just five or six years? Was Britt the ghost of Annie yet to come? Probably yeah: factor in a few bad years of foster care and another bad break or two for the little nine-year old…

I found I didn't want to think about it.

"You should come with us," Annie suddenly said to Britt.

I choked heavily, and began coughing. I found I just couldn't stop, and my spasms grew worse until I was throwing off a real spectacle. The

147

girls were visibly alarmed, but after a few minutes I started to get myself back under control.

"I'm sure that's the last thing Britt wants, Annie," I finally said, composing myself. "We're not going to be up here that long anyway, remember?"

"He's going to get me my mom back," Annie said, ignoring me. "He's a lawyer. Maybe he can help you, too."

"Help her what?" I said, wanting to put my fingers around the little kid's throat.

"We're better than Dennis, I bet," Annie said.

"Okay, okay..." I said, trying to laugh it off, forcing a chuckle. "That's not the—"

"Dennis isn't so bad, really," Britt said. "Seriously. Better than some of the foster homes I was in." She paused for just a second. "So, 'come with you guys'? What does that mean? Where're you guys going?"

"We're tourists," I laughed desperately, my voice getting high again. "We're not going anywhere. We're just visiting Canada for a few days until—"

Annie turned to me in shock. "But you said you'd get my mom out," she said, her face falling. "We came to Canada! You *promised*—"

"I'll still try to get your mother out," I assured her, cutting her off before the tears came. "Just,...first we have to—"

"*No*," Annie said, her voice suddenly dropping and octave, her eyes narrowing, looking at me hard now. "You were lying."

"No, no, no—I wasn't lying. Look I—"

"You're a *liar*. You just said those things to get me to..."

We were heading out of town at this point. It was decision time. And maybe it's 'cause we were desperate and on the run anyway. Maybe it's 'cause my brain was bruised from the accumulated traumas of the last forty-eight hours. Or just maybe the mental image of future Annie, hypothetical potential Annie growing up in the sick and violent world of pimps and hookers and heartless losers like the one Britt appeared to hail from was too much to bear. But whatever the reason, at that exact moment in time it sure seemed like there was no other choice.

"ALRIGHT ALREADY!" I practically shouted. "You want to come with us, Britt?" I asked.

"That would be great!" Annie exclaimed, her face transforming immediately back to happy, so excited was she, she was literally bouncing on the seat.

At that Britt looked at me somewhat sideways with a frown, clutching the lockbox tight in her lap, and I suddenly realized she was probably used to offers of help that came with an ulterior motive. Or maybe she was just playing hard to get. Or maybe she was just after a handout, hoping for some cash in hand from me as compensation for allowing us to dump her out on the street somewhere, and that striking out with us instead was not at all the attractive alternative that Annie had supposed it to be. In any event, I gave up trying to guess; Britt's life experience was so very different from my own that I had no frame of reference for understanding what was going through her head—amongst other things, she was a teenager.

"Is Annie right? Are you really a lawyer? Can you help me, too?" Britt asked.

"Well, I'm not sure what your—"

"I want to get my landed immigrant status? That's all I want. To be legal here in Canada."

"He's a lawyer, alright," Annie said, with absolute confidence. "Of course he can do that!"

I hesitated, for a second or two, and Britt was waiting for the other shoe to drop, I guess, 'cause her eyes never left my face. It was all fucking nuts, of course. I can see that now. Madstone was on the job to fix things up for me back to Santa Fe. With a little luck it was entirely possible I could have my old life back in days—with thirty grand in my pocket that I didn't have before. But truth be told it was just as likely Madstone might be weeks straightening things out rather than days—I simply didn't know. If it turned out we had to wait up here a couple of

149

weeks anyway, what the hell else was I going to do with my time. I might as well sort things out for these two girls along the way.

You can't save everybody, but sometimes you just want to. Stupid.

"I'll see what I can do for you," I mumbled.

Britt's cracked a smile at that, and by such avowals, covenants are made. And now I was some kind of pathetic wannabe Atlas holding up two worlds. There was a long pause after that.

"So what now?" Annie finally said.

I suddenly wanted very badly to join those good folks peacefully having their dinners in the Suchi Ichiban, to sit down with a beer and eat some great sushi and pretend we were normal.

"Get something to eat," I said.

I sent the girls on in ahead of me. There was one more box to check off, before the day was done. I had borrowed Britt's cell phone, and there was at least a very small chance chance her plan allowed for international calls. I needed to check in with Madstone.

Chapter 24 – Life in the Great White North

IN LESS THAN twenty-four hours we had set up temporary housekeeping under a month-to-month lease in a cinderblock eight-flat up in Crescent Heights when the first serious snowstorm hit. It was still only October, for chrissake, and only a few days after our encounter with Dennis down in Princes Island Park, but suddenly we were in a seriously different season. And I don't know if you've ever experienced cold. I can tell you, I hadn't. Not before. Not really. The temperature dropped like an anvil by about sixty degrees, and the world immediately shifted from really chilly, but still livable, to deep freeze polar-Winter. That arctic air hits you in the face like a hammer, too, by the way; vehicles stop working, snot freezes and every trip to the store becomes an exercise in survival. The harsh reality of it left Annie and me in shock, if you want to know the truth. We weren't used to weather that can kill you. Even Britt—who apparently claimed some relatively serious cold weather chops ("Spend a winter as a kid up in Inuvik, and then come talk to me about the cold.")—was taken aback.

A few more days passed, the cold persisted, and bitter experience pretty quickly taught us the necessary survival skills: for a kickoff, never go outside with your hair wet; never suck in deep breaths of that frigid air; and always, *always* plug in your vehicle over night. It took just one fifty dollar jump before I clicked to that. Fortunately for me, since poor dead James had purchased the truck up here in Calgary originally, it was already equipped with an oil pan heater; there was a line of electrical sockets up the side of the apartment building installed there for the purpose, and once we got ourselves a heavy-duty oversized extension cord, we were set.

But although the environment was harsh, the flat itself was a snug little place. A modest little "safe-house," and more than enough for a "dad" and his two "daughters" to live in credible comfort without drawing unwanted attention. It was furnished, too, with a couple of bedrooms, a pullout couch and flat screen TV in the living room. We were on the second floor of the place with a picture window that gave us a panorama of the Calgary skyline that was really quite nice, and I immediately invested a portion of my thirty-thousand dollar nest egg in an Apple MacBook to commence my transformation into an immigration lawyer. It's amazing what you can do with just a computer and an internet connection, by the way. But before I even started looking up American immigration sites, I took my new MacBook on a quick trip 'round the web. Everybody does, I suppose, and after checking my e-mail accounts, both work and home (nothing of note in either), and shooting off a rather insane e-mail to my ex to explain why I would be unable to pick up our daughter for visitation (I actually said I had gone into rehab, which she'd find easy enough to believe), my first stop was local news. I was rewarded immediately with a headline in the Calgary Herald:

Man Still in Hospital Following Shooting in Prince's Island Park

The man named was Dennis DuBois.

"Is that your Dennis?" I asked.

Britt looked at the article. "Yup," she said. "That's him."

"I hope he's going to be okay," Annie said.

"He'll be fine," Britt said, shoving in front to read the story over my shoulder, sounding like she thought Dennis was quite the baby for having even gone to the hospital in the first place. "It was only a flesh wound—it says here they're just keeping him for observation. He's probably out already."

152

I didn't care much about poor old Dennis, but there was one thing that concerned me. "What about us? I there anything in the article about us? or suspects or…"

Britt shrugged. "This last paragraph says 'Calgary police continue to investigate the incident, which appears to be gang related.' 'Gang related'," she laughed. "That's the Calgary cops for you. Everything unsolved for them is gang related. Doesn't sound like much for us to worry about."

"I guess," I agreed, dubiously.

"If Dennis had squealed, they'd have had more than just *that* in the paper."

I cruised through a few more websites, checking out the New Mexico papers, too, but there was nothing new out of Santa Fe that I could find. Nothing about us, anyway.

"All quiet on the western front," I muttered.

Ours was a strange arrangement, I have to admit. Me and Annie and Britt. We had been thrown together by circumstances beyond our control and had become partners out of necessity. I didn't know what to make of Britt yet, though I'd have to say she and Annie seemed to hit it off well enough. That's the way it is for kids, I guess—every day's a new day for them anyway, and even the craziest state of affairs can seem normal given the passage of about five minutes. For me, not so much. And I'd have been a whole lot more uncomfortable about our arrangement if it weren't for the fact that the entire world had seemed to have been tilted off its axis anyway. I mean, for a kickoff, I'd been practically chased out of the good old you-ess-uv-aye—my home for almost forty years, my daughter's native land, the place where all my stuff was! The Border Patrol had shot at me, for god's sake, and because of it I was a wanted man down there now, with live warrants and Amber Alerts and all. I'd turned it all over in my head at least a hundred times and it still made no sense! How can a safely-lived life be turned on its head so easily?

And then there was Dennis, of course. I'd never shot a pimp before, so I could tick that off my bucket list now. James Quintana was dead—I didn't want to say murdered, but I sure was thinking it. And let's not

153

forget Annie's father. I didn't know anything for sure there, but there had been plenty of sinister hints around the edges, and I suspected knowing more about him would not help me sleep any better.

What about the father?

By comparison, and all things considered, setting up housekeeping with two underaged girls in a strange city seemed almost prosaic.

I spent a little while longer messing around with the computer—believe me when I say, *You-Tube* can become quite addictive—and out of boredom the girls eventually drifted off to the living room and turned on the TV. I'll be the first to admit that I was just putting off the inevitable, not wanting to get down to work, but am quite proud of the fact that after screwing around for only another six or eight hours with my new toy, I immediately got my focus back. Pretty quickly I found some serious Intel on Annie's mum. And I have to hand it to the Homeland Security folks, by the way—if nothing else, they do give good website. They had an easy to access lookup function for folks in custody that actually appeared to be more or less current. I punched in "Michelle Chretien" and sure enough, about seven seconds later her name popped right up. She was lodged in the Northwest Immigration Detention Center in Tacoma, Washington.

"Hey, Annie," I called to the other room. "I found your mum."

She squealed and came running into the dining room, favoring one bare foot as she loped across the hardwood floor (one set of toenails freshly painted in lively colors), with Britt right behind her.

"*Where!*" she demanded, lodging herself at the top of my right shoulder. "Where is she?"

"Northwest Immigration Detention Center in Tacoma," Britt read off the screen from over my other shoulder. She held a little glass jar of green nail polish in her hand. "Due for a hearing, too, according to this," she added, pointing at the bottom of the screen.

"Your mum's going in front of an Immigration Judge on December 13th," I read, and instantly regretted not having bought a printer when I got the computer. I seized a dirty paper napkin to write the particulars down.

154

"Where is she, again?"

"Like I said. Tacoma, Washington. It's an American city just south of Vancouver. About a thousand miles west of here."

"Can we get there by December thirteenth?" Annie asked.

"We'll be done and gone back to New Mexico a whole lot sooner than that, I hope." I calculated our return coming up in days, maybe weeks at most. Certainly not months. I had no intention of living here on the ice-planet Hoth for two months. Nor waiting that long to rejoin my family and return to work, neither.

"So, does that mean we should we should go to Tacoma *now*?"

"Look, we can't do that yet."

"But you promised to help my mom," Annie insisted.

"And you hate this cold," Britt pointed out.

"You hate the cold. You say that a lot," Annie agreed. "Is Vancouver cold?" she asked, as an afterthought.

"No, Vancouver's quite nice in the winter," Britt said. "Rainy, but—"

"No! We're not going anywhere," says I, growing a little testy. I knew where this was leading, you see. I'd been down this road before with Annie, where you start talking about some crazy damn thing and next thing you know you're there. That's how we got to Canada in the first place. "Look, we're sitting ducks without ID. We have to stay here in Calgary for a few weeks at least. Just so I can get an Alberta driver's license, if nothing else. And we need more information about a lot of things before we start driving all over the planet again."

Not the least, about immigration law, I thought to myself. I was already writing some pretty big checks with my mouth that I wasn't entirely sure my legal abilities would ever be able to cash.

"What else does the computer say?" Annie demanded, impatiently. "Does it say if she's okay?"

I poked around the screen a bit, looking for additional links and came up dry. "No, nothing I can see."

"Can I call her? Can I call my mom?"

"Good question. It doesn't say here, but I'll try to find that out," I promised. "Probably you can. In fact, I'll try to figure out how you can call your mom now, so you can at least talk to her. *But in return*," I said, before Annie could start clapping, "we stay here until I get my Canadian ID. Right? No more of this taking off for Tacoma stuff? At least not until I get things squared away here. I get an Alberta driver's license and a Canadian passport before we do anything."

This illustrates an old lawyer practice point, by the way: you never give something up to an adversary without getting something in return. And I'd offered up a fair and appropriate deal. We'd get Annie on the horn with her mum right away, and I'd get to stay in Calgary long enough to square away my ID.

I waited. Annie was reluctant about it, but couldn't argue with the sense it made. "Okay," she finally said.

Britt signaled her approval.

"Right now what I need, though, is some peace and quiet to read some of this immigration law."

"Sure," Annie whispered. "Let's go, Britt."

"Actually, what I really need is some clients to practice on," I mused to myself. "There's nothing like the doing of a thing to learn it."

"I gotta make a call," Britt said, suddenly. She pulled her phone out of her back pocket and punched in a number.

Dark suspicion clouded my thoughts, and I started to say something, but reckoned she wasn't about to put Dennis on to us. Her making a phone call kind of took me off guard, though. Total radio silence made better sense to me right now, but I felt funny telling the girl she couldn't use her own damn phone. I wondered what sort of folk would be hanging out in Britt's particular milieu, though, who could she be calling—for reasons unknown the mental image of a huge tattooed biker with a bald head and sleeveless jeans jacket, pockets bulging with crystal meth or some other such contraband came to mind.

Four minutes later Britt came back into the kitchen. "Well, I got you a client."

"You what?…" I said.

156

"Ike. He's coming over."

"He's coming now!—*here*?"

"No. Not here. Around the corner. The Moose and Antlers. I figured we probably don't want to have people come up here to our place."

"Yeah. That's good. Protocol. Right. That's good."

"Not everybody likes him, but people who like him really like him. His wife's American and he wants to move down to the States, but he's got a bit of a history. I said you might be able to help him. You said you wanted clients."

"It's drugs, right? He's got a problem with drugs?"

Britt gave me a disgusted look. "No. It's not drugs."

"Does this guy know Dennis?"

Britt laughed. "I know people besides Dennis, you know. Ike's on his way up from Black Diamond right now, so he'll be here in about a half hour. I told him you'd meet him in the bar."

"Right now, huh. Well, that's great," I said. My "great" sounded a little weak, even to me. But I *had* said I wanted some clients. I was just a little stunned at how quick Britt had come up with one. Suddenly I felt more than a bit ambivalent about being thrust back into private practice. Panicked, actually, I realized. It was a long time since I'd been out there, and all this talk about doing some immigration law had so far been pretty abstract. Now I was really and truly facing the fact that I'd been nothing but a government hack for the last dozen years or so. You see, I wondered quite seriously if I'd lost my touch. No, I didn't really wonder—almost certainly I had. And even setting that very fundamental question of my general professional competency aside for the moment, the good sense—or lack of it—of dipping my big toe back into the legal profession in an area of law that I was almost completely unfamiliar with, at least in terms of practical experience, was questionable.

But there was no denying the pressing need to get up to speed on immigration law if I was going to do anything for Annie's mum. Like it or not, it looked I was going to be practicing in this area in a fairly big way in the very, very near future, and I might as well start by getting my

157

game on now.   I didn't have to range about too far to reckon what Madstone would say about it:

Don't be a pussy, McKenzie...

I could almost the disgusted look on his face as he chided me, too.

"Thanks, Britt," I finally said.

"Oh, look, Annie—" Britt hollered into the living room, "lawyer-man just gave me a 'thank you.' Look out the window and see if there's any pigs flying by."

Chapter 25 – Ike

SO I DELIBERATELY got down to the Moose and Antlers early to mentally prepare for this: the first "client interview" of my new career.

The place was a weird combination of north-woodsy and oil patch, and practically empty. I had some time to kill, so I flipped lackadaisically through a Calgary Herald I'd just picked up, checking out the hockey scores and such, trying to be a good Canadian. My mind should have been on preparing for the interview, but I couldn't help flashing-back to when I'd talked to Madstone a few days before, sitting alone in the truck outside the Suchi Ichiban, and trying to predict my future by turning over all he'd told me then. It wasn't much, by the way, that he'd told me, but there was some cause for optimism as it turned out: everything that had happened that fateful Tuesday night at the Santa Fe Police Station had been recorder by security cameras. Thank god for body-cams and dash cams, surveillance and such like. Who knows what kind of damning bullshit story they'd have come up with otherwise. Oh wait—we did know, since the initial police reports said I'd had a gun, shot at the cops and kidnapped a nine-year old girl. Now everyone knew the truth had been recorded by those ubiquitous cameras, and SFPD was scrambling not to release 'em. But I knew Madstone would eventually have the better of that fight.

Of course he didn't want to get pinned down on a timetable, no lawyer does, but he reckoned a day or two at the very least, maybe more—

two to three weeks, tops—and we'd get the all free to return. Undoubtedly right now the prosecutors and the cops were scrambling, desperate and in full damage control mode, in all probability going through the seven stages of grief, knowing full well the truth was coming out in the end, and wrestling with how best to present it. Still, waiting on those morons just so they could undertake a self-serving voyage of self-discovery and spin things in their favor was a touch annoying.

Also on the plus side, it turned out they'd somehow gotten my name wrong on the Amber Alert: somehow the authorities were officially looking for one "Robert McNoisy" of all things. There was no explanation for it ("Fly got caught in the printer ribbon?" Madstone had suggested, half in jest). Whatever the reason, it was practically too good to be true.

He did have one surprise for me, though:

"Well, you're square at work at least, I took care of that."

"What did you tell 'em at work?"

"That you are in rehab."

"*Rehab!*" I cried, amazed that he'd told the folks at the office the same story I'd spun for my ex.

He took it the wrong way, reckoning I was appalled and getting a little defensive. "McKenzie, they can't fire you if you're in rehab. Alcoholism is a disease. You're protected by the ADA, State personnel rules. Turns out you've got plenty of sick leave, too. You're golden. And with rehab, it *is* the kind of thing where you might just drop out of sight on a dime—exactly the way you did. Totally believable."

It was perfect. As a cover story it dovetailed perfectly with the e-mail I'd sent my ex.

"Well, thanks," I said. "They'll think I'm a drunk, though."

"You are a drunk, McKenzie," he said.

I had to admit the truth of it.

The entrance to the Restaurant and Bar darkened and I looked up, jolted out of my reverie. My jaw dropped a bit, 'cause what walked in was a nothing if he wasn't a giant in a jeans jacket. Six foot six, his cannon ball head was bald, and clamped under one slab arm was a motorcycle helmet.

160

The man spotted me across the room, and made his way over.

"I'm Ike," he said, a little bit sheepishly, still standing. He extended his hand down toward me. His gigantic mitt swallowed mine whole, and he stood all scrunched in then, like he was embarrassed by his massive bulk, that it was somehow inappropriate to the circumstance. He waited for me to ask him to sit down, and I did.

He set his helmet down on the chair between us, and asked the waitress who had just re-appeared what they had on tap. She was wearing one of those paper poppies that seemed to be growing out of lapels all over town, and for the first time, I noticed her name tag read "Sammy." She ran down a lengthy list of beers that included Tar Sands Porter and Petroleum Amber and Peace River IPA, amongst many others.

"Labatts," Ike decided, disappointingly me by not springing for something more exotic.

"A beer sounds pretty good." I pushed my coffee away. "Gimme a Petroleum Amber, will you please Sammy." She smiled and disappeared once more.

I turned and looked at Ike. The seconds ticked by. He saw me staring at him, and gave me that universal look that shrugs and says: "what?"

"I'm sorry," I said, waiving him off. "It's amazing—you look just like I thought you would—" I froze up a little at that, embarrassed that I'd said it out loud. What I'd thought he would look like was a giant tattooed drug dealing biker, and sharing the fact that he actually did look like that seemed impolite at best. I abruptly changed tack. "Britt said you and your wife have a bit of an immigration problem?"

A gold tooth glinted in the firelight. "Great kid, that Britt," he said. "She's gotten me out of a few jams." A chain of barbed wire was tattooed around his great bull neck, with a tattooed padlock holding the loop together just below his right ear. "She says you kind of stepped up for her, too—though she was kind of quiet on the details."

I found myself feeling a little embarrassed at that. And surprised to find Britt giving me credit. Suddenly I was doubly embarrassed for having thought so little of the girl. "Kind of cold out here, ain't it?" I said, wanting to shift away from Britt.

161

"Are you kidding. I guess Britt did say you were from down south. Hell, here it's full on winter by Halloween. Kids wear parkas over their costumes, and slog chest deep through snow just to ring the doorbells."

"Jesus."

"Yeah. Screw that, right?"

"So, how can I help you, Ike?"

"Well, Britt said you was a lawyer. And that you do some immigration stuff. See, I want to get an American visa so I can go down and live with my old lady in Spokane, but I got a problem."

"Drugs?" I reached down into my satchel and pulling out a yellow legal pad and pen.

"Killed a guy."

"Oh. Well, right….Tell me about it."

"It was a bar fight about ten years ago. My old lady was living up here as a landed immigrant, working as a nurse over in Victoria, and I was bouncing at a bar in Nanaimo. Some skinhead asshole come in one night and didn't like her complexion, if you know what I mean. He said a few things, whereupon I suggested—real polite, mind you—that he consider tempering his language. No go, right, and he pours a beer over her head. Well, I go to eject the guy, and out comes a knife. I had the inside ball bat handy, of course, and went to break his arm and knock the knife away, but he lunges at me at the same time, and his head got in the way. Of the bat," he added, by way of clarification.

"I figured."

"Gentlemen," Sammy the waitress announced, appearing at our table with a tray. She placed a draft Labatts in front of Ike and a Petroleum Amber in front of me. She produced a slice of cherry pie I had ordered before Ike had arrived, set that gently down in front of me, too, and then disappeared again.

"Dead?" I asked, as I continued scribbling down the details. I'm a compulsive note taker, so you know.

"Yeah, dead," Ike said, with a look that shrugged *what else would you expect?* "And get this," he added. "— *I* got charged. It never went to trial, though, 'cause the judge ruled self defense."

162

"So you were acquitted?"

"Yup. After a year. Then, last July her mum—my wife's mum, that is—she get's sick, right. Well, she'd been sick for a while. Lupus. She lives down there in Washington state, so my wife had to move down to Spokane to take care of her. She's working there as a nurse now, taking care of her mum, and all, and now she wants me to move down there too, to be with her. And I would, too,—I want to, in fact, but, you know, this murder thing…" he trailed off.

"Have you applied for a visa?" I asked.

"No. Hell no. We been afraid to. We've both heard stories that if you have a criminal record it's a problem with the American immigration people."

I sat there and took a sip of my beer and turned Ike's story over in my head. "Look," I finally said, "your situation doesn't sound that bad to me. If it was drugs, the United States is pretty unforgiving, but murder? Murder they can live with. The USCIS grants visas to murderers all the time. But you're right to be cautious. You were arrested and charged, after all, but you say your record shows an acquittal? I can put together an I-130 Petition for you, and we can tell 'em your story in there." Ike nodded, understanding. "They'll eventually interview you at the American consulate here in Canada, and we'll have another chance to explain your situation then. You should be fine."

"You really think so?"

"I'll be with you every step of the way." I paused again, mentally checking off the boxes that needed to be checked. There was one more. "I'll need to talk to your wife, of course—she's the one who actually has to file the petition."

"How's that work?"

"She's the American citizen, right?"

Ike nodded again.

"So she petitions the United States for the benefit to you of a visa. She's the petitioner and you're the beneficiary. I can't guarantee a result, obviously, but it certainly looks good—"

He erupted out of his chair, and just about exploded with gratitude.

"Britt said you was okay! Thanks Mr. McKenzie. Thank you so much!" For a moment I was afraid he was going to throw a bear hug around me, but instead he reached into his jeans jacket and pulled out an envelope.

"Look, there's two-thousand Canadian in there," he said, shoving it across the table between our two beers. "You get me that visa, and there's another grand on the back end, too." He hesitated a moment. "Is that enough?"

I was dumbstruck. To tell you the truth, I had fully planned on doing the work for free. But the notion of making money at it suddenly made a lot more sense. Funny how a fat envelope full of dough can change a guy's attitude.

"Sure," I said. "That'll be perfect."

We actually sat and chatted after that for a while and finished our beers; interestingly enough, it turned out Ike had been a roadie for Metallica for a couple of years back in the nineties. "Used to party with Lars and James Hetfield," he said, matter-of-factly. "Some of the Guns 'n Roses guys, too..." He was a font of practical information, and shared with me the best place to hide contraband on an airplane (the bathroom), how to role a six-paper joint (carefully) and the fact that a bunch of little barky dogs are better than one big one to guard your house ("They just come out of the dark from everywhere, biting and scratching."). Interesting stuff.

I split the cherry pie with him, he gave me the contact information for his wife, and we left out onto the icy Calgary pavement and went our separate ways.

"Hey, what's your phone number?" Ike called over his shoulder.

Shit. My American phone didn't work, and we didn't have a land line at the apartment. "I...for now just call Britt," I shouted. "I need a new phone."

Chapter 26 – Plus 15

WELL, THAT WAS PROFESSIONAL.

I need a new phone. What the hell kind of lawyer doesn't have a phone.

I had money and an address, though, I thought as I unplugged the goddam truck from the line of plugs in front of the Moose and Antlers, and rolled the goddam frozen extension cord into a goddam manageable ball. And I was out of the house anyway, so a quick trip downtown seemed like a good use of my time; I reckoned the girls'd be fine. Why not get a phone.

Of course, I could have called and told them where I was going, but of course, well, I didn't have a phone.

I stowed the stiff orange tangle behind the front seat, and got in. It was bloody bitter out, and the engine only turned over after several reluctant *WRR-RR-RRRS*. I let the motor run and warmed it up for a bit, not wanting to crack the block—which is what will happen if your engine's frozen and you try to make it to go too quick; then I put the thing into drive, and moved out onto the icy streets of Calgary. The cab of the truck was still quite cold, by the way, on account of it was kind of a shitty heater that old Chevy, and it was only just starting to get warm by the time I got into downtown.

That's my one complaint about the truck, by the way. You'd think a Canadian vehicle would at least have a decent heater.

I was anxious to get back to the apartment with a new phone before darkness fell, so I was in a bit of a rush and parked up in front of the Library again, where Annie and me had done the first time, back when we'd pulled into town just a few days before. I got out and immediately felt the lethal snap of that bitter cold. I hunched down and stepped lively for the nearest Plus15, which is what they call the City's system of enclosed walkways, and they're a hell of a thing, too, by the way—perfectly insulated from the harsh outside, they run along the second stories of almost all the buildings in downtown Calgary, with glass skybridges between 'em and over the roads, too. You can get all over without ever coming back outside. Supposedly they call 'em Plus15 on account of they're fifteen feet above the regular sidewalk, but I don't really know if that's true or not.

Anyway, I found my way to one of the access points, and once up the stairs and inside that second-story world of halls and windows I did have some idea where I was going, and made the Verizon shop after only having to hump a couple of blocks up from the library.

"Bloody cold out, eh?" the codger behind the counter said. It's a weird trick of the global economy that you are as likely to see seniors behind a service counter these days as you are kids.

"*Oh* yeah," I agreed emphatically. "At least we're warm and dry in here, though, right?"

"Oh, sure. Plus, could be we see a Chinook coming through anytime, eh. That'd be nice. Melt some of the ice off."

"A Chinook?"

"Sure, a Chinook." He waited, and then saw the blank look on my face. "You're not from here?"

"Just moved to Calgary."

He nodded in sort of a neutral way, neither hostile, nor particularly interested either. It caught me a bit off guard, 'cause of course in Santa Fe or St. Louis or Chicago—in short, back in America—announcing you're from somewhere else would have led to a follow up question about where you had moved from, an effort to connect based on some shared travel experiences or something, but apparently that was not the protocol here.

"Chinook's our winter wind," he continued, willing to share this little piece of local lore with me, at least. "Comes in from over the mountains and gets things pretty breezy, but warms things up a treat. You can see the thermometer rise by maybe thirty, forty degrees."

"Really?"

"Oh, sure, eh. I grew up the badlands over in Drumheller, and when I was a kid you'd see that arching sky coming at you from over the mountains and you knew a Chinook was on its way. The wind'd blow and the ice would melt away." He chuckled an old man sort of chuckle. "My dad used to joke about how if you were out on a horse drawn sled, you'd have to rush to get back to the barn 'cause the Chinook would be melting the snow out from under the runners!"

I laughed in an obligatory way. I kind of liked the idea of a summer wind blowing in on a dime, though, and said so.

"So what can I do you for today," he asked, getting us down to business.

"I'd like to buy a phone."

"Okay, well, you came to the right place. Are you on a plan already?"

I couldn't very well put him on to my one in the State's, of course— and when I told him I wasn't, he spent the next eight or ten minutes filling the air with words about the wireless company's various products and plans and options and so forth. It's torture. You have no choice but to listen to it all, of course, but I waited for a likely opportunity, and when it presented itself, I jumped and said: "I'd like that one!"

There must have been a certain desperation in my voice, 'cause he smiled and obviously knew he had me.

"Well, let's get you signed up, then." He drew a contract out from under the counter. "Name…" he began, clicking his ball point pen.

I told him, and then we went back and forth for a while, and after I'd provided all the appropriate responses, including our new Calgary address up on 13th Street, NW, he asked for my ID.

167

"I just lost my wallet," I said, having mentally prepared for the question. "They told me I have to get a copy of my birth certificate before I can go ahead and get a new drivers license and whatnot. The whole thing's going to take a week or two."

His expression suddenly changed. "Oooh, that's a problem."

"Can we just go ahead and get me the phone, and I'll get back to you with my ID when it comes in? You've been so helpful, I'd like to make sure you get the commission," I added, thinking the notion of a little cash in pocket might help push him over the top.

"I'm afraid not."

"Can I just get one of those prepaid jobs?"

He shook his head.

"I do have a bank card," I offered as a last hope.

But the bank card wasn't government issue, and with that, I was back out on the Plus15 walkway, phoneless, but on the other hand, way ahead of schedule.

I wasn't too anxious to step back outside into the cold, though, and the sun was still almost an hour from setting, and frankly, without a phone there was no real need to get home immediately. The girls'd be fine; truth be told they were probably only barely aware of my absence. I realized, suddenly, that I was on my own for the first time in a week, and I was kind of enjoying it. Exploring for a bit couldn't hurt. I'd wander about Calgary's climate controlled Plus15 system—chalk it up to research—and see what I could see. Who knows: familiarity with the ins and outs of this vast downtown labyrinth could come in handy sometime.

And it *is* a labyrinth. I crossed over the first skybridge to the next building, and from there down a long nondescript hall that led to the another glassed in walkway over a frozen road, and followed that to another one, and then another one, aimlessly making my way through an endless indoor world of blank corridors and glass walls and hotel vestibules...

And, mind you, the wandering really turned out to be a treat. I started to relax, and my mind wandered freely, and whenever I fetched up against a wall or a giant window or metal bulkhead, there was always

168

another turn or a stairway or a door or a bridge that lead to the next segment of the thing. I frankly lost my way pretty early on, and had only the vaguest idea of where I was in relation to the truck when I stumbled upon someplace called the Devonian Gardens, a second story Jurassic-Parky sort of place, with lush trees and waterfalls and ferns and bronze sculptures and such. In truth, it was a remarkable indoor botanical garden, and I paid my admission and went in. I must have spent a good half hour breathing in the warm humid air and looking at the hydroponic trees before I reckoned it was time to start finding my way back.

I emerged onto yet another skybridge, this one over a thoroughfare called Stephen's Avenue. Somewhere out of sight and off to the south the sun was setting above a ceiling of clouds, but even in the growing gloom the street was familiar—an outdoor pedestrian mall that runs for about four blocks in either direction and serves as sort of the retail axis of downtown Calgary. I paused on the skybridge and looked down at the pavement one story below

"Well, at least I got some idea where I am," I said to myself, and tried to mentally plot my return route to the truck. And if that route took me through someplace where I could treat myself to a quick beer or two, that wouldn't be the worst thing in the world. That Petroleum Amber I'd enjoyed with Ike had kind of given me the taste for another.

I noted that beyond the plate glass fifteen feet below there was plenty of evidence that outdoor pedestrian malls in winter were not a particularly popular item in Canada. What a shock! Indeed, the street was all but vacant in the frozen gloaming, but for one solitary citizen striding up the middle of it in nothing but blue jeans and a black hoodie.

That's a Canuck for you, by the way—always under-dressing for the season.

I paused in the middle of the skybridge, and looked down at him, wondering what set of circumstances could possibly have had the poor soul standing outside on an evening like this. At that very moment, he looked up at me.

Our eyes locked.

169

We were close enough I could make out his features (he was only fif-teen feet below me, after all) and I could see he was a brutish little fel-low, and not so little, frankly, with distinctly Slavic features and what looked like a puckered scar below one eye.

And slowly, a look of recognition came over his face.

My guts turned to water at that. There were no strangers up here in Calgary that had any business recognizing me, *if* that's what had just happened.

I wasn't about to wait to find out. I pivoted back toward the Devoni-an Gardens.

I walked away at a self-consciously normal pace; a muffled "Mon-sieur!" floated up to me through the glass from down below.

The recollection of Dennis's parting words at the park gave me a jolt—*I'll be seeing you, Monsieur!*, but this guy definitely wasn't Dennis. And anyway, Dennis was in the hospital. Plus, there were lots of French people in Canada, right? Getting called "Monsieur" couldn't be that unu-sual. Could it?

I tried to ignore the guy, hoping he was just some kind of weirdo Gallic panhandler, but out of the corner of my eye, I saw he was pacing me along the skybridge. I didn't like this one bit.

"Monsieur!...*Monsieur!*..." he called out again, his voice hardening beyond the window. He tossed his cigarette aside, his pace quickened.

What the hell!

I rounded the hall, backtracked past the Devonian Gardens, away from the skybridge I'd been on, and could hear him no more, but some-how I knew he was still on my trail.

It's nothing, I thought to myself, just a panhandler. Just a deadbeat whose probably already been distracted by another victim....But I knew it wasn't true.

I hustled up the hall, not knowing where I was going, but wanting to get away quick. I rounded another corner and was fairly jogging along now, part of me fully expecting to hear the suddenly eruption of a *Mon-sieur!* behind me in the hallway—but it didn't come.

I ran along the gangway, my spider senses still tingling like crazy, and made for some likely looking double doors. I burst through 'em, and suddenly I was in another world.

I was in Calgary's Core.

The Core is a Chi-Chi indoor shopping Mall in the heart of downtown Calgary, several stories of department stores and boutiques, all stainless steel and shining glass and potted palms under a massive broadly arched glass ceiling that covers the length and breadth of the place. It's actually quite high and open, and relatively attractive, as malls go—the sort of thing I suppose you'd expect in a rich oil town like this one.

It was presently crowded with shoppers, too—absolutely packed with many, many prosperous Canadians amiably wandering its smart landings, and looking idly for places to spend their colorful money.

I wandered into the mass of humanity with my head down, and breathed a small sigh of relief. There was probably nothing to worry about anyway, but I didn't slow down much. The quicker I got out of downtown, the better.

Dead ahead of me, one floor below, I marked the grand glass entryway to the mall. I shoved my way past mothers pushing prams, old people, teenagers, men in overcoats, and arrived somewhat breathless at the top of an escalator. Slowly but surely, I started moving down toward the first floor, and freedom.

"*Monsieur!*" I heard someone call out from high above and behind me.

My heart skipped, but I resisted the urge to turn. Just then, I saw something worse up ahead: on the landing opposite and just above, it was another gangster, this one holding a piece of paper in one hand and looking at it—looking at it up and down, from it to me, and back again. A smile of recognition lit up his face.

And suddenly he was simultaneously talking to someone on a cell phone and making his way toward the bank of escalators.

What the hell!

Who were these guys?

171

Dennis was the only person in Calgary who knew me. He had an axe to grind, sure (I still felt badly about his foot, if you really want to know), but how could his mates—if that's who these guys were—possibly have spotted me? Annie and me together might stand out in a crowd, but me *by myself?* That was ridiculous. I'd be surprised if Dennis himself could actually have recognized me, much less some minions of his to whom at best I could only have been described.

Panic reared in my chest, and I shoved myself past the stationary crush clogging the escalator. Some of 'em cursed at me as I knocked 'em aside, packages flying, bags falling down the metal stairs. I called back apologies, but welcomed the spirited confusion it was sowing in my wake.

How had they made me?

The question ran through my head like a red banner as I burst from the escalator onto the first floor. Nothing made any sense. If they weren't working for Dennis, then who were they? Snatch squads? Bounty hunters from south of the border? It was all too fantastic.

Well, this was just *great*, thinks I.

I moved quick across the broad marble floor, and in a flash I was out the great glass doors, and into the cold Canadian night.

I hit the pavement running without any real idea of where to go. I pumped my legs harder than I had in a long time, and looked up ahead desperately. About a two blocks ahead I could see a C-Train platform with a couple of waiting cars on it, and I made for the thing like a bat out of hell.

I could hear 'em behind me now, shouting, feet pounding the pavement, but I didn't turn to look. I just kept running as fast as I bloody could. Half-a-block…one block…a block-and-a-half…

I was losing my wind and I fancied I could almost feel a powerful hand reaching for my collar. I reached the steps of the outdoor train station and leaped over them up onto the platform. There a train was, the doors still open, and I made for one of 'em—

I jumped.

Safe inside, the doors *shuffed* shut behind me.

I looked up and one of 'em slammed into the window, but the train was already moving. As it slowly accelerated away from the platform, he jogged alongside. He drew a pistol from under his jacket, and tapped it on the glass at me. I could see the puckered scar under his eye clear as day, though this time there was no cry of *Monsieur!* This time he just stared at me, tapping the window with the barrel of the pistol, scary as hell, and cool as you please.

And then we left him behind. He vanished into the night and out of my life for now, though at the last I could see him talking into his cell phone.

The other passengers were staring at me like I was John Dillinger. I hopped off at the next station, dashed into the darkness between two buildings, and made for the Library by dead reckoning. I hugged the shadows, keeping my top-eye out for villains, but never saw any. It probably took no more than five or ten minutes to make the truck, but it seemed like forever.

I quickly climbed up into the cab of the thing, and blessed it a thousand times for just being there. They couldn't know about the truck, at least, I reflected. It had to be as safe a refuge as any.

It was full on dark, now, and I was as anonymous as any other vehicle on the street. But my heart didn't care—it was still pounding like a hammer. I drove slowly back to the house, observing all traffic laws, and following the speed limit, and I pulled up outside our eight-flat apartment building still massively freaked out, my hair mussed but breathing almost normally now.

I plugged in the truck, took a few more deep breaths, and went inside.

Apropos of absolutely nothing, I suddenly realized I hadn't thought about the cold for almost an hour.

"Try and guess what just happened to me," I called to the girls on the way to the kitchen.

I bumped right into Annie as I rounded the corner. She had her stuffed bunny under her arm, her Hello Kittie backpack over her shoulder, and she was dressed for the road.

173

"Britt's gone," she said.

Chapter 27 – Bienvenue, Canada? — *Oui!*

WELL, *SONOFABITCH!* I thought to myself.

Pretty quickly I calmed down, though, reckoning a fourteen year-old kid couldn't have gotten too far in the few minutes she'd been gone, and moments later it was Annie and me together again on the high bench seat of our big blue truck, this time driving slowly around our dark and frozen Crescent Heights neighborhood looking for a teenage girl in a big blue parka. After my recent adventures downtown I was too exhausted to be fully panicked; I was more than a little bit pissed, though—what could she be playing at? Whether she knew it or not, she was putting our whole operation at risk. And for what? She said herself she had no-where to go?

Except the back seat of some filthy john's car, I thought to myself, darkly, though I didn't say it.

I swung out and around onto Highway One in a wide arc, and started back east toward Center Street, widening our perimeter. If Britt was re-ally intent on splitting, she'd have to be looking for a bus or something, and all the stops were on the main drag. And if we didn't head her off before she got to one, all would be lost.

On the other hand, maybe she was just out wandering around, look-ing for a place to score. That flat she had been living in with Dennis was littered with the evidence of chronic drug use: maybe Britt was on the rock; maybe she was a full-on junkie, strung out and—

"There she is!" Annie said, pointing across at a Safeway north of the highway.

It was Britt, alright. I pulled the truck over into the parking lot where Annie had pointed, and sure enough, there was our girl, just coming out of the store.

"What are you guys doing here?" Britt asked through Annie's window as I pulled up next to her. She appeared surprised, and more than a little happy to be getting picked up.

"You ditched Annie," I said.

"Yeah, to run around here and get her some dinner," she answered rather sharply. "There's nothing in the house, and she kept saying she was hungry."

I turned to Annie. "But you said that Britt..." I trailed off, 'cause when I thought about it, all she'd really said was Britt was gone. And she *was* gone. And I *had* left them without food in the house.

"Oh," I said, a little sheepishly. "Well, that's alright then." I looked at the bag Britt had just set in her lap, as she pulled the door closed behind her. "So...," I added, weakly, once again feeling like a bit of a shit, "what's for dinner?"

Britt smiled brightly. "Sausages and mashed potatoes. And I got us some ice cream, and some milk and eggs and bread and cereal and bacon for tomorrow." She looked at Annie, and slowly pulled the top of a bottle out of the bag so the nine-year-old could see the label: "*And* apple juice."

"Yay!" Annie squealed, clapping her hands.

Little snowflakes started kissing windshield and I pulled us back onto the road, and by the time we got back to our flat it was coming down like crazy. Britt whipped up the dinner, and as we feasted together over our sausages and mashed potatoes, the snow coming down in the dark outside, I told 'em of my adventures downtown.

I weighed whether or not to do that, by the way, it being a scary thing, and not wanting to upset 'em. That may seem a bit naïve after all

176

that had happened—they had already seen so much of the world, and I supposed them both to be pretty sophisticated consumers—but they both were just kids, remember, and I reckoned all the crazy they had witnesses just while they'd been with me was enough between 'em to last a lifetime. I didn't want to add to it any more than I had to. But sadly knowledge is your friend, and this was definitely a problem situation for which we'd need to adopt some shared protocols: disguises when we went outside: hoods and scarves, like that; dark glasses; staying away from hot zones like downtown…

I did share with 'em my interview with Ike, too. "Britt, thanks so much for that," I said, as I shrugged out of my parka back at the flat. "You were right, Ike's okay. Can't imagine why anybody wouldn't like him."

"Could you do anything for him?" Britt asked.

"Probably, yeah—I think I might be able to help him. Really it's just writing up a petition. Truth be told, I don't even need to be physically here in Calgary for that. With a computer and the internet I could actually write it up and file it from Santa Fe."

"That's great, 'cause I got three more for ya."

"You got what? Three more what?"

"Two fiancés and a removal hearing."

"A removal hearing?"

"That's really cool—the way you repeat everything I say. Yeah, a removal hearing. It's in Seattle Immigration Court."

"We're not in Seattle…" I started, a little disoriented. I wanted some quick experience with immigration law yes, but I hadn't expected to get dumped into the deep end like this quite so quickly, or with quite so many cases. Certainly not in Seattle. Was Britt teaming up with little Annie to move us west? That sounded about right. On the other hand, I thought, switching gears, that fat envelope full of colorful Canadian cash Ike had put in my hand was quite nice. "Oh, what the hell, I'll take whatever you can get me. Just not the Seattle one."

"You said Annie's mom was there."

"I said her mum's in Tacoma, and I didn't say we were going there. It's just not practical to—" I held up immediately on account of Annie's face. There was no sense reopening that painful can of worms. "What about Dennis?" I asked, changing tack. "Could any of these folks you happen to know with immigration problems have some kind of connection to—"

"No. "

"No?" I asked, finding it hard to believe.

"Seriously, they don't. Not even close. I wouldn't bring them in if I though there'd be that kind of problem. But you're right to worry. Dennis has a lot of friends," Britt agreed. "And not just in this town."

"If you don't want to be recognized, you should grow a beard," Annie added, looking at my face critically.

Britt looked me up and down at that. "You really should," she agreed. "You'd look more manly."

"Thanks a lot," says I, but felt the rising stubble on my chin, and thought maybe the girls had something. I decided then and there to quit shaving, and believe it or not, less than three weeks later I'd actually raised a respectable beard: red and bushy, it completely changed my appearance. To be honest with you I'd been afraid much of it would come in white—I'd not had a full beard since college—but the thing actually looked pretty good. I looked like Yukon Cornelius, if you can believe it.

Three weeks was longer than I'd expected to be up there, of course, but Madstone was still wrestling with those idiots back in New Mexico about releasing the security videos. He had filed an IPRA request, which sought the materials under the state version of the Freedom of Information Act, and knowing the bastards would drag their feet had requested a court date to set up a backstop to the process. The outcome was no longer in doubt, and Madstone reckoned they'd turn the tapes over on the courthouse steps the day of the trial. I guess I should have been beside myself with the delay, but frankly our rehab cover story had removed any work or family questions about my enforced absence. And god help me, despite the cold part of me was enjoying being back in Canada.

178

I used those weeks well in other ways, too. In the end, the girls had promised not to bug me about the future until I'd squared away my government identification issues, so I reckoned I'd better put the time to good use. The funny thing was—the ID part turned out to be easy: I was Canadian, you see. It's frankly amazing how friendly the world can be when you are in the right category. So like I'd told the old man at the Verizon shop, I went about getting my birth certificate first; that was the predicate to everything—and there were actually a few minor hoops to jump through there, 'cause I'd been born in Montreal. Quebec at that time issued birth certificates through parishes and hospitals—mine was issued by the Royal Victoria Hospital where I was born—but Canada tightened things up after the attacks on the World Trade Center and changed things so that only government issued birth certificates would do for official purposes. That got me down a bit, but after a few false starts and several bloody-minded recitations of The Rules by The Bureaucrats, the authorities were nice as hell, and sent me a brand spanking new Birth Certificate issued by the Province.

Welcome to Canada, eh!

Bienvenue, Canada, oui! My French was shit of course, having been so many years away from *La Belle Provence*, but fortunately for me there was no language test for any of this, and from my birth certificate, all else flowed. Applying for other government documents became a pro-forma exercise. In short order I got my social insurance card, an Alberta driver's license, my passport. I had to pound the pavement a bit, and there were several short waits while things got mailed back and forth, but it's really quite amazing how quickly you can do things when your papers are in order. I even scored an Alberta Health card in double-quick time, which amazingly proved to cost nothing—no fee or premiums or anything! I had to blink, and look twice, but it was true: *viva la* provincial health care!

It all started to make me feel like a Canadian, which I suppose I was. I liked it, and that's the truth.

I went back to the phone store, of course, this time a different one out in the Boonies, and got myself a smart phone on a nice plan, with

179

some built in apps for Annie to play with and provisions for international calling. I reckoned I'd break it in by checking in with Madstone, once again from inside the freezing cab of the big blue truck while I waited for the blower to start kicking out some heat.

"We're getting a court date on my request for those security-cam videos any day now, and you want to back here when they come through. You follow?"

I had to remind myself for the umpteenth time he didn't know I was in Canada. "I understand, Madstone. We'll get back there whenever you give us the high sign.

He paused for a moment, seeming satisfied on that score, then said: "McKenzie, I'm afraid I have some more news for you. It definitely edges to the bad end of the spectrum."

"Hit me," I said.

"I have a contact over at CYFD, an old girlfriend—one of the few I didn't marry. She tells me Annie's father if actively looking for her."

"Oh."

"That's actually not the news. The news is this is a man of seriously low character. A bad man, McKenzie. Turns out he came down from Montreal to St. Louis almost ten years ago, just ahead of a human trafficking charge up there. When he left Montreal, the cops up in Quebec dropped everything, just happy to have him gone, and he's been clean as a whistle down in the States ever since. Officially, anyway. Been here for the better part of a decade on a legitimate green card, ostensibly working as a florist. However, the smart money says he's still in the business, as it were."

"Human trafficking?"

"Yes."

"So, what does that mean? Annie's father is some kind of an international whore-monger."

"I don't know, McKenzie. Maybe. He was a human trafficker with all that implies up there in Canada, and he's probably still doing that down here in the States. And right now he's looking hard for Annie."

180

It was unpleasant news, for sure, but entirely consistent with my theory that Annie and her mum had been running from him. Michelle Chretien—beauty of the black eye—was trying to get away from the guy and start over with Annie somewhere else, I was surer than ever of that, now. It all added up: popping up in a remote desert location in the middle of the night, not having any papers—she was on the run, escaping from her violent gangster husband.

And though Annie and me had crossed half a continent since then, and our whereabouts were unknown to the authorities, I reminded myself that Annie's father appeared to be buddies with Dennis. There was some kind of connection there, anyway, as our exchange in Princes Island Park had clearly shown. And if Michelle Chretien's violent gangster husband was looking for Annie, as I now knew he was, and if he knew Dennis, which I knew he did, the conclusion was obvious: Annie's father knew we were in Canada.

More specifically, her knew we were in Calgary, Alberta, Canada.

And at that exact moment I had the proverbial epiphany: the Amber Alert! That's how Dennis' people had spotted me three weeks before in the Plus-15. Information flowed both ways. While Annie's father had undoubtedly come to know we were in Calgary from Dennis, Dennis had just as surely learned about our jail-break, and that Annie and me were on the run. From that all else flowed. He'd done a little internet research. clicked to the Amber Alert, and *voila!* Robert McNoisy or not, they'd have a current and accurate picture of yours truly to hand about to Dennis' many friends:

The gangster was holding a piece of paper in one hand and looking at it—looking at it up and down, from it to me, and back again...

They knew what I looked like. QED baby.

I gulped uneasily. "But Madstone, child services surely would't hand the girl over to him now, will they?" I suggested.

"What planet are you on? Of course they will. Social Services *likes* to keep families together. At least that's their legislative mandate. And there's no criminal record on the father. Never even charged in Canada,

181

not so much as arrested down here in the U.S. Innocent until proven guilty, rememberMcKenzie—it's a fundamental principal of law…"

He held off a bit at that, reckoning rightly that there was no need to buy trouble. "Cheer up, McKenzie. Family law, domestic relations—it's a bitch. I did it for a while, and it was horrible. Who knows what will happen."

We agreed to stay in touch, and in the meantime, everything else in New Mexico remained in suspense.

Chapter 28 – Calling Annie's Mum

VERY SLOWLY I clicked off the phone and hung up. It was a lot to digest all at once. As a practical matter, the best way to minimize any risk *vis-a-vis* Annie's father, was to get Annie back together with her mother. Madstone hadn't given me any new info about her, which was alright. I figured as a practical matter we probably already knew as much about Michelle Chretien's current status as he could, and the time had come to act on that information. Indeed, for the last three weeks Annie had been perfectly patient about it. However, connecting with someone by telephone at the Northwest Detention Center proved to be a little more complicated—and restrictive—than I had initially hoped. I knew this now only because at the same time as I'd been organizing my forms of Canadian identification, I'd also been boning up on American immigration law, and the administrative apparatus and detention centers associated with its enforcement.

Unsurprisingly, the Northwest Detention Center where she was being held turned out to be another private prison run by one of those shadowy profit-engines like Correction Corporation of America that pretty much have taken over the American penal system and put it on a paying basis. Of course, with immigration, I'd noticed several times already that the powers that be are frequently at pains to point out these are not criminal matters, and that those in their particular houses of detention are not in prison, but of course, they are. In some ways, it's worse: theirs are prisons without due process, incarceration without limits. Hell, from what I had read, some of those poor bastards had been locked up for five or ten years or more, with no resolution in sight. Many couldn't speak English, some were mentally handicapped, and none of 'em had the right to an attorney. *Miranda* and *Gideon* were of no effect in this parallel universe.

It got me pretty angry, too, the more I read the law in this area—the more so because nobody seemed care what was happening to these poor souls. For most of us, they were essentially just off the books. The images I'd seen of the place on-line (and not yet shared with the girls) left no doubt as to its character—they were photographs of a modern penitentiary, replete with orange jumpsuits and bunk beds and concrete walls and linoleum floors and uniformed guards and barbed wire fences. And the prison rules, apparently enforced without exception (completely absent the Canadian bureaucrat's coda of "...but here's how we can help you"), said that we could *not* call Britt's mom.

Period, full stop, end of discussion.

Turns out, though, we could leave a three minute voicemail message, but that we'd have to pay for the privilege of doing it. And then her mum could call us if *she* had money in her prison—I'm sorry: "Detention Center"—account to pay for the call, that is.

Annie accepted this limitation better than I had expected, because she reckoned that her mum would indeed call us back, and pretty quick, too.

There were protocols to be considered for this venture, however. To a certainty the ICE was listening in on everything that came through the pipe, so circumspection was the rule of the day. After some discussion, we agreed that rather than having Annie herself leave a three minute message for her mum that the jailers could hear, and later share with the Children Youth and Families Department back in New Mexico, it would be safer if I called, leaving a message as a lawyer—her mums' lawyer—with all the associated protections that implied. I'd identify myself, leave my name and Canadian phone number, and a short plain statement that would contain an obscure message Ms. Chretien could understand, but

184

not the bums guarding her; something that would clue her into the fact that her daughter was safe and with me. Of course, leaving our phone number was a calculated risk. It was a definite link to us, but lawyers of various stripe were undoubtedly calling the detention center every day. The ICE eavesdroppers couldn't follow up on every message left for every inmate. And I reckoned if I did it right, mine would in no way stand out. Even the Canadian area code shouldn't raise too much of an eyebrow, since their charges by definition all had international contacts.

So we called. I wrote up a little one paragraph script, and the girls and I spent a little time refining the "coded messages" in it, and then we reviewed it one more time all together.

"Yup," Britt said.

Annie simply gave a thumbs up.

We gobbled a quick lunch of McKewen's meat pies—*With the Taste you Canna' Forget*—and after that we cleared away the dishes, sat down at the kitchen table, and I put the I-phone on speaker, and punched in the number to the Northwest Immigration Detention Center in Tacoma, Washington. We were on pins and needles, anxious as hell; somehow we knew that by making this first contact we were crossing a bridge, turning a corner, further braiding our fates together with the stakes high and our prospects unknown.

The phone rang,

...and then again.

There was a click, and a disembodied voice asked me to identify the inmate I was calling. I punched in Annie's mothers "A" number, then there was another sharp click and a beep.

I looked down at my script for "Michelle Chretien" and started reading:

"This is Robert McKenzie, attorney at law, calling for Michelle Chretien.

"Ms. Chretien, I have been hired to represent you in your removal proceedings and all related immigration matters. Please know, arrangements have been made with regard to any legal fees which may accrue, and you are in no way personally responsible for my compensation.

185

"Please call me at your earliest convenience to discuss my representation of you at the hearing presently set for December 13th, and other attendant matters. I have been asked further to tell you that 'Blankie is okay.'"

Blankie, of course, was Annie's stuffed bunny.

And with that, I left my phone number, and hung up. A protracted silence followed.

"Whaddaya think?" I finally asked, looking at the girls, one to the other.

After a moment's thought, Britt said, "That was great."

"You really sounded like a lawyer," Annie agreed, as if she could never have imagined such a thing before.

It was somewhat anti-climatic—we'd taken this huge step, and now there was nothing to do but wait. If I had to guess, Annie's mum would call back as soon as she possibly could, but when would that be? An hour? A day? More? There was nothing for it but to watch the phone.

And being a lawyer, even as we filtered into the living room and turned on the television, I mentally began making contingency plans for the worst case scenario: no response at all. Of course, there are many who would say don't think about that or hope for the best or don't jinx it or some such other thing. But we lawyers aren't like that. We are pessimists by training, paid and programmed to prepare for the worst. And the worst case scenario here was that her mum wouldn't call back. And then what? I didn't like it, but the answer was obvious: if her mum didn't contact us, we'd have to go to her. Somehow. If it turned out we couldn't do it by phone, the only the option left would be to physically go to the Northwest Detention Center, into the belly of the beast, as it were, and look her up in person.

The very thought sent a shiver through me. There was no way *that* would work. It was a thousand miles away. And how would we go about entering a detention facility in America without getting pegged as the famous fugitives from Santa Fe? I was pretty sure such a thing would have to involve my new Canadian identity documents, freshly

186

grown beard and some dodgy abuses of American immigration law that probably wouldn't survive any conventional risk analysis.

Just thinking along those lines seemed like buying trouble. I could almost certainly handle her situation long distance, same as I reckoned I could Ike's, and I decided to stop thinking about it.

One thing I did know was I needed a drink.

Chapter 29 – Bob McKenzie – Immigration Lawyer

ANNIE FIDDLED with the remote until she found another episode of *Wander Over Yonder*, and the two girls immediately commenced staring at the screen. Lord Hater was in the midst of chasing the intergalactic hippie and his pal Sylvia across some colorful exo-planet, and in spite of myself, I found myself being drawn in.

"Ike likes you a lot," Britt suddenly said, her eyes still fixed on the television. "Says you really sounded like you know what you're doing."

"That's good. I haven't really done anything for him yet, though."

"Probably I know even more people with immigration problems. People who could really use some help."

"I haven't even met the other two you got me yet. I talked to Mrs. Pearson, but—"

"*Shhh!*" Annie hissed.

"Sorr-*eee*," I winced.

I held my water water for a bit.

"*Much less that removal hearing in Seattle,*" I whispered very cautiously to Britt, not wanting to draw another rebuke from the nine-year-old *enfant terrible* on the floor. "*Did you call that guy back and tell him I couldn't do it?*"

"*There's lot of the girls from when I was with Dennis who need help,*" Britt whispered, ignoring me. "*Most of them aren't from here, you know. Almost all of them have status problems. No documents. That's how he stays on top of a lot of them."*

"Probably don't want to connect with anyone who could tie us to Dennis."

Britt shrugged, eyes still on the TV. The doorbell rang.

"Easy there, lawyer-man," Britt said, seeing the look on my, face and climbing to her feet. "It's Renee. Speaking of docs. I told her to come by and get hers."

Before I had a chance to protest Britt was at the door ushering the young lady into our flat. She was a petit thing in a tight fitting snow jacket, tights that revealed some nice gams underneath and heavy snow boots with cute fur fringes around the tops. I reckon it's hard to look sexy under layers, but this girl was definitely giving it a go, and succeeding at it, too. And as I looked on her further I realized she wasn't quite so young as I'd first supposed, though not so ancient as me by any means.

"She works for Dennis, doesn't she," I said, not sure if I was more pissed or alarmed.

"Did," Britt said. *"Did* work for Dennis. Past tense. Renee Aguinaldo, meet Robert McKenzie; McKenzie, Renee. And this is Annie I told you about," she added, completing the introductions. "Wait here, Renee. I'll get the lockbox."

There was an awkward pause. Renee smiled shyly.

"Do you want to see my room?" Annie asked.

Renee continued to smile but didn't say anything. My brain was still reeling from the notion that Britt had contacted someone from her old life. Contacted her and brought her directly to our safe-house, nonchalant as hell, like they were friends from high school or something, like they were getting together for some TV and snacks after volleyball practice.

"Here we are," Britt said, returning with the lock box she'd taken from the crack-house Annie and me had helped her move out of. She put the thing down on the coffee table and opened it up. The papers inside were passports and travel documents, different colors, different countries, plastic identity cards of various stripes, visas, a few birth certificates. It didn't take much to figure out where they'd originally come from. Britt's narrative had already given the backstory: *That's how he stays on top of a lot of them*, she'd said. Dennis had confiscated travel papers from his girls and held on to 'em for "safe keeping"—read leverage. Easier to keep your girls under your thumb when they can't travel or get a job or a drivers license. There was a lot of 'em in there, too—way more than I would have thought you could have crammed into that good for nothing little lock-box. If I'd had to guess, judging by their papers most of his hookers appeared to be from East Asia, though at a glance I could see there were a bunch from Europe, too, and couple from South America, Nicaragua and El Salvador. The damn thing looked like Jason Bourne's safe deposit box.

"I was really hoping there'd be a wad of cash in there, too," Britt said, "In addition to all the papers." Wistfully, she picked out one of the passports. It was brown with "Pilipenes Pasaporte" emblazoned in gold letters on the front. She thumbed through it, scanning the contents. "Aguinaldo. Renee Aguinaldo. You look really pretty in this picture," she added, showing me the photograph. I agreed. Deceptively young and very pretty.

Renee smiled and nodded, taking the thing.

"So where will you go?"

"I have…girlfriend…a girlfriend…in Winnipeg," Renee struggled politely in heavily broken English.

"McKenzie here could get your papers straight in Canada, if you want. He's an immigration lawyer. He's already helped Ike—you know Ike, right?…"

It looked to me like Renee probably wasn't getting a word of it, or I'd have stepping in forcefully. I didn't need any more of a workload than I already had, and was already feeling more than a bit overwhelmed, what with the clients Britt had already lined up for me, and Annie's mother and all.

Renee just smiled and shrugged.

Once she was safely out the door I buttonholed Britt: "What was that? Are you kidding me!"

Annie shot us the stink eye from her criss-cross applesauce seat in front of the screen, and pointed urgently at the TV.

"*What's the problem lawyer-man?*" Britt whispered behind a cupped hand.

"What's the problem? What's the—?" I continued in a substantially lower tone myself. "*You just brought Dennis right to our door.*"

"*I took that box of passports from Dennis so I could give 'em back to the girls. Renee's one of the girls. They deserve to get their lives back.*"

"*Do you think this is a game? Dennis wants to kill me.*"

Britt stood her ground and looked me in the eye with a resolute stare I'd not have credited her with before. "*No, I don't think this is a game, McKenzie. And there's going to be more of them coming by, too, so you know. I took that lock box so I could help those girls and that's what I'm going to do. Nasareen's coming by tomorrow and Angel, too. And I'm going to give them their papers back.*" She paused and seemed to sort of collect herself. "*You should be helping me with this, you know. Not just throwing stones.*"

"*You just put our whole operation at risk. Your the one who keeps saying Dennis has a lot of friends—*"

"ShhhHHHhhhHHH!" Annie hissed once more, pointing at Wander and Sylvia.

"Sorry," I whispered. "Sorry." Between the two of 'em, these two girls were seriously stressing me out.

"*I know a lot of people with border problems,*" Britt whispered. "*Kicked out of America, or wanting to get back in. Or here in Canada without any ID. A lot of times that's why they're on the street in the first place.*"

"*I can't help all of those people,*" I said, appalled.

"*You could do a lot of good for some of them. I spent a fair amount of time on the street myself, McKenzie, and it's not too nice, so you know. The folks that are out there all have problems of one kind or another. Most of them, anyway. And a lot of the time it's 'cause they don't have a*

191

visa or a social insurance number, and no way to get one. They can't work regular jobs, then. And a lot of times they're on their own, too. Try that—try being on your own with no papers, no way to get a real job, especially if you don't speak English. There's lots like that, and I know plenty of them, too. And don't think there aren't always animals ready to take advantage of us. Here, check this out":

Before I could protest Britt had pulled up her top. Her adolescent breasts popped out one, then the other, her pink nipples protruding, demanding attention, but immediately losing my attention to the cigarette burns that crossed her young belly in an ugly crescent moon.

"I was twelve when that happened."

She dropped her top back down. Annie's back was still toward us, her eyes fixed on the cartoon space travelers.

I didn't know what to say.

"I'm not looking for you sympathy, McKenzie," Britt whispered, reading my expression. *"Some women like the sex business. Or at least don't have a problem with it. It's a legitimate living. But you ought to have a choice about it. Renee—she didn't like it, okay. I just gave her back her choices."*

"I see," I said, not really seeing at all, my voice bobbing back up from a whisper to its normal register.

"The heck with this," Annie surrendered softly, clicking off the TV and heading to her room. "I'm gonna read."

"I'M SORRY..." I cried ineffectually after her, but she'd already disappeared down the hall.

"Don't worry, McKenzie," Britt said, not unkindly, before padding off after Annie. "How would you know any of this. You'll get it eventually."

And then I was standing there alone, realizing something had just happened. What Britt was tee-ing me up for? Some kind of noble charity work? The loser ex-pat attorney version of *Medicines Sans Frontiers. Lawyers* Without Borders, maybe? Make no mistake, none of this was going to be part of my life's plan. For now I was just taking on a few clients to bone up on immigration law for the sole purpose of getting

192

Annie back with her mother and me back to New Mexico, not to win the Nobel freakin' Peace Prize.

Still, I would have been more than human if Britt's scars hadn't shocked me. But I'd already promised to help her get her landed immigrant status, hadn't I? I hadn't promised any more than that. Now that I thought of it, she still hadn't told me what her own problem was. Britt was of ambiguous ethnicity, with a western accent that betrayed nothing of her origins: hell, she could have been Filipino, too, for all I could tell. Maybe she was. All I knew was, as soon as I got her paperwork straightened out, as soon as I got Annie back with her mum, and Madstone had things squared away for me back in Santa Fe, I was gone baby gone.

And maybe, yes, I *was* feeling kind of generally guilty, if I'm honest—you look upon the scars of a teenage prostitute, and then you can be the one to cast the first stone. And truth be told, I was finding that immigration was not like any other area of law. Some cases are hard cases. Others, well they seem kind of hard, too. I'd talked to Mrs. Pearson, one of the clients Britt had lined up for me. I'd talked to her by telephone, not in person, and found hers wasn't a finance case at all as Britt had originally said—she was a paraplegic, it turned out, and had been going on a March of Dimes trip to Disney World.

"There's a lot to it for a trip like that, Mr. McKenzie, when you're in a wheel chair."

Her voice was kind. Older. I pictured a grandmotherly type in her wheel chair at that exact moment I was talking to her, next to a frozen snowy window looking out of a tiny apartment mid-way up a pathetic high-rise apartment building up on Centre Street or some such place. The long and the short of it, she told me, was American customs stopped her before she got on the plane on account of she'd tried to kill herself a few years before. Apparently Homeland Security had it down chapter and verse: she'd been treated for depression for years before, and ate a bottle of pills at some point back in 2012.

"How did they know, Mr. McKenzie? How could the Americans possible know about that?" I reckoned there'd been a police report or something that got shared across the border, but she insisted not. She'd

193

never had any kind of interaction with the police. I was sorry about the old lady's trip, of course, which was obviously an inconvenience for Mrs. Pearson, and another body blow to someone life hadn't been overly kind to, but I had to wonder where she was going with this. I reckoned it would fetch up with her asking me to file some kind of hopeless lawsuit for reimbursement of her tickets, which wouldn't really have been immigration law at all, and something I probably couldn't do anyway unless I was licensed up here in Canada.

In the end, though, she didn't want money, she just didn't want her mental health records all over the place.

What did she want?—"I want you to make them stop doing that, Mr. McKenzie." Like that was even a thing.

Chapter 30 – All Clear

TWO DAYS LATER I got the all clear from Madstone.

He'd left a message on my new cell earlier that day, which I didn't click to until it was rather late. I hesitated to call him back, given the time, but knowing Madstone, even given the advanced hour there was a good chance he was still sitting in his office up in the Tower back in Santa Fe, sipping a Martini.

As it turned out, he was.

"Okay, the short version is, you're golden," Madstone said when I asked him where things stood.

"Seriously?"

"Yup. I just got done watching the video from the security cameras. It's the shit, McKenzie. Hell, they'll be happy if you don't wind up suing them—which we can talk about later. Anyway, for now just get your ass back to Santa Fe, and I'll walk you through a pro-forma interview with the DA, and you're done."

"That's fantastic." I could hardly believe it. I inwardly groaned a little bit at the burden of three days on the road and the challenge of getting our butts back across the border coming up again, but it was worth it. It was worth it.

"We'll turn the girl back over to CYFD, and you can be back at work on Monday."

"Well, it might take a couple more days to….Wait—what?"

"The girl. Children Youth and Families still has legal custody. Until they can officially hand her over to her dad, that is. They've agreed not to pursue this kidnapping thing with you, but they were pissed, McKenzie. Seriously pissed. Truth be told, they were the tough nut to crack. Santa Fe PD and the DA's office just want to get this sorry episode behind them, but those social workers are a vicious lot, vindictive, you know. You don't want them coming after your ass, believe me."

"So the girl has to go back to them?" This was not something I'd really thought about. The insanity and chaos of the the weeks just passed had distracted me so completely that Annie's ultimate fate—an alternate fate to the one we were currently pursuing with her mother—was not something I'd seriously contemplated until now.

"Yes. And, like I said, probably then off to the father, but that's their business. CYFD's, I mean. You're already out of it."

"So they collect the kid up, and just hand her over to the father?"

"He's her *father*, yes. And probably that's what they'll do. Who knows."

"You were the one who said he was a gangster! How can they just hand her over to a gangster!"

"He's clean on paper, McKenzie. But if she doesn't go to her dad, then it's off to foster care. We've talked about this."

"What about the mother?" I said, unable to let it go. I had a family of my own to worry about, but to just drop Annie like this now didn't sit well with me at all.

"McKenzie, her mom's in the Seattle detention center. You know that. C'mon. Get real. Do I really have to be the one to tell you the world's not fair. She's probably tied up in immigration red tape that could have her in limbo for years. Some of those poor bastards go months without even talking to a lawyer, much less seeing the light of day."

"But—"

"You're in the clear, and she's not your kid," Madstone said sharply. "What is this any of your business. You're frankly incredibly lucky they're not trying to hang a multiple count criminal complaint around your neck for this."

"Can I think about it?"

"*Are you fucking kidding me!*" Madstone shouted, sounding more than a little pissed. "*Think about it!*" He paused, and then added in a more measured voice: "Don't fuck this up McKenzie."

I glanced over at Annie sitting criss-cross applesauce on the floor reading a Percy Jackson book. Her chin was in her hands, and her full attention was on the Olympians.

I turned away, and cupped my hand over the receiver. "Look Madstone," I whispered, "I've got to talk to her about this. I can't just say I'm taking her back and handing her over to CYFD. They're the people she escaped from. C'mon."

Madstone was silent for a long time. "Okay," he finally said in a formal tone that was actually more disconcerting than his shouting had been. "Talk to the little girl, that seems fair. But the DA's waiting to hear back from me. Talk to the girl and get back to me." There was another short silence, and then he added, repeating his admonition: "Don't fuck this up McKenzie."

There was another long pause while he calculated up the reasonable time we had. "Get back to me tomorrow."

I held the phone to my ear until the line went dead.

Annie was still reading when I hung up the phone. I felt rotten at even the notion of betraying her—*strike that*, as Madstone would say—it wasn't a betrayal: CYFD had custody and that was the law. And Annie was a kid. Kids don't know what's good for 'em. That's why adults make their choices for 'em all the time. And I had problems of my own. I had a life and a job and a child of my own back in New Mexico. If I followed the rules, and returned Annie to the authorities, I could pick up where I left off. And I didn't just want to—I had a *duty* to. A duty to my daughter, amongst other things. Any other choice than following Madstone's instructions was ridiculous. And illegal.

By all appearances Annie hadn't moved, and was completely oblivious to me and the phone conversation I'd just had. Because of that, and

197

with history as a guide, I concluded it was extremely likely she'd heard every word. How much she could have inferred based on just my half of the conversation, though, was a mystery.

The doorbell rang. Again. Another one of Britt's former associates had arrived.

The process had become routine: every day or so another heavily made up young lady dressed in a sexually suggestive and very eye catching way showed up at the door, and disappeared for a few minutes into the back bedroom with Britt. While back there, Britt would pull out the lockbox, dig around in it until she found her friend's passport, via, birth certificate or whatever, return the papers to her, and the girl would leave. Truth be told, the kids—and they were mostly kids—never seemed to stick around for more than a few minutes.

More Joan of Arc than Mary Magdalene seeming now, Britt had to be seriously depleting Dennis' ranks of hookers. *Some women like the business*, she'd once said. *It's a legitimate living.* Those that don't, well, Britt was literally giving 'em their passport out.

"Hi, Julie," Britt said, greeting that particular day's contestant. She was a teenage wet dream with blonde hair. "C'mon in."

As Britt undertook the introductions, I notice this one was different from the others: she spoke English with an accent right out of Nebraska, and looked like she'd been born on a farm. An American farm. Or Canadian. The point was, she didn't look like the sort who'd need papers. Of course, then, I didn't either, I recollected sourly.

I needed to clear my head. This almost continual contact with Dennis' former employees was making me very uncomfortable.

We needed groceries, anyway, and I reckoned it was probably wise to make a quick exit before Britt started advertising her Lawyers Without Borders thing, and lavishly offering my services to this Julie person. Plus, I needed a drink after what Madstone had just laid on me.

"I'll be back," I said, as I shoved into my parka, and pulled my hood down over my eyes. Seconds later I stepped outside, and my beard flash froze to my face.

It was cold out. Colder than it had been since we'd come to Canada, and frankly up 'till now it had been pretty darn cold.

"*Jesus*," I sobbed, as I unplugged the truck and stowed the stiff orange extension cord behind the seat. I climbed into the cab and twisted the key. The engine growled very slowly, and I grew alarmed lest it actually prove too cold to start, but it finally turned over, and I set in for the Long Wait whilst it warmed up. There was plenty to think about while I sat there, of course, but I really didn't want to wrestle with those existential issues just then, so I just focused on the grocery list. Ham, apple juice, eggs…

Time ticked slowly by. I looked at my watch. One minute, three minutes, five minutes, ten minutes…

The heater was blowing out something, but it definitely wasn't anything warm; still, I'd already been sitting there in the cab of that freezing truck for way too long, and my feet were starting to go numb. I reckoned ten minutes was long enough; the engine must be ready.

I reached up and pulled the shift lever on the steering column into drive, and the thing snapped off in my hand.

I looked at it blankly for a long moment. It was loose in my fist. Now the shifter was just a stick.

The stump that was left on the steering column was irregular, like a broken chunk of grey ice, and I realized pretty quick the goddam metal had been frozen. It was so brittle the shaft of the thing had just cracked like an icicle. And I am not proud of this, but at that exact moment, well, my reaction was…well, I had a bit of a break down just then. I started screaming and crying and thrashing around. It was the accumulated frustrations of living on the run, exiled in this frozen north country that had finally come together, you see—the broken shifter was simply the last straw.

For quite a while I pounded the dashboard with my fists, tears freezing to my cheeks. I tantrumed long and hard for what was, quite frankly, an inappropriate amount of time, but after a bit, I did slowly compose myself, and set about evaluating the situation.

And I was fucked.

There was no question about it. There was nothing but the barest stump on the steering column now, and without the gear shift lever I was stuck in Park. There was simply no way to move the goddam truck transmission into Drive. I could still start and stop the thing with the ignition key, but other than that, we were essentially immobilized.

There was nothing for it but to call the wrecker.

Chapter 31 – Vancouver

"WE'RE PINCHED," Britt said, as I came back inside.

I knew instantly what she meant.

She said the words matter-of-factly, but her eyes were apologizing without reserve.

"How?" I said, already having a pretty good idea, keeping myself under control. Our plane was going down, and exploding at Britt right now wasn't going to help our cause.

"After I gave Julie her passport her cell phone rang. Julie tried to silence it without me seeing, and shoved it right in her purse like it was a hot potato, so I knew something greasy was going on. She wasn't the quick about it either, so I got a look, too. I know Dennis' number. We all do."

"How long?"

"It was maybe three minutes ago."

"No—how long do we have to get our stuff together and get out of here?"

"I don't know. If she wants to tell him in person, we might have some time. She might want to do that. Half hour for her to get to the hospital, another ten for her to tell Denis and then for Denis to get someone over here."

"Why would she want to tell him in person?"

201

"I don't know," Britt said, clearly flustered. "Some people are like that. But I don't know what she'll do, except that for sure she'll tell Dennis about us. Look, I'm really sorry about—"

"Forget it," I snapped, cutting her off. "First things first: we need to get out of here right now. *ANNIE!*..."

I didn't know if we had the gift of time or not. If so, it wasn't going to be much, that was certain. But whether Julie decided to go to the hospital in person, or decided to call Dennis back as soon as she was on the street outside our flat, the clock was ticking. Nonetheless, there would at least be a few minutes for us to work with.

Minutes, that was all. We had minutes.

Annie came bouncing into the room.

"We gotta pack up, kiddo," I said.

Twelve-and-a-half minutes later I watched from the window as the tow truck guy chained the Chevy up; it gave me a nasty flashback to the beginning of my adventures, when my own good car back in Santa Fe got towed. In fact, I was alarmed to realize getting towed was starting to become a bit of a theme with me—a karmic transitional marker that heralded things to come. And sometimes things are just a coincidence; but sometimes they're not. And in this case, I reckoned all this together was pretty obviously a sign that it was time for us to go. I mean, the very immediate and terrifying threat of Dennis aside, and putting Madstone's demands regarding Annie on the back burner, I'd already squared away my Canadian ID, and frankly Calgary was just too bloody cold. Metal freezing and shifters breaking off in your hand are not things that are supposed to happen in the world. Add to that the fact that Annie's dad— given his connection to Dennis—knew we were up here in Calgary, and the decision was an easy one.

The bags were packed, the girls were out in the taxi and I was ready to go.

"Where are we going?" Annie asked, as we buckled ourselves in.

"Hotel until the truck gets fixed," I said as the cab surged forward. I peered around nervously for Julie; the thought that she might have stuck around to spy on us until the bad guys could get here had been in the back of my mind since Britt said we'd been pinched, but if Julie was hanging around I sure didn't see her. I couldn't really blame the girl. She hadn't really been dressed for forty below.

"And then where?"

"Well, apparently I still have a hearing in Seattle immigration court..." I began.

Annie began bouncing in the seat.

"So, Vancouver?" Britt asked, tentatively. She knew she was in the doghouse.

"It's what I was thinking."

I pointed out that we'd have to wait for the truck to get fixed, of course, but that turned out to be less of a delay than I expected, and we had the thing back in three days with a brand new shifter on the column. I ordered up an oil change and four new tires for good measure, had the brakes checked, and we were back on the highway again before Thanksgiving.

American Thanksgiving, that is.

"Next stop, Vancouver," says I, dramatically, and popped the shiny new shifter into drive.

As I turned the truck onto Highway One, and pointed us west toward the Canadian Rockies, I noticed a broad arching cloud coming at us from over the mountains. It loomed like a heavy blue-grey rainbow.

"Chinook coming in," I said, guessing that's what it was, and glad to have at least seen one.

"Should warm things up a treat," Britt agreed.

"Could you pass me some jerky, please," I said without turning my head.

Annie passed me an overlarge fistful of the stuff that I then stowed in my lap, and started to munch on absentmindedly. "What's a wild rose?" Annie asked, pointing at the license plate on the rear of the car tooling down the highway in front of us.

I looked, and for the first time I saw the "Wild Rose Country" motto on the Alberta license plates—really *saw* it, you know. The license plate has got a little picture of some actual wild roses on it, too, all red and pretty, and quite evocative.

"Oh, you should see them. They're beautiful," Britt answered her. "Wild roses. They grow all over in the summertime. All along the sides of highways and stuff."

"I wish I could have seen some of them."

"Next time," says I, silently lamenting that I hadn't actually seen one either. Wrong season, obviously. Still, it was a nice image to leave Alberta with, and it gave me a sense that we might be back someday.

In the summertime, of course.

It gave me pause then, that I'd been thinking of the three of us doing things together in the future. That our association would continue. We were accidental tourists, companions of necessity and the notion that we'd be taking summer vacations together after this was all over was probably not a healthy line of thought. That said, I'd already come to the conclusion that my commitment to Annie would prevent me from turning her over to CYFD. Madstone wouldn't be happy to hear that, but even thinking about surrendering Annie made me feel dirty. Yeah, Madstone'd be pissed. But it's not like I didn't have a plan...

Britt reached over and switched on the old Delco radio. Of all things, Gordon Lightfoot came on the CBC singing about the Canadian railroads or some such thing, and we drove west. As the hours rolled by we climbed past Banff and Lake Louis, then across the divide at Kicking Horse Pass; we dropped over onto the winding B.C. side, growing breathless, and gassing up in the high mountain town of Golden, passing up Revelstoke. A winter storm that had started up high around ten o'clock had followed us, closing up the passes behind almost on our heels, but as we dropped steadily down in altitude the snow changed to a steady gray rain. Before long we were out of the high country and found ourselves passing through a muddy world of lakes and rivers, timbered with orchards of bare fruit trees, and pocked with marginal looking lumber camps and off season storage yards filled to bursting with houseboats and RVs. We eventually bottomed out in the Shuswap Lake district at

Sycamouse and proceeded through Salmon Arm, marching onward quite literally into the fog.

Annie was asleep, now, and it suddenly occurred to me this was as good an opportunity as any to talk with Britt about getting her landed immigrant status. She'd mentioned it that night we'd first met, of course, a while ago now, and I was a little ashamed that I hadn't followed up on it. But my days had been way full with learning the immigration game by way of on-line seminars and various governmental websites and meeting with the clients Britt had ginned up for me, and getting my identity organized and keeping a house and managing two girls. We'd packed a lot into those weeks. Yes, there were reasons enough, and good ones, why I hadn't tackled Britt's legal status up until now, but I didn't want to put it off any more than I already had. It was a promise, and I intended to keep it.

I looked over at her, and she appeared to be mesmerized by the falling rain and the slip-slap of the wipers. "So I promised I'd help you get landed immigrant status," I said, awkwardly broaching the subject.

She looked back at me and smiled. "Nice of you to remember, lawyer-man. Yeah, I would like that. Landed immigrant status." She seemed to consider the thing for a moment, and when I didn't say anything right away, added: "So is this when I give you my whole back story, or do you tell me how the process works, first? You're the expert, right?"

"Well," says I, "for a kickoff, yes, I do need to know your backstory. Where you came from, why you don't have papers and so on—"

"Well, the last time I saw my mother was when I was twelve years old—"

"But also I need to describe the process for you. So you understand what it is I need to know. And also so you can let me know if there's anything in your background, like arrests or brushes with the law or anything else that could cause a problem with Canadian Immigration. If you've had any problems like that, you need to tell me up front. Like drugs—"

"I don't do drugs."

"Sure. And by the way, we want to avoid any legal problems at all while you're going through the process. For a kickoff, I'd recommend you quit the drugs"

"Really. I don't do drugs."

"Okay. Look—I can't help you if you're not honest."

Annoyingly, Britt seemed to grow irritated at that.

"*Honest?*" she repeated, in a tone dripping with teenage attitude. "Seriously? First of all, I *am* honest. I never lie—except if it's in the line of work, and then lying is actually part of that job. Customers in the sex trade want you to lie. That's part of what they pay us for. But this, here, now," she said, waving her hand between her and me, "between us—talking about me using drugs—no, I'm not lying. I *don't* do drugs."

I thought she was done, then, but she swiveled away from me, folded her arms across her chest and added, "And you're a fine one to talk, by the way—the way you drink!"

I winced a bit, and counted to ten.

"Look…I'm not the one who's applying for landed immigrant status," I finally said, in as reasonable tone as I could muster. "And if you want to become a Canadian eventually, you need to be—"

She turned back toward me savagely: "*Look*, I have smoked the occasional joint and I've been known to have a glass of wine, but—"

"So you admit you were lying—"

Britt cut me off then with a string of profanity like I'd never heard before—it was truly impressive, and actually scared me a little. I immediately backed down. We were talking at cross purposes anyway, so I reckoned the best thing now would be a little benign neglect. I'd bring it up again another time—when Britt could let go of some of that denial she was clearly holding onto for dear life.

Dealing with kids is difficult, if I haven't mentioned it before.

Our fracas had woken up Annie anyway, so we pretended all was well and began the yellow car game. Britt cottoned on how to play right away, and the two girls were clobbering me something horrible until I spied a pocket of yellow school busses in the parking lot of some church off the side of the road that got me back in the running.

After another couple of hours of driving we eventually punched out into the desert of central B.C.—which actually looks a lot like New Mexico, surprisingly enough—and as the clouds opened up a bit, caught our first glimpse of the sun that day just as it was setting. Another monotonous hour or two passed, and it was full on dark when we made the central city of Kamloops. We stopped there to stretch our legs, feast on platters of fish-and-chips, and gas up once more for the last leg to Vancouver.

And indeed, after a grand total of thirteen hours or so of driving we eventually found ourselves closing in on the end of our journey, passing up the outlying towns of Hope, and Chilliwack, and then through the suburbs proper—Surrey, then Burnaby, and then finally into the City itself. I didn't know a goddam thing about Vancouver, but I knew we were just about done driving. I was shot.

"I'm getting to old for this," I said, as we got out of the truck. Once again, my ass hurt miserably.

"Yes," agreed Annie, pointedly.

Britt said nothing.

It was eleven-thirty, it was raining and it was dark. We scored a cottage at some retro Motor-Inn type hotel that had captured our fancy, and where the innkeeper was a tweedy, button-down sort with wire rimmed glasses. There were pictures of the Duke and Duchess of Cambridge on the wall behind the counter, and we were soon to find that Vancouver generally had much more of a British-y feel than anything I'd seen in Calgary.

"Room for me and my daughters?" I asked, indicating Britt and Annie.

"That'll be two-hundred and twenty for the night, sir."

I literally choked, and probably would have done a spit-take but wasn't equipped with a beverage. Slightly alarmed, I wondered how expensive living in this town would prove to be. I counted out the money, and reckoned I'd think about it tomorrow, and we walked back outside and through the downpour to our expensive little cottage.

207

I woke up the next morning and could hear the rain still coming down unabated. It was remarkable—relentless, hypnotic, endless. After I got the coffee on, I parted the drapes with the flat of my hand and looked outside. Everything around us was soaking wet and emerald green.

"Weather's something of a factor here," I whispered to myself.

"At least it's not cold," murmured Britt, still half asleep on the pull-out couch. Annie stirred briefly, and rolled away from her.

Britt was right. I guessed it was about fifty degree beyond the glass. Fifty degrees fahrenheit, of course. All the time I was up there I never did get the hang of centigrade or celsius or whatever.

We got up slowly that morning, recovering from the brutal drive, and spent the day exploring the city, checking the paper for more permanent lodgings. It's beautiful, Vancouver is, with its immaculate green-glass skyscrapers reaching upward, mirroring the heavily timbered mountains and the sea all around. It's a bit intimidating, too—crowded and expensive, and bewilderingly international, and I began to wonder if we'd have a problem getting a place to live.

I needn't have worried. Within forty-eight hours we had forked over first and last month's rent on a one bedroom suite in an anonymous high-rise near Stanley Park, and moved our stuff in.

V. Lawyers Without Borders

Chapter 32 – Annie's Mum Calls Back

THE SYLVIA HOTEL was right around the corner from our flat, and the Restaurant and Bar of the classic old place was almost deserted; I helped myself to a table by the fireplace with a clear view of the door. In the few days since we'd arrived in Vancouver, I'd made the Sylvia my refuge, my Fortress of Solitude, as it were; a handy little spot where I could hunker down, briefly shed the mantel of Father Goose I'd been wearing lo these many weeks now, grab something to drink and enjoy a few precious minutes of quiet and privacy each day. The bar was wood paneled, and clubby, and I ordered a scotch and soda, and bought a copy of the Vancouver Sun to read. I enjoyed the cozy warmth of the fire burning next to me, and flipped slowly through the paper; a headline at the bottom of page five caught my eye:

Calgary Shooting Victim's Foot Amputated

It was Dennis, of course.

"Jesus Christ," I said aloud, as the waitress dropped off my cup of coffee.

"I'm sorry, sir?" she said, looking at me expectantly.

"Oh, sorry—nothing. Just some…news. Friend of the family. Have to remember to tell my daughters. Could I get a piece of that cherry pie?"

She scuttled off, and I looked across the room through the plate glass windows onto Morton Street. It was drizzling again, and the soggy black trees dripped water heavily from their bare limbs. Past the trees was the sand, and then the old lonesome grey sea beyond. It was December in Vancouver, and outside it wasn't quite day, and it wasn't quite night, but there was a certain appeal to the monochromatic gloom. It's not for everybody, mind you, but I was starting to find I kind of liked it. It brought on a comforting melancholy.

But despite my efforts at relaxation, the issues of the day raced through my head even as I tried to read the newspaper—it's tough to chill when your life has become a paranoid's fantasy nightmare. We'd dodged a bullet and picked up a bit of a breather by getting out of Calgary, no question. But no matter how many miles we put behind us, James Quintana was still dead; a killer pimp from Calgary still wanted to get his hands on me in the worst way; Annie's dad was still apparently the head of an international ring of human traffickers, hot on our trail, too; and as if all that weren't enough, just about every law enforcement entity in the United States was probably still looking for me.

Did Amber Alerts stay on the books until they got the guy, I wondered idly, or did they expire after a certain time?

Of all our concerns, though, James' death was maybe the most puzzling. It loomed large, vague and ominous—a square peg that I couldn't convincingly fit into any available round hole. Another wave of guilt rolled through me. A fall in the bathtub was a plausible enough accident for the Santa Fe County Coroner, perhaps—a bureaucrat whose main purpose in life was moving files off his desk—but to me it was an exclamation point. It was a tragedy and a warning; it was a marker unambiguously signifying the possible stakes involved in whatever shadowy enterprise it was that was dogging us, because I was certain now he'd been murdered, you see.

212

Or maybe not. I honestly couldn't make up my mind. It seemed like a hell of a coincidence, though.

But if he had been murdered, who would have done it? And although it was most certainly an open question, the front runner to my mind had become Annie's father. He seemed the obvious ringer. He was definitely looking for Annie. Following Annie's and my trail from the Santa Fe police station that night in October might have led them up the arroyo to the wrecking yard on Airport Road, then maybe, *maybe* to someone working there who remembered the truck and its weird, foreign Alberta license plate, and possibly then to James.

It seemed like too much, but James *was* dead.

And Annie's dad was a bad dude: a consorter with pimps, and a personally violent man, too, as that shiner Annie's mom had been sporting suggested, and as his line of work assuredly demanded. As a practical matter, I reckoned it was pretty safe to assume that simply *being* a human trafficker meant you actually had to like hitting and maybe killing people.

QED.

I thanked my lucky stars once more that we had moved our operation to Vancouver. Even if we'd tried to set up housekeeping somewhere new back in Alberta, we'd still have been playing a numbers game: like Britt kept saying, Denis had a lot of friends.

But one less foot, I reflected, not without some satisfaction.

I had to admit, though, Annie's father was not the only possible candidate for James Quintana's killer. I kept coming back to the Border Patrol—its actions were extremely suspect as well. Their gunplay back in Santa Fe the night Annie and me escaped out of there in a stolen cop car seemed absolutely nuts. Homicidal. It certainly couldn't have been their standard protocol. But I had to admit it didn't necessarily follow they'd been vengefully coming up on our heels ever since—killing James, tracking our truck, pursuing us like frickin' Jean Valjean or something. In fact, the notion seemed downright crazy.

I was left scratching my head. There was so much we didn't know.

And then there was Annie's mom. Wife to the Human Trafficker-in-Chief, mother to my travel companion. Beauty of the black eye, tosser of colorful mittens. Prisoner of the American immigration authorities.

And sitting there on that wet winter day in the Sylvia Hotel, I could at least reflect that we had a slightly better handle on her situation, 'cause as it happened we'd made first contact with Michelle Chretien just the day before.

"*Hi Mom!*" Annie had shouted into the phone.

The little nine year old had literally started jumping up and down the moment the phone rang, and now that she was actually talking to her mother, the raw enthusiasm of it spewed out of her like a fire hose.

"...No, he's really nice!" she sang, "kind of dopy, but real nice and Britt's with us and we have this blue truck that's really cool and..."

Kind of dopey?

I kicked back in my Lay-Z-Boy and looked past the balcony at the thick mist floating along the upper reaches of the heavily timbered mountains across the Harbor, and listened. Annie's stream of consciousness paused occasionally while she gave her mum a chance to talk or caught her breath, but then she'd rev it up again, and the bright and happy monologue would roll on. The pure energy of their reunion continued unabated for almost ten minutes, and it was a beautiful thing to see, if you really want to know. I'd been watching the clock, though, looking for the right time to break in, worried that we'd get cut off and not wanting to miss the opportunity to take care of my business—exchanging information with Michelle Chretien was definitely critical path stuff.

Annie knew it, too, and reluctantly passed the phone over to me.

"Hello, Ms. Chretien?"

There was a long pause. I had no idea what she was thinking away down there in Tacoma, alone in that detention center with the phone pressed tight to her ear, but I reckoned she had to be torn in two. I would have been. She didn't know me from Adam, you see, and her daughter was at the other end of a long dark phone line, and from what I already knew Michelle Chretien was a woman who had had some experience with the worst of humanity, and likely a correspondingly strong index of

214

life's darkest possibilities. I hoped that hearing Annie's happy voice would have gone some way to allaying her fears, but exactly how far I didn't know.

"Yes," a woman's voice finally spoke up, and immediately that beautiful bruised face I'd seen at the CBP checkstop in Las Cruces came floating back up in front of me. "Is this Mr. McKenzie?"

"Yes," I said. "My name is Bob McKenzie. I'm very glad to see you got my message."

There was a short silence—maybe hesitation—and then she said:

"I got your message." She said it in an unnaturally neutral sort of way—the guarded sort of way you might talk to a kidnapper.

"Look, I'm sorry about all this," I said. "There's a lot here that we probably shouldn't go into on the phone, but I would suggest the best thing we can do right now is talk about how we're going to get you out of that detention center, and back with your daughter."

There was another pause, and then she said: "Where are you?"

"In Vancouver, British Columbia," I said, and gave her the address. Of course, sharing our location was a big risk—and if the ICE pencils were busily scratching away, we were screwed, but I reckoned not telling Annie's mum would be worse. We had to get her on board with this venture, or we were dead before we started, and to do that I knew pretty well I'd have to give her some evidence of my bonafides. Plus, if I was too cagy about answering such a natural question, it might possibly alert The Listeners to play closer attention. And that would be bad.

"We're about three hours north of where you are in Tacoma," I added.

"Annie's in *Canada*?" she said. "But how did she—"

"You have a very single minded and very resourceful little girl there, Ms. Chretien. She was of the belief that you also were in Canada. Annie thought that you had been deported here by Homeland Security after you were detained at that Custom and Border Protection checkstop in New Mexico. But please know, she is safe up here. And quite anxious to see you just as soon as we can make that happen."

"You really are a lawyer?"

Was that a softening in her tone?

"I'm a licensed attorney, yes. Licensed in the United States," I added.

"Are you working for my husband?"

"I am not. I've never met your husband, Ms. Chretien. But even if your husband contacted me, which I have no reason to expect, I represent you, not him. Anything you tell me is protected by attorney-client confidentiality."

"Good," she said.

It was a hard "good," and I could tell I'd made some points there. My theory that he was the one that gave her the shiner, that he was the person she was running from when the Border Patrol netted her down in Cruces, was starting to seem all too right. Add to that her husband's apparent status as a gangster, and suddenly I had a feeling I might not be looking so bad. As they say, it's all in who you stand next to.

"Ms. Chretien, I assume you are aware you have a Master Calendar Hearing coming up on December 13th with the Immigration Court. That's a little less than two weeks away. I would like to represent you at that hearing. Would that be acceptable to you?"

"To what do I owe this generosity? I still don't understand how you and my daughter come to be—"

"We can talk about that when we get together in person, Ms. Chretien," I said cutting her off. Obviously sharing *all* the details of Annie's and my adventures with Michelle Chretien at that exact moment meant they might also be shared with any Detention Center eavesdroppers and scriveners who were currently plugged in to our conversation, and that would have been fatal. "I'll be happy to answer all your questions as soon as I can get down to the detention center in Tacoma, at which time we'll have to talk about your case, too, of course. I'm hoping to get down there in the next day or so, and—"

"I want to see my daughter," Michelle Chretien suddenly burst out. "I want to see Annie! Can you do that? Can you bring her with you?"

I thought about that for a moment.

"Yes. Maybe. I don't know. Maybe there's something we can do. For now, you can certainly call her any time you wish."

"Should I call this number?"

"That would be perfect. Would you like to talk to Annie now one more time?"

I handed off the phone, and the two of them had another chat, this one a little more subdued. After about another five minutes or so, it was over.

I set the smart phone down on the table, and suddenly felt very tired. I had tried to sound professional and lawyerly throughout, the better to put Annie's mum at her ease, but maintaining that tone, and keeping my dialogue tight and controlled with so much at stake was exhausting.

"So, it looks like I'm going down there to the Tacoma Detention Center in a coupla' days," I said to the girls.

"You're really going to see my mom?" Annie said.

"It's the only way," I said, certain that it really was. "I have to be able to talk to her without the government listening in. The only way to do that is in person."

"Can I go?"

"She asked if you could go, too. Yeah, that'd be nice. But that's perhaps a bridge too far right now."

I was becoming reasonably confident that between my beard and my Canadian passport I had a reasonable chance to make it past American customs without getting stopped. They were undoubtedly still looking for me in the States, but they were looking for American me. I reckoned Canadian me might well fox 'em. If I was traveling with Annie, though, maybe not so much.

"A coupla' days" was all I had to figure it out, though. And it wasn't just on account of having to get down to the States to meet with Michelle. I had a removal hearing in Seattle Immigration Court coming up in forty-eight hours.

That was when I realized a drink at the Sylvia was called for. And it bears repeating: there's nothing like having a Fortress of Solitude to retreat to.

Settling back into my leather chair in my new favorite bar, I took another sip from my whisky and soda, had another look out at the lonely sea and the sky beyond Morton Avenue, and decided it was time to stop daydreaming. I set the paper aside and pulled the laptop over and opened it. The screen came on and I typed in the words "EOIR REMOVAL HEARING."

Immediately Google gave me a bright blue list of options.

Beyond the window the waters English Bay lapped endlessly against the soggy sand.

Chapter 33 –Seattle Immigration Court

YOU MIGHT THINK I'd have been shaken by the notion of doing an actual hearing at this point, advocating for client in front of a judge and on the record, having initially been so ambivalent back in Calgary about simply meeting up with Ike for something as easy as a consult, but the big guy had shoved a pretty sizable retainer at me for a pretty easy piece of work, and if I'm honest, the money kind of had me feeling it. I'd used the short time available before the removal hearing to purchase a new suit, along with a silk tie, dress shoes, a dope pocket square and a trench coat. If you're going to play lawyer, after all, you got to look the part.

Before they rang up my purchases, I noticed a display of hats on offer, and added a top-end Fedora to my collection.

Excellent, I thought.

And with that, the next morning I was on my way back to the good old U.S. of A. That had me in more of a sweat than the idea of doing the hearing, to be perfectly honest. Would my Canadian passport and new red beard be enough of a disguise to get me safely across the border? Or would my name alone be enough to get me pinched the second I entered American territory? There was that detainer, after all. Would they click to that, seize me, and bundle me off to the ubiquitous green room for a full body cavity search? And then onto the prison bus like they'd done Annie's mum?

And then what?—detention for me too, I supposed, while I awaited extradition to New Mexico, and the arrest warrants that awaited me there. Or possibly immediate removal back to Canada, because I was a foreign national who had broken the law...

Removal to Canada?

That was an interesting notion. If they just removed me to Canada, I'd be no worse off than I was right now. Back to square one. No harm, no foul. Hell, I could even volunteer for that, and they'd probably kiss me for it, too. A short plane or bus ride, and then I'd simply be back in Vancouver. It'd be like having a do-over.

But no. If I *did* find myself deported from the United States, that would be the end of my life in America. No more practice of law, no more house in Santa Fe. No more weekends with my little sweetie. My legal status in the States would be dunzo.

I chewed on that for a bit. No, it definitely wasn't for me. Getting deported to Canada was not a reasonable option, would be a disaster, in fact. But maybe there was still something there. Not for me, mind you, but as it happened I was about to find out that stepping up for voluntary deportation was not the craziest idea in the world. Not for some people, at least.

In the end, the border crossing proved to be nothing. Despite the fact that there were enough law enforcement tags associated with my name to set off a hundred alarm bells at any outpost, they were set for American me. I was a different person now, I was Canadian me; Canadian Robert James McKenzie, with a Canadian car, a Canadian license plate, a Canadian beard and, most important, a Canadian passport. So after an overlong wait, and a cursory look at my documents, and none at my face, they passed me on through.

Amazing.

Canadian me—the perfect camouflage.

Now that hump was passed, and the border behind me, it was good to contemplate getting back into the courtroom. Surprisingly so, actually, and I was feeling correspondingly large as I piloted the truck through thickening commuter traffic south toward downtown Seattle. After I'd safely locked up the big blue machine in some anonymous underground parking lot by Westlake Center, I returned to street level and headed downhill toward the water. I'd made arrangements to meet my client for breakfast at the Athenian Restaurant in Pike Place Market, and he was there waiting for me in an upstairs booth overlooking Puget Sound when I arrived.

"Bacon and eggs," I told the sweet sister who came to our table. "Over medium."

"Coffee?"

"Oh yeah."

She waitressed off to get our order going, and I turned to my new friend. He was less than I had imagined—indeed, so inoffensive a character could not come to mind. He was young and mild, maybe twenty-one, if that, wearing wire rimmed glasses and a short sleeved button down shirt. He seemed nice enough, with a face unblemished by any particular virtue or vice, and about the least likely illegal alien I could imagine.

"So, Mr. Kim. Very nice to meet you," I said, shaking his hand.

"Thank you, Mr. McKenzie. I really appreciate this."

"Well, Britt said you were an okay chap." I smiled. "I'm just sorry you have this problem."

He sighed. "It's okay. Like I said on the phone, I've been going to school at U dub and I guess my student visa expired. I never did get any renewal notice, and now they want to—" He looked down at his hands and shook his head, then looked back up at me. "Out of the blue they sent me a notice of this hearing, Mr. McKenzie. They said they want to *deport* me. The whole thing is so stupid. I don't even care anymore. All I need is a few days to move my stuff."

Beyond the window, the ferry was coming in from Bainbridge Island, churning up a polite wake behind it. Elliott Bay was green under the lowering clouds, and a light drizzle was falling.

"What are you studying?"

"Physical chemistry with a minor in physics."

"And Britt said you're a Canadian national."

He was nodding. "Mum and dad live in Burnaby. And I actually wanted to do my doctoral work at Dalhousie in Halifax, but University of Washington offered me a research grant, so I wound up here."

"Well, all this doesn't sound too bad," says I, checking off the boxes in good sound lawyer-like fashion. "It sounds like we could fix your visa problem fairly easily. We could ask the immigration judge to stay your removal pending application. You might have to post a bond, and we might even get that waived if..."

He was shaking his head. "No. I don't want to fight removal. The opposite, in fact. And it's not even the visa renewal process, Mr. McKenzie. I know I could get past that. It's the..." He paused. "It's the *attitude*. It makes you feel like a parasite. Like I said, I just want to be able to get my stuff and get out of here." The poor kid looked absolutely miserable.

"Oh," I said, suddenly feeling a little embarrassed. "But I don't really see the problem. Can't you just load up and drive back to B.C?"

He was shaking his head again. "My car's *in* B.C. I have to go get it. And I need a trailer, too. All my stuff is in storage down here in Lynwood, and without my car I have no way to get it all home."

"So you just want to make sure that if you leave the States to go get your car, you can get back across the border? Just to come back and get your stuff?"

"That's it!"

"And you don't contest removal?" I repeated, wanting to make sure I hadn't missed anything.

"No. Not at all. I just want to go home."

"Bacon and eggs," the waitress said, laying a platter before me. We paused long enough for me to eat, and then young Mr. Kim looked at his watch.

"It's eight forty-five, Mr. McKenzie," he said, a tad urgently.

I scooped up the last shovel full of congealing egg with a crust, washed it down with the last swig of coffee, and wiped my mouth with my napkin.

"Let's go!"

222

We walked up Pike, and then over on Second Avenue toward the building where the Immigration Courts were. The drizzle continued down, but it wasn't that cold out, and between my new Fedora and my trench coat I was feeling pretty dry and comfortable. Mr. Kim walked at my side the way clients always do, and we jointly searched out the street numbers to identify the skyscraper we were looking for. There was nothing to mark the place out, particularly, and when we did find it, it proved to be just another anonymous downtown tower: thirty stories of shops and offices, and a little more than half way up, on the twenty-fifth floor, the Executive Office of Immigration Review.

As we got off the elevator, I reflected that Britt had done pretty well finding me an easy case to cut my new courtroom chops on. We would undoubtedly be telling the Immigration Judge and the DOJ attorney exactly what they wanted to hear: *No problem here, your honor; frankly, my client can't get out of this country fast enough!* Another victory for Lawyers Without Borders.

Nonetheless, when we got off the elevator, the butterflies were dancing high in my belly, as they always do when you're about to walk into a courtroom to advocate for a client. You could do a hundred hearings a week, but it's the same every time, and I learned years ago, back when I was in private practice, that the quicker you could make anxiety your friend the better. People manage it indifferent ways, of course, but the way I did it was simply by channeling that anxiety in to my performance—you actually come to crave that jumpy feeling, if you can believe it. Before the end of that previous phase of my life, I had actually become a bit of an adrenaline junkie.

Of course, that all ended when I sold myself into government practice.

We went through a scuffed door, and found ourselves in the wide vestibule of a gray and grimy office suite, standing in line to go through a metal detector in a chute already clogged with people. Families, little kids, old people. Some of 'em were undoubtedly in line to get kicked out of the country themselves; others were the family members of those soon to be deported, or the lawyers coming along to represent 'em. And that's one thing you knew for sure, by the way, they were all there pending a deportation hearing of some kind. That's pretty much all they do, the immigration courts. It's almost all removal stuff. And it's a sad fact too that they don't have much leeway about even that. The immigration judges can grant stays and extensions, sure, and in extreme cases they might even be able to rule a particular individual *can* stay in the country—if there's a well developed court record that supports such a thing. But mostly it's just a few minutes of hearing, then the Immigration Judge's entry of yet another order of removal, followed by the bailiff's cry of "*Next!*"

We found ourselves in Hearing Room No. 3, which was very small, but did have a window. There were already maybe thirty people in the gallery, waiting for their cases to be heard, and the morning call was a long one. We had to sit patiently through a dozen or so bond hearings and master calendars and so forth, and it was a good thing, too, 'cause I got to observe for a while, and get a sense of the rhythm of the process.

"Jeffery Kim," the clerk finally announced, looking around the gallery. "Mr. Jeffery Kim."

"Our table's ready," I whispered to my young client.

We stood up and made our way to the front of the room, and stood together at the podium below the judge's bench.

"Robert McKenzie, entering my appearance for Mr. Jeffrey Kim, your Honor."

He gave me a quick up and down over his tortoiseshell glasses, and seemed satisfied enough. "Very good, counsel. Okay, then. Apparently Mr. Kim is with us today because his student visa has expired. Counsel, is Mr. Kim currently attending—" He glanced down at the document in front of him. "The University of Washington?"

"That is correct, your Honor. Mr. Kim is presently a doctoral candidate in the area of physical chemistry."

"Counsel, Mr. Kim's visa renewal issue is—"

"Your Honor, if I may. I'm very sorry, Mr. Kim does not contest removal."

"Oh," the Judge said, mildly surprised.

"He would like to voluntarily leave the country, your Honor. Voluntary removal. And he's prepared to do that immediately. The issue for my client, though, is that he has personal belongings in storage down here, and he would like to be able to reenter the United States briefly to retrieve them."

"That shouldn't be a problem, counsel. How soon does he anticipate doing that?"

Mr. Kim and I had a quick whisper back and forth. "Within the next two weeks, your Honor."

The Judge was nodding. "That would be perfectly fine. I'll enter an order to that effect. However, counsel, I must let you know, CBP will not necessarily respect an order from this court."

"What?"

"I'll go ahead and enter this order, but I just want you and your client to be aware that Customs and Border Protection will do what Customs and Border Protection will do. I have no reason to expect that Mr. Kim will have any problems, but I want to make you both aware of that fact."

I was flabbergasted. The notion that a writ of the immigration court was discretionary, a mere suggestion to the Department of Homeland Security was mildly shocking. All I said though, was: "Mr. Kim will be mindful of that, thank you, your Honor." And so saying, we gathered up our materials from the podium, and made our way out of the room.

Behind me as we emerged into the hall I heard someone cry: "*Next!*"

Back out on the street, I collected a check from a melancholy Mr. Kim, made some reassuring noises about the IJ's order he clutched tight in his fist ("After all, why *wouldn't* the CBP let you back in?..."), and saw him to his bus stop.

Then I went off to gather up the truck, and in minutes was flying south on Route 5 for the day's main event.

It takes about forty minutes to get to Tacoma from downtown Seattle, by the way, and the clouds and rain masked the scenery in a claustrophobic gloom; the swish-swash of the windshield wipers provided an appropriately monotonous soundtrack. As I piloted the big blue truck in and out of traffic, and having nothing else to do, I spared some thought for the unfortunate Mr. Kim. After all, a more messed up situation would be hard to imagine. Kicking a doctoral level chemist out of the country? It didn't seem like smart policy. I wasn't sure why, but it seemed like we might need people like him sometime. I wondered idly what other indignities he must have suffered, humiliations he hadn't told me about that led to his not wanting to contest removal, 'cause if ever there was a place that could make you feel the asshole for not having been born here, this was it—America the Brave. But whatever the reason, I had a feeling there was more to Mr. Kim's decision than just a visa renewal form that went astray.

I reached over and clicked on the radio, and twiddled the knob until I found a station playing some Sleater-Kinney and Nirvana and Macklemore and other such Pacific-Northwesty stuff. For a moment, the world began to make sense again.

A Mini Cooper with a Seahawks logo on the back window swished by me and made for the HOV lane. The old Ranier Beer brewery (long turned into condos now), Boeing Field, the turn-off for Sea-Tac Airport. The music played, the wipers slapped and before long, and without incident, I made Tacoma. But once there I had to circle around a bit looking for street names because I stupidly had forgotten to print up a map of the area before I left Vancouver. I had an address and a general idea where the place was, but the area was unfamiliar and no handy spot to obtain directions offered itself.

I got reasonably lucky, though, and in short order I located the Northwest Detention Center set down solidly in the midst of the numberless grim industrial yards that occupy Tacoma's Tidal Flats.

As I pulled up on the street out front, a modest crowd was milling around in the light rain in their coats and mittens, carrying signs and obviously having themselves a protest. "NO ONE IS ILLEGAL," "STOP ICE POLICE TERROR," "SHUT DOWN THE DETENTION CENTER" were parading around in endless soggy circles. Behind them, the prison loomed, an American Lubyanka, a sinister wet Bastille. And the Northwest Immigration Detention Center *was* a prison, by the way. There was no mistaking it for anything else. The building was low and menacing, made of formed concrete diced vertically to allow for slit windows; chain link and razor wire marked its exterior perimeter, and guard turrets punctuated the corners. It was depressing as hell to look at, and probably worse inside.

And for the second time in one day I found myself waiting in line to go through a goddam metal detector.

And in that exact moment, standing in line to go through security, the fact that I wasn't an American Citizen hit me like a shovel. I looked around—I was a stranger in a strange land. Jesus, I thought, they currently had a detainer out on me. If ICE ran my name—and it was ICE contractors running the place—it would come up cherries for sure! I could feel myself start to freak out.

I'd thought this through every step of this before, and in detail, of course. But thinking about it at the kitchen table in Vancouver, and coming face to face with the reality of it now were two different things. This was brazen as hell! I was a Jew walking into Gestapo headquarters! My instinct was to cut and run, and without meaning to, I glanced behind me at the exit, but cowardice was no way to run a railroad. I'd come this far. The rational part of me knew the only way back was forward—through security.

Keep it together, keep it together, keep it together...

I breathed deep to try to get myself under control, and looked around at the trolls guarding the place with their great bull necks and giant bellies—they could smell fear, of that I was certain. If I was to have any chance at all, I'd have to look confident.

Next!

The guy in front of me stepped through the machine. He was Mexican. He wore canvas work clothes and had on muddy boots. They looked at him suspiciously. One of the guards made him turn around, then quick as a blink reached down between his legs and grabbed his crotch from behind. Hard.

The Mexican man winced. The guard nodded and passed him through.

Jesus Christ! I thought with alarm.

227

"Next!"

I stepped up, and they beckoned me through the portal.

I hesitated for one split second before the machine, then took a step forward: the beeper didn't go off, one of the guards glanced at my Canadian passport, and he waived me through. I walked up to the end of the conveyor belt and retrieved my Fedora, coat and briefcase.

I was in!

Chapter 34 – Meeting Annie's Mother

IT WAS MY ALTERNATE Canadian identity that got me through, of course. Once again. That and the fact that I was pretty obviously a lawyer. Plus, they might even have thought I was sent by the consulate, thinks I—puffing myself up accordingly. Sure! I rambled on in my head, indulging the fantasy a little further as I pulled my shoes back on: And why not? I could pass as a diplomat in the ordinary course of business: graying hair, nice suit, good teeth and so forth. I'd used my passport as identification, after all; I was clearly an upper-crusty Furenur.

It's amazing how self-important international travel papers can make you feel.

But whatever the reason, my suit or my passport, or possibly even my new red beard, the name Robert James McKenzie—despite the fact that it was radioactive in various ICE bad guy databases—when appended to a Canadian ID morphed into a handle that didn't draw unwanted attention. At least in these Detention Center circles.

They led me down a broad linoleum hallway, bright with Florescents and piney with the smell of disinfectant, to the heart of the middling level security area to which I'd been admitted (the high security area where they housed the inmates was off limits, of course); and without ceremony they lodged me in some bland vestibule where other interested parties were also waiting to talk to the "detainees," as they were euphemistically

229

called. In truth, and as I had already noted numerous times, Prisoners was clearly the proper noun.

Those come to visit the prisoners—the poor souls I was sharing the waiting room with—all looked like civilians, meaning non-attorneys, of course. One old codger, noting my assorted badges of office (tie, suit, briefcase, good haircut, etc.), glommed on to me immediately and without preamble.

"My son's American," he said.

"Oh."

"Can you help him?" The old man's hair was pure white and very fine; it was quite thin and patchy, too, and I could see his pink freckled scalp underneath.

"Well, I...probably not today. I'm here to see a client, but..."

"We couldn't pay you."

Never lead with that, by the way. Not that I was even thinking about doing anything, mind you, but knowing that money *wasn't* involved was an immediate buzz-kill. Frankly, I was finding I liked getting paid. Receiving that fat envelope from Ike and a check from the melancholy Mr. Kim had whetted my appetite, and my DNA was changing a little. It's nice receiving money, no doubt about it. On the other hand, this guy obviously had a real problem, and I was starting to feel like maybe I *could* help people like that. And it was starting to seem like there maybe weren't many like me that could. Or would.

"They don't appoint you a lawyer, here," he added, rheumy eyed. "It's not like with criminal stuff."

"It's a hell of a thing," I agreed. My mind flashed back to the cop back in Santa Fe. "*No,*" she'd responded to the question from the Mexican kid in red Chucks, "*you can tell him he's definitely not entitled to have a lawyer appointed for him!*" I thought about the notion for a moment, and couldn't help speculating aloud: "I suppose one way to get around that would be to make sure when you get pinched for an immigration violation, you try to get charged criminally as well. You know, throw a few punches, resist arrest. That sort of thing. Then I expect *Gideon* would apply, and they'd have to give you a lawyer."

And that's a happy choice, thinks I.

"Gideon?" the old man said tentatively.

"Yeah, *Gideon versus Wainright*. It's the Supreme Court case that—"

"Robert McKenzie," a stout lady guard with a clipboard in her hand called from the door. "Robert McKenzie!..."

"That's me," I said, jumping up.

"Mister?..." the old man commenced once more, imploring.

I looked down at him, and an unfamiliar impulse suddenly grabbed me. I wrote my number down on a piece of paper.

"Mr. McKenzie!" the guard called impatiently from the door.

"Coming," I said to her, passing the paper to the old man. "Call me. We'll see what we can do."

Even as I followed the lady guard with the clipboard, I was already mentally kicking myself. What the hell did I just do? No money, but more work. Brilliant! It went against my history—as far as pro bono work went it sounded hard and there was zero potential for free lunches. I didn't have time to think about it further, though, because she had led me only a short distance to a room, empty but for two chairs and a table.

In one of the chairs sat Michelle Chretien.

For a moment, she took my breath away. Her thick red hair was brushed back, and pulled tight in a bun, very severe; but her pretty freckles and upturned nose softened the effect. Her oval face bore no sign of the sunset bruise that had colored her eye when I'd seen her the first time, but she was Annie's mum alright—the woman from the checkstop north of Las Cruces, though that crowded night seemed like a million years ago now. A formless white ICE issued jersey and loose white pants disguised her petit form like some kind of bland burqa, and she sat there with her hands folded in front of her, hiding the handcuffs, and looking at me blankly, like she'd never seen me before—which of course she hadn't, not that she'd remember, anyway.

"Could you take off the handcuffs, please?"

The good lady guard ignored me, and read from her clipboard without looking up:

231

"Alright, you're an attorney, so you know the drill. This here is a client interview and will not be monitored, but you will be visible through the window, there. During the interview, there will be no physical contact, no exchanging of materials of any kind, no food or drink will be allowed,…" The list of prohibitions went on for some time. I think "chewing gum" and "farting" were actually in there somewhere, but finally she finished up.

"Very good," I said. "I understand."

She turned to depart.

"Handcuffs?" I said again, catching her before she could withdraw.

Without a word, she turned, undid the handcuffs, and left the room, and suddenly Michelle Chretien and I were alone.

"How is Annie," She asked, rubbing her wrists. As it had on the phone, her soft French accent sent a quiver through my chest.

"Good," I said. "Really good. She's safe in Vancouver with Britt, and can't wait to see you. You have quite a little girl there, Ms. Chretien." I laid my briefcase on the table, and sat down.

"How is it *you* know her?"

It was a hard question, hard as steel, no-nonsense and direct. And none too friendly, either. It's probably the one I should have asked had our situations been reversed. Fortunately I had a good answer, if a little fantastic:

"Ms. Chretien, we've actually met before. About a month and a half ago, back in Las Cruces, New Mexico. When you were detained and Annie was first taken into custody. I'm a Canadian national, too, and got pulled aside at the same CBP checkstop where they picked you up. At the same time, too, actually. I sat next to Annie in the waiting area while you were being…processed. You may recall tossing me her rainbow mittens afterward. On the pavement outside. You know, when they were taking you to the bus?…"

Was there a glimmer of recognition there? Hard to tell. Maybe. I held off a second, but she said nothing.

I kept trying: "There were two of those CBP guys taking you out to the bus, and you tossed 'em at me? You said to give them to your daughter?..."

Nothing.

I cleared my throat. "Anyway, long story short, I ran into Annie again the very next night, four hundred miles north of Las Cruces in the City of Santa Fe. At the police station there. She'd got picked up by Santa Fe PD because she was walking along the side of the road without an adult. She'd escaped on the way to foster care, you see, which was where they were going to put her after they'd taken you away. She was trying to get to you, of course. Annie was under the impression that you had already been removed to Canada, so she was heading north—"

"Why were *you* in the police station?"

Another hard question.

"Well, I actually live in Santa Fe. That's where I went after the Border Patrol let me go the night before. And the next day I got pulled over up there 'cause some idiot pinched my license plate." It sounded so lame when I said it out loud, I think I might have flushed a little. "That turned out not to be too big a problem in and of itself," I went on, "the license plate, I mean. But the cop who pulled me over asked if I was a citizen— apparently they do that *all* the time now—and I told him I was Canadian. And proud of it, too, by the way. But then he asked for my papers, just like they had the night before in Cruces, and I still didn't have my visa in my pocket, so they arrested me."

Such a stupid, embarrassing reason to be arrested. Describing it out loud, the humiliation of it stung a bit.

"I'd been in the State's for years," I explained, defensively. "Legally there, I mean. I'm an attorney, for god's sake, licensed to practice in State and federal court; I have a house, a wife—ex-wife, anyway—and a daughter down there, too. None of that mattered to the cops. And 'cause I didn't have my visa actually with me, they booked me in and contacted the immigration authorities. Anyway, while we all waited for ICE or whoever to come and round me up at the police station, they lodged me in some kind of makeshift waiting room for illegals. That's where they had Annie waiting too. They were holding on to her for the Children Youth and Families people."

"I don't understand," Michelle said. "A little girl left alone in a room with adult prisoners?"

Those green eyes.

"Go figure."

"What kind of police are these?"

"Wait. It gets better. I mean worse," I quickly corrected, not wanting to seem in any way flip. "The cops stuck her in there to cool it until the child services people arrived, right, but she was so desperate to get to you she decided those four walls wouldn't hold her. So when they took the other immigration detainees out of the room to talk to a translator, she gave the delivery door a push, and out she went. That's when things got extremely insane…"

Her eyes never left mine. She was taking it all in, and I could feel the intelligence of her, the *presence* of her in the exchange, weighing everything I was saying.

"I went out after her, then, and they started shooting at us."

"Shooting!"

"They started shooting at us. Right. That is correct. The Border Patrol guys did, anyway. I think the local cops were pretty horrified, though they didn't do nothing to stop 'em that I could see. Anyway, yeah, a *hail* of bullets. No warning, no order to halt. Maybe they didn't see Annie, I don't know. By the way, did you know your daughter could drive?…"

I told her the rest, then. The escape, the run to Canada, the encounter with Dennis and Britt, the murder of James Quintana, and some of it was so unbelievable I could hardly credit it myself, but there was no denying that we were presently lodged in Vancouver, and that I was actually with Michelle herself right now to make arrangements to get her and Annie back together. And that Michelle had actually spoken to her healthy happy daughter only the day before. The reality of those things, at least, bore some witness for my story.

234

"I didn't want to deal with you falsely," I said, when I finally finished up, "but I couldn't tell you all that over the phone when we talked before. We have to assume the ICE listens in on everything except these attorney interviews, and it wouldn't do for them to know our whole back story. All that stuff in Santa Fe amounted to a series of horrible misunderstandings, but it's not straightened out yet."

"How could you possibly straighten that out?"

"Actually, out of this whole wretched puzzle, that's the part that seems to be coming together. I have an attorney back in New Mexico—Madstone. He got ahold of the police station surveillance videos from the night Annie and I were shot at, and they're pretty damning. Frankly, the cops just want this to go away. It was the Border Patrol agents who went nuts, after all, and the fact that it happened at the local police station four hundred miles from the Mexican border makes everybody look bad. It's really the social services people that are the problem now. They want Annie back in their custody in the worst way."

Michelle's expression was still veiled, but no longer openly hostile, though she was obviously still chewing on it all.

"And if I can reunite you and Annie," I said, "that takes care of them. Once the kid's back with a parent, then social services—CYFD—they have no jurisdiction. At least, I hope that's how it's going to work."

"So you have self-interest here." It was a statement, not a question. Self-interest was obviously a motive she could understand.

"Yup," I admitted, nodding. "And my selfish interests and your parental interests are the same, by the way. Getting you and Annie back together gets me my old life back," daughter, pension, house and all, thinks I. "A win-win-win."

She seemed to get it. It's funny how that works: somebody does something nice for no reason—beyond just holding the door for you or passing the ketchup, anyway—and suddenly folks start looking at you squinty eyed and mothers are pulling their children away. It makes sense, I guess. It's what I'd do.

"You were right to watch out for Dennis," she said, in a new, slightly less guarded tone. "I know him quite well. He's a very sick person."

235

"Annie felt very badly for him after the gun went off."

"She would." Michelle gave off a very thin smile then—either a crack in the ice or simply an ironic comment on Dennis, I couldn't tell which.

"Look, the goal here is to get you out of this place, and back together with Annie as quickly as we can." I lifted a yellow notepad and a pen from my briefcase. "I'm not sure how much time they'll give us, and we have some boxes we need to check off, so I hope you won't mind if we get down to business." She nodded. "Okay. Number one, are you okay with me representing you with regard to your immigration issues?" She nodded. "Okay. Can I ask you a few questions about your status then?"

"Sure," she said, resignedly, with a Gallic shrug.

"Citizenship?"

"I'm a Canadian." She paused briefly, and then added with mock brightness: "*Je suis un Québécoise!*" lifting up her hands to imaginary accolades. Her nails were a shade of green that fetchingly offset her red hair. Somehow well manicured, too, despite the fact she was incarcerated.

"Not an American citizen?"

"No," she said.

"That's alright," I said. "If you're not, you're not. No green card or visa of any kind?"

"No. My husband just brought us down here. To America…St. Louis. There was some trouble for him in Montreal, and even though I was pregnant with Annie we had to leave in a hurry. We had passports once, but he has them. I think mine would be expired by now, anyway. It's been almost ten years."

"So you are completely undocumented?"

"No, of course not. I have a birth certificate, somewhere."

"Province of Quebec?"

"Oui."

"Do you physically have it?"

"I could get it, of that I'm sure. I am Canadian, after all."

236

"But identity or travel papers currently in you possession? You don't have any?"

"No."

"Well, I can get to work on that right away. Apply for a certified copy of your birth certificate," I said aloud, making a note on the yellow legal pad. As it happens, something I actually knew how to do, I thought to myself—Hurrah! I'd literally just been through the same process rebuilding my own identity back in Calgary. Indeed, I had begun in exactly the same way: getting my birth certificate from *La Belle Provence*. "I'll prepare some forms for you to sign," I continued, "and then that'll be one box we can check off. Your husband?"

"He's a piece of shit," she spat.

"I'm sorry, no. I mean, what's his nationality? An American piece of shit, or a Canadian piece of shit?"

She laughed. "Canadian. Naturalized Canadian. He came over from Nigeria with his family in the nineties. He's a naturalized American, too. I believe he paid somebody. It was underhanded."

Underhanded or not, this was welcome news, thinks I. Madstone thought the guy had a Green Card, but apparently Michelle's husband had gone one better and become a citizen. Sounds like the bastard made a hobby of collecting nationalities, too—Nigerian, Canadian, American. Who knew what other papers he might have in his own safe deposit box. "Well, if he's actually an American citizen, that opens up some options. There's U-visas and V-visas; either could provide you status in the States," I said, repeating some of what I'd read off the internet. "Sufficient to keep you in the country. They're designed for victims of domestic violence and human trafficking, and I don't want to be presumptuous, but the night I first saw you, you had quite a shiner."

Her face flushed bright red. "Oh, *oui* -- yes, he gave that to me," she said, becoming animated. "That...'shiner.' *That's* when I left him."

I wasn't the least bit surprised to hear it, of course. Indeed, it's pretty much what I'd thought from the start.

"Well, the Violence Against Women Act allows that if you are victim of domestic violence by an *American* family member, and it sounds like you are, we can actually pursue a V-visa. You'll get it, in fact. It sounds like all the other boxes for that one are checked off, too—"

"He's a pimp, you know. A slaver. He brings little girls from eastern Europe, girls who can't speak English, and puts them to work. He takes their passports, too, and then he thinks he owns them—like the slaves."

"I understand," I stepped in, definitely interested, but wanting to keep her on track. "And because of him, because he victimized you, there are some real alternatives for us to keep you in the country. One of the few things United States citizenship and immigration law is actually somewhat progressive about is domestic violence..."

Chapter 35 – Michelle's Secret

WHAT WAS SHE doing with this guy? I wondered about that as I ran on about VAWA, and showing off my relatively narrow newfound expertise a bit. How could she have been married to him? I don't want to seem to naïve, but frankly I was a bit horrified. I mean, here was this stunning woman, far from clueless—hell, from what I'd seen of her so far, she was the opposite: she was smart as hell, elegant, and not the sort of woman to be misled, and yet she was hooked up with a gangster, a sick human trafficking gangster with...

I realized she was suddenly looking at me very critically.

"Money," she said, successfully reading my expression. "I wanted a good life. He was sexy and dangerous. And he drove a Lexus."

"I'm sorry, I didn't—"

"Am I the first woman you have met, Mr. McKenzie, who chose poorly? I think you mentioned previously that you yourself are divorced."

"My apologies. I meant no disrespect."

She was shaking her head. "I'm not upset. I only want you to understand. I made a mistake. And now my daughter and I, we are trying to find our way back."

She paused and looked at me, her hands—her milk-white hands with the green nails—upturned on the table top. Those green eyes looking at me across the table, wide open, moist, her gaze level. She was opening up, reaching out to me. I think. I could have taken those slim hands in mine just then; she wanted me to. I think. But I didn't. Just then, at least. I wasn't sure of my footing, you see. And I was sitting across the table from a woman who needed me, whose daughter needed me, who was entirely dependent on me; I was too much a Canadian to take advantage of that, you see.

But there was something else, too. There was something missing in her story. She'd been truthful in what she'd told me—I'd no doubt about that. But absent anything else, the corollary was, Michelle Chretien had had no objection to her husband's monstrous profession until he'd struck her, until she herself was victimized. She'd obviously been enraged by that, and by her own admission it was why she left him; that was why she'd been running away with Annie on a remote New Mexican highway the night she got picked up by the CBP. Not because she'd had any particular epiphany about the source of her husband's wealth and the criminal foundation of her probably very high lifestyle.

Or had she? Was there more to Michelle's volte-face change of heart than just a one-off act of domestic violence? Was Michelle Chretien's midnight flight across the American continent then just pure self-interest, or did it suggest something more?

Part of me definitely wanted there to be more.

"You should know, he's trying to get his hands on Annie," I said, breaking the spell.

"He is?" She drew her hands back.

"That's the whisper from Madstone—my attorney back in Santa Fe. And he expects that if the Children Youth and Families people in New Mexico get physical custody of Annie again, that they will hand her over to him." I saw the expression on her face, and temporized. "I'm sorry, I'm not trying to freak you out, here. You should know about that, though."

"I understand."

"The CYFD contacted him. Your husband. It's their standard protocol when one parent is deported. Child Service's prime directive is to

240

keep a kid with at least one of the biological parents, and it wasn't that hard for them to find him, I'm sure. They had a name and a state—the rest is just checking government databases." I held off a bit there to gauge her reaction.

She went quiet for a bit, then spoke in a whisper: "Then it's very good for now she's with you in Canada."

"We should keep that in mind, though, whatever way forward we choose. That he's waiting out there in the wings. But for now, let's talk about your options for a bit," I said, undertaking an awkward segue. "How we're going to get you out of here. Being from Canada you're obviously not a candidate for asylum or refugee status. And a family based petition isn't an option, obviously, since you and your husband are no longer together. So by process of elimination—"

"There are many here in the Detention Center like that. Stranded without an American sponsor or money or…anything. There are some who have been locked up for five years. Ten years. Longer, even."

"That's a category you don't want to be in," I agreed. "Fortunately, as I mentioned before, we have the option of a V-visa, so—"

"No, Mr. McKenzie, I *am* in that category. That's something *you* should know."

I was puzzled by that, and said so.

"They work for my husband. Some of these immigration officials. Even when we were still in Canada he had friends in America of this type. It was some of these who sent me here from the prison in El Paso. They transferred me because there are more who work for him up here. At this place," she added, waving her hands vaguely around to indicate the Northwest Immigration Detention center generally.

"People here work for him? You mean he bribes them?"

"Bribes, I suppose. Yes," she said. "They work for him, and they're to make sure I don't go anywhere until he gets what he wants."

"Annie?"

She shook her head. "No. He doesn't care about Annie except as a hostage to control me."

"What then?"

241

A grim look overcame her, and her jaw tightened; she looked me over hard, weighing, me, of course; my character, my motivation; my five week history of looking out for Annie. She was adding it all up, and weighing whether to cross the Rubicon, I suppose, weighing whether or not to tell me her deep dark secret, and I must have come out okay, on balance, then, 'cause she went ahead and launched into it:

"Our daughter is only a means to an end for him. It's not Annie he wants, although he will pretend so that he can then hold our daughter over my head. No, I took something of his before I left. Something very serious, something he wants returned very badly."

"I'm guessing they didn't find it on you when you were arrested."

"Do you know what 'the Cloud' is?"

"Sure. I mean, kind of. It's computer stuff, right?"

"I have a lot of information about him and his 'Friends.' When I came to know what he was we'd already been married and had a child. It was too late, then. He owned us. That's how he sees things. I knew he would never let us go. Not willingly. And if we were ever to escape I'd need a chip. A bargaining chip. So I pretended to be happy and started collecting things. Information. And I put it all in a safe place. A place no one can ever get to."

"You collected information about your husband's criminal activities and you saved it in the Cloud?"

She touched her nose. "In cyberspace, yes. I saved lots of names and dates and numbers, and I wrote it all in little ones and zeros and stored it in the virtual world. Away from me. Away from everyone."

There was something there that didn't add up. "But if you have that bargaining chip, as you say, then how come—"

"I didn't expect to be caught in New Mexico. I wasn't ready yet. I thought I'd have more time, time to make arrangements."

"So that if he hurt you or Annie, the information would be published automatically?" I guessed. "He'd destroy himself if he destroyed you?"

She nodded. "*Oui.* So, now, the information is safe. I saw to that. It's in the Cloud. But he's safe too, because while I'm in here I can do nothing."

"But you still have access to computers. Even in here. You can get at anything in the Cloud as easy as I can, I'm sure."

"There's a password."

"So?"

She said nothing.

"C'mon—what're you telling me? You don't remember it?"

"I knitted the password into Annie's gloves so I wouldn't have to remember it," she said, somewhat irritably.

The gloves! Rainbows with the numbers for Michelle Chretien's Cloud account knitted right in. It was brilliant. Especially so for a woman with such a poor memory. I mean, my god, there couldn't have been more than ten numbers knitted into those little mittens. It was a goddam social security number for god's sake! How hard could it be?

"That means we can burn him. Annie's got the gloves."

"They will never let me go."

"I don't get it."

"There's more than the password."

"More than the password?"

She clammed up at that. And to be honest with you, I was becoming more than a little bit irritated by it, 'cause as any good lawyer will tell you, it's a bad idea to keep secrets from the guy representing you. I also knew we were running out of time. I didn't have the luxury of being able to slowly tease more secrets out of her.

In any event, whatever "more" there was to her story, I couldn't see how all our problems weren't solved by simply getting Michelle Chretien out of the Northwest Immigration Detention Center. Gloves, Cloud and all of it were irrelevant at this point. "Look, we're not dealing with the ICE or the staff here," I said to her. "I represent you in court now. It's why we have the judiciary, for crying out loud – so some out of control government agency can't keep you locked up indefinitely. Like I mentioned earlier, a V visa is something we could certainly apply for, and almost as certainly get. Problem is, the standard USCIS protocol would undoubtedly be to investigate the petition. Which is okay, of course;

243

everything's on the level. But that would mean interviews and forth, and to a certainty it would take a while."

"A while?"

"Months probably. Hopefully it would just be months. But the advantage of a V visa is, although the transaction would take some amount of time, it *would* keep you in the States. The obvious downside is you could remain stuck in this detention center for a while longer while we tried to arrange bond. And that's if we can even get bond. And in the meantime, Annie's father's not going away, right? There's no universe where his getting a hold of Annie would be a good thing for anybody, and there's a chance that could happen. Time's a real factor." I paused, thinking that what I was about to suggest was maybe just too easy to be good. "So—there's another possibility, one that would actually be pretty quick, comparatively speaking."

"And what is that?"

"The no action alternative."

"The no action alternative?"

"No action. Not fighting removal. In other words, you just let 'em send you back to Canada. You wouldn't be the first, believe me," I added, thinking of the surrealistic proceeding before the Immigration Judge I'd participated in that very morning. "If you don't have strong feelings about staying here in the States, it'll be the quickest way to get you and Annie back together."

She thought about it hard for a second. "What does that mean?"

"As a practical matter? You tell 'em you want to leave. We post a bond, and they release you. Look, I won't lie. If you admit you are here illegally, and you get removed, even voluntarily, it could cause problems for you in the future. Problems with maybe ever being able to return to the United States. At least for many years. But you tell the judge you want to opt for voluntary removal—in other words, you promise to leave the country—and they will let you go. Hell, you're actually doing 'em a favor."

"And?"

"And that's it. Basically, they'd let you go upon your word that you will leave voluntarily, and then I would just drive you to Vancouver. Right then. Simple as that."

"And Annie's in Vancouver," she said, completing the thought.

"That's right. You guys'd be back together a few hours after you walk out of this place. We could all be having dinner together in British Columbia that very night. Depending on the line up at the border, of course."

"Well, *yes*," she said, emphatically, as if I had been an idiot to consider anything else. "I have nothing down here."

"Great. In my opinion that's the best option. So let's get this show on the road. I'll enter my appearance for you and let 'em know you don't contest removal. You have a hearing already scheduled for the thirteenth, but I'm thinking we can probably get a court date and you out of here sooner than that."

"They will not let me go easily," she said, the clouds gathering again. "Be prepared for that."

I glanced up at the window, and saw the good lady guard there tap her watch. I wondered briefly if she was on Monsieur Chretien's payroll. Whether she was or wasn't, my time with Michelle was coming to an end. "Is there anything else, as long as we have a few moments?"

She shook her head. "Take care of Annie."

"I will. Stay safe. We'll have you out of here in no time."

By the time I hit the road the streetlights were already coming on in Tacoma, and it occurred to me that though the climate was milder (and wetter), we were amazingly still almost as far north as frozen ice-berg Calgary. Not quite, but almost. The black December night came on just as early, and though the drive back north proved to be relatively painless, the darkness made it seem rather over long. I passed up along the length of Route 5 through the bright city lights of downtown Seattle, the Space Needle, Lake Union, and then on up into the northern suburbs beyond— Lynwood, Edmunds, Everett. At that point I finally allowed myself some congratulations that things were actually falling into place. I was still distracted by the fact that there was more to Michelle's story then

245

she was willing to tell me—*There's more than the password*—and I could have pressed her I suppose, but what was it my business anyway? I wasn't here to solve all the problems of the world, and if I simply managed to reunite the two of them, Annie and her mum, that would be good deed enough for one day, and I could skip back to Santa Fe with a song in my heart and resume my old life.

Yup—if things weren't exactly coming up roses yet, then the buds were out at least.

It was in that frame of mind I tried to call the girls. I'd left 'em with the new I-phone I'd got in Calgary, and had with me the old one—my old I-phone, the one I'd snatched out of my Scion XB in front of the Denny's back in Santa Fe about a million years ago. The one that apparently only worked in the U.S.

Well, for at least another half hour I was still back in the gold old U.S. of A, and I reckoned it was time to test the old girl out.

I whipped it on out and went to dial 'em up, and realized instantly that it was dead as disco—a lifeless lump of metal and plastic in the palm of my hand. Like an idiot I'd forgot to charge the thing.

I set it back down on the bench seat next to me and sighed.

"We'll give it a go next time," I said aloud to the otherwise empty cab of the truck.

Heading up the Pacific Highway, the ocean endlessly dark and off to the left, eventually I reached the border, and the Peace Arch, set in its lush and lovely little pocket park. Between the north and south border crossings, the Arch sits in no-man's land, so to speak, appropriately peaceful and lavishly lit at night. There wasn't much of a line and I flashed my passport and crossed through Canadian customs no problem, popping out safe and sound and very relieved back up in B.C.

"Welcome—British Columbia, Canada," the sign read, "The Best Place in the World."

Maybe so, I thought to myself. Maybe so. And despite the crush of traffic, I made it from there to downtown Vancouver in under an hour. I parked the truck on the street outside our high rise and rode the elevator up to our floor, weary but relaxed.

I deserved a drink, I decided, and opened the front door to our modest urban flat with the image of several tall frosty ones dancing in my head.

"Hey, I'm back!" I shouted down the hall, heading for the kitchen.

No response. The apartment was empty.

Chapter 36 – Tuck and Roll!

I WASN'T TOO WORRIED, of course. I'd been down this road before, as you may recall, and back in Calgary had learned the foolhardy consequences of jumping to conclusions where the girls were concerned. Though it was full on dark, it wasn't particularly late, and Britt and Annie had undoubtedly gone out—to a movie or on a shopping expedition or to the playground or some such thing. Totally expected. I took the opportunity to enjoy some quiet time, doffed my Fedora, peeled off my trench coat, set down my briefcase between two half finished bowls of congealed oatmeal.

I made a mental note to talk to the girls about dishwasher protocol, and liberated a Labatts from the fridge.

My body was still buzzing from the drive back from Tacoma, my brain full of the events of the day, and I wandered out onto our small balcony with my first frosty beverage and sipped it under the bright lights of Vancouver in the soft misty drizzle. Winding down from the day's adventures, I reflected that this strange life we were living had started to seem normal, that in some ways it was even weirdly enjoyable. And it was coming to an end soon. Annie's mother would be back in Canada; Annie would be rejoining her; I'd be heading back to Santa Fe to resume counting off the days 'till retirement. And Britt…

Britt.

There was no quick answer to that one. There was a promise so far unfulfilled there. A promise I'd have to keep before I left Canada. And truth be told, it wasn't just a duty—I actually wanted to do it. Britt was acerbic and annoying, yes, but she had surprised me all around: pitching in at every opportunity; conjuring up clients for me almost from the moment we arrived in BC; managing Annie like a little sister. The notion of her returning to the mean streets of anywhere was something I didn't want to contemplate. But was she was prepared for any life other than hooking or stealing or dealing drugs? After our adventures were over, what would she do? She actually wouldn't make a half bad paralegal, I thought to myself, vaguely. If I could nail down that landed immigrant status for her before I left, she'd at least have the option of trying that on for size, working at some kind of law office job here in Vancouver, maybe. And as a landed immigrant there'd be health care for her, too; educational opportunities; there'd be safety net and status, all courtesy the equitable principals of Canadian socialism.

The heartless horny oil men of the Great Province of Alberta had been happy to exploit her youthful assets for the last couple of years; it seemed entirely appropriate that she should now be able to avail herself of the benefits of this Land of Promise as well. I mentally renewed my commitment to get Britt's immigration status squared away before our happy band split up, and we went our separate ways.

Better make it quick, though, I thought to myself.

I tipped the beer bottle up high and drained the last of it. The thing was empty, and I rotated it in my hands, looking thoughtfully at the Maple Leaf emblazoned on the label. I'd easily earned another, I decided, and I went back inside to retrieve one from the fridge. I popped it open with a smile: here I was, your typical Canadian "dad" recreating at home after a long day's work. I'll be the first to admit that it wasn't an entirely accurate characterization, but I liked the notion just the same.

Standing in the kitchen I realized I had gotten a little soggier than I would have liked standing out in the mist, so instead of returning to the balcony I commenced to stroll aimlessly around the house feeling oddly serene. The quiet was lovely, if you really want to know, and the living room was starting to accumulate the comfortable detritus of domesticity—a jacket here, a pile of books there, a couple of magazines. Britt's light blue rain jacket was draped on the arm of the chair. Odd for her to be outside in this drizzle without a coat, I thought to myself...

For the first time, I really started to wonder just where those guys had gone. It was past eight, now, and getting kind of late for a shopping expedition.

I poked around the living room and the kitchen for a note or something, and came up empty. Nothing. I wandered back to the bedrooms. There was Annie's backpack and bunny on the bed, but no note or sign of where they might have gone.

I felt a shiver climb up my back.

Oh, yes, her bunny's okay, I had told Michelle. *She actually carries it with her all the time...*

The girls were gone without Britt's coat, and without Annie's bunny. It was drizzling outside, and had been all day. This was starting to become marginally worrisome. They wouldn't normally just launch out the door with nothing but the shirts on their backs. Not in the rain. Why would they leave in such a hurry? Without coat or stuffed animal?

My brain began reeling through horrible alternatives.

I reflexively pulled my smart phone out of my jacket pocket, and tried to figure out what to do—it took me a full second to remember it wasn't the new one, and it wasn't charged. All I had was a dead rectangle that didn't work in Canada.

It was then I noticed the blood.

It was a crimson smear on the carpet on the far side of Annie's bed, just under the window. About a foot long, it suggested an injured hand or knee had been involuntarily dragged or shoved across the white pile.

I instantly went numb.

Calm down, I thought. I'd panicked before under similar circumstances back in Calgary for what turned out to be no reason. I tried to take a step back and think. What did I know for sure? That they'd left in a hurry.

Okay. There was that. They had definitely left in a hurry.

And there had been violence…

Wait. Back up—blood on the floor didn't *necessarily* mean violence. At least not violence at the hands of someone who meant to do harm. They were kids, after all. Kids play and get injured all the time. Cuts, scrapes, bruises. Had Annie banged herself up, and had Britt taken her to an emergency room?

Did they have emergency rooms in Canada?

A hollow feeling in my chest told me the emergency room, or its British Columbian equivalent, probably wasn't it. I stalked around the house trying to think, looking for more information to inform my analysis. Evidence might be the better word at this point. I worked my way around the flat, lifting some things, looking under others; living room, kitchen, bedroom, balcony…That was about it, really. It was a small place, and I managed a reasonably thorough search in about ten minutes.

I went to the front door and peered out into the exterior hallway, saw nothing, then started over again with the living room.

As I commenced turning over cushions for a second time, I began to question my approach. What was I was looking for, exactly? Anything was the answer. Anything that might tell me what happened.

I lifted up an armchair and scanned the area underneath. The darker possibility—the likelihood—that The Bad Guys had snatched 'em, started to work on me. That scenario fit the meager evidence at hand of an empty apartment and blood on the floor. But how would any possible Bad Guys know where we were? How could anybody? Moving on to the kitchen, I went down the list of those few we'd been in contact with: Annie's mum, of course. Then there was Ike and Mr. Kim; there were the two other clients Britt had spoken to which included Mrs. Pearson who I had spoken to also, and some guy named Dave whose number I hadn't yet dialed. And we had been in touch with the Northwest Immigration Detention Center when we left that phone message for Michelle. And then there was whomever the girls may have called when I wasn't around…

Okay, there were lots of people who might know about us and where we were. It's amazing how hard it is to stay off the grid.

251

Absentmindedly I picked up Britt's blue coat.

And there the phone was. The new one, the one I'd bought in Calgary. It sat on the arm of the chesterfield under where Britt's coat had been.

"*Shit!*" I said aloud.

They'd left the phone. I stared at it for a moment knowing now something bad had gone down, that to a certainty something had slipped very badly sideways.

Of course, if they'd taken it with 'em, that'd have been another chit on the normalcy side of the ledger. Indeed, if they'd had both the time and the presence of mind to take the phone, that would have meant the two girls had had things under control. But they didn't take it with them. They'd left the thing behind, along with Annie's bunny, Britt's coat and a fairly sizable blood stain on the bedroom carpet. The only reasonable conclusion was that person or persons unknown had arrived at the apartment and roughly escorted the girls to another location.

It was also apparent that they'd had a few moments warning, and as the ship was sinking had shoved the smart phone out of the way, stuck it in a place where they knew I'd find it.

Why? Why had they done that?

To send that very message to me, I supposed. To alert me to the fact that they'd been taken. I mean, adolescent girls don't absent-mindedly leave their cell phones. They live their lives on the damn things, and to the extent they can, have them on their persons at all times. Britt and Annie were both smart enough to click to that, to the fact I'd expect them to keep close track of the phone, and that I'd know there was something up if I found it here without 'em.

It also gave me the phone to use. Whether that was part of their purpose or intention I did not know, but regardless, I had a tool now that I didn't have before.

So what was I supposed to do? Wait for 'em to call me? That wasn't going to happen—at least, it didn't seem very likely. My best guess was at the moment they were tied up in a car trunk or locked in a basement somewhere, or worse. As a practical matter, I had to assume they were incapacitated.

Were there any other alternatives for me then? Call the cops, that would be one. Not a very good one, but maybe it was time to start thinking along those lines.

What else did I have?

The thing suddenly buzzed in my hand. I practically jumped through the roof.

Then I struggled to push the answer button, realized I was reaching for the delete button, and shifted back. I pushed the right button and clumsily put the thing to my ear.

"Hello."

"Lawyer-man," a girl's voice said, "It's me, Britt."

"Britt! Are you all right?—"

"I'm good. But the Mounties got Annie."

"Got Annie? What happened?"

"The RCMP showed up here, McKenzie. Dennis is dead. They know about Canadian you and about me—McKenzie, they know everything."

"How the hell did the RCMP get wind of this."

"Dennis. An infection. It was the gangrene that got him, but they're saying he died of the gunshot wound. And from Dennis they clicked to us."

Well that all sounded about right.

"It's murder they're saying, McKenzie. They're looking for you."

My face suddenly went numb. The RCMP were probably pretty good at tracking down dogs like me once we came on their radar, and I could easily imagine the dominos falling. Dennis knew who I was. Julie had told Dennis where we were staying back in Calgary, just like Britt had said. Dennis had undoubtedly shared that information, too, with probably just about everybody else he knew, all his gangster friends, including the dude with the puckered scar that had chased me to the train platform in Calgary. And with Dennis dead now, it was frankly unsurprising that the RCMP had our number. It wouldn't have taken much

253

police work to get that; if Dennis hadn't told 'em during a deathbed interview, subsequent interviews with a few pimpy lowlifes and whatnot would've put the Mounties on my trail.

"I should have seen this coming, Britt," I said, although to be perfectly honest, I don't know what I'd have done if I had. "Where are you?"

"They got us both but I slipped the lead. There's a story there, McKenzie. They were leading Annie to the police car and—"

"Where are you?" I growled, a little more urgently.

"We're at my brother's. Annie's still with the RCMP."

Britt had a brother? That was new, but there was nothing for it. I had a hundred questions, but now was not the time. The quaver in Britt's voice told me all I needed to know for now. She gave me some quick directions, I gave her some words of encouragement and headed for the door.

On the way downstairs I punched the address Britt had just given me and drew up a map of West Van with a little flag to punctuate where her brother's house was located. From where we were on English Bay it was just through Stanley Park and over Lions Gate Bridge. I reckoned I could make it in about twenty minutes.

I flung open the front glass doors to the building and exited into the drizzly night.

Chapter 37 – One, Maybe Two Ways Out

I WAS IN A feverish sweat as I made for the truck, scanning the street up and down for any suspicious looking folks. Britt hadn't given any details sufficient for me to really know what had gone down with her and Annie, but I knew enough.

The Mounties got us, McKenzie.

The authorities were involved here, and a reasonable caution suggested they might still be about. There was literally no one I could see out on empty wet Morton street, but as I climbed into the cab and switched on the engine I didn't feel one inch safer. Things were going south like Sherman, and when the Ju Ju goes against you it's wise to expect the worst. I lifted the shiny new shifter into Drive, and headed out into the night keeping an eye in the rearview mirror.

The chilling notion hit me that if the RCMP found us, the late unlamented Dennis' goons could, too, and Annie's father wouldn't have much trouble, either. My Canadian camouflage was apparently in tatters, at least on this side of the border, and I felt visible all around. Still, while I could easily work out how the RCMP could have caught up with us at least as far as Calgary, it remained a mystery what breadcrumbs they'd followed to catch up with us here in Vancouver. It was a murder investigation now, so I reckoned they had pulled out all the stops, but even with that it was quite a leap. We'd only just fetched up on these shores and couldn't have made much of a footprint.

Finding my way to Britt's brother's place was job one, of course. The leafy world of Stanley Park opened up onto Lions Gate Bridge, with the black salt water far below, the Harbor heavy with ships off to the right, and the bright lights of West Vancouver directly in front. I reckoned I'd better look lively so as not to miss the turnoff. I needn't have worried; the directions were straightforward enough, and in minutes after crossing the water I was pulling up in an alley behind a two story red-wood structure with a deck-cum-balcony wrapped around the second floor and one of those mobile basketball hoops standing in the driveway.

I walked up a short flagstone path to the nondescript green door and ding-donged the bell.

Concentrating on directions, traffic and street signs had kept me from thinking too much about Annie on the way over. Britt said the RCMP had her. It's hard to imagine how things could get any worse than that, but I braced myself for what I was about to learn from Britt.

An elderly black gentleman came to the door. "You must be Britt and Pablo's uncle," he said. "You're not what I expected."

"Yes, I get that a lot."

"Well, come on in. Welcome to West Van School for the Deaf. I'm Leonard, sort of the head honcho around here. You can hang your coat there if you like."

He directed me to a line of hooks against a wood paneled wall with perhaps a score of raincoats and fleeces and windbreakers occupying most of them. Below were wellingtons and tennis shoes and boots, most in what looked to be children's sizes. I selected an empty hook from the few remaining and hung up my own soggy trench coat and Fedora.

"Follow me—the kids are in the common room."

He took me up a short hall that opened into a thrift-shop decorated rec room: cozy and nice with mismatched furniture all around and a stone fireplace at the far end of the room. It was an over-large space, with tables for Fussball and pingpong that sat along sliding glass doors that appeared to open onto an enclosed yard.

On the nearest sofa Britt sat next to an adolescent boy of about eighteen or nineteen. The room was otherwise empty. As they stood to greet me, the resemblance between them became unmistakeable.

"McKenzie, this is my brother Pablo," Britt said.

Simultaneously her hands flew into a series of shapes and gestures that I couldn't follow, but which Pablo seemed to respond to. He was a moderately tall youth, filling out from a childhood only just left behind, with a fringe of beard testifying to his first assertions of adulthood. He wore a soccer shirt, jeans and red chucks.

The boy smiled at Britt, and then nodded at me. His hands and arms flew into a similar series of gestures as Britt's had done.

Britt turned to me, "He say's he's very pleased to meet you, and says thank you for helping me."

Pablo undertook another series of gestures, including tugging at an invisible tie and slapping the back of one hand.

I turned to Leonard. "What'd he say?"

"Britt?" Leonard asked, turing to her.

"Wait? You can't understand it?" I asked, a little perplexed. I reckoned a head honcho for a school for the deaf would probably know sign language.

Leonard shook his head. "They have their own sign language," He explained. "It's really quite remarkable. Britt and Pablo are from Guatemala and Pablo was born deaf. It was some backwoods cantonment, and they wouldn't let him go to school or learn to read and write. Pablo didn't even know his own name until after Britt was born."

"When I was little I started talking to him," Britt said. "Like this," she added, and made another series of gestures at Pablo, who smiled.

"I just told him I was explaining how we came up with our 'language.' I was three or four, then, I guess—that's what they tell me, anyway, and Pablo was a few years older and he started making signs at me. We started playing games and stuff, and after a while I started passing on things he'd told me to our mom and dad. Translating, you know."

"You made up a language?"

"I guess," Britt shrugged. "It's just ours, though. Me and Pablo made it up together. No one else understands it."

"He's learning American Sign Language now, thanks to Britt," Leonard said. "If it wasn't for her, I don't know any way we could have opened him up. Not only has she helped with getting Pablo to communicate with us, but she's been paying his tuition here, too. She's an amazing kid. We don't see enough of Britt now, though, do we Pablo?" This time Leonard made some gestures at Pablo which appeared to be a little more conventional—the American Sign Language Leonard had referred to before, I assumed.

Pablo scowled for a second, like he was trying to piece together what Leonard had "said," and then clicked and smiled and gestured back.

"He says he wishes Britt could live here, too."

Britt smiled uncomfortably and didn't say anything.

A stunning realization washed over me all at once, then—the obvious one, of course, and I reckoned for the first time I really did have a pretty good idea what was going through Britt's head. I flushed red at all my earlier assessments of her. Britt had worked for Dennis back in Alberta to score money for her brother's tuition at this school for the deaf. It couldn't have been cheap, and a sanctuary like this for those like Pablo was no doubt supported, like everything else in the world, with dollars.

I didn't know what the rest of their backstory was, but it had to be pretty rough.

"Look, I'll leave you guys to it," Leonard said. "You want any coffee or anything, Mr. McKenzie? Kitchen's still open for a bit?"

I said I rather would like a cup of coffee if that wasn't too much trouble—it had been a long day and a cold wet night, and the aroma of a steaming cup of Joe sounded just about right. Not least 'cause it was plainly apparent that I'd need to keep my wits about me for a few more hours. Leonard disappeared upstairs, and Britt and I sat down on the couch opposite Pablo.

"Mom and dad took us to the U.S., McKenzie. Cross country across Central America, over the Rio Grande at night. That old chestnut," she

258

added, ironically. "I was too young to really remember any of it, of course—I have flashes from time to time, you know, like we all do with our little kid memories, but I guess the gangs were after Pablo back in Guatemala. He was deaf, couldn't communicate, he was strange in a small town—mom and dad got us out of there with our skins. We made our way to New York and Pablo eventually got asylum status in the U.S. 'cause of the gang stuff, but the fuckers were going to deport *me*. Can you believe it. I was a little kid for heaven's sake. Mom and dad knew we couldn't be separated: if I got deported, Pablo would be alone again. And the worst part was, I could never come back. That's the deal, you know. If the Americans deport you, you can *never* come back. I was only six by then, McKenzie. Six! Worse, if I left voluntarily—*at the age of six*, Pablo could never come visit me in Guatemala, 'cause it would call into question his asylum status. They'd say, 'well the gangs aren't a problem enough for you to stay away from Guatemala, so...'"

"So your mum and dad took you to Canada so you two could stay together," I said, filling in the rest of it.

"Right you are, McKenzie," Britt sighed. "You make it to the Challenger's Round. Somehow mom and dad got us up here. But before they could make the trip themselves, the American's deported them. They sent them back to Guatemala."

"Can you get 'em up here to Canada?"

Britt's voice got real small then. "We haven't heard from them McKenzie. It been a lot of years now."

She let that sink in. It was a lot to digest, but I really wanted to know more. Why couldn't the American immigration courts or Homeland Security or whoever decided things have let the family stay together. A deaf boy and his little sister who was the only one who could talk to him? Separating them? Separating them from their parents? What the hell! It was cruel on the face of it, but almost worse than that it seemed willfully arbitrary. It made no sense.

And what was their status here in Canada? I knew I could help, and I needed to know more. Why hadn't Britt told me any of this before?

"Okay, Britt, we're going to fix that. Do you believe me?—"

"Look, McKenzie, I appreciate it, I do. But we got bigger problems right now. Like, for one, they're after you for murder, and Annie's under lock and key."

"Okay. Right," I agreed, remembering the force-five shit-storm we had just sailed into. "Well, we'll have figure that out first I guess...for starters just tell me what happened."

"They showed up at the door looking for you. The RCMP guys. There were two of them and you were who they were interested in, not Annie and me. Tell you the truth, they were pretty surprised to find us there. They weren't prepared for that at all—they really didn't know what to do with us at first."

"But you got away?"

"Those Mounties are just too damn nice. When they came to the apartment I thought it was you, right—that you had forgotten your keys or something, and I just opened the door right up like a dummy. Fresh-man mistake. Slap me one for that, lawyer-man. And there were these two guys with trench coats standing there, and they flashed their badges and said they were looking for you. I stalled them for a bit, and I guess that's when Annie hid the phone—you found it, obviously."

"Yeah. That was smart to stow it. I found the blood in your guys bedroom, too."

"Annie made a break for it. Probably just to distract them from her hiding the phone. She cut her knee when they dragged her out from behind the bed, but nothing too serious."

"My god that little girl's quick," I said.

"But here's the best part: after they got Annie, but while we were still at the apartment, I told them I had to go to the bathroom. And when they said okay I just walked out of the living room, and instead of going down the hall to the bathroom I just walked out the front door. Just walked right out. When the heard the door latch they must have thought it was the bathroom door that had closed, 'cause they didn't come looking around for me for whole minutes..."

"My god, you and Annie are a pair."

Suddenly Britt's expression darkened. "But I left her."

"Don't worry about that," I said quickly. "You did absolutely the right thing. We'll get Annie back. It wouldn't have been any good if the Mounties had gotten you, too."

"Maybe she'll escape," Britt suggested, brightening.

I held on to that hopeful notion for a moment. She'd done it before, of course. If history was a guide, Annie would definitely take the opportunity to duck out if it came her way. "No," I concluded reluctantly. "The RCMP ain't New Mexico child services."

"So what do we do, then?"

We both went quite for a bit, trying to think it out. Leonard came back in with a couple of cups of coffee and a plate of cookies. "It's lights out. Other kids are down, so we try to keep it quiet, if that's okay."

"We'll keep it down," I whispered.

Leonard shook his head. "You guys are fine. Just wanted to give you a heads up."

"Thanks for the coffee."

Britt and I returned to noodling our problem. "Look," I finally said. "Let's parse this out. What has really changed?"

"Everything."

"Nothing. The plan all along has been to get Annie and her mum back together. It almost doesn't matter that the RCMP has our girl. The calculus is the same. If we get Annie's mum out of the lockup down in Tacoma and up here to Canada, problem solved. Michelle's done nothing wrong. They'll have to hand Annie over to her own mum—it'll be a mother and child reunion with the official blessing and imprimatur of the Mounties."

"C'mon, McKenzie. No way it's gonna be that easy. They'll put her in foster care before that happens, and then there's a whole bunch of official crap to undo. She's probably been fobbed off on someone already. It's what they always do," she added, gloomily.

"Maybe we have some time, though. I mean, you said those Mounties didn't expect to find you and Annie at the apartment. It's just me they were after." I had a sudden flash. "And if Annie gave 'em a fake name, then it might take them awhile to connect all the warrants and Amber Alerts back in New Mexico to us. They won't know where she came from or who she is—they won't know what to do with her."

"You're dreaming. Like they're not going to put you an Annie together in about a ten seconds."

She was right. Canadian law enforcement was connected to the States via a robust umbilicus. Even I knew that. I flashed back on Mrs. Pearson and Homeland Security's amazing knowledge of her mental health status, information that seemed to go well beyond simple law enforcement data. We had to assume the U.S. and Canada would share everything: the Amber alert, any warrants, the shootout back in Santa Fe, the ICE detainer and probably our earlier interactions with the Border Patrol. If all had not yet been revealed to the RCMP, it soon would be.

And by the same token, in all likelihood the American authorities were soon to find I was up here in B.C.

"…And even if they don't connect you and Annie here with the you and Annie from back in New Mexico," Britt went on, "So what. They'll still hand her off in the meantime—to foster care, or some institution. The Mounties aren't in the business of taking care of children. Not for any length of time." From her tone I reckoned Britt knew whereof she spoke.

"Well, we've just got to head 'em off before that happens."

"So how are you going to do that, lawyer-man? And don't forget, you're wanted for murder now. I mean, that's as big a problem as Annie. What the hell are we going to do about that!"

Murder. The kid was right. Things had lit up into such a major trash can fire that the charge that actually brought the RCMP into our lives had briefly slipped my mind. The hell of it was, I really was a murderer now.

Britt must have seen the look on my face. "You didn't kill him, McKenzie. I mean, you actually did kill him, I guess. You shot him and he died. But it was self defense. I saw it and so did Annie."

"No. I'm the problem," I said. "There's a big bright target on me now." I started to contemplate all the practical difficulties that suggested. Movement for one. If I got stopped for so much as a parking violation they'd run my license and that'd be it. And what about Michelle's hearing: if the CBP didn't snag me when I tried to cross the border on the way down, it was pretty damn likely there'd be Marshall's waiting for me with handcuffs at immigration court in Seattle. One thing we did know: the cat was half out of the bag—and time was not on our side.

Time was not on our side.

"Okay," I began, needing to nutshell for my own benefit: "One, we need to get Annie out of custody quick so she don't get handed off to foster care. Or at least keep the RCMP from surrendering her to some other person or entity for the next few days. Two, I need to cover Michelle's hearing down in Seattle immediately, and get her back up here to Canada as soon as possible. Three, once that's done, we gotta connect Annie and her mum up here in Vancouver, and get the Mounties to surrender our girl, step back and get out of the picture."

"And four," Britt added, "You' re radioactive and have to avoid getting pinched before we can accomplish the three aforementioned tasks. Easy peasy."

"Yeah," I agreed, sarcastically. Easy peasy. "Tomorrow I'll call and set up Michelle's hearing.   In the meantime, we'll lay real low so as to not draw unwanted attention here. As for crossing the border...," I hesitated for a moment. "When the time comes, we'll just have to trust to luck and providence, I guess. If we move fast, I'm guessing I can at least get across the border going south. I'm not so crazy about what might be waiting for me at immigration court down in Seattle, though."

"And Annie?"

"At this exact moment the RCMP's maybe the biggest problem," I agreed.

"So what do we do?"

That's when the lightbulb went on.

"Well, we have something they want," I said. "And they have something we want."

"What are you talking about?"

"It's me they're after. They want to charge me with murder, right? And we want 'em to hold up doing anything with Annie for a few days."

"I don't follow."

I couldn't believe she wasn't getting this.

"How 'bout a trade," I suggested.

The scales fell and Britt looked at me like I was nuts.

VI. The Big Switcheroo

Chapter 38 – The Hearing

ANNIE CALLED 'EM BEARDED BUMPS: the great green hills of the Pacific Northwest. Bearded bumps because the rain populated 'em so thick with timber you could hardly see the water gushing off their sides in steep muscular falls, braided torrents in wet weather that thrashed heavily down the steep slopes to plunge onto the shoulders, and drain into wide culverts that ran under the roadways. Lush and lively both north and south of the border, the Bearded Bumps are really something to look at—especially whenever you're driving between Vancouver and Seattle.

Except I *couldn't* see 'em 'cause I was driving in the dark.

Dawn comes late in December to these northern climes, and Michelle's hearing was set for nine, so I found myself parking the truck at a still dusky eight o'clock in the morning in some underground lot on Fourth Street. It left me a good hour to spare to find my way back to the high rise where Seattle Immigration Court was located, and twenty minutes later a rainy monochromatic dawn was only just coming on as I found the place. Before I went upstairs, though, I reckoned it was entirely appropriate to take care of breakfast—have one last meal, as it were. A quick review of the premises confirmed there wasn't much on offer, so I settled myself into a wrought iron chair at a precious round glass table in the coffee shop in the Minnie-Mall that occupied the first floor of the building. I bagged a cup of coffee and a scone, and noted that the breaking day didn't bring with it much in the way of additional light. The unrelenting shower came down outside and I slowly sipped my dark caffeinated brew and let the dull tattoo on the window relax me.

I do love the smell of coffee, if I haven't said it before, and held the ceramic cup up to my muzzle to fully enjoy the aroma. This is one of the few pleasures of life I'll be able to enjoy just as well in jail, I thought without irony, and glanced up at the clock on the wall. There were ten minutes or so left before I had to head upstairs, allowing time for security, to find the courtroom, and scout out the scene before the hearing started. For the hundredth time I mentally worked my way through what the day's likely agenda was going to include. Ostensibly, it was simple—we were here to get the court's stamp of approval on the voluntary removal of my client, Michelle Chretien. Straight forward enough. But in reality, the whole thing stunk. The notion that a hearing was necessary for this simple procedure, that the process for an illegal immigrant who simply wanted to leave the country, a Canadian who just wanted to be shown the door, required a hearing seemed odd in and of itself. Truly suspicious. Pretextual. Maybe it wasn't; maybe this was all on the level. But prepare for the worst, I always say. And the notion that my Canadian identity had somehow come unglued down here as well as back in the Great White North, that my cover was finally slipping and the powers-that-be had set up this hearing as a ruse to get their hands on me when I showed up in Court today seemed all but certain. To be fair, I'd had a good run. I'd stayed one step ahead of the authorities for far longer than I had any right to expect. But now things were unraveling and law enforcement down here in America may well have matched blameless, innocent Canadian Bob McKenzie with his evil New Mexico twin. Probably had. In any event, I assessed the likelihood that I had a burley deputized welcoming committee waiting for me upstairs at this very moment as being very good.

But once again, there was nothing for it. The only way back for me now was forward. The only path to my old life in New Mexico—to my

268

daughter, my job, my retirement—was through whatever ordeal was waiting for me upstairs.

Trial by fire, baby—on the thirty-eighth floor in a room with no windows...

Oddly enough, I felt remarkably calm, almost complacent about it. Part of me had known all along that this would probably happen, that they'd eventually catch up with me. The fact we'd all jointly made it this far seemed truly incredible. And no matter what happened, if today's results included nothing more than getting Michelle out of the gears of this infernal machine, back to Canada and reunited with her little girl, that would just be alright. And if the collateral damage was to be me, so be it.

This is probably what those Freedom Riders felt like, I thought to myself idly, with melodramatic self-importance. Back in the sixties. Those guys knew they were walking into a dark fate—that they were going to get hauled off the buses or shoved from their lunch counter stools to be horribly, viciously beaten by racist southern mobs—chains, tear gas, dogs, truncheons, fire hoses, the whole bit—yet they went into it voluntarily; and they did it not so much with a smile as with a strange beatific calm...

Yeah, this was exactly like that.

I quaffed down the rest of my coffee, took a polite and rather unnecessary pee in the first floor men's room, washed my hands quite thoroughly, then climbed into an elevator with a crew of oblivious wage slaves wearing their bland business casual: GAP, JC Penney, REI. Together we jointly headed up and out of the lobby. I was a few minutes early, but why wait, after all? No sense putting off the inevitable. Rip the band-aid off! that's my motto. And in any case, while I didn't know for sure if the bastards had me, whether they were waiting for me upstairs or not, I still wanted this unpleasantness over with as quickly as possible.

But sooner than I would have liked the elevator doors slid aside, and I stepped forward onto the cracked and yellowing Linoleum of the thirty-eighth floor.

269

As they closed behind me, I oriented myself, and across the way spotted the familiar words, "Department of Justice," spelt out in big letters on the door just opposite. Down below in slightly smaller type were stenciled the words "Immigration Court." The door hadn't changed much since the last time I was there, though there was a child's handprint at knob level. That was new. Peanut butter, I was guessing. I took a deep breath and approached the grimy, dirt-smudged, hand-printed entryway, opened the thing and stepped through.

The foyer was every bit as unlovely as I remembered it: Florescent lights, faded white paint, dog-eared informational posters, and of course the usual long ramp of the sad and slump-shouldered, the hopeless people waiting to proceed through the chute into the metal detector. Only this time there were more of them than I remembered from my last visit—so many more, each in various stages of undress, taking off belts and shoes and jackets, putting wallets and keys into the blue plastic bowls provided for the purpose. Piles of purses and backpacks and briefcases disappeared into the x-ray machine, and the line marched forward. I praised myself for having allowed extra time for this. My turn came soon enough though, and despite the fact that I expected the same extremely thorough attention others appeared to be getting, instead they simply waived me through without ceremony, apparently once again judging by my clothes and demeanor that I was a respectable member of The Establishment. They didn't bring out The Wand and didn't even ask to see my Bar card.

The sons-of-bitches may have been on to me, I reflected, but word obviously hadn't made it down to their gatekeepers.

Once inside security I retrieved my Fedora, overcoat and briefcase from the conveyor belt and looked around. My god, there were so many people. Could there have been this many when I was here before? Had I just not noticed? They stood alone and in pairs, some in larger groups; they filled the halls and open spaces; they milled or sat or stood with their lawyers; they filled the benches, conversing about what was coming up, commiserating with family members or calming their children. Some looked scared, some resigned, some just blank. And I wondered if this, after all, was the truth of it—that up 'till now I had just missed the fact that the population of this temporal purgatory was truly numberless. Indeed, the whole world seemed to be here: it was a goddam United Nations—every shape, size, age; every nationality; every hair color; every religion.

And all of us endlessly waiting. It was our sole shared experience. And that might have been the worst of it, too, really: the waiting...

There are some who have been locked up for five years. Ten years. Longer, even...

As I made my way through the crush, I decided that that was pretty fucked up—that the waiting really could be the worst of it. Because the exile at the end of the process was pretty bad. I'd had a taste of that, too, as you may recall. But having now had some practical experience with the matter, having been a participating observer in this sad shadow world, so to speak, I'd have to say it really wasn't the exile *per se* that had aged my heart and had already started my hair toward the grayer end of the spectrum. It was the uncertainty. It was having my future tossed up for grabs. And it was knowing that our ultimate fates were being decided by a system that was not just arbitrary, but mindlessly cruel, probably incompetent and completely unaccountable. By all appearances, *no one was watching the shop.*

CBP will do what CBP will do...

And of course it was not just us; thousands—millions of people in this zombie system were being eaten up by a machine that was completely automated. Soul-less. Baffling. Impenetrable and unsupervised.

Who's managing the managers, Madstone had asked me once an age ago about our own sorry Agency. I'd had no good answer then.

I shoved my way between the crushing masses in the hallway, rebounding between bodies, briefcase in one hand, coat and Fedora in the other. I stepped around a mother juggling two toddlers, wound my way between another man and two women, and advanced myself toward the docket sheet posted on the wall: an eight-and-a-half by eleven computer printout which announced where each person's court call was going to be held. I ran my finger down the vertical column:

271

Chretien, Michelle: Bond Hearing, Courtroom Three - 9:00 a.m.

Courtroom Three, the only one with a window. Well, that, at least, seemed like a good omen.

I turned, and began shoving my way down the seething hall toward Courtroom Three. So far I'd observed nothing untoward. The burley deputized welcoming committee I'd expected hadn't turned up so far; no U.S. Marshalls or Men-in-Black; no official looking types paying me any attention at all, as it turned out. Perhaps my concerns had been over-blown; maybe much of the paranoia of the last few weeks had been mis-placed. Maybe the Immigration Court really did need to sort of punch Michelle's ticket, as it were; hold a hearing to validate her removal in some more formal way then just saying "okay,...see ya!" After all, who was I to second guess DOJ protocols. I was pretty new to this stuff, after all.

My initial fears calmed and I stood a little more erect, a little more clear eyed as I wound my way through the crowd. Maybe this was work-ing. Maybe this plan would go through without a hitch. And why shouldn't it!

Nothing succeeds like success, and I held my Fedora, and continued my slow motion forward progress.

Courtroom Three had a window just as I remembered, but it was still a closet. Court was already in session, and I scanned the tight room for my client, but couldn't see her anywhere on account of all the heads and shoulders in the sardine gallery confusing the view. Up above, the Judge was taking evidence on some poor soul's removal, and I tried to be as unobtrusive as possible as I looked for a place to light. I locked in on to the one available seat I could see, a place away at the back that was actu-ally next to the window. Once safely ensconced there, I resumed looking over the thick sea of heads for Michelle.

This time I spotted her right away. She was away at the front, on the opposite side of the packed courtroom from me, and not in Detention Center white, either. They'd allowed her to come in Mufti: a green silk blouse and her loose red hair flowing down the back of it was all I could see, on account of her facing forward and being obscured by the many folks in the gallery between her and me.

She quickly turned just then, and looked right at me.

"Are you okay," I mouthed to her across the room.

Her pale white oval face, emerald eyes and freckled cheeks were motionless for a second. Finally she nodded "yes."

We stared at each other a bit longer, and normally I'd have tried to work my way up there next to her for a quick attorney-client confab before our hearing started, but there was really no way to easily approach her. The place was just too packed. And since there was a hearing already in progress I reckoned I'd hold my place until we got called. We had already gone over everything we needed to anyway, and were as prepared as we were ever going to be.

She smiled at me then, and turned back to face the front.

I wasn't sure if we were the next ones up, but the presentation we were sitting in on was practically done, and the subject of it appeared to be a tubby Hispanic guy in his thirties—a father and Mexican National with his American family filling a good part of the gallery. Based on the testimony, his wife and child were U.S. citizens, and the kid had cystic fibrosis; nine years old, and chronically ill. She was there in the Courtroom, the little kid was, and I could just make out her tiny head and the top of her oxygen tank in the front row, two seats away from Michelle.

At that exact moment, some doctor was currently testifying telephonically about the little girl's condition: "...She requires special care, yes," her voice crackled over the speaker-phone. "Daily care, the constant supervision of an adult. Medication to be administered and monitored, of course, not to mention regular and emergency visits to health care professionals. Trips to her GP, the emergency room when necessary..."

"Anything else?"

"Oh, the prescriptions, the cost of care. Yes, I'd say this is an extraordinary family situation. The management of Mona's care, the costs of her treatment are not insignificant."

The Mexican man's defense counsel tapped his chin with a pen. "So, would you say in your expert opinion that removing Mr. Rodriguez from the household would work a particular hardship on the child? On this family?"

The expert witness didn't hesitate. "No question. There is no possible way—or I should say, I cannot imagine one parent alone taking on those tasks. Physically, emotionally. Financially."

"Could Mona's mother reasonably be expected to take on these tasks alone?"

"No. As I said, not without the support of a co-parent. Such a thing would work an extraordinary hardship on any parent or caregiver. And on the child. It's not too much to say we could expect it to have a significantly deleterious effect on Mona's health."

"Removing the father, Mr. Rodriguez from the home would negatively affect her health?"

"To a certainty."

By now, the Judge was nodding. More interestingly, opposing counsel was too. She was a browny-haired DOJ lawyer, cute enough, and serious, and if I wasn't mistaken, judging by her body language and facial expression she appeared to actually be sympathetic to the family's plight.

There's something you don't see every day, I thought to myself. A prosecutor with a heart.

"Anything else, counsel?" the Judge said to Mr. Rodriguez' lawyer.

He shook his head. "No, your Honor."

"Anything else from the DOJ?"

The browny-haired DOJ lawyer shook her head. "No, your Honor."

"Well very good, then. And I'd like to thank both of you for an excellent presentation. You were both prepared, helpful and professional, and it's a pleasure to be able to preside over a hearing like this. And it's also a pleasure to be able to rule for a family," the Judge said, turning to Mr. Rodriguez. "As you know, removal may be denied in the case of exceptional hardship. The statutes and case law are clear that extreme hardship does not mean simply the loss of a parent from the household,

274

or the loss of that parent's earning potential. However, given the extraordinary medical condition of the type your daughter suffers from, removing you from the household to deport you from the country would indeed work a severe hardship of a type that is recognized at law. It is my pleasure to be able to rule that your removal order is reversed. You may stay in the country, Mr. Rodriguez."

There was a gasp in the gallery, as the Rodriguez family realized they had won. A harrowing, protracted and costly ordeal was over, and the dad got to stay.

The Immigration Judge's gavel came down with a splintering crash just then. The Crack! of it split the room.

"Your petition is granted!" he said with a smile. "We'll have a short five minute recess."

Chapter 39 – You Are Free to Go, But . . .

THE SCENE WHICH FOLLOWED was amazing: there had to be about a dozen or more Rodriguezes there, and they all rose, crying, laughing, happy as hell. They surrounded the dad and the mum and the little girl, and slowly exited to the hall *en masse*. I imagined them out there after the doors closed behind 'em, the years of uncertainty come to an end, the hemorrhage of money and time over. They could move on now, this whole immigration horror-show nothing but a memory, and the whole lot of them then off to some local family restaurant to celebrate that fact, to commiserate, laugh and resume their lives.

Of course, the kid still had cystic fibrosis, but one thing at a time, I suppose.

As the DOJ attorney packed her stuff up in the quiet that was left, I marveled that she and the Immigration Judge had seemed almost as happy as the family had been to see Mr. Rodriguez stay. It was a different tone than any I'd ever witnessed at a hearing before. I mean, usually a prosecutor is bitter and vituperative to the very end, never quite so happy as when they are prevailing over a hapless defendant regardless of the justice realized by the proceedings, or the lack of it either. Maybe it was a mark of this uniquely terrible system, I reflected; a system where the law is so completely fucked up even the government lawyers were happy when you could find a way around it.

I threw an involuntary shudder at that, like I'd just looked into the heart of the Universe and for one endless second understood its perfect indifference.

Before I could do much more than that, though, the Immigration Judge had gaveled his Court back into session, and bade the Clerk announce the next contestant: "Michelle Chretien," announced the Clerk, peering about the sea of heads crammed into his walk-in closet of a Courtroom.

"Michelle Chretien," he repeated, and read out her "A" number.

Michelle and I stood, and I began inching my way up toward her, around peoples' knees, between backpacks and briefcases. And now that she was standing I could see she wore a rust-colored silk ascot around her neck, fixed loosely over her breast with a modest gold broach. Together with the silk turquoise top, the colors all together worked really well; they really brought out the light in her face. The face I remembered. She lifted her forearms a bit and touched my arm as I joined her at the front, and with a jolt I realized they had her wearing chains again. This was outrageous. I could hardly believe such a thing was allowed.

"What the f—" I commenced, visibly furious, but before I could speak further the Immigration Judge jumped in.

"Can we please have Ms. Chretien's manacles removed," he said.

"These restraints are standard for master calendars, your Honor," said a woman ICE agent who suddenly popped up out of nowhere. Apparently she had been sitting next to Michelle there in the front row the entire time, acting the custodian to my client's prisoner. (Civil matters my ass.) In support of her grim thesis, she waved around the room behind her.

Prompted, I looked back and couldn't believe I hadn't noticed it before: At least two rows of defendants were seated behind us, all similarly in chains, all probably there for their master calendar hearings.

"Yes, I'm well aware you ICE folks like to keep your charges bound," the Immigration Judge said to her, wearily. "But I don't think anyone in this room seriously fears violence from Ms. Chretien. I would be much obliged if you would please remove her manacles."

The female ICE Agent reflexively went to protest again, but thinking better of it, hesitated, pulled back, and quickly did as she was told. I think she yielded solely out of respect for this particular Immigration Judge, 'cause already I was getting the sense that, sick as it was to contemplate, the twisted rules that governed this place probably did allow for prisoners to be shackled. I guessed that if she'd sustained her protest it was the Immigration Judge who would have had to back down, not the ICE, and then I'd have had the privilege of representing a client in chains.

And as she unlocked the cuffs and released Michelle, I realized the others in the room probably wouldn't be so lucky. And soon they would be appearing in front of the Immigration Judge in chains, with all that implied, too: which is to say if you look like a prisoner, even with the best of intentions everyone including the judge will probably treat you like one—with predictable outcomes.

Michelle's "chaperone" resumed her seat, remaining fully on alert, Michelle's chains held in her fingers and at the ready.

The two of us finally stood at counsel table. The moment had come.

"Appearances, please," the Immigration Judge said.

"Good morning, your Honor," I said with a smile, hoping to catch on to any good feelings that remained from the previous trial. "Robert James McKenzie appearing for respondent Michelle Chretien."

"And Rhonda P. Flemming for the United States," said the DOJ attorney. I snatched a look at her and noted she was a different lawyer than the one who had represented the United States at the last hearing. She was very tall, and not unattractive, but her face was flat. Emotionless.

"Thank you both, counsel," the Immigration Judge said. "Please, please—be seated."

He looked down his nose through tortoiseshell glasses at the docket in front of him. "Apparently we are here for a master calendar for Ms. Chretien." He squinted at the thing a little more. "Or does this say a bond hearing? I'm sorry, Mr. McKenzie, can you help me—is that correct? Do I have this right? Is your client seeking bond in furtherance of her voluntary removal?…"

"That is accurate, your Honor."

"Okay. Good. Well, thank you, counsel. So, backing up a little bit, apparently Ms. Chretien was originally interviewed at the Las Cruces, New Mexico permanent Customs and Border Protection checkpoint several weeks ago. She was determined by the Border Patrol to be a Canadian national…and undocumented…she was detained." He paused, then, continuing to read to himself. "Interesting," he finally said. "Transferred up here from the detention center in El Paso, Texas to the Tacoma Detention Center for reasons which aren't clear…"

He glanced over at the Court Clerk, who perked right up. "Special circumstances, your Honor," the Clerk said.

A wrinkle clouded the Immigration Judge's brow. "Okay," he said, drawing out the word. "But given the fact that she's up here now at the Northwest Detention Center, why isn't her case being heard in the hearing room in the east wing down there in Tacoma? Instead of up here in Seattle? I mean, that's why they *have* an Immigration Court down there in the first place." This time his question was directed at the government's attorney

"Special circumstances, your Honor," she said, without inflection.

At that, the Clerk leaned forward and whispered something to the Immigration Judge that caused him to look at me. This isn't good, thinks I, and felt my guts leap a bit. I didn't have time to think about it much more than that, though.

"Okay, then," the Immigration Judge immediately carried on, sitting back up in his seat. "Well, in any event, as a practical matter we *are* all physically here today, here in my Courtroom, and Ms. Chretien is no doubt anxious to have her situation resolved, so let us proceed. It's what we're being paid for, after all. Mr. McKenzie, does Ms. Chretien contest that she is a Canadian national?"

"No, your Honor. She does not. My client is Canadian who does not hold United States citizenship."

Same could be said for me, I thought ironically.

279

"She does not contest that she is here in the United States without documentation?"

"No she does not, your Honor."

"And she seeks bond?"

"The United States would object to that, your Honor," the tall and emotionless Ms. Flemming suddenly interjected firmly, but without any evidence of actual interest.

"Mr. McKenzie?"

"Your Honor, Ms. Chretien is fully entitled to bond. She does not contest removal, she has no criminal record in the United States, and seeks only to return to her home country. If allowed to do so, she will leave from here today and attend straight to the Canadian border crossing into British Columbia. As such, I would like to move for her release on her own recognizance, pending her immediate and voluntary removal to Canada."

The Immigration Judge turned to the apparently irascible Ms. Flemming. "Counsel?"

"Your Honor, the United States would have to object to that."

"Yes, so you said. But do you have anything to say in response to Mr. McKenzie? His client wants to return to Canada, she has no untoward history in this country, and nothing I have so far heard suggests that upon release she would do otherwise than leave the borders of the United States."

"She is here in this country illegally, your Honor," the DOJ lawyer said, almost robotically. "She is a lawbreaker by her own admission, and by that very fact is not entitled to bond, much less a release on her own recognizance."

I felt anger welling up in my chest as I realized there was no legal argument here—she was simply objecting for the sake of objecting. She knew nothing of my client, had no reason to be concerned about her bonding out, probably couldn't care less one way or the other, and yet out of habit was being bloody minded about it. It was pretty fucked up, if you really want to know. It's one thing to do your job, it's another to be a dick about it.

In any event, the Immigration judge was having none of it. He looked over the tops of his tortoiseshell glasses at the DOJ attorney. "Alright, counsel. So by your logic, no one who comes through my Courtroom would ever be entitled to bond out, or to remove themselves from the country voluntarily."

"Correct, your Honor."

The Immigration Judge's face twisted a bit into something that wasn't exactly disgust. "I'm afraid I don't share your view, Ms. Flemming." He sat back in his seat, and turned to me. "Mr. McKenzie, your motion is granted. Ms. Chretien, you are hereby released on your own recognizance pending your voluntary removal from the United States." He glanced up. "Would two weeks be sufficient time for you to get your affairs in order and leave the country?"

"Your Honor, we will be returning to Canada today."

"I'll allow two weeks," the Immigration Judge said, glancing back down and writing something. "...to allow for any unforeseen eventualities." He looked up again, and smiled. "Ms. Chretien, you are free to go. Get a copy of the Order from the Clerk before you leave," he added.

"Thank you, your Honor," I said, and glanced at Michelle, who was smiling. She never looked so much like her daughter Annie as at that exact moment. Just beyond Michelle, still seated in the front row of the front bench of the Gallery was "Chains," as I'd affectionately christened her ICE guard. It was probably my imagination, but to me Chains now looked sad—sad and deflated, the empty manacles in her hand a bitter reminder to her of what might have been.

"Too bad, Chains," I thought to myself. "Maybe next time."

Though this time there was no gavel, Michelle and I rose to leave. As we did, the Immigration Judge brought me up short: "However, Mr. McKenzie, I'm afraid I have some bad news with regard to yourself..."

Chapter 40 – In Which I Get Pinched

"WELL, I'M FUCKED."

I didn't say it out loud, of course, but that was the exact thought that went through my head, because as you'd expect, I had a pretty good idea exactly what was coming next.

"I'm afraid I've never had anything like this come up before," the Immigration Judge continued, "but are you Robert James McKenzie of Santa Fe New Mexico?" He was frowning, but not with anger. It was puzzlement and curiosity that crossed his brow.

And possibly dismay.

"Yes, your Honor," I said, with as bluff and manly a look as I could muster, though my guts were really churning now.

"Robert James McKenzie?...Robert McKenzie of Santa Fe New Mexico?" he demanded again, unable to believe it.

"As I stated in my appearance before the Court, my name is Robert James McKenzie. I am licensed to practice law before the State Bar of New Mexico, the U.S. District Court for the District of New Mexico, and the Tenth Circuit Court of Appeals. I am a resident of Santa Fe, and am here in Seattle today for the sole purpose of representing my client, Michelle Chretien before the Executive Office of Immigration Review."

Michelle's smile had begun to fade a bit.

The Judge sat silent for a moment, lowering his massive head between mountains of shoulders, and I realized for the first time what kind eyes he had. It's funny how something like that will suddenly hit you. Strands of hair were combed over his broad freckled pate, and the combined effect of it all was the appearance of a good Judge—a man who ruled fairly and controlled his courtroom well. But now we were probably dealing with issues that were out of his hands and beyond his control. Unfortunately for me.

"Well, Mr. McKenzie," he finally said, "Apparently these are yours." He held up a fistful of documents where I could see 'em, each packet folded in thirds like a letter before you put it in the envelope, and an impressive stack they made together, too. He began thumbing through 'em: "These are several warrants for your arrest, Mr. McKenzie, six of them by my count, and—oh! Bit of a surprise, here. A detainer from the ICE." He laughed ironically at that one. "My, my, Mr. McKenzie, it would be truly distressing if I were to learn you yourself were an illegal alien representing the undocumented in my Courtroom."

"No, sir. I would never do that." I reached for my Canadian passport. "I am here in the United State's on a—"

"Take care, Mr. McKenzie," he said, waving me off. "I would not want you to say anything here today that could cause you difficulty later on. And nothing I have seen, including these documents, suggests you have been anything but entirely candid with this tribunal. I have no complaints about your conduct before me today, counsel. However, I'm afraid there are some folks here in the gallery who would like to talk to you further about these warrants."

He laid the stack of 'em, and the detainer, too, carefully down on the desk in front of him. I should have been ashamed, I guess, but I couldn't help take a certain perverse pride in the gargantuan significance of it. If you're going to be a villain you might as well go full Dillinger.

Directly behind me I could hear the bustle of spectators. They were shoving aside to let the people through. I reckoned whoever was moving toward me from behind had been waiting in the back of the gallery for just this moment, big, burly and badges at the ready.

"This is it," thinks I, refusing to look around.

Michelle urgently tugged at my sleeve. "*Monsieur McKenzie!*" she whispered. She had gone from caution to concern, and now full blown alarm.

Quickly, I handed her the keys to the pickup and the parking receipt, shoved 'em tight into her pretty little fist, and whispered urgently, talking fast: "Look, the truck's at an underground lot up on Fourth Street. The address is on the ticket. It's an ancient Chevy, okay. Blue, with a wooden bed. Hail a cab out front and have the driver take you straight there, 'cause if you're seen on the street by any of—"

"But these people here," she whispered, glancing over my shoulder. "What will you do?"

"We talked about this, okay. You have the address in Vancouver, and Britt's waiting for you. She'll explain everything and get you together with Annie."

"What about Annie?"

"She's okay," I emphasized. "And she's in Vancouver. Britt'll take you to where—"

Hard hands suddenly gripped my right shoulder and with cruel efficiency lifted my forearm up into the center of my back from behind like a lever. My captors were on me. Pain screamed in my shoulder, and I lifted up onto my toes in response with an involuntary groan.

The croissant and coffee from earlier climbed up in my throat, and the zip of handcuffs being opened sounded in my ear.

"Mr. Robert James McKenzie," one of the unseen persons behind me started, "You are under arrest. I hereby take you into—"

"Hold it right there!" the Immigration Judge said. I had taken my eyes off him while my arm was being wrenched behind me, and looking back now I saw he had become visibly furious.

"What the *hell* do you think you're doing!" He literally shouted it. "Stand down immediately."

The thug holding tight to my arm was indignant. "Sir, this person is a fugitive from justice. He's—"

"*Stand down!*"

"Have you read those warrants? He is an escapee, your Honor. A kidnapper, *an illegal immigrant, for God's sake!...*"

"Anything else?" I gasped out ironically, giving the goon a gratuitous hip check, though standing on my toes with my arm behind me it was a pretty weak bump. He ground my fist up even higher into my back, paying me back with sufficient interest to make my shoulder scream again.

At that, the Immigration Judge took his gavel in one massive fist, and by the look of him was getting ready to use it on my captor: "I've had several firsts in my Courtroom today, sir, but this one takes the cake—seizing an attorney while he is actively engaged in the representation of a client! It is not something I'm willing to permit."

"I am required to take him into custody."

The Immigration judge started to stand. "Not while you're before this tribunal you're not!—"

In the back, the sound of the door to the Courtroom opening: "Your Honor," cried a familiar voice. "I may be of assistance here."

I turned to the rear: God bless the man—He had come! Halle-*fucking*-leulia. It was Madstone!

Chapter 41 – Madstone Saves the Day

I'D CALLED THE SONOVABITCH THE NIGHT BEFORE, but neither one of us reckoned he'd be able to make it here to Seattle in time for the hearing. The fucker must have found a red-eye flight or something. It was enough to make you believe in miracles.

The bent bastard stood in the doorway, wrecked hand gripping a twisted walking cane, his breath undoubtedly smelling of liquor. The Immigration Judge, Michelle Chretien, my captor and his two associates all turned to look, bringing the instant proceedings to a greasy halt.

Once all eyes were on him, Madstone began stepping painfully up the center aisle, the wet Seattle climate no doubt playing hell with his arthritis. He was a great lawyer, Madstone was, with a true master's sense of the theatric. Everybody just waited. He was that kind of guy, you see. He didn't have charisma or charm, exactly, but somehow Madstone did dominate a room, no question. He was tall and lanky and bent, and he always came heavy.

By the time he was standing in front of the Immigration Judge, it had become his show all the way. At least for the moment.

"Your Honor, I apologize for the interruption," he began, slightly breathless (whisper if you want to be heard, he always told me). "If I may, I'm an attorney from New Mexico, and I represent Mr. McKenzie."

Madstone stated his name for the court reporter then, and stood as straight before the Immigration judge as his twisted, broken chassis would allow.

The Judge gently set his gavel down, though his jaw was still out. "Well, Mr. Madstone, you just saved me having to start throwing down contempt citations and possibly worse."

"Your Honor, I am truly glad of that," Madstone said. He was always respectful as hell of the Court. Any court. A real old school gentleman.

"At the same time your appearance for Mr. McKenzie has created something of an interesting legal conundrum."

"How so, your Honor?"

"You are entering your appearance for Mr. McKenzie, are you not?"

"Correct."

"But Ms. Chretien is the party before the Court today. A party who is in turn represented by that same Mr. McKenzie you now speak for."

"Yes."

"So you represent him? You represent Mr. McKenzie? You speak for Mr. McKenzie? An attorney who is currently engaged at this very moment in the active representation of someone else?"

"That is accurate, your Honor."

"Okay. Just wanted to make sure."

"I represent Mr. McKenzie, who is in turn representing Ms. Chretien, who is herself the party before this tribunal."

The old man sighed, and looked at the six of us—me and Michelle and Madstone, as well as my two guards, who I still couldn't see, and another who was with 'em—her I could just see out of the corner of my eye, and she looked to be a business woman in a short skirt and a long jacket. There was no question but that she was in charge of their little party.

The Judge turned to the Court Clerk: "Sam, are we still on the record?"

"Yes, your Honor."

"Okay. Well, then. Time to cut this odd Gordian knot. Let us all be clear: first—this is *my* Courtroom. I am not about to let law enforcement of any kind come in here and start seizing lawyers while they are advocating for their clients. That said, it has been brought to my attention that several warrants have been issued for the arrest of Mr. McKenzie, and there seems to be no question or doubt that the Robert James McKenzie named in the warrants is the Mr. McKenzie standing here before me today—and he, apparently, is your client, Mr. Madstone." He spared a glance in Madstone's direction at that, then took a long moment to contemplate the ridiculous situation. "I think where we are here," he finally decided, "is I need to conclude the proceeding Mr. McKenzie is involved in. Then Mr. McKenzie and his entourage—including yourself, Mr. Madstone—need to remove yourselves from my Court and sort this out elsewhere. These warrants and the issues they present are clearly outside my jurisdiction, and the matters involving Mr. McKenzie are not presently in front of me."

"I would have no objection to that, your Honor," Madstone said.

"We can take Mr. McKenzie into custody just as easily out in the hall," one of the knuckleheads behind me said.

"At that point it would be none of this Court's business," the Judge continued. "And with regard to Ms. Chretien, there simply remains the matter of my entering an order, and—"

"Your Honor," Madstone piped up, "I'm very sorry to interrupt, and I have no objection to concluding Ms. Chretien's hearing. However, before we adjourn, and pursuant to Rule 34, I'd like to move the Court to take a short moment and identify for the record the other parties to the unfortunate incident."

"Why?" demanded of the woman in the short skirt and the long jacket. "The Judge just told us to leave."

"An unfortunate incident is occurring here regarding my client," Madstone said coolly. "And I will almost certainly be identifying these three persons in our subsequent lawsuit."

"That's ridiculous," the woman said.

288

By turning my head as far to the right as possible, I could just make out her legs. They were sheathed in white stockings of the sort nuns wear, making them look like plastic prosthetics.

"Good catch, Mr. Madstone. We do want to have a complete record. Please release Mr. McKenzie, sir," he said to the man behind me. "We'll start with you. Identify yourself for the record."

The pressure on my arm was suddenly released, and my hand freed. Apparently putting the proceedings back into some kind of on-the-record context had a salutary effect on the thug. It's funny how shining a little light on people can change their attitude. Or their behavior, at least. I stretched out my elbow and slowly rotated my shoulder bone to loosen it out.

"My name is Brad Whimple, your Honor," the man said, "and I'm a deputized officer with—"

"Why do you need to know his name," the woman cut in. She was looking laser-beams at the Immigration Judge.

"Because you have placed yourselves before my tribunal," he said mildly, "and because I have ordered you to state your identities for the record."

"You have no authority over me."

"You've clearly not spent much time in Court, young lady," he said with a patient smile that did not involve his eyes.

She snorted with indignation. "I'll have you know I've testified before hundreds of administrative custody hearings, and never once—"

"Enter your name for the record, please," he said, obviously underwhelmed with her verbal resume and growing impatient.

"Julia Barnes," she finally admitted. "I'm deputy manager of district six child services department in Santa Fe, New Mexico. And this man," she was pointing at me of course, "kidnapped one of our charges."

"That is not correct," Madstone said, calmly. "And I have a Writ here to prove it."

"Annie Chretien is ten years old," the woman said, pretending Madstone didn't exist. "And was in the custody of Child Services on October 25th when Mr. McKenzie here kidnapped her. In *my* custody!"

"Again, that is not correct. First of all, young Ms. Chretien is nine years old. But of greater significance, she was provably not in the custody of Child Services on the night you describe. In fact, Child Services—in the person of Ms. Barnes, here—had actually lost her the night before. Indeed, her Agency's incompetence put at hazard of extreme danger the daughter of the senior Ms. Chretien, present here next to me, and for reasons unknown—"

"That's a lie!" Julia Barnes of Santa Fe District Six Child Services shouted. "I have *never* lost a charge."

"You don't have her now, do you?"

"Of course not," she spat. "Annie Chretien ran away. She escaped!—"

Madstone rolled his eyes in classic cross-examining lawyer fashion. "Ran away? Is that it? Really? Escaped? A moment ago you said my client kidnapped her. Now which is it? Did she run away or was she kidnapped?"

"He did it, he kidnapped—I mean she…first she ran away, but then he…"

"Was little nine-year-old Annie Chretien in your custody the night she disappeared from the Santa Fe police station, or not?" Madstone asked, wearily.

"No."

"Has she been in the physical custody of Child Services at any time between then and now?"

"It doesn't matter. Child Services has legal custody."

"How can your agency have legal custody when they don't have physical custody?"

"As you well know, Mr. Madstone, and as a matter of family and domestic relations law Child Services can have legal custody even over a child that has fled."

"You do not have custody."

"We do."

"That is not correct. The girl's mother is right here. She can testify her daughter is safely at home, in Canada. Annie Chretien is not in your

290

custody, legal or physical—nor has she been for some time. In point of fact, your agency's claim to custody has been flawed from the outset, hasn't it, Ms. Barnes?"

"This is nonsense, your Honor," she blustered. "There is the warrant for the arrest of Mr. McKenzie, right there. Right on the desk in front of you. He broke the law by taking Annie Chretien, and removing her from the state of New Mexico. God know what he's done to her while she was in his control."

A gasp ran through the Courtroom.

"Yes, that's right," she said, addressing the gallery, which as any experienced lawyer will tell you is a real freshman mistake. "He is a sick, perverted criminal who belongs under arrest."

"Please address your comments to the bench," the Immigration Judge cautioned her, looking vaguely amused. "And that is neither here nor there with regard to this Court. As I told you Ms. Barnes, I am not in the business of enforcing arrest warrants. Once I get your names properly in the record, I shall thank you for your time, and ask that you remove yourselves. As the bartenders are known to say, you don't have to go home, but you can't stay here."

"Thank you, your Honor," Madstone said, "Yes. And I would add, for Ms. Barnes' benefit, I hold two writs in my own hand here, and one of them withdraws warrants for Mr. McKenzie's arrest on that score."

Let me see that!" She snatched the document from Madstone's weak hand and commencing to examine the thing.

"Ms. Barnes actions this day smack of false imprisonment and defamation at a minimum," he continued. "Adding that to her and her Agency's incompetence with regard to the management of young Annie Chretien, I'd say they have much to answer for."

Julia Barnes looked flummoxed. The Immigration Judge was beaming. "I assume the other document in your hand withdraws the other warrants for Mr. McKenzie's arrest?"

"That is correct, your Honor. The City of Santa Fe wisely decided not to pursue the matter. The events of 25 October proved to be more problematic than they at first thought."

291

"There's still the detainer," snarled the nasty from Child Services. "Robert James McKenzie's an illegal!"

"This detainer is directed to law enforcement," the Immigration judge shrugged. "If Mr. McKenzie is ever taken into custody, the Santa Fe police may decide to hold on to him for ICE. But as for today—this Court will do what this Court will do. Mr. McKenzie, Ms. Chretien, you are free to go.

"The three of you, stay here," he added, indicating Ms. Barnes and her two goons. "Our business is not done yet."

Chapter 42 – Drinks on Elliott Bay

"ANOTHER VICTORY FOR LAWYERS WITHOUT BORDERS," I said, and instantly regretted it. I still had to tell Michelle about Annie's situation, and though we'd just gotten past a couple of big hurdles it wasn't time for self-congratulation and levity just yet. Nowhere near.

"Where to?" the cabbie finally asked, not wanting to drive randomly around all afternoon.

"Salty's," I said, with a look at Madstone, who indicated his approval. "The one over in West Seattle."

Without a word, our guy turned the cab around, and headed west along the coast of Elliott Bay.

"Okay, I need to tell you some things," I said, shifting in the back seat so I could look directly at Michelle. I hesitated, and then decided to pull the band-aid right off. "The RCMP got Annie. But listen, she's *okay*. She's in Vancouver and she's okay. And the plan for us is pretty much the same—"

"Monsieur McKenzie, where is my daughter?"

"Let me explain. Britt's been in touch with the RCMP, and they know you're on your way back to Canada. And that's good—that's a good thing. We may have a few more legal hoops to jump through, but the result's going to be the same. When you get there, we should be able to get them to surrender Annie to you."

293

"I thought she was safe with you."

"I thought so too," I said, any remaining feeling of triumph from our recent success in immigration court fully squelched by this stark reminder that I'd lost my client's nine-year old daughter. "I have no excuse—I didn't see this coming and I should have been prepared for it." I described then the events of that night: coming home to an empty apartment, getting the call from Britt, crossing over into West Van, connecting with Britt at the School for the Deaf. "Your girl's still in Canada," I said. "She's in the custody of the Mounties and has been for the last few days. But Britt's been in contact with them, and alerted them to your arrival. As a matter of law, once you have entered Canada—"

"I am not worried about the RCMP."

"Yes. I know."

"My concern is her father. If the RCMP have Annie, they will attempt to notify her father, will they not?"

"Yes, I expect they will. They may already have done so. But it's not first come, first served. Like I said, Britt's alerted them to your arrival and we are scheduled to meet with them at the RCMP office in Vancouver tonight. I'm not saying we don't have a few hurdles to get over yet, but at least it's not a race."

I didn't bother to mention that the quid pro quo, the reason for my confidence, the reason Mounties had agreed not to dispose of Annie until Michelle was back in country and able to defend her parental rights was me. I had agreed to turn myself in. I would surrender to the RCMP to face charges for the murder of Denis DuBois so long as the RCMP agreed to hang fire on Annie's custody issues at least until then. Britt had made the arrangements, and given 'em no more information than that I'd be there by nine o'clock tonight. This night. They'd grumbled about it, of course, but in the end there was really no choice for 'em. They had agreed, and they were Mounties so I knew I could trust 'em. Of course, there was no way for Madstone or Michelle to know anything about this, and I wasn't about to tell 'em. For one thing, it might spoil lunch.

Indeed, traffic had been light, and already we found ourselves pulling up in front of Salty's seafood restaurant It was well before noon and the parking lot was largely empty. Inside my jacket pocket I felt the reassuring bulge of my old smart-phone—Smart-Phone No. 1 I'd taken to calling it—fully charged now and ready to use. I reckoned spending twenty, thirty minutes to eat, debrief with Madstone, and to check in with Britt back in Canada to let her know we were right on schedule would be fully justifiable. Michelle and I'd have plenty of time left to get across the border and up to Vancouver before nine. Plus, this might be my last meal as a free man for a while, so I might as well make it a good one. I paid off the cabbie, and minutes later we were seated by a window looking out on Elliott Bay, the skyline of Seattle bracketed by the Space Needle at one end and Smith Tower at the other.

A light rain had returned, but the view beyond the plate glass was well worth the price of admission: the skyline across the water remained clearly visible, with ferries coming and going across the grey waves; below us, a clutter of kayakers braved the returning drizzle, and bobbed and paddled their way up the coast, past the wet deck of Salty's empty outdoor seating area and off toward parts unknown. The wood planking outside was slick with water, reflected the grey-white sky and at one end the lone form of a seagull perched atop a fat log pier.

Steady drops endlessly dimpled the water's surface, but despite the returning rain, the day had brightened somewhat. The waitress arrived and commenced to take our lunch orders.

"Blackened salmon and a Red Hook for me," says I, and Michelle ordered the same. Madstone went for a cup of chowder and crab cakes. And a pint of Red Hook.

"Madstone – thanks, man," I said, after our waitress scudded off, lifting a toast to the man. He tried to wave me off, but I was having none of it. "If it wasn't for you I'd be in the Hoosegow right now. Seriously. How the hell did you get here in time, anyway?"

Madstone was downing his beer like a man truly in need. I knew his to be, like mine, a thirst beyond quenching, but at length he placed his empty glass on the table, and neatly patted his lips dry with the linen napkin. "Private plane," he said. "My own plane, that is. It took all bloody night. But the getting here wasn't the hardest part. The hardest part was those arrest warrants. After we talked, the more pissed I got about it. The fact that they wouldn't quash those things until you came back to Santa Fe and turned yourself in was utter bullshit." He glanced at his empty glass, looking mildly surprised to find that he had already drained it.

"Goddamit, McKenzie!" he almost spat the words, "we had films of those knuckleheads shooting at you and the little girl, and the DA knew how fucky that was, and so did the cops. It was those idiot Border Patrol agents who did the deed, but all of it took place on City property; all of it went down at a Santa Fe police station. It all happened in the presence of, and under the supervision of the City of Santa Fe PD. So Border Patrol or no, you and the girl have a lawsuit against the City first and foremost. And that liability lawsuit shit-rifle was pointed right at their chest and they *still* wouldn't drop the charges against you!"

"They reckoned if I came in from the cold in chains I'd look guilty, right?"

"Exactly right. That's all it was. And correspondingly it'd make them look quite solid. Santa Fe's boys in blue frog-hopping another orange jump-suited slime ball off the streets and into the courtroom. Hurrah, right? Your mug shot would probably make the front page, and that would define this transaction. Until we filed our lawsuit, of course. But by then no one's watching. The best we could hope for is two years from now there'd be a page two story below the fold about how the City had to settle a lawsuit for wrongful arrest or some such bland thing for an undisclosed amount. Those fuckers knew damn well knew it'd be old news by then, the settlement money wouldn't be coming out of their pockets anyway, and what people would actually remember out of this whole thing, the only thing they would remember, would be that first photograph of you in chains."

"That is cynical as hell," I agreed with a chuckle.

Madstone frowned at that. And say what you will about the guy by the way: he might be a drunk, and he liked the ladies maybe a little too much, but he was still moral as hell. Injustice and dishonesty didn't sit well with Madstone, and once he got the wind at his back on something like this there was really no talking to him. His character was rock solid and he had a spine of pure titanium; it's just the way he was built. How he survived in state government, I have no idea.

"No," he continued, "You're dead right. They wouldn't quash the arrest warrants until you came back to New Mexico and turned yourself in and it was for the sole purpose of setting up the optics—making them look good and you look bad. At least for the foreseeable future. I swear to god, McKenzie, it really had me spitting nails."

"Hold that thought, Madstone," I said, turning to Michelle. "I should have done this sooner." I pulled out "Smart Phone No. 1" and handed it to her. "Here, would you mind calling Britt," I said, pulling up the number. "Let her know we're on our way. Britt's worked as hard as anyone to make this happen, and she's been a good friend to Annie. I'd really dig it if you guys connected."

"It should be working, I charged it up last night," I added. She smiled, and withdrew to one of the many vacant tables to call the one partner to our joint enterprise she hadn't met yet. At the same time our waitress brought me and Madstone more beers.

More beers. The secret to a happy life.

"Anyway," Madstone continued, "Long story short, I worked myself into such a lather just thinking about it that I couldn't sleep. I couldn't read or sit still, so I just started writing. I was up until dawn and wound up putting the whole thing down on paper, McKenzie. I drafted up a Complaint against the City sufficient to make the gods weep. I know their attorney did when I showed it to him, anyway. Hell, I spent twelve pages just laying the factual predicate, describing the shooting, the injury to you, their negligent abuse of the girl— my god, shooting at an eight year old! We win automatically on that alone—"

"Annie's nine, actually."

"—And it's all on video. I know the City attorney pretty well. Mike Trujillo. I took the Complaint over and showed him what we were going to file the next day if he didn't come around."

"I'm guessing it changed his attitude."

"It took about thirty seconds. Then he called over the DA. And she didn't want to bend, of course, but that type never does. Both knew I had them by the short hairs. though."

"They quashed the warrants, then, obviously."

"With extreme prejudice."

"And you agreed to drop the lawsuit in return."

"*Hell*, no. I can't settle a lawsuit without you signing off on it. You know that, McKenzie," he scolded, like the law school professor he once was. "Nor would I counsel you to do so, by the way. No, I just told them I'd wait to file it, and talk to you about it first, that's all. There was no trade here except that I agreed to give the bastards a little breathing time to position themselves. Plus, I let them know to a certainty I'd see to it things'd go worse for them if they didn't stop screwing around with you."

Michelle returned to the table, phone in hand. She stood waiting for Madstone to finish. "Britt wants to know when we will be in Vancouver," she said, when he paused. "She is very excited!"

I looked at Madstone, then back at Michelle. "As soon as we can get there. Let's just eat, then go back to Canada. Is that okay, Madstone?"

"Sure. Don't worry about me. I'll share a cab with you guys back downtown, then figure something out."

"You sure?"

"Yup. Hell, I might even stay in Seattle a few extra days. I know this gal in Fremont."

"Pot's legal here, too."

"Don't think that hadn't occurred to me."

I turned back to Michelle. "I'm guessing we can make Vancouver by seven if the traffic's with us. Maybe a little later depending on how the line up at the border is."

She went off to give Britt our ETA. At the same time the waitress brought us our entrees and Madstone took the opportunity to order us more beers.

Always thinking ahead, Madstone is.

I tucked into my blackened salmon, savoring the buttery goodness of it. Blackened salmon and beer. What a reward. I looked over at Michelle three tables away comfortably chatting with Britt in Vancouver over the smartphone I had just given her. Sharing anecdotes about Annie, I reckoned. Cell phone technology is so obscure that I can only chalk the operation of 'em up to magic. I'm not a physicist, or an electrical engineer, neither, and all I really know is, when I turn 'em on, they work.

That said, though, when all this was over, when there was blood on the floor and bodies to be counted, I took the time to look it up. 'Cause in the end, and as it turned out, the science of it directly affected us.

When a mobile phone is switched on, apparently it sends a signal to a base station or tower where a computer checks to see if you're allowed to use a given network. Each base station is associated with a geographical "cell,"—hence the "cell" in "cellular phone"—and once connected to a cell, the user then can make a call. During a call, a cell phone user can move about from one cell to another and experience uninterrupted continuous service, but a phone is only ever communicating through one tower at a time, so correspondingly the network always knows the cell where your phone is located. And thereby the electronic gods-that-be know your geographical location, and can route incoming calls to your phone at all times. Handy.

It also leaves a trail. It's how they got Bin Laden, I think.

I could be wrong about that. Maybe it wasn't Bin Laden. Maybe it was some other famous bad guy they got. Pablo Escobar, maybe? Or Silvio Burlusconi? But as a tool for wronged spouses, weirdo stalkers and government agencies attempting to track drug couriers, cell phones have proven to be a godsend. Indeed, the Supreme Court has said you have no reasonable expectation a privacy when you use one of those things (although to be fair, your average Supreme Court Justice is so far removed from the world we share that's it's hard to see how any one of them could confidently state what it is you or I reasonably expect about any day-to-day thing—when was the last time Clarence Thomas bought a carton of milk at the Seven-Eleven, for example?).

Michelle returned to the table smiling, and handed me back the beautiful white rectangle. "Britt said to say 'Hi' to you, Mr. Madstone. She is very happy."

I took the phone from Michelle, switched it off, shoved it deep down inside my jacket and thought no more about it. As we laughed and drank and finished our lunches, electrons leaked from my pocket.

Chapter 43 – Back to Canada

THE RAIN was sheeting down again as the cab dropped us off onto Fourth Street. Not for the last time I was glad of my Fedora and overcoat. I popped open the umbrella I'd brought for the purpose, and held it over Michelle's bare head as we made our way upstream against the flow of pedestrians toward Westlake Center where I'd parked that morning.

She slipped a hand gently around my bent arm as we walked, edging up next to me, under the umbrella and away from the wet. I felt her hip against mine. Above us the rumble of the mono-rail, below clots of pedestrians, and the smell of concrete and exhaust.

Madstone bid us adieu and disappeared into the bustling street, and minutes later we were underground, back in the truck and not too soggy.

And a few minutes after that we were back again at street level, safe in the big blue vehicle, perfectly anonymous and on the road home.

The wipers slapped back and forth and the rain splashed lavishly off the sides of the windshield and I reckoned we'd be home and dry back in Vancouver well before nine, just as I'd said. The prospect of actually getting Michelle and Annie back together in what was really just a matter of hours seemed almost unreal. Christmas in December!—I could hardly believe it was happening. Neither could Michelle, I'm sure. I looked over at her oval face, tattooed with the liquid rain shadows that moved over her, shifting with the lights from the oncoming vehicles, and

301

searched for her mood. The indistinct, ever changing view of her revealed nothing, but she looked back over at me and smiled. I held her gaze for a long moment before turning back to the road.

In no time we were out of downtown, past Edmonds, then Everett, then closing in on Blain, Washington, which was perhaps the most boring name for a border crossing anywhere, but nevertheless heralded the approaching hump of Canadian customs, and the last leg of this marathon journey. The traffic was thick as hell, growing thicker the further north we got—inclement weather meets rush-hour, I supposed. But even factoring in the traffic, and somewhat unbelievably, I was going to keep my promise to Annie, reunite her with her mother, and get my old life back. Or something like my old life, anyway. To be truthful, the imminent prospect of a return to New Mexico, the high desert sun and my precious retirement was affecting me rather less than I had expected. I ascribed it to the distracting intensity of the last several days, and decided it was time to start looking for signs to the Canadian port of entry.

Easier said than done, as it turned out.

I'd been through here a couple of times before, of course, but the traffic and the rain together were quite disorienting. Plus it was a real circus milieu this time 'round—far busier than when I'd crossed going north before, with an overabundance of signs that I hadn't recalled, disorienting arrows and speed limits and exits and cautions, each equally significant, all demanding my full focus and attention. Around me, the rain refracted red and green stars from taillights and street lamps, providing really wet Holiday optics that distorted the view, and slowed our progress but gave a festive tone to our world, nonetheless. Meanwhile, the traffic crushed heavily around us, six lanes side-to-side; cars and trucks and buses jockeyed for position, moving constantly up and in and around, each probing and pushing, each searching for the path of least resistance home.

To my right a red Corvette found a gap, and quickly leaped past; a moment later an old school VW Beetle cut in front of me, and then just as quick it swung over to the turn-off lane, exiting nimbly off the freeway, and up a ramp to some nameless suburb.

At the same moment, a green and white truck shwooshed up next to us, and stayed even for a bit.

Emergency lights from behind flooded the cab.

Michelle gasped.

The swirly red, white and blue washed away the Christmassy feel in an instant with a disorienting Tsunami of authoritative patriotism. The green and white truck to the side of us suddenly exploded with emergency lights itself, and for the first time I saw "Customs and Border Protection" printed in big black letters on the side of the thing.

I cursed.

Another truck, this one in front, abruptly slowed, and blinkered a right turn. It was obvious we were supposed to follow.

"What is happening?" Michelle's voice was plaintive: panicked and not fully understanding.

"Border Patrol," I said, stating the obvious.

"But the Judge..." she began.

"These guys obviously didn't get the memo."

However, counsel, I must let you know, CBP will not necessarily respect an order from this court—

The astounding words of the other Immigration Judge, the one from just a few days before at the removal hearing for the melancholy doctoral biochemist Mr. Kim, sounded in my ears. This situation suddenly seemed like something I should have foreseen. CBP were clearly—and perhaps somewhat predictably—off on their own hook.

Michelle looked at me with alarm. "But the Judge said we could go," she said. "I have his Order." She pulled the document from her purse, and held it up for me to see.

"Good," says I with a bluff smile, pretending to glance at the document. "We'll need that." But it was a false confidence I offered, and I knew the piece of paper would be of absolutely no effect. The Border Patrol was a law unto themselves, and for reasons unknown we had drawn their full attention. I still didn't fully understand how they fit into this. Were they connected to Michelle's better half and running this errand for him? It was possible they just resented being undone by the court. Or maybe they just didn't like us. But regardless of their motivation, and whether they were aligned with Annie's father, or just pissed about this morning's hearing hardly mattered. It was pretty clear they meant us harm and we'd best duck 'em if we could, ideally with an international border between us and them.

The emergency lights endlessly whirled around us and I ranged about for a possible escape route. Running was nuts, of course, but I was desperate.

There was no chance, anyway. The truck that I'd originally noticed to the left edged dangerously closer, well into my own lane. It was shoving me over to the right pretty effectively, emphasizing that there was no way out for me, and I was to follow the truck in front.

I eyed up the shoulder—there was none. Instead, to our right was a thirty-foot poured cement retaining wall, with the barest ribbon of hard pavement below, maybe four feet wide at most, that the truck to our left already had us encroaching.

The truck in front was already half over into the thing, too, completely blocking our way forward.

A glance in the rearview confirmed the same was now true behind.

They had us—we were moving forward at sixty miles an hour, boxed into tightly by the three trucks.

I glanced over once more at the truck to our left, and realized I could see the driver's silhouette through the rain: he was gesticulating wildly for me to pull us off to the right. His movements were abrupt and forceful, with the firm and righteous anger of law enforcement defied squarely behind them.

There was nothing for it. I swung the wheel of the truck, and pointed us up the ramp the three CBP trucks were edging us into, like a steer into the chute. I should have known they wouldn't let us go quietly into the dark night. It had all just been too good to be true.

"What is this!" Michelle said. "What is wrong? What is the problem?"

She was negotiating with me. Apparently she had skipped the denial and anger phases of grief, and had gone right to bargaining.

"The problem," I said, feeling lightheaded, "is we're still on the American side of the border."

We weren't the only vehicle on the road, though, and out of the mass of cars on the freeway pitched a little black coup, a late model Porsche Boxter as it happened, which attempted to cross our path onto the exit ramp. It cut off the CBP truck in front of me at high speed with utter contempt.

Me first, I thought to myself—what an asshole: obviously some jag-off attorney or hopped up bio-tech boss in a rush to get home and screw his trophy wife. He nearly made it, too.

The collision with the front end of the CBP truck exploded in front of me before I could grasp what was happening. The green and white vehicle went into a one-eighty across the wet pavement that fetched it up on the grass to the side, and left the road in front of me suddenly open.

"Holy shit!" I cried in triumph, gunning the engine.

"Fuckin'-A!"

I sailed past the backward-facing green truck, and the still moving black Boxter, too, and headed on up to the top of the ramp. A glance in the rearview mirror confirmed that the other two green and white CBP trucks were stuck behind the wrecked, now sideways-facing Porsche, their emergency lights angrily whirling further and further behind us, impotent and furious.

Another glance behind, and Mr. Attorney asshole-slash-biotech guy was already out of his car yelling at the Border Patrol agents.

I smiled.

I brought us to a halt at the stop sign that marked the top of the off-ramp, good responsible law-abiding driver that I am; I looked to the right and then to the left—safety first—then proceeded forward. I crossed the road, and drove casually down the on-ramp and back onto the express-way and into traffic.

Easy-peasy.

In an instant Michelle and I were headed north again, unimpeded and blending in well with the traffic. We were anonymous once more. And closing in on the line-up for Canadian Customs, as it happened. We looked at each other with our jaws in our laps.

"What just happened, Monsieur McKenzie?" Michelle asked, her husky Quebecois accent still sexy and charming, but coming through a little shell-shocked, nonetheless.

"I don't know."

To say that I was a little bit dizzy from the whole business was an understatement.

"How did they find us, do you mean? Or what did they want?..." I was thinking about these questions at about a hundred mental miles an hour, but had absolutely no idea what the answers were.

"Annie's father, he wants the password. I told you he would never let me go free."

The password. The numbers in Annie's mittens. Maybe that was it. The ghost of James Quintana sent a shiver down my spine.

I slowed the truck to a crawl, gelling with the rest of the north bound traffic into the line-up at the international border crossing. The Peace Arch was immediately off to port now, screened and blurred by the hard, endless, vertical rain that just wouldn't stop. It marked the boundary between the State of Washington and British Columbia, which was cause for a half-sigh of relief. We were home, now, but not yet safe and dry. Not quite.

As usual, the queue on the other side, the half-mile column of vehicles heading south, waiting to go through American customs, was quite a bit longer than the one we were in going north. But the delay on our side proved to be more than I'd ever experienced before. It wasn't 'cause of us, by the way. As it turned out, Canadian customs were on a work slowdown, of all things. I didn't find that out until later, of course. When all of this was over, back in the safety of our flat in Vancouver. But it was a hell of a thing. They were stopping every car, asking numerous questions, very, very thoroughly instructing people about the Canadian law on long guns, bringing drugs into the country, and so on. And all the while, of course, being genuinely and sincerely polite and helpful. Polite and helpful quite literally and deliberately to a fault.

As we slowly drew ever more slowly toward the Border Services kiosks, I had too much time to think about our situation.

On the one hand, I strongly suspected the American CBP had not been on the clock, so to speak, when they were chasing us just now, and wasn't too concerned about them having contacted the Canucks about us. Truth be told, I reckoned one way or another they were dirty as hell, and correspondingly might well fear the spotlight authoring an international alert for our arrest would throw on them.

And there were other good reasons to think we had nothing to fear from official channels, too. We'd just come through a hearing in Immigration Court, after all; there was nothing new on us—nothing at all. The CBP had had no legitimate reason to pursue us, or take us into custody. There was no probable cause. And to the degree they had been empowered to seize us, it was only due to the fact we had been within their infamous Constitution-Free Zone, that hundred mile apron that runs around the border of the United States where Homeland Security can pretty much do as they please.

We were now out of their jurisdiction and had effectively entered the no-man's-land which exists between our two nations.

But what if there was more to it than that? What if they had actively set us up? What if the Border Patrol had planted drugs on us, or some such thing? Whether these particular guys were working for Annie's father or not, I wouldn't put it past them doing it out of pure vindictiveness. In fact, now that I thought about it, it would be surprising if they *hadn't* engage in such behavior. The notion that if you drew the animus of CBP, they'd do you dirty to their utmost, seemed entirely consistent with everything I'd seen and learned about them over the last several months. Planting drugs might well be a standard part of their repertoire. A packet of cocaine "discovered" taped to the undercarriage, and then they would have had reason enough to take us into custody back in the States; indeed, they would have reason now to contact the Canadian authorities and alert them to a crime committed on American soil, and to contraband located in or on our vehicle.

Drugs discovered in our vehicle by the Canadian Border Services folks. That would be some pretty sweet shit.

I shook my head to clear it. The whole idea of the CBP planting drugs on us was silly. They hadn't known where our truck was parked back in Seattle. Hell, they never expected the hearing to go they way it did. Every reasonable expectation on their part would have been that with all those outstanding warrants, a kidnapped girl and a pending detainer on me, I would be locked up tight in one of their antiseptic jails at this exact moment, wearing a jump suit and receiving rolled up bedding and a cot assignment. There would have been no foreseeable need to plant drugs on us. And their efforts to take us down back in Blaine had likely just been them lashing out one last frustrated time. A blind, reflexive swing by an arrogant unaccountable monster now safely in our rearview mirror.

The line inched forward, and like everyone else, I craned to see what was going on in front of us. Periodically, a car would get pulled out of line for "further review," but mostly the Agents were just taking their sweet time and being very, very thorough with each and every car that arrived at their booth.

At long last I pulled us up under the high canopy, and the Canadian Border Services Agent greeted me. I put on my standard bemused middle aged man face.

There was no point to that, by the way; she didn't even look at me.

"Could you pull your car just over there, sir."

Surprisingly, I kept my cool. Customs in every country have their own invariable protocols. Sometimes its SUVs that get stopped, sometimes cars with certain license plates; people having a bad hair day get noticed sometimes, as do those who have stamps in their passports from watch-list type countries. If you've just driven in from Yemen, for example, you can count on some time and a lot of attention in the Green Room. There's nothing you can do about that, of course. But even if you do catch their attention, even if you get randomly marked for audit and further review, often as not you can brazen your way through. And we had nothing to hide, after all. Just a couple of Canadians coming home. What could possibly go wrong.   We had been pulled aside for further review, yes. But no matter what they did, we were still Canadians on the Canadian side of the border.

It was only then I remembered with horror that the pistol was still in the glovebox.

Chapter 44 – Annie Gets Her Gun, Redux

"OVER THERE," as it turned out, was an enormous parking area behind the large main structure. The Canadian Border Services Agency had apparently set this aside mainly as a repository for the inspection of trucks, judging by the large number of eighteen-wheel rigs parked in neat, discrete lines up and down the wide expanse of pavement. But there was a pocket area for smaller vehicles to park near an unmarked entrance to the building, and a handful of sedans, hatchbacks and SUVs had been left there, the owners undoubtedly inside undergoing "further interrogation," or whatever the appropriate euphemism *de jour* was.

Across the lot, looking north, I could just make out the taunting sign: "Welcome—British Columbia, Canada—The best Place on Earth."

It is, too, I thought to myself. Now if they'll only let us in.

"Michelle, have a look in the glove box, will you please. Do you see a gun?"

Maybe the rotten thing wasn't there. I was grasping at straws, of course, but miracles do happen, don't they? It was worth checking.

She opened the glove compartment, surveyed the space, then looked at me. A slight nod told me the fucking loaded Glock was still in there. Christ fucking leaping jesus. The sudden realization of it washed over me all at once, but I still couldn't help reflexively making a mental note for the umpteenth time to get rid of it at the first opportunity. Like I'd ever have a chance to do that again.

I reached over Michelle's lap, and pushed the glove box closed again. "It's mine," I said. "The gun's mine. Don't worry. I'll tell 'em that. They'll have to let you go. You still be together with Annie before the day's out."

What the hell. I was going to turn myself in for murder anyway, why not add a gun charge. The notion was vaguely freeing. What could an international gun charge could cost me in terms of jail time? Additional jail time to whatever I was going to get for killing Denis, that is. In legal speak, I reckoned the likely answer was quite a lot.

Michelle reached out and took my hand in hers. I could feel her shaking slightly, and squeezed her hand tight.

"Don't worry," I said. "Seriously. What's the worst that can happen? They can't kick us out of our own country. Right?"

She laughed thinly. "*Oui.* I know."

"What's the worst that can happen?"

"They don't know about the gun," she sensibly pointed out.

She was right. They probably didn't know about it. Yet. But idiot that I am, I'd inadvertently run the border gauntlet in both directions too many times with the thing in there and not gotten pinched before now; in my heart, I knew my karmic number was up.

The minutes ticked by. What could be taking them so long to come out and engage us? It was the work slowdown, of course, though I didn't know it at the time. While we waited, I tried to look on the bright side. On balance we were still far better off for having made the border. I'd take getting pinched by Canadian customs over the tender mercies of the American Border Patrol anytime.

The unmarked door in the building in front of us finally opened up, and a troop of Canadian Border Services Agents filed out. I say a 'troop,' but there were really only four. Enough to cause me some concern, though. There was something very military and out of the ordinary about it.

311

They walked toward us in a line, the four black clad Border Services officers, sporting black baseball caps and body armor, which might otherwise have seemed kind of sinister, but I must say the word "Canada" on their shoulder patches mitigated the effect somewhat. As did the Maple Leaf waving above us.

Two of 'em advanced toward my driver's side window, while the other two held back. Michelle looked at me, her face a question mark.

"I don't know," I said, answering the question she hadn't uttered but was going through both our heads.

I rolled down my window as the two Agents approached. On my left arm I could feel the spattering of raindrops, ricocheting off the door panel and into the cab.

"Sir, good evening," said the taller of the two agents. "Could you step out of the vehicle, please."

"Of course," I responded, and reached for the door handle as the officer stepped back, allowing me to exit.

Beyond where the Border Services officers were standing, about thirty feet away, the door to the main building opened again. A man—a civilian—stepped into the light; a Border Services Agent stepped up behind him, holding an umbrella over his head.

From the inside of the cab of the truck we could hear the pelt-pelt-pelt of the drops on the thin umbrella skin.

He was a black man, very tall and very well dressed, you could see that even at a distance. And big. He was maybe thirty feet away, but you could sense some kind of weird authority about him—or menace, perhaps. Maybe that was it. It was raining, and kinda' hard to tell. Whatever it was, I didn't like it much.

He stepped away from the building, pulling someone else behind him.

"Annie!" Michelle whispered at the closed window. Her breath made a perfect white circle on the glass.

Across the tarmac I saw Annie's red hair and her bunny and her backpack, too. It didn't take any time at all to reckon who the man holding on to her hand was. And they say you can't tell a book by its cover.

312

I'd never seen a human trafficker before, but Annie's father did look the part. Greasy. Greasy as hell.

This was not good. This was no good at all. What the hell had happened? Was Britt okay?

Michelle put her hand to the steamed-up glass of the passenger side window. Thirty feet away Annie's face wore no expression I could see. Maybe this wasn't so bad. Michelle was her mother, after all. If we could just get a chance to explain things, we should be alright. Michelle had done nothing wrong, after all.

The Border Services agent standing in the rain next to my door was growing impatient. "Sir, please get out of the vehicle."

I had been staring at Annie and her father for rather an overlong time, and the Border Services agent was already fingering a canister of pepper spray and handcuffs. I opened the door and climbed down. Once outside, the rain tapped annoyingly on my bare head, and I instantly regretted leaving my Fedora on the seat.

"Could I get my hat, please," I asked the Agent.

Before he could answer I heard the passenger side door of the truck open.

"*Annie!*" Michelle cried.

There was a brief pause before Annie shrieked back: "*Mommy!*"

The big greasy bastard under the umbrella yanked Annie's hand hard, yanking her into his greasy arms.

"That's them, officers!" I heard him say. "They're the two that kidnapped my daughter!"

There was a brief pause at that, and Annie's father took a step forward.

"Stay where you are, sir," one of the Agents cautioned him.

"She's the girl's mother," I shouted, across the truck and over the rain. "She's Annie's mother."

"What did he say?"

"He said the woman by the truck is the girl's mother I believe, sir," one of the Border Agents said.

"That's a lie," I heard Annie's father say.

313

"Everybody calm down, here, please," one of the Agent's said. "Let's get out of the rain and go sort this out." He said "out" almost like "boot," in the good old Canadian way. He was holding up his hands, palms out toward both sides of the conflict, taking things down a notch, acting the peacemaker.

This was going okay. Sitting down and sorting it out sounded just fine to me. Truth be told, at this point we had nothing to hide. Michelle was Annie's mother, we'd already got things sorted out south of the border. I still had my business with the RCMP to deal with, but I was reasonably confident the truth would come out on that, too. Eventually.

But what about Britt...

Before I could think on that disturbing concern further, someone shouted: "She's got a gun!"

A loud crack slashed the air, and the world froze in the flash of its single strobe.

314

Chapter 45 – One Bullet

EVERYTHING CAME to a complete stop for that atom-short moment—
a million raindrops hung motionless in the air around us.

Then time started up again.

All Canadian heads turned south—the shot had come through the
fence, you see; it had come from south of the border. From the American side.

It was the CBP, of course; previously unnoticed a hundred yards
away, half in the dark on the other side of the chain link that separated
the two countries. I could clearly see three green uniforms and three sets
of jackboots, one of 'em with a smoking pistol in his hand.

I say it was smoking, but truthfully I don't remember any smoke. It
hardly mattered anyway: there was no question who had fired the thing.

And it was only a glimpse I caught anyway, 'cause from the other direction, from behind me from across the tarmac came a wrenching moan.

It was Annie, and I knew it.

In the slow-motion time it took me to turn my head back around to
look, I wondered how I knew it was her, 'cause it didn't sound like anything I had ever heard come out of that sweet little girl before: I mean,
I'd heard laughter and weeping, I'd heard annoyance and disgust and
amusement; in fact over the last several months I'd heard pretty much the

full range of human emotions come out of her, but never anything like this.

But it was Annie just the same.

The blood, even in that weird monochromatic light was unmistakable. Gore was rapidly accumulating on the pavement just below Michelle's head, and in that black-and-white night it looked like chocolate syrup. She hung out of the truck at a broken angle, one arm pointing to the earth, the seatbelt the only thing keeping her from falling to the ground.

Twenty feet away, Annie stared at the wreckage of her mother in silence now, her eyes wide, that unearthly moan still filling the space between us.

The sound of it faded, slowly rising into the air above the parking lot, growing ever thinner as it lifted above the clouds and floated up toward the freezing cold of space. And under the steadily pounding rain the bloody pool grew and ran.

The Mounties were all looking across the southern border now—staring and pointing through the chain link fence at the American Border Patrol murderers standing safe and sound across an imaginary line away in another country. Those three men in America might as well have been a thousand miles away, across an Ocean for that matter, secure on a foreign continent, in Iran or North Korea or Somalia or some such similar place, some similar land located on the far side of justice.

Two of the Mounties ran over to where Michelle was, and released her from her seatbelt, spreading her out on the ground where they began working on her: administering CPR, pounding her chest, applying pressure to the wound. A third Agent was standing apart, talking urgently into his shoulder mic. Calling for an ambulance, I supposed, calling for backup. Already the sound of emergency sirens was rising.

I glanced back over at the American border fence. Or maybe Canada owned the fence—who knows. The two countries have about fifty-thousand miles of unguarded frontier between 'em, unguarded and most of it unmonitored, with people by and large free to travel across one way or the other, and we just happened to be in one of the few spots where there's actually a barrier. The American Border Patrol Agents had gone. Slipped back into the rainy night—not wanting to hang around for what came next, maybe? Appalled and shamed by what they'd done? Doubtful. Run off to get their stories straight, and prepare an official alibi? Almost to a certainty.

Time had ratcheted up to full speed, now, or maybe even a little bit faster. The ambulance was suddenly there; Michelle was strapped to a gurney with EMTs ministering to her violently, with a sort of "live, damn you!" desperation; a newly arrived squad car with the RCMP crest on its side produced a likely looking fellow with a peaked cap who inserted himself the milieu. They were ignoring me at this point, but across the bloody pavement my eyes locked with Annie's.

I mouthed the words "I'm sorry" through the rain at her. She looked back at me with blank eyes, here Hello Kitty backpack and bunny sagging in the rain. I started toward her:

"Sir! Please get back!" someone said to me.

Across the tarmac, the father's hand grabbed Annie's arm and yanked her hard toward the door.

"Annie!" I shouted, and launched toward her.

"Sir—sir!" the Mountie shouted at me. "Sir, please restrain yourself!" He didn't pull a gun like they would have down south, but was on me quicker than I could get to Annie; quicker than I could close any real distance, truth be told. To be fully honest, there was no race at all. He was fit and young and extremely competent.

Efficient gents, these Mounties are, by the way. Real professionals, and I don't mean that in any kind of ironic sense, 'cause quick as a wink he had me cuffed and on the ground. And without any unnecessary clubbing or beating, either. No gratuitous punches. No grinding my face into the tarmac. Just hard, polite restraining. Although, frankly I couldn't have been much more than a tackling dummy for him, and who's going to waste their brutality on a that? Indiana Jones I'm not.

We were finished. I knew that now. There were no more cards to play. The worst had been done, and out of my line of sight I waited for the sound of that door slamming shut, the sound of Annie's father pulling

317

her into the building, and off to whatever grim and irredeemable fate awaited her—a flat punctuation mark, our story ended, Annie's fate sealed.

I waited, but the door didn't slam.

Chapter 46 – Who the Hell is Captain Riley?

INSTEAD, A POLITE, but unmistakably official command punched through the night rain:

"Hold it, please sir!"

I couldn't actually see any of this, of course, being trussed up and pointed in the other direction, but Annie's father was clearly the target of the injunction. Hesitation followed. A brief and uncertain silence filled the air.

It was a powerful pause, pregnant with calculation, and followed shortly by Annie's father's parry:

"It's okay. Captain Riley's on board with this."

It was a high voice for such a large man. Thin and high, and almost soft.

There was the sound of movement then, of the casual footfalls of Annie's father making once more for the exit. Apparently the R.C.M.P. and Canada Border Services were made of sterner stuff than to be thrown off by causal name dropping, though, and another official voice immediately commanded:

"Stand fast, sir!"

There was no "please" this time. An urgent kaleidoscope of dialogue commenced, the staccato rush of it oddly muffled by the steady rain:

"Look constable, this is my daughter."

"Stand down, sir!"

"Captain Riley is aware of my—"

"STAND DOWN SIR!"

There was a light scuffle, and then a wet thump, and a rather weak and pompous *"How dare you!"* followed by a cry from one of the EMTs away on the other side of the parking lot:

"Hey, I've got a pulse!"

"We've got a pumper!"

"Strap her in."

"Watch her head, now…"

The human mind can only stand so much, and it actually took a few seconds for the words to sink in: Michelle had been sent on the long gone, and yet these guys had somehow brought her back. This was an emotional u-turn so profound I could almost feel the centrifugal force of it—but incredibly, and at least for now Michelle's heart was still beating!

"ANNIE!…" I cried out into the night as loudly as I could.

"Please sir, you'll have to control yourself."

It was my own personal guard who said it, still standing tall above me.

Back over by the building, where they'd brought Monsieur Chretien to ground, one of the RCMP fellows announced:

"I've got the little girl."

"You've no right!"

"We've a lot to sort out here, sir."

"…Captain Riley shall hear of this!"

"Captain Riley's already in custody."

I was cuffed and face down, my cheek cold against the wet blacktop, and I couldn't see a goddam thing except the dark and the rain, but it was pretty obvious things were going south fast for Annie's father. And for Captain Riley, whoever he was. But I was growing tired of not being able to see anything, and having to imagine what was going on, so I shoved over hard.

A sharp pain stabbed deep into my shoulder due to my hands being cuffed awkwardly behind me, but I succeeded in making a complete roll. Through the dark and driving rain I finally got a good look at Annie.

My guard became agitated. "Sir, please—sir," he admonished, but I was already repositioned.

I caught Annie's eye just then, just as she was being turned away from me.

"YOUR MUM!..." I cried at her, hard.

"*I KNOW I KNOW I KNOW!...*" she squealed back at me over her shoulder.

And the last glimpse I had of the tough little tyke that night was the very back of her, one hand on her bunny, clutching that stuffed animal tight as they pulled her out of the rain and away from the bloody mayhem. A burly Border Services chap escorted her not ungently in through the doorway and out of sight.

Simultaneously Annie's father was being loaded into the back of an RCMP cruiser. And for the first time during those crowded minutes I had time to contemplate just what the hell was going on. First off, it sure sounded like the authorities had Monsieur Chretien's number—had Britt met with some success? This morning she had gone to tell the cops I'd voluntarily turn myself in to face a charge of murder for Dennis, so long as they held off on disposing with Annie until the end of the day. And it was beginning to look like that deal had been done. Kind of.

Jesus christ, I thought—could it be that this bloody catastrophe was sort of going to plan?

Maybe.

Except for Michelle. I did not see that coming.

But Annie's mum had apparently survived the cross-border assassination attempt. She was alive—for now, at least—and with all that implied: secret code word, access to incriminating evidence stored in the cloud, and not the least, the fact that a certain very annoying little red-headed kid still had a mother.

It was tiring holding my head up trying to look at stuff, so I let it drop back down to the wet pavement. I know that sounds weak, but it's hard on your neck holding your mellon up when you're laying sideways on the ground with your hands tied behind you—just try it sometime. And once again I couldn't see very much at all, but through the rain from across the pavement I could hear them provide Annie's father the universal caution familiar to all of us who have ever been loaded into the back of a police car:

"Watch your head sir."

I could hear another vehicle arrived just then, too, and the sound of a car door opening and someone jumping out.

"The American's say it was self defense."

"*Self defense!*" the Mountie who had been first on the scene suddenly shouted with outrage. "That's ridiculous."

"Sir, she was no danger to anyone," one of the Canada Border Service Agents protested.

no danger to anyone…

Except to Annia's da, and to those corrupt U.S. Border Patrol villains who'd just tried to do her in. The bastards had tried to murder her, and they'd probably get away with it, too. Fuckers. The nihilistic scars of an agency gone mad mutilated the borders of that great country to the south, and no one seemed to know or care because all this collateral damage was quite simply off the books.

One thing I could see, and just out of the corner of my eye, was the nine-millimeter Glock was still lying on the ground below the truck. In all the excitement and confusion, it had not yet been retrieved. It lay there in that grim half-light, water drops bouncing off it, black and gleaming like original sin.

The Border Services Agent guarding me saw I was struggling, and helped me get up into a sitting position.

He was a young man. I spied a ring on his finger, and reckoned he and the misses might well have children. He might appreciate what proved in the event to be Annie's last words to me, a joke she had told me back at the apartment before I'd gone off to Seattle to meet her mother for the first time:

"What do you call a cow with no legs," I said to him.

322

He looked down at me with obvious uncertainty. Not fearful of course, not by any means. Just—I guess he didn't know what to make of me. But in the end, his humanity took over—what person with a soul could not take the hook on that bait—and he said what any of us would have said:

"I don't know? What do you call a cow with no legs."

I smiled at him briefly. "Ground beef."

He hesitated then, and he didn't really want to, I know—probably thought it was unprofessional or inappropriate or something—but he smiled. Kind of a half smile, the kind that grudgingly admits something.

"That's a good one, sir. I'll have to tell it to my daughters."

I was sitting on the pavement, sitting criss-cross apple sauce, my Fedora in the car, my overcoat hanging open and no help at all. The ground was wet, and the rain poured relentlessly down upon my bare head.

VII. All's Well That Ends Well... In Canada, Anyway

Chapter 47 – Banff

WE WERE BACK IN BANFF.

On the street it was cold, quiet and still. There was ice already on the windows all around us, and our breath made distinct white clouds. It was after ten, but neither of us wanted to go right back to the motel. We strolled up frozen side streets for a bit, poking around the dark mountain town at random, warm and cozy in our new winter coats.

Eventually the restaurants and gift shops thinned out, giving way to rows of modest private homes. We rounded a corner onto a sidewalk that ran along the side of a neat picket fence, and suddenly, and without any kind of warning came smack up against a goddam Elk.

Annie froze.

"Hold it," she ordered in a whisper, and held up her arm to stop me.

It was a real full sized honest-to-god Elk, just standing in the middle of the sidewalk right in front of us. It was surprising as hell, and the last thing either of us expected to see in a town, even this particular town, located as it was in the high mountain heart of the Canadian Rockies.

The animal stood there, about ten feet away, doing whatever it was it was doing, and took no notice of us whatsoever. Antlers and all, it stood as tall as my shoulders. Annie and I just held our places and marveled. It was a hell of a thing, I've got to tell you.

"I'm going to pet it," she said.

"I don't think that's such a—Annie—Annie, don't touch the thing…"

She was already upon the beast before I could comment further, and like with the delivery door at the Santa Fe lockup, she took no notice of me, and slowly reached her hand out to touch it.

Slowly, slowly she put her arm out, and then her little hand was on its shoulder.

For five or six seconds she gently petted the thing. The creature turned its head and looked around at her. For just the briefest of moments, they were eye to eye. And then it gave a light snort, twin puffs of white steam floated up from its snout, and it just walked away.

Just like that. It didn't run, mind you. It walked, sauntered actually, down the sidewalk.

Annie trotted back to where I was. "That was cool!" she said, her face lit up bright and happy.

"That *was* cool," I agreed. And it was, too.

Then I woke up.

I was back in Vancouver again. I'd already had the same dream several times now, and much as I liked it, I was puzzled. Annie and I had never been to Banff together. Was I walking in my dreams with the little girl away in some parallel universe where I would be able to save her mother from being shot? Or was it just my brain trying to heal the raw wound with kindness; with a sweet memory that never existed.

Whatever it was, it did make me smile.

Beyond the window it was summer now. Summer in Vancouver. But other than the leaves on the trees, it was hard to say what was different. The rain still fell, it was about fifty degrees out, and the grey sea surged over the sand in the park opposite just the same as it had the December before. So much had moved on, but the world, the world it still kept turning. For some of us, anyway.

After the shooting The RCMP had briefly taken me into custody, but it became quickly apparent they already had a reasonably good understanding of what had gone down by the river on that October night in Princes Island Park back in Calgary. Leonard brought Britt in to provide

328

a statement in support of my self-defense claim, and I was back on the street before Christmas. I guess it's one of those life-lessons: if you're going to shoot someone, shoot a pimp with a knife.

Madstone had had the warrants from south of the border quashed before Michelle's hearing, of course; the Amber Alert was resolved without further question; and the ICE's detainer became a dead letter when I decided to remain in Canada.

Remain in Canada? Why do that, you ask? Well, why not. My ex had decided to remove to Virginia with her boyfriend, taking our daughter with her, so even if I had gone back to Santa Fe I was looking at a long distance relationship with my little girl anyway. And truth be told, long distance ain't so bad. It *is* a relationship. I'll see her all the time, maybe more now, what with summertime and holidays and school breaks. And the kid's Canadian after all—through her father of course, though she's never seen the place, but I've been sending her maple leaf post cards and pictures of Vancouver and such like every day to ease her into it. She's flying up next month. Britt's excited as hell to meet her.

None of what happened was Britt's fault, of course. But as I'd known she would be, Britt was destroyed by what happened. She'd reckoned it was her job to make things right, to protect us all, and in her own eyes she'd let the side down. She'd taken on the mantel of blame completely, and is there anything more Canadian than that?

Not that in anyone's wildest dreams Britt could have done anything about bullets fired across the border by Americans. Try telling that to a teenager, though.

The bullet lodged in Michelle's brain, as it turned out. It didn't kill her outright, but sent her into a long Sleeping Beauty coma that's lasted now a good six months. Maybe a tad longer, if I wanted to look at the calendar and be exact about it, which I don't. As anyone can tell you who's been through something like this, it's the uncertainty of it that takes the real toll.

But Michelle's still alive, and that's the good news.

And whether or not Britt wants to believe it, she was definitely the hero of the hour. She had gone to the RCMP just as we'd planned, told

329

'em I'd turn myself in if they'd just hold on to Annie 'till I got Michelle back up there, but nothing's ever that easy. For several hours Britt got to live that horrible Casandra nightmare where she knew the truth but no one would listen—the curse of any kid or teenager, I suppose. But the Mounties aren't stupid, and in the end they agreed to our deal after a fashion. Agreed to it without actually agreeing to it, if you know what I mean.

Turned out they had another motive besides taking me into custody: they already knew about Annie's father, you see—they just lacked the evidence necessary to bring him to justice. And Michelle had that, and Michelle was with me. Problem solved. But thanks to the Americans, for the time being they've had to make do with half a loaf. Monsieur Chretien is locked up for now, the key to convicting him locked in the brain of that beautiful Quebecois who was currently flat on her back with a tube down her throat, hooked up to a machine that goes "ping."

Britt and I try to get up to see her at least a couple of times a week.

Yeah, that's right—in the end, Britt elected to stay on with me. She's going to school now, and doing a damn fine job of it, too, by the way. That part, at least, turned out to be kind of an easy transition for the both of us.

She's able to see her brother all the time now; she takes the bus over to West Van a couple of times a week, and he comes over and hangs with us on occasion, too, which is terrific. It's just good to have family around to help deal with stuff. I think Pablo helps Britt a lot. To get through it, you know.

As for my part, could I have seen what was coming and kept Annie and her mum safe? I think about that a lot. All the time. There are never any answers, though. Anger might help, but I can't make it work. Although there are individual villains aplenty—Annie's father, Dennis, the anonymous American guard who fired the killing shot from across the border, the Border Patrol flunkies who pulled Michelle and Annie over a hundred years ago back north of Cruces and started this whole damn adventure—at the end of the day it's hard to focus on any given

330

one of 'em. There was so much more wrong than just the bland malefactors who played their individual parts in the tragedy.

Who do you get angry at when it's the system itself that's pathological?

As I made my way into the kitchen in bathrobe and slippers I saw Britt had made the coffee before she left. Good 'Ol Britt—she knew my vices well. I poured myself a steaming cuppa and exited to the balcony where I could sit and revelate beneath the great green skyscrapers and green mountains that surround English Bay. She'd left me a note by the coffee machine like she does every morning, and under the bright grey skies of British Columbia I sipped my coffee and read her message penned in red ink on a yellow sticky:

"Annie's still alive," her note read. "and so's her mum—never forget that lawyer-man."

Indeed. For the millionth time I resolved to remember. Annie was in foster care with some farm family over in Chilliwack, her mum was in the hospital, and Monsieur Chretien was in stir. It wasn't the best result, but there was some cause for optimism. At least for now.

I spared a glance for the rainbow colored mittens that perched atop the small wicker basket at the end of the kitchen counter.

Don't get the wrong idea about the bathrobe and the late hour, by the way. I'm not retired. Far from it. My quest for same back in America had accrued me an almost decent enough pension for whenever I do finally hit the silk, but that's a ways off. Today I'm still a working man— an immigration lawyer, as it happens, and a damn good one. Well, starting to become a good one, anyway.

Well, adequate. Let's say adequate. For now: adequate.

But it was an area of the law that suited me as it turned out, and one where I don't need a B.C. law license, or a State of Washington one, neither. At fifty-six I haven't got another bar exam in me, so I'm practicing on both sides of the border solely on the strength of my New Mexico legal credentials. Happily it turns out they're all I need. I'm doing the work I want to do, helping people who need my help, setting my own hours and making enough to keep my child support current and me and Britt in the green.

Or in the blue or the red or the gray or whatever the hell colour this country's money is.

I padded back inside, poured myself another cup of coffee and headed to the bathroom for a shower. It was time to get ready. I had a few things to take care of before my first client meeting of the day.

A few hours later, errands done, I pulled the big blue American truck that had been made in Canada out of traffic and parked it on Morton Street, in front of the old Sylvia Hotel. I switched off the engine and headed along inside.

Chapter 48 – Tow Away

"YOU CAN'T PARK THERE."

I cringed, looked about and saw a young couple—young Asian hipsters as it happened: him with a chin-beard and horn-rims, and her with pink hair—jointly pointing at a sign: No Parking Any Time, it read. Tow Away Zone.

"Hate to see you get towed," the girl said, in a shy English accent. She held an oversized pink umbrella over the two of them.

I nodded thanks to 'em and moved the truck.

How had I not gotten towed before now, I wondered? I parked there literally all the time. It was a miracle—or maybe the sign was just new. In any event, I gave the young couple a tip of my Fedora, though they were long gone by now, and strode into the foyer of the classic old Hotel. Britt had set me up with another client and it was time to meet him for an interview. I preferred doing that at the Hotel, by the way—the Ike thing back in Calgary had started a sort of tradition. We still had the flat, of course, Britt and me, but that wasn't an office—it was pure refuge now; the Sylvia had become my de facto place of business: overstuffed and clubby, it had proved to be a welcoming sort of place, both for me and for my clientele. As a practical matter, everybody should have a neighborhood bar. It makes life so much easier.

I took my usual table near the fireplace, and unfolded the Vancouver Sun and waited for my new immigration case to arrive.

"Mr. McKenzie, how nice to see you again," the waitress said with a smile. "Your usual?" I nodded a big yes, engaged her in some polite badinage, then she bustled off to get me a pint. While I waited for her to come back with my beer I scanned the headlines, which was the usual tripe about the NDP and the Liberals splitting the provincial vote; the Tories having good things to say about the Tar Sands, old stock Canadians and business generally but not much else; and some Canadian pop star getting caught with her pants down. Literally.

Page two had an item about missing prostitutes, and once more I said a silent atheist's prayer in thanks for Britt having come through the extreme shite of the last year safe and sound.

"Your beer, Mr. McKenzie," the waitress said, returning to the table. The glasses were big at the Sylvia. Not your standard British pint glasses, but the sort with a handle, you know. Bulbous, round and deep, with cut glass indentations all round the outside. They held a lot of beer. A robust amount of beer. The amount of beer you might expect to get at the Hofbrauhaus in Munich, or some such other teutonic sort of place.

Another good reason to make the Sylvia my home away from home, thinks I. You don't get served with mugs like that just anywhere.

Interestingly enough, this new client was just "technically" new—that is, he was new only in the sense that I had not met him yet. He was in actual fact one of the three original clients Britt had set up for me when we were back in Calgary. We'd had to skedaddle so quick from that oil and gas town last November, and the intervening months had shot by so quickly that I'd not been able to connect with him until now. Story was he'd been a roughneck up in Fort McMurray, a temporary foreign worker; one of the many brought in by the oil companies to keep wages low and ditched once the bottom dropped out of the oil market. He was discarded now, and distressed at the notion he'd have to leave Canada. I didn't know the rest of his story, what his situation was here, or what awaited him in the Old Country, wherever his Old Country was, but since Britt thought his claim sympathetic he'd get my full attention and the benefit of any doubt.

This time, for obscure reasons, I expected a miner to walk in: that is, someone in canvas overalls and size fifteen steel-toed boots, with a pick-ax in one hand and a helmet sporting a flashlight upon his head. Childish and ridiculous, I know. But if you recall, I had been right about Ike.

I was wrong about this guy, though.

"Mr. McKenzie?" he said.

He was a diminutive East Indian, with the name of Gujarat Singh.

I shook his hand and handed him my card. "Mr. Singh, how nice to finally meet you. Please, have a seat."

I wondered what tale Mr. Singh was going to tell me. I reckoned it would commence with the country we were in having used him for whatever purpose, legal or no, and now having done with his services wished only to see the back of him. Whatever his story, there was some cause for optimism. The west was still somewhat welcoming and reasonable to immigrants—the rule of law still applied. Our governments still paid lip service to their post-war commitments to provide sanctuary to the stateless and oppressed. For now.

I say this knowing full well that we were always only another terrorist attack or two away from closed borders and rising nativist violence.

But I couldn't control that. You can't solve all the problems of the world. I had been a wannabe Atlas attempting to hold up two worlds, and had dropped one of them rather badly. All I could do now was...well, listen:

"So what's the story?"

"Mr. McKenzie," he began, "I have a problem..."

My Canadian Exile

Edward Charles Bagley

Ted Bagley is an ex-pat, a Canadian and a lawyer much like the protagonist in *My Canadian Exile*. He was born in Montreal in 1959, came to the States in 1964—the year of the Civil Rights Act and the Beatles debut on the Ed Sullivan Show—ultimately received his law degree from John Marshall Law School in Chicago, and currently practices in Santa Fe, New Mexico.

Visit

tedspad.com

And watch for the next confusing madcap rage-filled
installment of

Edward Charles Bagley's

Bob McKenzie, Immigration Lawyer
series

THE
NEW
ORDER

Coming in 2017

www.ingramcontent.com/pod-product-compliance
Lightning Source LLC
Chambersburg PA
CBHW030406180626
46812CB00005B/1938